WALK AWAY DREAMING

by

Mike Lenio

Copyright © 2018 Mike Lenio. All rights reserved.

For Meri

TABLE OF CONTENTS

PREFACE 5
PROLOGUE I: REVOLUTION 9
PROLOGUE II: A HARD DAY'S NIGHT 17
PROLOGUE III: WATCHING THE WHEELS 21
CHAPTER ONE: TOMORROW NEVER KNOWS 24
CHAPTER TWO: WITH A LITTLE HELP FROM MY FRIENDS 41
CHAPTER THREE: GETTING BETTER 56
CHAPTER FOUR: THE FOOL ON THE HILL 71
CHAPTER FIVE: FIXING A HOLE 85
CHAPTER SIX: IT'S ALL TOO MUCH 96
CHAPTER SEVEN: ALL TOGETHER NOW 108
CHAPTER EIGHT: ACROSS THE UNIVERSE 129
CHAPTER NINE: FLYING 140
CHAPTER TEN: MAGICAL MYSTERY TOUR 156
CHAPTER ELEVEN: OH MY LOVE 170
CHAPTER TWELVE: AWAITING ON YOU ALL 183
CHAPTER THIRTEEN: DON'T LET ME DOWN 201
CHAPTER FOURTEEN: BAND ON THE RUN 223
CHAPTER FIFTEEN: COLD TURKEY 236
CHAPTER SIXTEEN: THE ART OF DYING 250
CHAPTER SEVENTEEN: ALL THINGS MUST PASS 266
CHAPTER EIGHTEEN: LETTING GO 280
CHAPTER NINETEEN: ALL YOU NEED IS LOVE 287

APPENDIX A: World Events 1941-85............................305
APPENDIX B: SELECTED DISCOGRAPHY.................332
APPENDIX C: PERFORMANCES AT LIVE AID.........370
AUTHOR'S NOTE AND ACKNOWLEDGEMENTS....380
NOTES..383

PREFACE

Douglas Yang, PhD

University of Eastern Pennsylvania

June 23, 2032

We live in a world of breathtaking changes. The scope of human knowledge and the boundaries of human innovation are being broken almost daily. There is no telling what sort of world our grandchildren will know. All that we can know for sure is that it will be vastly different from the one we know.

The advances that have been made in recent years in science and technology have been truly astounding. Just consider the recent discovery of the Cotton-Hamel carbonization process, by which depleted coal veins and oil wells can be essentially "refilled" with a new form of their carbon-based fuels through reprocessed atmospheric carbon dioxide. The introduction of this process promises to create a virtually perpetual source of clean-burning fuel. Likewise, the development of alkaline compounds to neutralize body acids shows great promise in addressing obesity, diabetes and related issues worldwide.

Running side by side with the rapid pace of scientific advancement in our time has been the growth of religious faith. An estimated 95 percent of the world's population as of 2030 consider themselves churchgoers of the various faiths. Indeed, as the long-perceived conflict between science and faith has been rendered ever more obsolete, the growth of faith has given greater focus to scientific discovery and innovation – after all, as the Good Book says, "seek and ye shall find."

Of course, probably no area in which we have sought, and found, in recent years has had the impact of the discovery of the O'Malley-Patel Wormhole Effect. This exciting discovery has been the source of seemingly constant discussion among the media and general public virtually from the date of its announcement. The focus of the many media outlets, unsurprisingly, has been on the fact that O'Malley-Patel wormholes appear to have provided the first real direct scientific evidence of the existence of the Deity, although that is still being hotly debated. No one needs to hear me reiterate that discussion. Almost as dramatic has been the news that O'Malley-Patel wormholes also would seem to have confirmed the existence of multiple universes. Both the scientific and religious communities – to say nothing of political structures – are still attempting to absorb the impact of these findings and their implications.

Less widely publicized, but potentially even more dramatic, have been the result of further experiments on O'Malley-Patel wormholes, which have provided for us a means of actually gleaning information from some of these parallel universes. While the possibility of sending information, to say nothing of traveling to other universes, is still speculative, the retrieval of information from parallel universes has already produced mind-boggling results. We have identified and opened studies on eight parallel universes so far. They range from universes in which no life appears possible to universes that closely parallel our own. The most intriguing universe we have come across thus far is one that appears to be very similar in many respects to our own universe, but that has a historical timeline that appears to differ from ours in significant ways. This universe we have dubbed the "HC Universe" (for "high correlation"). As an example of the differences, we have discovered that in the HC Universe, an individual named "Barack Obama" was in 2008 elected President of the United States. Subsequent research within our own universe has been able to locate only one individual in the United States with that name, a relatively obscure personal-injury attorney who was born in Honolulu and worked in Chicago until his retirement.

In my ongoing efforts to make scientific knowledge accessible to all, I sought a way to make a comparison between the events of the HC Universe and those of our own universe, to note both the close correlation and the differences in events. I eventually decided that popular culture would prove a fruitful area, as popular culture tends to be "noisy" in that it generates data that can be gleaned with relative ease via O'Malley-Patel wormholes. The Beatles, we were quickly able to determine, were major pop-cultural figures in both universes, and so my research team and I believed that comparing the events revolving around that popular musical act of the 20th Century would enable us to draw a sharp distinction between events in the two timelines. Our results succeeded beyond our expectations.

With the goal of scientific education in mind, I have decided to annotate WALK AWAY DREAMING, the well-known and popular history of the Beatles that was published in 1989, with footnotes. The footnotes, which appear in the republished version of the book that follows, illustrate the differences our research team has noted between the HC Universe and our own. It is our hope that these annotations will allow the reader to clearly delineate what is, and what could have been, across the vast scope of time.

PROLOGUE I: REVOLUTION

June 30, 1941

Josef Stalin stared at the rustling trees out the front window of his dacha. The beauty of the Russian summer did not at all match his mood. His hands trembled, and he was pale.

He rubbed his deeply pockmarked face. If there was such a thing as God, if he still believed the lies they had told him back at seminary, he would pray now. But he knew that he would only be attempting to make himself feel better. The dark cloud of depression that had hung over him for over a week now would not abated with more lies.

He had failed the revolution. He had failed the people.

For so long, he was sure he knew the way. He had worked loyally for the revolution – robbing banks to finance the Bolsheviks when they were still illegal, carrying out assassinations – doing the dirty work that girlish philosophers like Trotsky would never touch. He was not afraid to get his hands dirty. He was not afraid to do whatever needed to be done.

When the revolution came, he found himself in the outer circle of the party, while windbags like Trotsky, or secret capitalists like Kamenev and Zinoviev – traitors to the cause – suddenly appeared beside comrade Lenin, stroking him, flattering him, making him think they and their destructive, counterrevolutionary ideas were something he could not dispense with. Lenin was the leader – no one disputed that. But surely the revolution required more than just windy philosophy – or outright treason. It needed a doer. Someone not afraid to take the actions he needed to take. All for the good of the people.

For the glorious workers' state that would shine like a beacon for all the proletariat of the world.

So he had bullied, and maneuvered, and backstabbed when necessary, until he was Lenin's first lieutenant. And when Lenin died, he stepped in. He was ready to provide the revolution with the leadership it needed. He was ready to push forward the great Communist state, in Russia and throughout the world.

They had fought him all along. There had been enemies everywhere. Trotsky had been a menace. He had made him leave Russia, and pursued him to the ends of the earth. Just last year, Stalin had gotten the grimly satisfying news: an ice pick through the head, in Mexico. No more of Trotsky's prattling.

There had been wreckers, saboteurs, counterrevolutionaries everywhere. They had resisted the march to collective farms, to the growth of Soviet industry. He had brought down the iron fist upon them. This was no polite bourgeois debate. This was the revolution. There was no room for petty bourgeois concern for propriety. Enemies must be crushed without mercy. And most of the enemies were within.

He had found them among the Bolsheviks, so many of whom had turned against him. If they were against him, they must be against the revolution – for he had brought Russia so far, so very far, and how could it be otherwise? So he had had them tortured until they confessed their treason, then killed them one by one.

The camps and prisons were full of enemies of the revolution. They had come from among the kulaks, the wreckers in the factories, the hidden counterrevolutionaries among the commissars, the leadership itself. The revolution had no room for sentiment. The workers' state was too important to allow for it.

Counterrevolution had been present, too, in the Red Army. Marshal Tukhachevsky had been a brilliant strategist, but he had become too important. No man could be bigger than the revolution – not even Stalin himself, though he embodied the revolution in any case. A cult had started to form around Tukhachevsky. A dangerous situation, for the possibility then would arise that loyalty to the field marshal would trump loyalty to the revolution, to the state, to Stalin, the indispensable leader of the revolution. This could not be allowed to happen. Tukhachevsky had been eliminated. And the Army had been taught its lesson – other potential centers of power, like Rokossovsky, were in prison, atoning for their own scheming. Loyal men like Comrade General Voroshilov served the Red Army, the Soviet state and Stalin instead, and that was how it should be.

But just as there were enemies within, there were of course enemies without – formidable ones, bent on the destruction of the Soviet state, though it was foolish on their part, for the revolution was after all inevitable. The capitalists of France, Britain and the United States nevertheless schemed for its destruction. The minute they saw an opportunity, they would try to thwart the workers' state. The capitalists were desperate – the world revolution was on the horizon, so they had increased their efforts against the vanguard state of the workers. They had already tried, at the time of the revolution, to stop it. They had failed. Inevitably, they would fail. But that did not mean that the going would be easy for the Soviet Union in the meantime.

Then the most menacing threat of all had arisen, in the form of the fascists in Germany. They made no secret of their hostility to Russia, to the Bolsheviks, to the revolution. They claimed to be carrying out a "national revolution" of their own, but any fool could see that they were merely mocking the true revolution.

At first, Stalin had approached the Western capitalists with the intention of making a bargain with the devil: the lesser threat of the Western states could be ignored for the time being while the greater threat of the Nazis was contained. But the foolish capitalist states had spurned Soviet help. The shortsighted imbeciles. So Stalin had done what he must do: ensure the safety of the revolution. He made a superior devil's bargain, by concluding a nonaggression pact with Hitler.

The irony was that Hitler, as it happened, thought very much like him. Both saw the need to crush internal enemies and bend the will of the people in support of their respective causes. Whatever he could say about Hitler, even now, Stalin observed to himself ruefully, he could not call him bourgeois.

He had never trusted Hitler. He was hardly so simpleminded as the weak-kneed French and British in that regard, who bowed and scraped before Hitler until he had gone to war with them. Still, the bargain with Germany was convenient, and it provided time for the Soviet Union to strengthen its defenses for the battles that would one day come. In the meantime, let the capitalists and the fascists destroy one another. Perhaps there would be that much less work to do when their own people rose up against the oppressors who had led them into another world war.

But he had been stunned by the suddenness of the fall of France and the repeated losses incurred by the British as well. True, Britain was still holding out. But it was obviously only a matter of time. Then the fascists would be victorious – and the Soviet Union would be alone, without even the possibility of allies.

He had clung over the past year to the hope that perhaps the bargain with Hitler was still as useful to Hitler as it was to him. Part of the treaty, after all, was the provision of vital resources, most especially oil, to Germany, which needed them in its ongoing struggle with Britain. The Soviet Union had not balked at providing any such deliveries to Germany – he had seen to that. And surely Hitler wanted peace on his eastern flank at least until he finished off the British. The Soviet state was clearly more useful to him alive than dead.

Stalin's face reddened. He had persisted in this belief too long. He had allowed himself to become blinded.

He ignored the warning signs. The British – Churchill himself – had sent him messages warning that their intelligence had discerned the possibility of a German invasion of Russia. The Americans, too, though still neutral, had picked up the signals from their own intelligence network and had tried to warn him. He had dismissed the warnings as capitalist provocations.

Soviet military intelligence had noted increased military activity on the German side of the border and had tried to pass on warnings. He had dismissed the officers involved, or had them arrested, believing they were yet more troublemakers.

Even one of our own best spies, Stalin observed bitterly, had tried to pass on a warning. Richard Sorge, at Germany's embassy in Tokyo, secretly a spy working for the NKVD, had passed on information obtained via the Japanese that an attack was imminent. He had ignored Sorge. It didn't fit with what he had wanted to hear, what he had wanted to believe...that Hitler would not go to war....

But he had been a fool.

Just eight days ago, some 4 million German and other Axis soldiers, some 600,000 vehicles – the largest invasion in history – had smashed across the border.

The front had broken at once. He had ordered the army to concentrate close to the border, despite the advice of his generals, who had seen how the Nazi blitzkrieg tactics had worked so effectively against such a static defense in Poland and France. Now all had turned into disaster. The Germans had already occupied Lithuania and much of prewar eastern Poland. Hundreds of thousands of prisoners were already taken. Worst of all, some 4,000 aircraft had been destroyed, leaving Hitler's dreaded Luftwaffe in total command of the air.

He had tried, at first, to reassure them – to reassure himself – that he was still in control of the situation. He had darted about the Kremlin, a whirlwind of frenetic activity, involving himself in every decision, large and small. He had given endless instructions to the Politburo. He had ordered Beria to have the NKVD, the feared Soviet secret police, take care of deserters and defeatists. Most critically, he had ordered the army repeatedly to stand its ground at all costs.

But, just three days ago – in five days of war! – he had demanded from his generals, Zhukov and Timoshenko, the hard truth. And they had given it to him: the enemy was on the verge of taking Minsk, already some 480 kilometers inside Soviet territory. He left the Kremlin then, muttering, "Lenin created our state, and we've fucked it up," and drove here, to his dacha at Kuntsevo.

He had failed them. He had failed them twice. Once by assuring himself against all evidence that Germany would not attack, and once by ensuring, by the disposition of the armies, that when she did attack, Russia would suffer the same defeat as France, Poland, Norway, Greece, Yugoslavia…surely the armies of the revolution could have beaten the invaders back, if not for his own mistakes.

It was then that he heard the car coming up the road.

He pulled the curtains aside and peered once again out the window. A black car, bearing official markings – the markings of the Politburo – was approaching the dacha.

He knew what they were here for. He had failed the revolution. And by his own lights, the revolution had no room for sentiment. If his decisions had produced such dire results, he was no better than a counterrevolutionary himself. And, the Politburo had no doubt decided, he deserved the fate of any counterrevolutionary.

He straightened himself out and withdrew his service revolver from its holster. He would not force the Politburo to put him on trial. He would not flee like Trotsky, nor deny his failure like Kamenev and Zinoviev.

Outside, Anastas Mikoyan scrambled breathlessly from the vehicle to the front door. He knocked sharply. "Comrade Stalin!" he cried. "Please, open the door! We need you to come back to the capital! The nation needs you!"

Inside, Stalin, having placed the pistol inside his mouth, pulled the trigger.

Mikoyan and the others heard the gunshot, followed by the thud of a body falling to the floor.[1]

PROLOGUE II: A HARD DAY'S NIGHT

February 3, 1959

For all the darkness of the predawn hours, the way ahead seemed almost a continuous sea of white. But not the good kind of white – the kind that suggests light and clarity. Instead, it was like a swarm of locusts, seemingly endless, relentless, the snow pelting against the windshield of the little red Beechcraft Bonanza.

Less sturdy than the similar Cessnas, the Bonanza had a V-tail tail design that made it rattle ominously anytime it flew into extreme turbulence. A number of fatal crashes had been attributed to the V-tail breaking up. The aircraft was fine for normal weather, but even Beechcraft did not recommend its use in severe weather. And this night the weather northwest of Mason City, Iowa, was most assuredly severe – a falling barometer, low ceiling, blustering winds, and increasingly poor visibility due to precipitation which had now turned to snow in the air, leaving the pilot, Roger Peterson, with no definite horizon.

Peterson, a pilot for Dwyer's Flying Service, assigned to fly the little four-seater chartered plane to Fargo, North Dakota, gripped the controls, desperately trying to see forward through the blanket of snow. All conversation in the plane had stopped from the moment the plane had hit the turbulence. Then came the jarring jumps, side-to-side lurches, and, worst of all, that loud, dissonant, terrifying rattle from the tail of the aircraft.

Buddy, seated next to Peterson, clung tightly to the sides of his seat. He had the most frightening view of the three passengers of the blanket of snow in front of the plane. His breath was short, escaping his mouth in quick bursts, each one a puff of steam that barely had time to dissipate before the next one came, and they were coming quicker and quicker. Behind Buddy and the pilot, Ritchie, fear etched into his face, quietly prayed the Lord's Prayer over and over in Spanish. J.P. closed his eyes, not wanting to see, wishing only that he were back on the ground with a good stiff whiskey.

    The plane lurched violently to the left, and the rattle from the tail began to compete with the sound of the engine. Peterson tried hard to see the ground.

    J.P. wasn't the religious type, so years later he would just shrug his shoulders over what happened next. But both Buddy and Ritchie would call it a miracle.

    The haze broke, and although the ominous clouds hung all around the little plane, it was just clear enough that Peterson could, at last, figure out what was sky and what was ground. Enough moonlight cut through the gap in the clouds to allow him to make out a cornfield below.

    They were only about five miles from the Mason City airport. Hubert Dwyer, the owner of the flying service, manning the control tower, could still see the taillight of the plane, gradually descending toward the ground.

    "Hang on!" Peterson shouted, as he made for the cornfield.

    The Bonanza hit the snow-covered field, screeching and skidding over the frozen ground. Pilot and passengers were flung about haphazardly. The luggage – mostly dirty clothes the passengers were hoping to get laundered before the next show in

Moorhead, across the river from Fargo – came loose and a flock of dirty white shirts billowed into J.P.'s and Ritchie's laps.

Before the plane could halt, the tail finally snapped off.

The plane spun around in circles, Peterson trying to brake it to some kind of stop, however bad. The right landing gear wheel punctured. The left wing began to shear off. Buddy was a mass of sweat. Ritchie, in tears, his voice a hoarse whisper, gasped, "*Granice Maria, llena de tolerancia, el Senor esta con Usted...*" J.P. just squeezed his eyes shut, his face pale white.

As the right landing gear collapsed, a final violent lurch flung everyone to the right. Buddy, thrown forward, broke his nose. His trademark glasses flew from his face and cracked against the broken windshield. Ritchie suffered a severe cut to his forehead as he was flung against a front seat. J.P. cried out in pain; he would soon learn his left ankle was fractured.

But, as the snowflakes fell onto the wrecked plane, they all peered out of the shattered windows. For all the injuries, for all the terror, their brief flight was over, and they had made it out alive.

The radio suddenly popped to life – it was Dwyer. "Roger, are you there? Roger, over! Do you copy?"

The pilot, gasping for breath, asked, "Is everyone OK?"

Buddy Holly, holding someone's shirt to his bloodied nose, and Ritchie Valens grunted their assent. J.P. Richardson, "The Big Bopper," rasped, "I think my leg is broken."

Still gasping, but sweating now with relief, Peterson opened the microphone. "Dwyer, this is Peterson, I copy," he said. "We need an ambulance here but no severe injuries."

Early on the morning of February 3, 1959, after being treated and released at the same Mason City hospital where Ritchie's forehead had been bandaged and Bopper's leg put in a cast, Buddy Holly swore up and down that, no matter what, he'd never, ever let himself get booked on any goddamn tour as awful as the Winter Dance Party ever again.[2]

PROLOGUE III: WATCHING THE WHEELS

December 8, 1980

It had been another successful day at the Record Plant recording studio, where John Lennon had been working at the mixing board on the new record. Now he was on his way home.

He sat in the back of the limousine, nervously tapping his fingers against the window. He and his wife had thought about going out for a late-night bite, but he wanted to get back to the Dakota first, to say goodnight to the children. He didn't want to take long, and he considered the limo entering the courtyard, and how long it would take to make their way back upstairs, and decided instead to jump out of the limo onto 72nd Street, where he could scoot inside the main door and take the elevator.

He turned every now and then and smiled at his wife, seated next to him, also silent. He was in a good mood, but his mind was preoccupied.

A nagging thought was bothering him. A voice seemed to be speaking inside his head, in the quiet of the limousine. *Something is wrong. Don't go back to the Dakota. Have the limo take a different way. Something is wrong. Don't get out of the car. Something is wrong.*

"Rubbish," he thought. But as he stared out the window, continuing to nervously drum his fingers against it, watching as the lights of Manhattan streamed past, the thought refused to go away. And then it suddenly became much more insistent:

YOU MAY DIE TONIGHT.

That thought, too, was surely rubbish – but what if it wasn't? A cold chill went down his spine.

As he continued to watch the Manhattan lights on this cold December night, he pondered. Then another thought flitted through his mind. It took him back to a conversation he had had a few weeks ago with Brian Jones.

Brian had dropped by the Record Plant to see how things were going and to add a few synthesizer enhancements to John's songs. After they'd finished working, they stopped to chat. John hadn't seen Brian in about a year, and it was always fun to reminisce with friends.

Like it so often did when Brian and John talked, the conversation gradually veered onto the topic of religion. Brian told John, as they sipped mineral water, that even now, after all these years, he was occasionally tempted to go back to the bottle, to the drugs – "back to the Rolling Stones," as Brian joked.

"Really?" John said. "You'd think by now it'd be second nature to you. Staying sober, I mean."

"Most of the time, yeah," Brian said. "But you have your moments. But I always remember something Buddy Holly said to me five years ago."

"Our resident dispenser of wisdom," John said, and they both laughed. John's caustic sense of humor belied the great respect he and Brian both had for Buddy.

"He said, 'Trust that voice, Brian. Trust that still, small voice.' That's what it's called in the Bible, you know – the 'still, small voice.' When that happens inside your head, that's God talking to you, through your conscience." Brian took another sip of his mineral water. "Buddy was right, you know. I've never known it to fail."

Those words, coming from Buddy Holly and Brian Jones, suddenly struck John. *A still, small voice.* The perfect description of what he was hearing in his head.

There was a time when he would have dismissed such a voice. His wife never would have. She would always have insisted that it was the voice of God – speaking through the conscience, just like Brian said. But there was also a time when he nearly dismissed her, too. And he'd nearly died once before, after all.

A still, small voice. Should he change his plans?

As John turned toward his wife, the limo swung off Central Park West, the headlights briefly illuminating the block next to the Dakota, including a mousy, nervous-looking man who paced the sidewalk in front of the entrance, clutching a copy of *The Catcher in the Rye* in his hands, a revolver in his pocket.

CHAPTER ONE: TOMORROW NEVER KNOWS

September 2, 1966

John Lennon stared out the window of the train, looking at nothing in particular, not that the landscape was especially inspiring. Just the same endless rows of cornfields he'd been seeing for miles and miles.

On the Beatles' previous American concert tours, Brian Epstein, the group's manager, the one who had discovered them in the Cavern in Liverpool and had taken a chance on them, plugging hard against the advice of family and friends when virtually no one else had faith in the fledgling group, had usually booked them on chartered jet flights across the United States, ignoring the substantial cost. Their 1965 tour had been especially grueling – back and forth across the country, since the venues and dates were not booked in any geographically useful pattern. Now, for the end of their 1966 tour, Epstein had decided to save a few dollars – and hopefully give the boys a chance to relax – by taking advantage of America's rail passenger system, one of the finest in the world[3], to travel to New York after the final show in San Francisco. From there they would board a plane back to England.

It had seemed like a good idea at the time. But, two days into the trip, John was bored out of his mind.

He turned to his left, looking around the first-class roomette, one of several booked by the group and their entourage. The tiny lights above the aisle, in this darkness, seemed inordinately bright, even as they illuminated only a few faces. Paul

McCartney, visible through the open doors across the aisle in the next roomette and seated next to the window, cradled a tape in his hand, holding it like a talisman, like it had some sort of magic power. John knew what the tape was – the recording they had asked Tony Barrow to make, of the last show. It would turn out that Tony had forgotten to turn the tape over, and it had cut off in the middle of "Long Tall Sally". John chuckled a bit as he saw the intensity with which Paul held the tape, as if he feared that letting go of it would mean letting go of everything else too. Still, he couldn't blame Paul. He'd brought out a small camera and taken pictures from the stage himself. For the Beatles had decided that, for the foreseeable future, they would not perform live again.

Next to John sat Buddy Holly. He was fumbling with his glasses, a nervous habit John always kidded him about, through all the long airplane flights, on what now seemed like a blur of touring. John couldn't blame him, either. Not after what he'd been through seven years earlier.

Buddy caught John's gaze, and smiled at him with a nod and a shrug. John shrugged and nodded back, then turned back toward the window.

On Buddy's lap sat a newspaper, the *San Francisco Chronicle*. John noticed a headline – "Kennedy and Chiang Berate Kremlin" – and concluded that it must be a story about the Soviet Union's "escalation" of its brutal war in Vietnam. "Bloody world we live in," he muttered under his breath.[4]

He cradled his head in his hand, propping his arm against the bulkhead. *At last it's over.*

It had seemed so unbelievably wonderful at first. Hordes of screaming girls, chasing them just the way they used to chase Elvis. Sold-out shows and number one smash hits and record sales like no one had ever seen, anywhere, ever. He chuckled again, this time at himself, thinking about how exciting it had once been to think that he would be appearing on *television*. Right now, if he never saw his face on television again, he wouldn't care.

Sometime during the last year or two, it had started to get old. Then it had gotten older and older, and then very old. The screaming was so intense, night after night, show after show. The fans couldn't hear the music. They never heard the music. And John wanted, more than anything else, for them to hear the music – for them to love his music, and love him, and make the dull feeling he got when no one heard his music go away for a while.

But they weren't listening. They were there to scream. It was so obvious. They looked on him as a doll, as a dad, as a sex object to masturbate to – anything but as what he wanted to be, namely someone that another person could love, for real. He'd already told a reporter they might as well put the four dummies of themselves from that wax museum out on stage and that no one would know the difference. Neither Epstein nor Buddy Holly had been happy to hear him say that. But he didn't care anymore. Fuck it. Especially not after this last tour.

They hadn't understood. None of them did. He hadn't meant that comment that had gotten him in so much trouble, that one about the Beatles and "bigger than Jesus" and all that, to sound that way – couldn't they get that? Sure, maybe, that day when he talked to Maureen Cleave, given her that long interview for that profile piece – maybe he shouldn't have smoked a joint before, maybe he'd have been more articulate, better able to make sense. But he was always so nervous before interviews. That had never changed, no matter how many of them he'd done. The press conferences were one thing – they were bullshit, and he could joke his way through them, at least until this tour. But a real interview was a different story.

Fuck them all. Couldn't they get it? He was saying that it was *bad* that people paid more attention to him. He'd never meant it to say that God was a lesser thing. What kind of fucking idiot did people think he was, that he would actually believe he was *more popular than Jesus*? It hadn't come out of his mouth the way he wanted, but it shouldn't have been that hard to understand.

But then he saw the footage coming in from America – the angry faces, mostly older but so many young, teenagers, fresh-faced blonde American girls, American boys with greaser hair with just the slightest hint of the shaggy bangs he and the lads had made the hippest look on the planet. The same kind of faces he'd seen hundreds of thousands of times, screaming at the concerts, laughing as they tore at his clothes as he had run from the concert halls, the hands that climbed atop the limousine and clutched at the windows and held on for dear life, their faces pressed against the glass, hoping against hope for just one look, just one second's worth of the sight of his own face. Now these same faces were contorted with rage. The hands were now throwing into bonfires posters, pictures, figurines with his image on them – and, worst of all, the records, the music, that into which he had poured his soul, the music he had given to these kids.

How quickly they had turned on him. How quickly they had listened to the distortions of his words, the angry voices that had always hated him, the same bastards who were so like his father who abandoned him, worthless punks every one of them. And now they had turned the kids – his kids – against him, and the kids had burned the records. And his soul burned every time he saw it happen.

His first instinct had been to say fuck it all. He wouldn't bother. If they couldn't understand what he had said – if they were willing to hear it not as he meant it but as some silly teen magazine had shown it – he wasn't going to bother to try.

But Epstein had begged him, and in the end he couldn't watch the records burn. So he had swallowed his pride, and gone to America, and apologized. And the press asked him about it again, and he apologized again. And it had happened over and over, right until the night before the last show – for he knew, now, that this was absolutely going to be the last show.

Knowing that was supposed to give him peace. But instead, knowing that only created another question: What the hell do I do now?

He mused for a bit. *I just want to be happy,* he thought. *I just want to feel like I belong. Like I have a place in this world. Like I'm actually loved....*

The nagging loneliness. There it was again. He thought that it would go away once he became famous. The Beatles had struggled to get to the top. Now, there was no one in show business bigger. And once he had arrived, all he felt was: *This is it? This is all?*

Being a pop star wasn't going to make him happy. He'd realized that by now. But what he didn't know was…what else is out there. *If I'm not a Beatle, what am I?*

October 18, 1966

The concert that night was like every other Rolling Stones concert over the past year or more – near-complete chaos. Frenzied girls, one after another, ran shrieking onto the stage, climbing through the churning mass of teenagers and flinging themselves toward one of the band members, before being grabbed by a cop and dragged unceremoniously offstage. The cops wore earplugs. They were less to protect their ears from the music, which was more of a faintly audible rumble of guitar noise, than from the constant wail of hundreds of girls' relentless screams.

Brian Jones loved every second of the show. He thrived on the chaos, laughing manically, thrilled with the sight of the frenzy. He teased the audience, throwing facial gestures here, pointing the neck of his guitar there, doing everything he could to draw the kids onto the stage, toward him. It was both a grand and beautiful joke to him and the culmination of everything he'd ever wanted out of being in a band.

Money didn't matter so much to him. He liked having it, certainly, but he'd been with it and without it before, and he knew how to have a good time either way. He wasn't obsessed with it, the way Mick Jagger was. Mick and Andrew Loog Oldham, their manager – they were the ones who worked themselves into a lather over every pound note the band was getting.

He knew he should be making a bigger deal about the songs, at least. He knew he should have gotten more credit – "Paint It, Black" was much more his and Bill Wyman's song than Keith Richards', whose name was on the writing credits. Bill had come up with the riff on the organ one day, and Mick wrote the lyrics, and then Brian had added the sitar – the buzzing, twanging, angry, exotic sound that took the song far beyond the realm of the ordinary. Even Charlie Watts' pounding drums had more to do with the song than Keith did – he was barely audible in the final mix. Sometimes stuff like this bothered Brian. But not all the time. The whole thing was going so fast, like a rocket blasting into space, that he barely had time to stop and think, even if he wasn't smashed half the time. Surely there was no time to stop and reflect on whether he was being adequately acknowledged or compensated for his contributions to the band.

And anyway, recognition was sure to come. He planned to start working on a film soundtrack as soon as the tour was over. It was for a thriller starring his girlfriend, Anita Pallenberg, called *A Degree of Murder*. The film was a piece of shit, but Anita had gotten him the "in" for doing the soundtrack, and he meant to make the most of the opportunity. Maybe then he could convince everyone that he really could write songs, that his name should be on songwriting credits. Maybe he'd finally even convince himself.

No, it wasn't the money, or the fact that Mick and Keith were making more of it because of the songwriting, that motivated him. It was nights like tonight – the raw thrill of seeing the audience in utter screaming frenzy, the rush of knowing that the fierce energy pouring out of each of those kids was being directed at the band – his band – the band he had put together. That was what really mattered. All that stuff about songwriting would straighten itself out sooner or later.

In the meantime, there were plenty of thrills, plenty of fame, plenty of hot nights basking in the attention that clung to the band like a magnet in the latest and greatest clubs, plenty of champagne and porterhouse steaks – and the acid, and the mind-bending visions that came with it, and the coke and the grass – and the dozens of girls who willingly parted their legs for him virtually without his having to ask, night after night, even as he looked forward to the sight of the woman he had come to regard as the love of his life. Anita – it was always a wild ride with her, but as far as he was concerned, she might have been custom-designed for him.

If only the rest of the band would get along with him. If only the band would recognize how important he was to them, how much his creativity, his musical skill, even his sense of style had been to the foundation of the Rolling Stones – and continued to be to them, no matter how much they tried to push him out of the spotlight. There wouldn't even *be* a Rolling Stones without him, he knew. If only the band would let him know how much he mattered to them – then he would finally be happy, instead of feeling somewhere behind apprehensive and downright miserable so much of the time. And that was all he wanted, really. Just to be happy.

He knew the Stones didn't appreciate the way he flirted with the audience onstage. Mick grumbled that he was trying to compete with him for the spotlight. Maybe he was right. Brian thought Mick was a good enough singer, at least for the blues, but he wasn't anyone you'd take seriously. And just being the singer didn't make him the center of the band, no matter what he thought. Brian had enough familiarity with jazz – something Mick didn't even *understand* – to know that jazz bands weren't necessarily led by their singers. The person who was most central to arranging the music may have been a trombonist like Tommy Dorsey, but he was still the leader of the band. Brian couldn't see why the Rolling Stones should be any different.

Then there was Keith. He still remembered the friendship he'd had with Keith in the early days. That was all but gone now. No matter how hard they tried, they seemed to get along less and less. It galled Brian that Mick and Keith had formed a little cabal and were acting as if they were the leaders of *his* band. And he was convinced that Keith was jealous of his talent. Maybe that was what kept coming between them all the time.

Keith would be angry again tonight. The last number, "Satisfaction", was like all the other songs, buried in the screams. They could barely hear each other, let alone play with any great skill.

But it was that riff – Keith had dreamed up the guitar riff to "Satisfaction," never seemed to tire of telling that damn story over and over about how he'd woke up in a hotel room one night with the riff running through his head. Brian believed the story was bullshit, but he had to sit and nod while Keith told it again and again. And the song had been the Stones' big breakthrough hit, and that was it – suddenly, Keith was like Beethoven, and Andrew and the band and everyone else forgot how much better

Brian was at his craft, just because lightning had struck Keith that one time. And Lord, how he treated that riff with care – you'd really think he was Beethoven, the way he wanted to make sure that stupid guitar riff, that *simple* guitar riff, was exactly right on stage.

It was absurd. The audience couldn't hear them anyway. And so Brian refused to take Keith's precious riff seriously, bending it, improvising on it – that's what a real musician was supposed to do, improvise - right? He might as well enjoy the playing as much as the thrill of the show. But Keith always thought Brian was making fun of it. He'd accused Brian of purposely ridiculing it, of warping it into the "Popeye the Sailor Man" theme among other things. Brian never said he *wasn't* doing anything like that, exactly. But he did think Keith was being childish and uncreative.

Now, as on every other night, they ended with a terse "Thank you" from Mick and the band all but fleeing for their lives, barely ahead of their fans. They tumbled down a flight of stairs backstage, then out into the waiting limo. By the time the driver got the car underway, the fans were already outside, the sound of their screams echoing into the dark streets, their faces pressed against the car windows, contorted with ecstasy at seeing their idols.

Brian smiled wryly at the kids, and waved to them. Bill, had he been sitting next to him, would have done the same, his onstage reticence notwithstanding. Bill's quietness was often mistaken for shyness, but Brian had seen Bill around the groupies, and knew better.

But instead it was Keith who had the seat next to Brian, and he let out a derisive snort. Turning to Mick, he sneered, "The fuckin' Queen is wavin' at the masses over here again."

Brian tried to ignore him, but then he heard Mick's answer – naturally, because Mick wanted him to. "Poodle should wash his hair again if he wants to impress them," he said with a laugh. "Poodle" – that insulting nickname again. He and Keith fell to muttering and chuckling – no doubt taking the piss out of Brian, they way they so often did these days.

Brian kept waving, but felt a choke. So what if he washed his hair and wanted to look good? He *cared* about the way he looked. Keith didn't, and if he had ugly teeth like Keith's, he wouldn't either, but Brian was proud of his good looks – they certainly hadn't hurt him. Why did it have to be like this night after night? Once they got offstage, and the thrill of being in front of the audience was gone, the bullshit started again.

He'd broken into tears before. He didn't want to do that again. That only made it worse, of course. Mick and Keith wouldn't let up all night then. He just wanted to get back to the hotel, get some brandy into him, maybe take a hit of acid…stop feeling this way.

November 7, 1966

The austere-looking Asian woman walked this way and that, checking the exact placement of pieces, the lighting, the overall look of the exhibit, noticing the tiny aesthetic flaws that would only capture the eye of a skilled visual artist. She adjusted the pieces, now this one, now that, a quarter of an inch or less, but just enough to make it exact, absolutely perfect. The tiny differences added up to a successful or failed gallery show, and she always took great care at her shows.

She had, by the fall of 1966, established a small but growing reputation among the avant-garde art community. She had worked with Fluxus, a New York improvisational group that sponsored performance art pieces. In one of these, she sat on a stage silently, inviting members of the audience to cut off pieces of her clothing with a pair of scissors. For the most part, *Cut Piece* proved a success, though several male attendees spewed insults when they cut pieces of fabric from strategic locations, only to have her modestly cover her private parts with her hands.

The current show, at the hip avant-garde Indica Gallery in London owned by John Dunbar, was set to open on November 8, but unexpectedly, a guest, invited by Dunbar for a private showing, ambled into the gallery a day early.

She was annoyed. Dunbar hadn't told her about this, and she didn't like people viewing her shows until they were prepared down to the finest detail. "Who is he?" she whispered with irritation.

"Just wait and see," Dunbar replied.

The tall, thin man seemed vaguely familiar, but she couldn't place him. He wore a paisley shirt, but that could have made him one of any number of wealthy young Londoners roaming the city, and that still didn't make her any more sanguine about his barging into her show early. He had short hair, though – he looked as if he had just started to grow it out, as if donning the paisley in advance of the changeover from buttoned-down proper Englishman to groovy new psychedelic "with-it" man, in the days when short hair was a dead giveaway that not too long ago he would have been comfortably sipping tea and reading the *Financial Times*.

His eyes were partially concealed, too, behind round wire-frame glasses, the kind distributed by Britain's National Health Service. National Health glasses on a wealthy snob who saw fit to interrupt a gallery show setup? It didn't quite compute. She puzzled over the identity of this strange man.

Coolly, with no outward show of emotion, she walked over to be introduced by Dunbar. She greeted the man politely, and they shook hands. Dunbar pulled her aside and quickly told her he had arranged for a special viewing. "Who's got more money to spend on art than a Beatle?" he said. Her eyes followed John as he began to stroll through the gallery, looking at the pieces. Only then did it dawn on her that he was one of the Beatles.

She knew who they were by reputation more than interest. They were a pop group and held minimal allure for serious artists, and she most emphatically regarded herself as a serious artist.

Still, they had pretensions toward being artists themselves, drawing them more and more into the world of serious art. More to the point, they had money, and money could come in handy. Already she had attempted to visit Paul McCartney at his home, in the hope of interesting him in a project – at least to the point of funding it – but she had been unable to see him. But now here was another chance, with a different Beatle – John Lennon.

John had just gotten back from Spain. He'd gone there to play a role – not a starring role, but a role nevertheless – in Richard Lester's film *How I Won the War*, as a soldier, Private Gripweed. Dick had directed the Beatles' two films, and asked John to be in the movie, and John agreed as a favor to a friend. But he also wanted to find out for himself if acting was a viable career option, which is why he'd taken the role seriously enough to cut his hair short.

The Beatles had stopped touring. There was no question about that. They weren't going back, especially not after the troubles that had plagued them all summer on this tour. It had long since ceased to be fun. Now it was frightening. John didn't care to put his life in danger just to be onstage, when no one could hear him sing anyway.

But if there was no touring, was there still a Beatles? He didn't know. He had been in touch with all the others. George Harrison had gone to India to study the sitar and kept talking on the phone about how the new faith Ravi Shankar was teaching him had the answers. Answers sounded good to John. His LSD experiments had already long convinced him that the world was not as it seems – though, really, he had known that since childhood, sensing that he saw the world differently from his friends, his teachers, his Auntie Mimi – from everybody. So when George spoke of things like "karma" and "sansara" and "atman" and all the rest, John listened patiently. If there was something there, he wanted to know.

Ringo Starr had mostly kept to himself, but Paul was the star of the London art scene – every gallery show, every theater opening, every party packed to the gills with the hip and the cool and the trendy seemed incomplete without the presence of the sophisticated young Beatle. This was everything John had ever wanted, but it was Paul who was experiencing it. Paul was getting to enjoy it all, while he, John – bloody hell, thought John, I'm the one who *went* to art school – was at home at Weybridge, getting out of his head on acid, missing it all. He had resolved to get into the scene more, to make himself visible like Paul, to experience the new artistic world and discover new artists first – for a change, he'd be on the telling rather than the receiving end when talking about a new artist with Paul.

Maybe this is what will make me feel like I belong, he thought. *Being part of the art crowd. Maybe being a pop star isn't enough. But maybe this is where I belong.*

So much of what he'd seen had annoyed him, though. It was all "smash" and "trash" and "destroy" and "anti." This wasn't what he and George were talking about on the phone. This wasn't the cosmic peace of his acid trips, when he felt all of existence flowing through him in utter perfection. This was back down to the dark, cold earth, where there was nothing but hate. He understood the idea of rebellion – he'd been a bohemian against the bohemians, no one more of a rebel than he, tearing up the orthodoxies of not only the orthodox, but of rock and roll and arty bohemianism alike. But he had sensed something greater, something genuinely moving, something that led him, even when he thought he was an atheist, to know with certainty of a transcendence, a truth beyond this reality. That was rebellion with a real purpose. Just smashing things didn't make it.

As John wandered through the gallery, the artist closely following him, he came across a piece entitled *Ceiling Painting*. The viewer was asked to climb a white stepladder and peer through a tiny spyglass at a white canvas suspended from the ceiling. John did so, and found a word written on the canvas in barely-legible letters.

The word was "RIPOFF." [5]

The artist had thought to write the word "Yes," but at the last minute decided that might be too twee for the London art crowd. So she substituted another word instead. A word that reflected Pop Art irony, that was supposed to convey the gray area between high art and commerce, where one could never be sure that the high art was not a ripoff and the commerce not real art, or vice versa.

But John Lennon either didn't catch this subtext or didn't find it interesting. His face fell in disdain.

Just more avant-garde bullshit, he thought. More division. Another artist who didn't know, didn't understand...who *cares* whether art is a "ripoff" or not? At the level of cosmic reality, where all things are both real and unreal, who can say what is art and what is life and why the fuck should I *care* about something like this? He began to grow angry, could feel his forehead getting hot, his eyebrows knitting. Another big pile of nothing masquerading as a statement, when all it had to say was about itself, totally self-referential, navel-gazing – no perception of reality here at all.

He climbed back down the ladder. He turned and stared at the artist, who gazed back impassively.

With a sneer, he muttered, "Lovely day for a ripoff, luv." Then he turned away, walking toward the door. Dunbar's face fell as John plodded toward the narrow stairs that led back up to the street. He passed Dunbar with a shrug, and a half-smile, feeling he was disappointing his friend even more than he was disappointed himself.

The artist turned back to the ladder and carefully climbed it with the intention of making sure that this horrible young man had done nothing to disturb the work prior to the opening. She let out a tiny chuckle herself. *Some "artists"*, she thought. A little money in the Beatles' pockets and they think they're the real thing. She knew for sure know – up close they were philistines. They could never understand or appreciate real art, no matter how often they arrogantly invaded art galleries with their money and their ridiculous pop celebrity, and they never would.

Yoko Ono had a genuine laugh that night, relating the anecdote to Roman Polanski, the film director, who lavished praise on her and her work. Here was a *real* artist. The night was the first of many for Roman Polanski and Yoko Ono, the beginning of a long and tempestuous romantic relationship. But she never saw any of the Beatles up close again. Nor did she care to.[6]

CHAPTER TWO: WITH A LITTLE HELP FROM MY FRIENDS

February 28, 1967

Keith Richards had been arrested that month, on drug charges, along with Mick Jagger, after the police raided Keith's home. An art gallery owner and friend, Robert Fraser, had been arrested too – but not a mysterious man known as "David Schneidermann." Schneidermann was a recent acquaintance. He was present at the house that day but – with a hasty excuse – left shortly before the police arrived. No one ever did find out if he was working for the police.

Jagger and Richards claimed the drugs found by the police actually belonged to Schneidermann, but he had conveniently left the country by the time he was identified the following day. The police charged Jagger with possession of LSD, having found several tabs in his jacket pocket. Richards was charged with possession of cannabis, a small quantity being found in a drawer in his bedroom.[7]

Shortly after Mick and Keith were freed on bail pending indictment for the raid on Keith's home, Keith and Brian Jones planned a brief vacation in Tangier. They both hoped that the deteriorating relations between the two of them might be improved by a bit of camaraderie. Keith also needed some stress relief after the immediate trauma of the drug bust. A few nights of hedonistic fun in the Casbah would seem to be just the thing.

But halfway down, before they even got to Tangier, Brian's asthma began acting up, and they had to stop and send him to a French hospital. Whether it was genuine or a product of his constant drug usage and general sense of misery, no one knew. He'd done *A Degree of Murder*. But it hadn't seemed to impress Anita.

Keith continued on without him, with the Stones' assistant Tom Keylock driving and Anita Pallenberg, Brian's girlfriend, sitting beside him.

Anita and Brian had been fighting again. She said Brian hit her. At the very least, he was verbally abusive – anyone around the band could see that. He was wonderful when he wasn't drinking. When he was, he became unaccountably cruel.

So Tom drove Keith and Anita, and they talked, and laughed, and by the time they arrived in Tangier, Tom had to look away to pretend not to notice Keith and Anita having sex in the back seat.

Brian, a few days later, sent a telegram to Anita. He demanded that she come back to France and help him get back to London to complete his recovery. Anita, torn between her new lover and her old one, left to meet Brian.

After another few days, though, Brian and Anita, accompanied now by Mick Jagger and his girlfriend Marianne Faithfull, left to rejoin Keith in Tangier. By now Brian had become sullen. He had started to sense what was going on with Keith and Anita.

The first night back at the Hotel Marrakech, he confronted her. Far from denying it, she was proud, told Brian that Keith stood miles above him, was more talented, a better man. Brian reacted by trashing the room. Anita fled, into Keith's room, into Keith's arms

The next day, Brian went out to the square of Jemaa el-Fna, alone. He had hoped to hear the sacred Master Musicians of

Joujouka, but was unable to secure the opportunity. Instead, he took a hit of acid. He stared deeply at the square, at the pink buildings, the dusty ground, and everything seemed to merge, to stand still, as if it were in a single moment, a single reality of time and space. The more he stared, the more every single object came into a sharp relief, accentuated, yet blending and pulsating with energy.

But then he saw the monkeys. They had been climbing about in the trees. Then, suddenly, they were laughing at him – and they were Mick, and Keith, and Anita. The monkey that was Anita was standing beside him, and laughing, and then she was gone. Then she reappeared, and she and Keith were laughing, then gone again.

He shook his head, trying to clear the acid visions from his mind, determined not to go into a bad trip, trying to focus his thoughts. Then at once he saw the figure of a man, who he didn't recognize, but who beckoned to him. Brian felt himself flooded with unearthly warmth.

Then the man disappeared as quickly as he had come, but the monkeys were gone too, and Brian heard only music, sweet, otherworldly, transporting. Then that was gone too, and he stared at the rippling shapes in the square, the palm trees swaying in the wind, the dust settling at his feet. And he felt alone, more alone than he had ever felt in that moment, as if his whole lonely life was compressed into one second on a sunny afternoon on a dusty square in Africa.

Suddenly tearing himself from the scene, he rubbed his face with his hands. He was beginning to break into tears. Oblivious to the puzzled looks of the onlookers who wondered who this strangely-dressed man with the long blond hair was and why he was moaning, he stumbled away. Somehow he made his way back to the hotel and collapsed onto the bed.

The next day, when he awoke, Anita hadn't returned. Checking around the hotel, he found that she had left with Keith for London. Mick had left as well; everyone had abandoned him. He returned to his room and sobbed uncontrollably for hours.

When Brian got back to London, he found that Anita had already cleared her things out of their flat on Earls Court. Again he wept uncontrollably. He called her and begged her to come back to him, pleading abjectly, but she refused. Brian curled up miserably on the floor in a fetal position, crying until his eyes hurt.

Then he called an old acquaintance – Buddy Holly.

He and Holly had come to know each other well. Holly, since moving to Britain in 1960, had in fact come to know almost everyone in British rock. He had been there for the explosion.

After that night in February 1959, that moment when he came so close to death, he had vowed to get off the rock and roll flea circus. The relentless touring, the frenzied schedules, the long hours, the exhausting shows, the shabby hotels, the lousy food, all was bad enough – but when his very life was in danger, well, no amount of fame was worth that. And it wasn't like it was an isolated mistake – the cheap plane flights and lousy buses and icy roads were a way of life in this business. It was a wonder he hadn't been killed already, even before the night that plane almost did a nosedive into an Iowa cornfield.

The rest of the Winter Dance Party tour was canceled. Buddy went back into the studio and worked hard to come up with the perfect hit. The 1959 singles "True Love Ways" and "It Doesn't Matter Anymore" were moderately successful, but they were not the smashes he needed. For he now had a plan.

He had concluded that the real money in show business didn't go to the performers. They did all the work, but the money never ended up in their pockets. All they got was the lousy food and the shabby hotels…and the plane crashes. The people behind the scenes – record companies, producers, promoters – made the real fortunes. He could rail against this situation all he wanted, but facts were facts. Or…he could cross over to the other side.

Britain seemed to him to be more fruitful for his plan than America. He didn't know much about the British music scene, at least at first, but he was sure they couldn't have much in the way of homegrown rock and roll. He saw a niche: he could act as a liaison, promoting American rock and rollers to British concert venues and record companies. He could then leverage that into promotion, production, who knew what else. All he needed was the seed money to get started.

And for that he needed a big hit. "True Love Ways" and "It Doesn't Matter Anymore" had gone the wrong way, he soon realized. They were too syrupy, too much of an attempt to go mainstream, to abandon his rock and roll roots. They didn't win him any new fans, and they disappointed his old ones.

So he had toured a bit more, just enough to promote himself – although he made it clear to his manager Norman Petty that there would be no hectic schedule this time requiring short airplane flights to get one's shirts cleaned. And then, in the late winter of 1960, he had released his newly written song, the song that laid out everything that was in his heart, his greatest work,

"All My Hopes and Dreams." It was a mid-tempo ballad, not unlike Ben E. King's later hit "Stand by Me," but it was gutsy, not mushy. Like many of the great rock songs, it was on the surface about a boy-girl relationship – but like many of the great rock songs, it went deeper, into a more profound fear, that of losing one's hopes and dreams, and the profound hope of finding them – and finding out what they really were.[8]

The record was a Number One smash not only in America but throughout the world. And that smash hit, and the accompanying album it had propelled into gold status, had given Holly the seed money he needed to plant.

He had not formally announced a retirement, at least not in so many words. He had simply taken the money, packed his bags, and gone to England.

His liaison work had paid off handsomely. He had established contacts on both sides of the Atlantic, getting just about every major performer he could manage to the British Isles. He wasn't able to get Elvis, but then Elvis had gone to Hollywood after leaving the Army. He also found he couldn't break British acts in America. At least not for a while.

But his contacts, and his involvement, had grown. He became an important figure in the British recording and performance circuits, making the money he knew he could make and resisting all calls to return to the stage or the recording studio himself.

He was right there when that group from Liverpool who had adopted his most-beloved hit into their onstage repertoire suddenly turned into the biggest thing to hit the island since Elvis.

He hadn't been on the ground floor with them, but once they hit, he had seen their talent right away. He'd befriended Brian Epstein, and worked closely with him, getting the Beatles into the best venues he could find in Britain, and using his contacts in America to help midwife their entry into the birthplace of rock and roll. It was Holly who convinced Capitol Records in a transatlantic phone call to release "I Want to Hold Your Hand," the boys' first American Number One. The boys, for their part, were in perfect awe to be not only so close to one of their idols, but to have him actively helping them, so appreciative of their talent that he would put such an effort behind them.[9]

So the Beatles had hit America hard, and then came the invasion – the Dave Clark Five, and Hermans' Hermits, and the Kinks, the Animals, Manfred Mann – with Holly acting as the conduit, becoming friends with all these new British acts and linking them to his old friends in the States, to the point where some argued that there could have been no invasion without him. The managers and the bands viewed him as indispensable, and he often made a point of traveling with them, helping smooth out issues.

There was that incident with the Kinks, for example.

Holly had worked his contacts hard to break the Kinks in America. He had gotten them on the Beatles' 1964 summer tour of the United States as an opening act, for at least a few dates. The Kinks had pulled out all the stops, Ray Davies mincing and winking at the girls, kid brother Dave pulling guitar-hero poses, and by the time they left, even though they didn't have a record out yet in the States, they were greeted with a phalanx of screaming girls at the airport in New York – a good sign. Holly then pushed hard again, to break "You Really Got Me," and it had gone to Number One, soon followed by "Tired of Waiting for You."[10] The Kinks hadn't even formally toured the States on their own yet, but they were already in the top tier of the new British invasion bands.

They finally arrived in America in the summer of 1965, with Holly accompanying them, in lieu of their managers, who inexplicably stayed at home – and a good thing it was that he was there. For on the Fourth of July weekend, they had been booked on a Dick Clark TV special, headlining a few other British acts. The Kinks were late, because they always were, and at the studio a union guy started complaining, bad-mouthing the "limeys" with no talent who, he declared, were taking jobs away from American musicians just because of their long hair. He was probably just looking for a payoff, but Holly knew the Kinks' reputation as pub brawlers, and he knew that if they heard this, punches would be flying. A backlash was beginning to develop against the British Invasion; a fistfight could end up getting the Kinks banned from the States for good. So he'd found someone to distract Ray Davies, and in the meantime found Dick Clark and got him to calm the union guy down and get him out of the way. [11]The show proceeded without further problems, and the Kinks continued having hits in America, reaching Number One again with "Sunny Afternoon" in the fall of 1966.[12]

Some of the other bands had been harder to break, their wildness off-putting to programmers and promoters, if not to the fans. The Who had gotten a Number One hit in the spring of 1966 with "Substitute," after Holly had responded to Kit Lambert and Chris Stamp's pleas to give their act the opening slot on the

Kinks' fall 1965 American tour – to the chagrin of the Kinks, who had honed their "wild" stage act only to see it blown away by the Who's auto-destruction.[13] The Rolling Stones, too, had taken a bit longer, but "Satisfaction" had been the clincher: the minute Holly heard it he knew it would be a smash, and it was. The Stones had swiftly risen to the number two pole position behind the Beatles, and while he had befriended all of them, he had a special sympathy for Brian Jones, who reminded him of a lost puppy, gradually being more and more sidelined by the confident and aggressive Jagger and Richards. He knew Brian had to be more assertive – but what band could function in the long term with members at cross-purposes like that?

Now, this night in February 1967, with the Stones on the eve of their fifth Number One hit in the States, he found himself on the telephone with Brian Jones.

"I can't go on like this," Brian gasped, between sobs.

"Do you want me to come by?" Holly replied. *Jesus*, he thought, *I've never heard him sound so bad. I hope he's not holding a bottle of pills or something.*

"No, I just need someone to talk to," Brian said. "It's everything, Buddy, everything. First they take my band away...and they freeze me out...and now this? I love Anita! Keith knows that! How the bloody hell could they do this?" He sobbed so hard he sounded ready to choke.

Buddy heard him take a long suck from his asthma inhaler. Well, if he's using that, Holly reasoned to himself, he's at least trying to stay alive. No suicide. Not yet, anyway.

"Brian...."

"I wrote 'Ruby Tuesday'!" Brian shrieked. "I sat down at the piano and I made up that melody! I WROTE that song! Why is my name not on the credits? Tell me that, Buddy. Why the fuck is my name not on the credits?"

"I don't know," Holly said, trying to sound calm. "Do you want me to talk to Andrew about it?"

"ANDREW DOESN'T CARE!" Brian howled. "Andrew's on their side! The whole lot of them, they're all trying to tear me apart!"

This went on for almost two hours. Buddy didn't really have time for this. The call had come while he was working on his financials, and he had a lot of work to do. But he made time. Brian was a friend, and he clearly needed someone right now.

"I don't even know how I can stay a musician," Brian said. "How can I do anything but quit now?"

"Because music is your life," Buddy said firmly.

"My life's been ruined," Brian said.

"No it hasn't," Buddy said, putting his foot down. "Not as long as you have the ability to make music. Keep making music. Forget about Anita. Any woman who could do that isn't worthy of you. And Brian?"

"Yes?"

"Start praying. I mean it."

May 10, 1967

When the scheduled date of Mick Jagger and Keith Richards' arraignment arrived, with what seemed like a thousand reporters and TV cameramen following them, Brian Jones was not at home. It wasn't supposed to be that way.

The night before, he'd been doing what he'd done most days since February – drinking a lot and staring at the empty space that used to be Anita. He didn't bother to answer the phone the first time it rang, nor the second, nor the third. But the caller was insistent.

Finally, with an angry growl, he got up to pick up the relentlessly ringing phone. He half-hoped it would be Anita. He half-hoped it wasn't.

"Brian Jones?" an unfamiliar man's voice said.

He almost hung up. Some fan who's got hold of my number, he thought. I'm in no mood for this shit. But something compelled him to mutter, his irritation showing, "Yes?"

"Don't be at your flat tomorrow or you'll be arrested."

At once he snapped out of his stupor. "Who is this?" he said angrily.

"Never mind who it is." The voice sounded stern, officious – the kind of voice an authority figure…a policeman…might be expected to have. "Just bloody well listen to me. The police are going to raid your flat tomorrow. They're looking for drugs. They expect you'll have them and they want to arrest you. They want it to be a big media sensation – on the same day the other two Rolling Stones are being arraigned, a third one gets busted too."

Brian couldn't believe it. Some crank was trying to scare him. But there was something about that voice that impelled him not to hang up. After a second or two of silence, he said, "Why are you telling me this?"

"A message from a friend."

"What friend?"

"Don't ask me that, you stupid wanker."

Arsehole. Still, Brian found he couldn't hang up.

"Listen and do what I tell you. Another friend will be at your flat in twenty minutes. You won't recognize him, but let him in anyway. You and he are going to go through your flat and gather up any drugs. Any at all, wherever they are. You've got to get everything – don't miss even a seed. Then get it all together and flush it down the loo."

"How do I –"

"Shut up, you little shit," the voice said. "I'm not doing this for you, and neither is the man you'll meet tonight. We owe a favor to a friend. So if you don't believe me and do what you want anyway, I won't bloody care."

Brian breathed deeply. "All right, what else?"

"After you get rid of the drugs, get out of there. Clear out of the flat and lay low for a couple of days. Don't come back till I call you again and tell you it's all right."

With a click, the line went dead.

Brian could feel himself starting to shiver. Even though the call seemed mad, it was quite unnerving.

He began to catalogue in his head, trying to clear the alcohol fog out of his mind so he could think clearly. Of all the people he knew – this couldn't have been Andrew, and he wouldn't give a toss anyway...was it one of his friends, somebody he knew from the clubs, the Ad Lib, the Speakeasy, a gallery owner like Dunbar – it didn't sound like something the Beatles would...

Holly!

He'd been talking to Buddy Holly on the phone so much lately. The only one who listened. The only one who seemed to understand.

And Holly had contacts. He knew people. As a promoter in London, he had to. It wouldn't do to have concerts busted all the time.

A friend, the voice had said. Now he was afraid not to believe.

The knock at the door came just about twenty minutes later, just as the voice said. Brian saw only that he wore a black cap, held his collar high about his neck and kept his face averted. It wasn't anyone he knew, not that he could get a good look. He tried to say something but the man abruptly shushed him. He remained quiet. It could have been the same person who called him, or it could have been a confederate. He had no way of knowing, and he would never know.

The man strolled into the flat, heading silently for the bedroom. Brian followed. In the bedroom, the man stopped in front of a chest of drawers, pointing at the top drawer. Brian slid it open. *So this is how it's going to work,* he realized.

The man silently rummaged through the contents of the drawer, finding a handful of blue and white pills. He withdrew a small canvas bag from a pocket and dropped the pills into the bag.

Throughout the rest of the drawers, then the rest of the bedroom, then the rest of the apartment, Brian assisted the man in searching every drawer. Every drug the man found – tabs of LSD, uppers and downers stuffed into shirt pockets, small plastic bags of with white cocaine powder or dark masses of hash – went into the canvas bag. Brian felt compelled to cooperate, even as he silently raged at the hundreds of pounds spent on those drugs going to waste.

When they had searched the whole apartment, Brian and the man proceeded to the bathroom. In three loads, so as not to block the pipes, the drugs swirled down the bowl and into the London sewers.

The man then made a beeline for the door. Brian tried to say thank you – he didn't even know why – but the man again shushed him.

He leaned against the door jamb, watching the man make his way down the hall. He closed the door and leaned with his back against it as he picked up the phone and dialed a number. His driver was already used to middle-of-the-night calls. This would be nothing unusual.

"Could you have the car ready about 10 o'clock?" he asked. Stopping for a minute, he realized he had to come up with a destination. "We're going…to Cheltenham. To visit my mum and dad. It's a surprise."

The next day, when the news cameras arrived, all they found was a gaggle of frustrated bobbies. Brian's regular cleaning woman had opened the door. They had searched the flat thoroughly. Jones wasn't there, but no matter – a warrant could still be issued for his arrest. Given his reputation, the police had no doubt they would find plenty to incriminate him with.

But after two hours of searching, the police had turned up nothing. The disarrayed clothing in the drawers surely seemed suspicious – but there was nothing criminal about it that the police could prove.

Eventually, the TV news people grew weary of watching the police fruitlessly searching the house and left. The news that day indeed carried images of Jagger and Richards arriving at the courts for their arraignment – but there was no Brian Jones drug bust to join those images.

The police were somewhere between annoyed and confused. Maybe Jones wasn't using drugs at all? On the other hand, if he was, they had already made fools of themselves once on camera – while the BBC chose not to air the footage and quietly buried the news of the raid, there was no reason to assume they wouldn't be made fools of again, and there was little point in carrying out further raids without the media coverage.

The police decided to wait and see what transpired before raiding Jones again, if only to make sure that he was indeed a viable target.[14]

CHAPTER THREE: GETTING BETTER

June 1, 1967

The first of the month saw the release of the Beatles' psychedelic magnum opus, *Sgt. Pepper's Lonely Hearts Club Band*. Critics worldwide acclaimed the album a masterpiece – an artistic statement in a medium that hadn't even been thought of as "art" until very recently.

Yet George Martin, the Beatles' producer, at least, read the reviews with ambivalence. Things hadn't gone as either he or the boys would have wished.

The first two tracks the group had begun work on in December had been groundbreaking, and Martin's importance to the Beatles as their producer had been clearly reflected in both. "Strawberry Fields Forever," that incredible montage, had been built around two separate tracks, one slowed down after Martin had discovered that when it was slowed to match the tempo of the other, it matched it in pitch as well. John's lead vocal was culled from the slowed-down track, and gave the song a world-weary, yet hesitant quality that underscored the confusion John's lyrics expressed.

Paul's "Penny Lane," a sprightly yet surreal reminiscence about Liverpool childhood scenes, was lifted by a solo cornet in the instrumental break, consisting of figures which Paul – unable to read music – had hummed to Martin, who had in turn transcribed them.

George Martin considered these two songs the strongest pieces the Beatles had coming out of the spring sessions and tried to convince the lads to hold them for the album. But Capitol was pressuring the group for product – it had been six months since *Revolver*, an unconscionably long time by mid-Sixties standards. The Beatles gave in, issuing the two songs as a single in late January. Almost immediately, they, and Martin, regretted it.[15]

For barely was the new single out when the Beach Boys released *Smile*, Brian Wilson's "teenage symphony to God." Like *Sgt. Pepper*, it featured thematic, deep music with the songs blending into one another. The Beach Boys hadn't come up with the Beatles' idea of creating a doppelganger – Sgt. Pepper's Band – but they hadn't had to; the presence of the increasingly-mysterious Brian Wilson was intriguing enough.[16]

The Beatles had little choice now but to include both songs on *Sgt. Pepper*. An elaborate, unfinished track called "She's Leaving Home" was set aside – permanently, as it turned out. Another, "When I'm 64," was set aside to become a 45 B-side. Paul was a little annoyed that both of the outtakes would be from among his songs, until Martin pointed out that even with the two deletions, he would still have more songs than John on the album – "Penny Lane," after all, was Paul's.[17]

The album was stronger now, but it wasn't a surprise, at least not a complete one. Two of the best songs would already have been heard by the world before its release. Ironically, this put them in the same boat as the Beach Boys, whose "Good Vibrations" was a hit months before *Smile* was finished. But Paul, in particular, had looked forward to unveiling a new collection of music before the world.

George Martin was deeply frustrated, and so was the group, with having caved in to Capitol's pressure. They had no fear that

Sgt. Pepper would be overshadowed in the long run by *Smile*, and indeed it wasn't – the Beatles were simply a bigger act than the Beach Boys, the biggest in the world, and their new masterpiece was sure to draw unprecedented attention. But never again, Martin and the Beatles vowed, would they let the record company pressure them into releasing something until they were good and ready.

June 18, 1967

First *Smile,* and then *Sgt. Pepper,* heralded the beginning of a "summer of love" – a summer when the yearnings and hopes and dreams of the youth movement burst into full flower.

A new generation had come up, in large numbers, looking hopefully but fearfully at the world around them. They saw a world riven by war and violence, a world consumed with greed and selfishness, a world where "getting ahead" was the most important concern of the nicest people on their block. They saw poverty where there should be abundance, anomie where there should be happiness, conflict where there should be peace, hatred where there should be love. And they were looking for a better way.

It was a deeply spiritual ache, one that was hard for those who felt it even to understand, let alone put into words. But it seemed to so many that life could be better, richer, more connected, more loving – that people could live authentically and without pretense, that life could be about genuine sharing and concern. "Peace" and "love" were the words on many lips that summer.

When John Lennon had said the Beatles were "more popular than Jesus," some had misinterpreted his words as arrogance.

But others, even the Vatican, understood what he meant: many had abandoned faith. Some paid it lip service, attending church every Sunday, wagging disapproving fingers at the clothes and music and behavior of their kids – but going to church was a matter of propriety, or public image, or simple habit, rather than something deeply felt within their hearts. They had come back from the war and its victory, and had given their children much in the way of material goods – material goods this Depression- and war-stricken generation had never known in their own youth – and, despite what they thought, their children were not ungrateful. But in creating a world that was materially full, it seemed, they had allowed it to become spiritually empty. At least, so thought a growing contingent of the young.

Few political radicals were to be found amid this group. Those who tried to co-opt the movement found themselves very much unwelcome. Political radicalism was seen by the "love crowd" as just another system, another means of dividing people, a new set of "Us" and "Them" when what was needed was "One."[18]

They had had some success in the past. The civil rights movement was a big deal. As young Northerners had volunteered to go South on the Freedom Rides, to participate in the voter registration drives, to march with Martin Luther King to Washington in 1963, the radicals believed they may have found their moment. For a while, it looked as though the left might have a "wedge," a chance to exploit the civil rights movement for their own purposes.

But then President Kennedy partially defused the issue by signing the Civil Rights Act into law in 1964[19]. Then, after his 1964 reelection, he moved immediately after the Watts riot in

1965, forming a special commission to study the needs and grievances of the black community. Even as some blacks drifted into the militancy of the Black Panthers, Kennedy's commission, and the recommendations acted on by the president, did much to alleviate the problems experienced by the black community. Indeed, during that "long hot summer of love," President Kennedy personally intervened to cut short an incipient riot in Detroit.[20]

Then, later in the Sixties, the political left suffered a blow to its credibility over Vietnam. The film showing up on American televisions was grainy, shaky, of poor quality – smuggled by way of Cambodia and Thailand by courageous journalists who risked (and sometimes lost) their lives to bring the news of the horrible war to the West. The images were sparse and scattered, but they were enough: Soviet airplanes bombing villages, Soviet infantrymen massacring innocent civilians, the indiscriminate use of napalm…it was getting harder and harder for leftist intellectuals like Bertrand Russell or William Kunstler to defend those monstrous acts. Beatle Paul McCartney had met Russell a year before at a gathering of the rich and beautiful in London – and shunned him.

So the younger generation wanted no part of political radicalism, but sought instead to find a deeper answer – a way, many insisted, to get closer to the God their parents excoriated them for abandoning. And so they experimented, with their clothes, their hairstyles, their lifestyles – most of all, with their music. The music was becoming more sophisticated, abler to express the hopes, fears and wishes of its fans. Rock was growing up.

There was *Smile,* and *Sgt. Pepper,* and now, there was the Monterey International Pop Festival, held on the weekend of June 18 in Monterey, California, the most prestigious event in live rock and roll up to this time – indeed, the first live show to which the words "prestigious" and "rock" could both reasonably be applied in the same sentence.

The opening act on Friday night was the lightweight pop band the Association, invited to open the festival for the purpose of making sure the sound equipment, lighting, and so forth were working OK. Whether or not anyone told the band this, they innocently played their hearts out, giving the festival a lively start.

Then the "real" artists took the stage, one by one. The Kinks led off a Friday night dominated by pop sounds, their cheery good spirits notwithstanding their recent Number Four single about poverty, "Dead End Street." [21] Then came the cheery folk-rock of the Lovin' Spoonful, followed by the elegant Italian-American soul of the Rascals, who made it into D.A. Pennebaker's movie of the event (*Monterey Pop*) with the Number One song in the country at the moment, "Groovin'." [22] Two Motown acts, the Temptations and Marvin Gaye, both already responsible for a bevy of classic soul hits, followed, and then the psychedelicized Eric Burdon and the Animals, their former dark and gritty blues sound replaced by a swirling, colorful (if pretentious) acid-rock sound featuring, among other instruments, a violin.[23] The literary, erudite folk duo of Simon and Garfunkel gave a typically stirring set. At the end of the first night, the Beach Boys appeared, with Brian Wilson joining them onstage for the first time since 1964, his intense stage fright seemingly tempered by the positive response to *Smile*. He sang just one song, "Surf's Up," with the boys before fleeing to the safety of the backstage area – but it was enough; no one ever doubted the Beach Boys' "hip" credentials ever again.[24]

The second day's sets began in the afternoon. The swamp-blues band Canned Heat got things rolling with their "Mississippi noise." They were followed by the psychedelic folk-rock of Love,[25] then the trippier acid-rock of Country Joe and the Fish. Following in order were the straightforward and earnest blues of the Paul Butterfield Blues Band, more acid-rock sounds from the Quicksilver Messenger Service, an exciting soul set from Stevie Wonder, the innovative blues-rock-with-a-horn-section sound of the Electric Flag, and the rough, unpolished, gutbucket soul music of Wilson Pickett.[26]

After a break, the Saturday program resumed with San Francisco's Moby Grape, one of the few San Francisco bands who played straight-up rock and roll rather than acid-rock excursions, up first.[27] Jazz artist Hugh Masakela was next, followed by folk-rock heroes the Byrds, whose set was one of the few disappointments of the weekend, with David Crosby clearly at odds with leader Roger McGuinn. The hard-rock power trio Cream and the stately, vaguely church-like Procol Harum, each making their American debut, were next, and Cream's stunning version of "Spoonful" turned out to be a highlight of the movie. The Velvet Underground performed a classic set, but one that was ill-received, as their New York street grittiness didn't translate well to the flower-power Monterey crowd.[28] The Jefferson Airplane, the acid-rock darlings of the San Francisco crowd, was more welcome, and appeared in the movie performing Richie Havens' "High Flyin' Bird." Finally, the criminally-neglected – at least until that night – versatile soul singer Otis Redding, with the skilled Memphis backup band Booker T. and the MG's, performed an astounding set, an appearance that made him an overnight star.

    Sunday afternoon featured two acts: a brief set by the gentle, flower-power folk singer Donovan, [29]with the rest of the afternoon devoted to Indian sitar player Ravi Shankar. The evening set was led off by the hard British-Invasion rock of the Yardbirds, on their last legs as a band by that point, but with Jimmy Page determined to give his all, partly to help lay the groundwork for what he was planning next.[30] They were followed by a legendary performance by Big Brother and the Holding Company, and the national debut of that band's singer, Janis Joplin, who like Otis Redding emerged from the festival a star, with the audience clearly overwhelmed by her performance of "Ball and Chain." The eerie sound of the Doors was next, with a set that would land them in the movie performing "The Crystal Ship" from their debut album. [31] Buffalo Springfield, folk-rockers in the mold of the Byrds, performed a somewhat indifferent set, marred by Neil Young's tension with the rest of the band onstage.

    The Who, the loudest and most anarchic of all the British bands, to no one's surprise, were stratospheric, with Pete Townshend smashing his guitar for one of the last times on stage on an unforgettable "My Generation." The Grateful Dead, granddaddy of the psychedelic San Francisco bands, should have had an equally unforgettable night, but as Jerry Garcia later complained, they were stuck in the most overlooked point in the program – after the Who, and before the Jimi Hendrix Experience.

Hendrix, making his American debut, and introduced by Brian Jones – who, with no drug charges hanging over him, left his bandmates behind to stop by the Festival – lived up to the breathless stories that had been crossing the Atlantic for months, performing a set that took the electric guitar into places no one in the Monterey crowd had ever heard before, and ending by lighting his guitar on fire at the end of "Wild Thing" (a suggestion from bandmate Noel Redding that he smash his guitar as well was nixed when Hendrix said, "That's old hat – the Who have been doing that for two years.").[32]

Festival co-organizers the Mamas and the Papas, with their jangling folk-rock and soaring harmonies, trying hard not to be forgotten – though their set, in large part, was - came after Hendrix. Finally, Bob Dylan, the enigmatic poet who had become the voice of his generation, and who alone could have closed such a night (apart, of course, from the now-retired Beatles), having recovered from his motorcycle crash the year before, made his first live appearance since the accident. The immortal scene, captured by Pennebaker's cameras, was of Dylan – ironically commenting on the abuse he had received from folkies on his last two tours after abandoning folk music and protest in favor of rock and stream-of-consciousness lyrics– saying "Some of you are even clapping" before leading his backup group, Levon and the Hawks (a.k.a. the Band), into "I Don't Believe You (She Acts Like We've Never Met)."[33]

August 3, 1967

"The Maharishi?" Brian Jones said, staring skeptically at George Harrison.

He'd been spending a lot of time with the Beatles lately. After all, Mick and Keith were behind bars, leaving the Rolling Stones idle, and most of the rest of Brian's circle of friends had been scared off by the drug bust.

When Mick Jagger and Keith Richards' case went to trial on June 27, both had been swiftly convicted. The evidence planted by the mysterious David Schneidermann had been damning, even though Jagger and Richards had insisted that the drugs were not theirs – few doubted that the Stones were heavy drug users. With LSD and cannabis found by the police, no Establishment figures stepped forward to defend the two rock stars.[34]

On June 30, the pair had been sentenced to three months in prison. They were released on bail pending appeal of their sentences. But on July 31, the Court of Criminal Appeal refused to overturn their sentences, although it did reduce them to two months for each.[35] Weeping and wailing Rolling Stones fans had lined the streets as Jagger and Richards were removed to Wormwood Scrubs. Some in the rock community protested – the Who announced that they were releasing a series of Jagger/Richards-composed singles to "Keep their work before the public until they were again free to record themselves." The first single, "The Last Time"/"Under My Thumb", was followed in August by a second, "19th Nervous Breakdown"/"Stupid Girl". However, neither Who single did particularly well, and the Who abandoned the effort after the second single.[36] (The Who had

65

enough work on their hands anyway; they spent the late summer in the studio working on their concept album *The Who Sell Out*, which yielded their second Number One hit in the States, "I Can See for Miles.")[37]

Brian Jones's behavior since May 10 gave very public evidence of an attempt to give up drugs and alcohol – he had checked into the Priory Nursing Home in London in July to dry out. The police, apparently satisfied with having bagged Jagger and Richards, left him alone. He came out of the hospital a few weeks later, but by then, Jagger and Richards were on their way to prison, and Brian had little to do.

Anita, of course, could go to hell as far as Brian was concerned – no matter that he still loved her desperately. He wanted nothing more to do with her. She'd called him, of course – Keith was in jail and she was bored. She offered to fuck Brian, to blow him, to do all the stuff to him that he used to love. But he had his pride. She'd torn him up, and that was that. Let her run to Keith if that's what she wanted. Filthy Austrian scumbag...

"Well, does it make any sense to keep doing that?" asked George, breaking Brian's train of thought. He was pointing to the table. Brian had hardly realized that he was reaching for his brandy glass.

"You just got out of hospital," said George.

Brian sighed. He was in no mood for a lecture.

"Bloody hell," Brian finally said. "I know I just got out of hospital. What do you want me to do? How else am I supposed to stop thinking about Anita? The Maharishi is going to do that?"

"No," said George. "But you learn that your fears and earthly wants don't matter. What matters is the Lord, the One."

Brian sighed again.

"Look," said George. "Think of it this way. You're hurting because of Anita. That's because of all the baggage that you have around her – you expected her to be a certain way, and she wasn't that way. But when you're one with the Lord you don't expect thing you can't control to be *any* way. They just *are*. You leave it all up to Him."

"I don't see how the Maharishi will make the pain go away," said Brian.

"He doesn't," said George. "But you transcend it."

This was now the third day in a row during which George had relentlessly spent hours trying to convince Brian that he needed to turn away from drugs and drinking. His heavy-lidded eyes, that had looked so sullen in many a Beatles photo shoot, stared across the room into the bloodshot eyes of the Stones guitarist. "So," Brian said, "transcend it – how?"

"You get beyond so-called reality," said George. "You get beyond what happens in this worldly reality."

Brian sat back and reflected deeply on George's words. Based on the small amount of reading of Eastern philosophies and religions he had done so far, this did seem to make sense. Still...

"So how much does he charge for this sage wisdom?"

"Two months' salary."

Brian chuckled. Two months' salary for him and George was more than most people made in a year. But it wasn't like he couldn't afford it. And if this cat WAS on the level....

He carefully set the glass down. "So...he gives you a mantra?"

August 17, 1967

Two weeks later, Brian Jones was at home, meditating.

It was a very hard discipline. Staying focused on the mantra, on that softly repeated, chanted phrase the Maharishi had given him, was enormously difficult. Brian's mind tended to wander, and random thoughts would interrupt the flow. Normally, this type of "chatter" flits through one's mind without being noticed, but it interferes with the love emanating from God, the Maharishi had said. It was necessary to remain conscious of the "chatter," even while meditating, and force it out of one's mind, to continue focusing on the mantra, in order to reach a state of pure consciousness and awareness, where one's mind was truly open to the divine One.

So the Maharishi had told him. He hadn't been able to get there yet. But he hadn't given up.

It was doubly hard for Brian, who had to discipline himself not only to meditate but to refrain from drugs and alcohol. He knew that the only alternative – to go back – was a road he did not want to take, even before the Maharishi had come along. But the urges were strong, and it was a brutal battle to fight them.

At least now, though, he had friends. Before, he'd been left to battle his demons alone by Anita and the rest of the Rolling Stones (other than Bill Wyman, who, also in a state of enforced idleness, had been phoning Brian regularly to check in on him and provide support). Now, however, his growing closeness to the Beatles, George in particular, had brought him into their circle, and George was an avid supporter of Brian's work on meditation. He also had the Maharishi – and his friendship with Buddy Holly, who while not a meditation "freak" was willing to do whatever he needed to help Brian through his alcohol problems.

It's like learning to play a musical instrument for the first time, Brian told himself. You need that same level of discipline as when you are first learning to play the guitar and the fingertips on your left hand haven't hardened and are bleeding, or when you're learning to play the saxophone and getting blisters on your lip. "If I didn't play so many instruments," he thought, "I wouldn't be able to keep going. I've got that well of self-discipline to draw on from those experiences. I know how to be disciplined; I've done it before. Maybe not for a while, but I can do it again for this."

That afternoon, as the sun streamed through the curtains of the little meditation room he had established in his King's Road flat in Chelsea, it finally happened. Deep into the meditation, he at last felt it.

It was not like the palette of hallucinations that came from LSD, or the rush of cocaine, or even the pleasant stupor of alcohol. Brian felt something utterly unlike anything he had ever before experienced. A sensibility of the deepest serenity and peace overwhelmed him, feeling as though it was not only pouring through his mind but penetrating into every cell in his body. Yet, at the same time, he felt an incredible clarity, as though he were aware of each and every one of those cells, and how they were working in harmony, even as he was working in harmony with the rest of the universe and with God. He felt the universe around him in absolute perfection, and felt the deepest connection to the Higher Spirit – the One – God – he had ever known, a sensation of pure joy that made every stimulant , chemical or human, he had indulged in his entire life seem as wispy as a cloud by comparison. He knew – he knew immediately – that this is how he wanted to feel forever.

And it was gone, just as quickly as it had come. He yearned for it. But even in the yearning he felt joy. He felt blissful happiness even in the pain of losing the momentary burst of spiritual consciousness, unlike all the other "earthly" drugs that had just left him craving more.

He suddenly felt as if nothing else mattered. Not the Stones, nor the recognition he had so long craved. Not Anita, nor his pain at her betrayal. Suddenly, all of it shrank to a vanishing point, becoming laughingly unimportant. He could get Anita back, and become recognized by everyone as the leader of the Stones – and it would be like a tiny drop of water compared to the rich ocean that lay opened to his mind. He knew, now, truly, how to be happy.

He had arrived. He knew it. He could seek and find it again. This, he knew at once, would change everything in his life.[38]

CHAPTER FOUR: THE FOOL ON THE HILL

August 26, 1967

As the Beatles left for a seminar that day with the Maharishi Mahesh Yogi in Bangor, Wales, their manager, Brian Epstein, planned to spend the evening at his country home at Kingsley Hill, East Sussex. He had planned a weekend of partying and sexual escapades before joining the Beatles in Bangor, as he had promised. Two employees of Brian's company, NEMS, Peter Brown and Geoffrey Ellis, joined him at his house. Brian, however, was more interested in the "boys" that had been invited up for the weekend. When no prospective sexual partners transpired, Brian, disillusioned and drinking heavily, left for his residence in London.

In the morning, Joanne Newfield, Epstein's personal assistant, was unable to wake him. Shrieking, she quickly summoned Brown and Ellis, who had no more success, and who called for an ambulance. Medical teams arrived, but despite their best efforts, they were unable to revive Epstein, who had taken a lethal dose of barbiturates.

It had been Jane Asher, Paul's girlfriend, who had answered the phone, that one that wouldn't stop ringing in the dormitory at the college in Bangor, Wales, where the Beatles were staying. They had only just been initiated by the Maharishi and had enjoyed a late lunch. Now they were standing in stunned silence, their faces blank. No one shed a tear. The shock was too great for that.

Paul quietly slipped out of the room, saying in a soft voice that he would head back to London to take care of arrangements there. The Maharishi came out and spoke to the others, telling them not to allow grief to overwhelm them but to send happy thoughts to Brian Epstein wherever he was. George seemed the most receptive to his words, clasping the Maharishi's hand and managing a faint smile. John and Ringo merely nodded, their faces ashen.

Meanwhile, the press had already begun to gather around the college entrance. Patti Harrison, George's wife, came inside the room.

"They're saying the press won't leave until they get a statement," she said, her voice a hoarse whisper.

No one broke the stony silence for a minute or two. Ringo, half under his breath, asked what there was to say.

Finally John, taking charge, said, "I'll do it," and stumbled, dazed, out of the door and toward the entrance. George and Ringo shortly followed.

They fumbled their way through the questions, barely able to answer. The reporters pressed them about the Beatles' future without Mr. Epstein. The three Beatles fielded such questions as best they could, saying only that they would return to London shortly. They said what nice things they could about Epstein and related how the Maharishi had tried to comfort them.

The interview was brief, but it was an ordeal. As John returned to the dormitory, to await the car that would take them back to London, the tears finally began to flow. Ringo sat down across from him, his eyes reddening.

"Stupid wankers," Ringo said. "How are we supposed to know what we're doing next?"

John had buried his face in his hands, his round wire-framed glasses riding up onto his forehead. Teary-eyed, he looked up at Ringo. "We've fucking had it," he said. "That's it."

Ringo said nothing but stared back with just the faintest hint of a nod.

"How can we do anything?" John said. "I mean...who can run it all...all that business stuff around and none of us knows anything about it...."

John broke down crying copiously. Ringo, his own eyes tearing, got up and walked into the next room. There he found the telephone, the one that Jane had answered.

Ringo looked back at John, then out of the window at the sunny warm day outside. Then, stoically, he made a decision.

Picking up the telephone, he dialed Buddy Holly's number.

September 4, 1967

The diner was nothing special. Just another run-of-the-mill greasy spoon, like hundreds of others in New York City, with its Formica counters and stools with vinyl upholstery, with a fry grill in the window for cooking burgers and hot dogs, and a list of daily specials – ham and eggs, tuna on toast, grilled cheese on rye – chalked up on the blackboard next to the hand-lettered menu. Certainly it wasn't the kind of place that had the cachet of the groovy coffeehouses of the nearby East Village, the kind of places frequented by the new young mods in their beads and bells and Nehru jackets. To those people, the little "coffee shop" would have seemed hopelessly old-fashioned.

Still, it had its regulars. One of them came through the door, breathlessly sauntering up to the counter.

"Hi, Sam," the attractive young woman said.

"Hello, May," the genial cook and owner answered from behind the counter. "How's your day today?"

"Fantastic," she said, sitting down at an empty stool. She could feel the sets of male eyes in the room landing on her legs as she crossed them, eyes that were grateful for the day Mary Quant had bestowed the miniskirt on the Western world. But she ignored them.

May was used to catching eyes. Petite but beautiful, with delicate Asian features, and long hair that swept down nearly to her elbows, she had been turning heads since she was barely a teenager. But right now dating, and men, were the last things on her mind.

"Look at this," she said, a grin crossing her pretty face, as she held up a check for Sam to see.

"Hmm…I wouldn't wave that around if I were you," he said. "That's a big payday. Congratulations!" The check was payable to "May Ling" in the amount of ten thousand dollars.[39]

"Thanks," she said. "Let me have a soda. I'm thirsty as hell. Talking and talking for the last two hours." She shook her head. "I'm supposed to be an artist, you know? Not a hustler."

"What's the difference, these days?" Sam said. She broke into laughter.

"Wait till you see the movie I make," she said. "That'll show you the difference."

"Hey, China doll" – the voice came from over her shoulder – "want to make some chop suey with me?" She turned around to see a thirtyish man, with slicked hair, probably a salesman, in a bad suit.

She rolled her eyes. "Do you always try to pick up girls by insulting them?"

"What?"

She dropped her New York accent and went into a fake Chinese-immigrant voice. "Oh, *most honorable* sir," she said, faking a bow. "Why you not *fuck off*?"

"Hey, sweetie," the guy said. "I'm just looking for some fun."

She pulled the crucifix out from under her shirt. "Well, first off, I'm Catholic," she said. "I don't fool around like that. And second, if I did fool around, it sure as hell wouldn't be with the likes of you." Sam suppressed a smile.

"Jeez, what a bitch," the odious man said half under his breath as he walked off.

"Want me to get rid of him for you?" Sam asked her.

"Nah," she said. "Just some asshole. Assholes can't ruin this day. Two hours of yammering with an investor – but I got enough funding now to do my movie!" she said, her voice rising with excitement. "Now I need to start getting things together – casting, film crew, equipment – "

"Sounds like a lot of work to me," Sam said.

"What my parents did was real work," she said with a coquettish smile. "I get to have fun while working."

Sam chuckled. Then he turned toward the small television set on a corner of the counter, and turned up the volume. "Are you following this Vietnam thing at all? The Russians are sending more troops, Cronkite said today."

She shook her head. "Not good. But Mao won't try going south – he's too afraid of losing Manchuria. As long as Chiang keeps his nose out of it, shouldn't be a problem." [40]She took a drink from the straw in her soda. "My parents still send money to our relatives back in Shanghai, you know."

"Your dad's got the money to send," he said, lowering his voice so other patrons wouldn't overhear.

"Well, that's why they came here. American dream and all that. Plus no war – sort of a big factor. And they bring up their youngest daughter to be a good Chinese and a good Catholic too, and then she decides to be a filmmaker and goes to film school, and screws them all up."

"Hey, they ought to be proud of you. First in your class, right?" Sam, it seemed, knew everything about everyone. "Yeah, but in film – what good is that, right?" she said with a laugh, and took another drink of soda.

She sat back and stared out the window, already beginning in her mind to piece together a script for the idea she had in mind. She noticed out of the corner of her eye another man staring at her legs, but he held no more interest than the dismissed bad-suit guy. She hadn't even had a boyfriend in over four months, she thought to herself, and she was much too busy now to think about one. "Art comes first," she said aloud. Sam, who had heard her say those words before, quietly wiped the counter down.

September 8, 1967

Buddy Holly, on payroll now as the Beatles' "business adviser," was finding himself more and more taking charge of events, stepping into the vacuum created by Epstein's death.

The Beatles had made plans to begin filming a new movie the following week. They had in mind a sort of British version of the psychedelic cross-country trip taken by Ken Kesey's group of sidekicks, the Merry Pranksters, in America a few years earlier. The Pranksters, early LSD advocates, drove around the country in a dayglo-painted bus, stoned out of their heads and filming everything in sight. The Beatles were impressed by the spontaneity of the concept (ignoring the fact that the resulting Pranksters' film was virtually unwatchable), and hoped to do the same for a one-hour special to be titled *Magical Mystery Tour* and aired on British TV at Christmas.

Buddy Holly, meeting with the Beatles to discuss the movie idea, said he thought the basic idea of a trippy, otherworldly "mystery tour" taking place in a bus that comes across surprising "happenings" wasn't a bad one, but that a proper director and scriptwriter should be hired to flesh the idea out more. Paul and John objected, arguing the concept would lose its spontaneity if it were planned in advance. Buddy dug in his heels. "This is the first use of the Apple name," he said, referring to the company the Beatles were in the process of setting up. "Do you want it to be a failure?"

If it were only Brian Epstein, John and Paul might not have been willing to listen. After all, hadn't John told Eppy once before to "stick to his percentages, and we'll look after the music"? But this was *Buddy Holly*. However close they had become as friends in the last few years, the Beatles all remained in awe of Buddy, one of the founding fathers of rock and roll, one of their greatest inspirations and influences – their very *name* was a tribute to Holly and his old band, the Crickets. So John and Paul listened a trifle meekly as Buddy said gently, "Look, fellows, you haven't written or directed a movie before, and it can be really easy to screw that up – look at what happened to Elvis, for

God's sakes. I'd never tell you what to do about your songs. But you could easily make a bad movie and make fools of yourselves in front of the whole country. Keep the idea, but let somebody with better film experience fill in the blanks. You can't just mess around like the Pranksters did. That was really just a home movie. This is supposed to go on national television."

It took some batting back and forth, but Buddy's line of argument finally began to convince Paul, always the most levelheaded Beatle and the one most reluctant to look foolish. Paul was the strongest advocate of the movie in the first place, so when he changed his mind, Buddy won the day. The group decided to postpone the filming of *Magical Mystery Tour* into October, to allow time to hire a film crew, director and scriptwriter. Also, to provide enough time for postproduction and editing work, they decided not to present the film to the BBC for a Christmas airing as planned, but instead present it for airing sometime in early 1968.[41]

Meanwhile, Brian Jones spent the month of September meditating fervently and discussing faith and the Maharishi with George, John, and Ravi Shankar, the renowned Indian musician and George's sitar teacher. The meditation was working wonders for Brian. Every day, the fear, the gnawing worry that he wasn't good enough, receded a little bit.

He was playing the guitar more and more now, using that as a substitute for the drugs and alcohol that had been his old means of staving off boredom. It was a slog at first – the drugs and booze had taken their toll, and he'd lost some of his touch. But the more he meditated, the more focused he felt, and the more he felt the presence of God. And with that, he prayed for his talent not to be gone forever. And slowly, as the days and weeks passed, and he jammed for long hours on his guitar, his old suppleness and inspiration slowly began to come back.

In late September, he spent a few days at Olympic Studios in London, putting finishing touches on two already-recorded Rolling Stones songs – "She's a Rainbow" and "Dandelion" – with the expectation that they would be used on the next Stones album, to be worked on following Mick Jagger's and Keith Richards' release from prison.

September 29, 1967

Paul McCartney stubbed a cigarette out, relaxing in his favorite easy chair in Buddy Holly's office, which was trendy-modern but functional, as sharp and to the point as its occupant. The musician and his "adviser" were deep in discussion.

Buddy ran down the checklist again. Almost all the divisions of the proposed new company seemed to make sense, and he could easily fold NEMS, Epstein's old company, into the framework. Apple Records – a given. Apple Music – important for publishing, and to create a home for John and Paul's songs if he could manage to persuade Dick James to sell his share of Northern Songs, the Beatles' publishing company that held the Lennon-McCartney copyrights, to the boys. Apple Films – of course. Apple Books – yes; who knows, maybe John would write something again that could be published under the trademark; and even if not, there were plenty of talented new writers out there. Apple Foundation for the Arts – well, a little vague, but the boys' philanthropic impulses were well-intentioned.

But Apple Electronics? And with Alex Mardas, of all people, in charge?

"Paint that plays music?" Buddy asked.

"Yeah, he's really a wizard with all that." Paul lifted an annoyed eyebrow at Buddy's stifled giggle, but he couldn't suppress his own sense of doubt. He was, after all, the Beatles' natural skeptic.

Magic Alex, indeed, Buddy thought. What a phony. He was a former auto mechanic, and he happened to be the son of a colonel in the Greek army – and that made him an electronics expert, and a brilliant inventor? The boys are so good-natured, Buddy thought, so willing to be helpful, and it's so damned obvious this bastard is just after their money...

"Paul," Buddy said gently, "you already know what I think of Alex..."

Paul shifted uncomfortably. He was prepared to defend Alex, but only so far. As the Beatle and the manager continued the discussion, Paul could hear his own voice wavering. Finally Buddy made a proposal Paul couldn't possibly find unreasonable.

"Look," he said, "neither of us is an expert in electronics. Why not get a more educated opinion? Alex keeps promising to design a new recording studio. Get him to produce a set of diagrams, and we'll take them to George Martin and the engineers, and then they can tell us if Alex is worth your attention or not. If it turns out he really knows what he's doing, I'll drop it."

For nearly a week, Paul phoned Alex daily, and each time Alex found an excuse why he could not send the diagrams. Finally, sensing that Paul was losing his patience, Alex hastily threw together a set and gave them to a courier. He hoped that John and Paul would glance at the diagrams, be duly impressed, and their faith would be restored.

Alex would have been more worried had he been at Abbey Road, at the EMI Studios.

The Beatles were taking the day off, but Paul had asked George Martin and Geoff Emerick, the Beatles' usual recording engineer, to meet him there. When they arrived, Paul presented Alex's diagrams and asked for their opinion.

Emerick suppressed a laugh. Martin looked gravely at the face of the 25-year-old musical genius he had worked so closely with since 1962.

Brushing a hand through his slicked-back hair, the Beatles' producer began speaking slowly and earnestly. "I don't know quite how to tell you this, Paul, but he's having you on." Paul's eyes shifted back and forth between the diagrams and George Martin's face.

Emerick now jumped in. "Half these circuits wouldn't even work, Paul," he said. "They'd short out. The console would be unusable."

Paul now felt himself growing angry. Not at Martin - George had brought *Sgt. Pepper*, so much his baby, to life, and he trusted him implicitly; and not at Emerick, who served Martin and the Beatles loyally. At himself. For letting himself be hoodwinked so easily.

He grabbed the diagrams and marched upstairs. Stuffing them into a garbage can, he began shouting angrily about Alex's "betrayal" of his and the group's trust. His amiable public persona aside, one did not try to make a fool of Paul McCartney.

Paul had been on the phone with John Lennon nearly an hour. He had expected this. He had been convinced relatively easily, but he knew John would be a tougher case. After all, whatever else Alex was, he was a weirdo, and John's taste for the weird was always acute.

"I don't know," John said. "I mean, they've good points and all, but George - "

"Bloody hell, John," Paul said in exasperation. "Has George ever lied to us? Or Buddy?" Into the wee hours the conversation ran, Paul repeatedly trotting out the words he know would most move John: "Buddy said...."

The next day, not having heard from Paul, Alex began to worry. Perhaps it was time to go make sure everything was still right. He took a cab to Abbey Road, where the Beatles were in session.

He walked up to the front door of the familiar white building – to be greeted by the most unfamiliar sight of Mal Evans, wearing a long coat, standing in front of the doorway. "Sorry, mate," Evans barked. "You're not allowed in here."

Alex was not about to put up with this. The imperious son of a Greek army colonel who had recently been part of a coup there, he was used to talking down to underlings. "Get out of my way, you asshole," Alex snapped. "Don't you know who I am?"

Mal, the Beatles' roadie and all-around gofer as well as ad hoc bodyguard, had protected the Beatles like they were his brothers, since the Liverpool days. He had loathed Alex from the day he met him, and he could barely conceal his wicked glee now.

Despite his bulk, he was an amiable teddy bear by nature, but he had no trouble putting his foot down with Alex.

"Course I know who you are, mate," he said, trying not to laugh. "That's how I know you're not allowed in here. The lads' orders."

"I want to talk to them-" Alex said, making for the door.

Mal's large form stepped directly in front of the door, and his coat opened just enough to allow Alex to see the brass knuckles on his right hand. "I *said*, you're not allowed in here. Now – off with you."

Alex backed away from the door, all the while shouting at Evans. "You fucking pig! You will be fired for this!"

Mal didn't answer, but allowed himself a smile as he watched Alex's form disappear up Abbey Road.

Alex didn't go far. He hurried a few blocks away to Cavendish Avenue, to Paul's house. He waited by the main gate, looking singly incongruous around the usual flock of giggling teenage Beatle fans. Surely, if he could speak to Paul…

Hours later, when Paul's car arrived, Alex, shoving a teenage girl or two out of the way, ran to the window. "Paul! Paul!" he shouted. The window came down.

"Fuck off, Alex!" came Paul's voice through the passenger window, sounding angrier than Alex had ever heard him. The window went back up, and the car disappeared inside the gate.

Ignoring the teenage girls who by now were pointing and laughing at the strange foreign man, Alex scurried down Cavendish Avenue, finding a red phone booth. Hopefully John would be home by now. Surely John would listen to him. He dialed the number of the house in Weybridge.

He breathed an audible sigh of relief when he heard John's voice come on the line. "John, this is Alex," he began. "I –"

John abruptly cut him off. "Sorry, love. Honeymoon's over." *Click*.[42]

After he hung up on Alex, John turned back to the piano, and refocused his attention back on the song he was writing – a sardonic putdown of his former friend, "Magic" Alex.

A year later, when it came time to record the tune, Buddy Holly, fearing a lawsuit from Alex (who by then had returned to Greece after repeated unsuccessful attempts to contact the Beatles) convinced John to change the title. John obliged, retitling the song "Sexy Sadie."[43]

CHAPTER FIVE: FIXING A HOLE

September 27, 1967

May Ling was becoming frustrated. They had just spoiled the third take of this scene, a scene she had hoped to capture in one take. She was burning budget, and she didn't have that much budget to begin with.

Moving in front of the cameraman, who held the Bell & Howell 8mm camera on his right shoulder, she clapped her hands and shouted, "Take four! Action!"

The soundman held the boom mike just out of camera range. The actor, playing a junkie reduced to living on the streets, muttered to himself. He was an unknown, cheap to hire, one of the dozens of anonymous would-be stars that could be easily found in New York, trying to break into show business.

May had no lines scripted for this scene – she had directed the actor to "mutter incoherently." He stumbled along the sidewalk of the West Village street where May and her little crew were filming her first independent picture.

They hadn't gotten a permit from the city, but film crews – even small ones – shooting on location were still unusual enough in 1967 that May and her crew were largely left alone. The camera focused in on the actor, backing away but keeping him closely framed as he staggered, junkie-style, up the street. The soundman kept the boom mike close. The hand-held camera – besides being cheap – would lend the film the cinema verite quality that was so in vogue.

The "junkie" suddenly came to an abrupt stop, peering at a garbage can. Atop the can was a book. Next to the book was a spray of white chrysanthemums, neatly arranged. He picked the book up and held it aloft.

"CUT!" May shouted in disgust.

"Goddamn it!" the actor shouted. Only now did he realize he was holding the book – *Revelations of Divine Love,* by Julian of Norwich – upside down.

May held her hands to her head, then sighed. "I need an aspirin. Everyone, ten minutes."

The actor sat down on the stoop next to the can. "I'll get it right this time, Miss Ling," he said. "Fifth time's a charm."

She said nothing, but gazed up at the sky.

The cameraman – an acquaintance from film school – walked over to her. "Are you sure we can't use the take? It was technically almost perfect."

"Joe, the book was upside down," May said. "How is the audience supposed to see the title?"

The cameraman sat down and lit a cigarette. "What is it with you and that book anyhow?"

"Changed my life."

He smiled. "That's right. I forgot. Catholic girl."

"I'm a woman, not a girl," she said. "And don't start about my being Catholic. Not in the mood."

"Hey, I'm not criticizing," he said. Like most of the men she knew, he was drawn to May for her intelligence and wit as much as her good looks. Like most, he found out before long that – bucking the trends of the time – she didn't sleep around. Not anymore, anyway.

"What's it about? Really, I sincerely want to know. Catholic prayers or something?"

"Catholic mysticism," she said. Gradually, her face broke into a smile – and May's smiles could warm a frosty night. "I'm sorry I'm being so short," she said. "Making this movie is…tough."

"You have it tougher than most, being a woman." He smiled. "Not a girl."

Now she was genuinely laughing. "You should read it," she said. "I mean, all the things people are getting into these days – all the mystical stuff, Buddhism, *Tao Te Ching*, all that – and here's a mystical book that people don't even know about. It really spoke to me. I did all the hippie stuff, all that exotic stuff, but this was the first thing I read that really spoke to me. It kind of reconnected me to my faith, you know?"

"I wouldn't recommend trying to preach with this movie. It's mostly hippies here in the Village who will go see it. They'll give you crap."

"I'm not preaching," she said, "but I'm not going to pretend not to say what I want to say, either. And anyway, it's not that weird – Warhol is a Catholic."

"Says who?"

"He did. To me."

"Holy shit!" the cameraman yelped. "You met *Andy Warhol*?"

Now May was beaming. "I most certainly did," she said. "A few months ago. Long story short, among other things, I told him I'm Catholic, and he said he's a believer and very interested in the Church too."

The cameraman shook his head. "Warhol is about as fucking far from a church guy as I can imagine."

"Hey," she said, "we're all sinners, right? That's what the Church says."

He shrugged. "Well, what about the white chrysanthemums?"

She gave him a quick, wry smile. "No symbolism. Just a personal favorite."

With a deep breath, she stood up, a look of resolve in her eyes. "OK," she said. "Enough church talk. Let's get this show on the road. Places, everyone. Let's get it right this time."

October 1, 1967

Mick Jagger and Keith Richards were finally released from prison, greeted by crowds of Rolling Stones fans, some of whom had maintained a vigil outside the Inns of Court during the entire two-month period of their incarceration. Somewhat to the surprise of the media, the two Stones made little comment to the assembled reporters, other than to thank their fans for their support during the past two months. Jagger, instead, jostled past the assembled reporters and made a beeline for the car. His face wore a haggard expression, one that no one could ever remember seeing on him.

Although both Jagger and Richards, in respect of their celebrity, had been isolated from the general prison population and in general given a "soft" version of the standard prison routine, Jagger had failed to adapt. He had cried when he was taken away after his sentencing, and had been withdrawn and morose throughout his time behind bars. He remained that way upon release, and was this morning slinking silently to his waiting car, not only not responding to the press but failing to answer anyone, even Marianne Faithfull as she tried to embrace and kiss him.

Indeed, over the next few weeks, even as he made a great show of trying to put his prison experience behind him, Jagger's behavior became more self-protective than ever, tinged with an air of paranoia. He appeared eager to pretend the whole experience never happened, declined to talk about it even to members of the "underground" media, and seemed to determine to isolate himself from anyone who could possibly hurt him. Keith Richards, by contrast, made the best of a bad situation, functioning well in prison and in fact becoming something of a folk hero to the other prisoners. Unlike Jagger, he spoke openly about his experience to the media and made a conscious effort to address his imprisonment in song lyrics.

The Rolling Stones lost a critical chance to get things back on track upon Jagger and Richards' release. Richards – along with the other Stones – hoped to begin recording almost immediately. "We really need to get back on the horse," he insisted to Jagger. But to the dismay of his bandmates, and the disappointment of fans, Jagger announced one day after his release that he had decided to take some time to "clear my head" before recording. Jagger then flew off to Italy, where he and girlfriend Marianne Faithfull lived a sybaritic existence for the next few weeks. It wasn't until early November that the Rolling Stones finally regrouped to begin recording.[44]

October 16, 1967

At last – and for Paul, not a minute too soon – the Beatles had begun work on *Magical Mystery Tour*. The American filmmaker David Maysles had been hired to direct the film. Alun Owen, who had written the screenplay for *A Hard Day's Night*, was brought back to polish up the Beatles' "spontaneity" just enough. The Beatles had accepted the wisdom of Buddy Holly's suggestions.

Owen and the Beatles came up with a loosely constructed storyline – loose enough to allow for unexpected "happenings" to occur, but tight enough that the film would not meander pointlessly. (A long sequence where the Beatles would watch a stripper perform was one of the ideas discarded.)[45] The storyline had the Mystery Tour bus picking up a group of tourists, among them the Beatles, who after a series of adventures went to see a group of wizards (also played by the Beatles), with the film ending with the tourists returning home "enlightened."[46] Most of the footage retained a cinema verite quality and an air of spontaneity and discovery, in keeping with the original concept, but Maysles' skills ensured that the result would not look amateurish.

Brian Jones, who was also distressed by Mick Jagger's decision not to return to work immediately, tagged along with the Beatles during the filming, and made his way into the movie footage. Most prominently, he and John Lennon are seen having a strange conversation about being inside a box that represents the whole universe: "If you're in the box, you don't know that there's an outside."[47]

November 7, 1967

"Are you ready, Brian?"

With a nod, Brian Jones assented, and the engineer began rolling tape. Through the earphones, Brian heard the opening notes of the track as he huddled in front of the Mellotron. A swipe of a chord on Keith's guitar, a thud of tympani, and then he began playing.

The Mellotron was not an easy instrument to play. It had an amazing ability – for its time – to sound like a variety of instruments, but those sounds had to be pre-programmed. Brian had spent a long time in the studio that night, fiddling with the Mellotron until it produced a fair imitation of a string section, exactly the sound he was looking for. Over the rumbling sounds of the guitars and drums, Brian added his Mellotron embellishment.

The track was called "2000 Light Years from Home." It was meant to evoke a journey through space. But the music didn't convey much of that, at least until Brian added his Mellotron overdub – an eerie, sweeping series of long notes that gave the song a chilling aspect, more H.P. Lovecraft than Buck Rogers. Brian frowned even as he played. Once more it was left up to him to provide the color and depth, to make Mick and Keith's ideas come to life.

He hadn't touched a drop of alcohol or smoked so much as a joint ever since *that night*, when he had meditated and found what he had been missing. Not an easy thing to do in the Stones, with all the rampant drugs and booze that surrounded the band. He was dismayed at the party atmosphere. He hadn't expected it.

Being in prison had surely been tough on Mick, Brian thought. But he had also thought it would change Mick's perspective a bit. Perhaps he would emerge from prison a bit sadder but wiser, with new songs that would reflect on his experience. Maybe he would grow a little from his ordeal.

Mick had indeed seemed shaken when the Stones had reconvened to work on a new album. There was something "off" about his personality – Brian couldn't explain it to himself any other way. He wore a constant expression on his face – morose, fearful – that Brian hadn't seen before. Brian, who had himself shown up to the studio more clear-headed and ready for work than he had been in years, was bemused.

But he had become frustrated when Mick announced that the Stones would complete the album they had begun working on before his and Keith's sentencing – a heavily psychedelic album that would match the Beatles' *Sgt. Pepper* and the Beach Boys' *Smile*. The prison sentence, the whole experience, was barely mentioned. Mick grunted and changed the subject whenever anyone brought it up. And he certainly had no song lyrics about it.

This was exactly the wrong approach, Brian thought, musing even as his fingers played the notes on the Mellotron keyboard. The fans would be waiting to hear what Mick and Keith had to say about their time in prison. To avoid it was a mistake. It would make the Stones look cowardly.

Besides, the album was already dated. *Sgt. Pepper* and *Smile* had both come out months ago. They had already spawned many imitators, both good and bad. Neither the Beatles nor the Beach Boys would likely make a similar album again. The Stones should be doing something different. This would seem like they were belatedly chasing after a trend, running for a train that had already left the station.

Brian hadn't tried to argue the point, sensing that Mick was not prepared to listen and not wanting to upset him in what seemed like a fragile state anyway. But he had put his foot down over the title of the album.

The album had originally been titled *Cosmic Christmas*. But it had quickly become clear that it wouldn't be completed by Christmastime. Then Mick had come up with the idea of naming the album *Her Satanic Majesty's Request* – a spoof on the wording on British passports, "Her Britannic Majesty requests and requires…" But Allen Klein, the group's new American manager, had suggested that in the wake of Mick and Keith's recent prison sentence, insulting the Royal Family was perhaps not the best course of action at the present time. So Mick had suggested altering the title to *Their Satanic Majesties' Request*.

Then Brian had balked. His newfound religious sensibility wasn't fully formed yet, but something about using the word "Satanic" just didn't feel right. He had dabbled in the occult with Anita when they were still a couple, but that was then, and he wanted no part of it now. He had insisted on dropping the word "Satanic" from the album's title. Mick had reluctantly agreed, but hadn't come up with a new title – the album would be called simply *Their Majesties' Request* – an awkward, clumsy title at best. [48]

For the first time, Brian felt embarrassed to be a Rolling Stone.

December 7, 1967

At least the Stones weren't alone in missing the Christmas holiday. Of rock's three top artists, only Bob Dylan, with his stunning new album *Woodstock*, would have a record ready by the end of the year (and then just barely).[49] The Beatles had decided to hold back the release of a *Magical Mystery Tour* soundtrack album until the film actually aired (it was now scheduled for the BBC for March 5, 1968, the weekend before Shrove Tuesday). They did release the single "Hello Goodbye"/"I Am the Walrus," but remembering the *Sgt. Pepper* debacle earlier in the year, refused all entreaties to rush-release the album. Buddy Holly backed the group up, despite a series of frantic transatlantic phone calls from Capitol, who for the second year would be going without the boon of a Christmas Beatles album like those that had brightened their 1964 and 1965 holiday seasons. Capitol was reduced to releasing an American version of the Beatles' 1966 British LP *A Collection of Beatles Oldies* in an effort to scare up Christmas sales.[50] It sold relatively poorly for a Beatles album, the fans sensing it was a hack job and already owning most of the songs on other albums anyway, and it was deleted from the Capitol catalog before very long.

Before the year was out, though, the first manifestation of the Beatles' new Apple empire was made public with the December 7 opening of the Apple Boutique at 94 Baker Street in London.

The boutique had been one of the many ideas tossed around during Apple's formative months, but it was Buddy Holly's attention to detail that made it happen. He placed Brian Epstein's brother, Clive, in charge along with many of the NEMS staff who had experience in retail from working in the Epstein family's old music store in Liverpool. The clothing and accessory items on sale were custom-designed for the boutique, but were carefully reviewed and chosen (one of the rejected design teams was a Dutch group calling itself The Fool).[51]

Within a year, the Apple Boutique was doing well enough to allow for the opening of another store in the trendy King's Road district in London, eventually followed by a New York store in 1970 and a Paris store in 1972. Buddy also approached each of the Beatles shortly after the opening about lending their names to a clothing line to be marketed by mail-order through the boutique. John and George both reacted with amusement, but the other two were interested, and before long would-be hipsters on two continents were buying clothes from the "Ringo's Gold Starr" and "Ringo's Silver Starr" lines, as well as the "Paul McCartney Collection" and the "Paul McCartney Country Scottish Collection."[52]

CHAPTER SIX: IT'S ALL TOO MUCH

February 20, 1968

To EMI's great relief, the Beatles finally released a finished version of their *Magical Mystery Tour* album.[53]

The songs on Side One came from the film. On Side Two, "Hello Goodbye" and "All You Need Is Love"/"When I'm 64" had been singles – the latter song left off *Sgt. Pepper* to make room for "Penny Lane," but made part of the next single release at Paul's insistence. "Baby You're a Rich Man" was an outtake from *Sgt. Pepper*, while "In the First Place" was a song recently written by George and originally intended for a side project, a film called *Wonderwall* that George was scoring (a version of the song was used as the movie's theme).[54]

On March 5, the *Magical Mystery Tour* film aired on the BBC for the first time. The whimsical, psychedelic tale, thanks to Maysles and Owen, was coherent enough to hang together while remaining trippy enough to have the freewheeling flavor the Beatles had wanted. The film received generally favorable notices, though some in the press objected to scenes that apparently depicted drug use or its effects. The Beatles cared little for such comments – for in their minds, they'd already moved beyond drugs, into the transcendence promised by the Maharishi.

Sessions early in 1968, intended to lead to a single to be released while the Beatles made their upcoming pilgrimage to India with the Maharishi, resulted in the selection of Paul's "Lady Madonna," backed with George's "The Inner Light," which he had recorded with Indian musicians in January. John had written an appropriately transcendent song called "Across the Universe," but was unhappy with the Beatles' recorded version.

"Lady Madonna" featured Brian Jones guesting with the Beatles as a key part of the instrumental track (he had also sat in with them on an unreleased comedy track, "You Know My Name [Look Up the Number]," the year before, but his saxophone at the end was more an afterthought than anything else). Brian added a bluesy guitar line that transformed the song, eliminating the need for the horn section Paul had originally envisioned for the gritty number.[55]

March 7, 1968

Three months later than intended – and, frustratingly enough, once again just in time to be overshadowed by a new Beatles album – the Rolling Stones finally released *Their Majesties' Request*.

As Brian Jones had predicted, the critics savagely slammed the album as a ripoff of *Sgt. Pepper* and *Smile*. Furthermore, its release date foredoomed it to no higher than a Number Two position on the charts, even with the cachet of being the Rolling Stones' "comeback" album (actually, it only reached Number Five).[56] The critics' estimation of the album would grow over the years, but the disappointment of the fans, who had expected the Stones to come roaring back from their prison experience, was inescapable.

Not long after *Majesties'* release, Brian, doing little to promote the album he hated, instead traveled with his new girlfriend Suki Potier to join the Beatles and their wives at the Maharishi's private retreat in Rishikesh, India. There Brian, the

Beatles, and other initiates including Donovan and the Beach Boys' Mike Love, had begun in late February an intensive instructional course in Transcendental Meditation at the feet of the Maharishi. Buddy Holly also flew out with the group for the first few days, but as planned he returned home to London to be on hand for the formal organization of Apple Corps, which was now proceeding full-swing.[57]

Whatever their enthusiasm when they arrived at the ashram, one by one the adherents began to drift away. Ringo, along with his wife Maureen, was the first to leave, citing the spiciness of the food. Paul left a few weeks later, along with girlfriend Jane Asher. He would break up with her by the summer.

John and George, along with Brian Jones and Mike Love, remained determined to stick out the course and stayed to the very end. By the time they flew home, though, John couldn't help feeling a bit discouraged.[58]

March 31, 1968

"So that's it, then."

John Lennon was sitting cross-legged on the floor in Brian Jones' flat. Brian's hair was a bit longer after the Indian sojourn, and he'd sprouted a beard, although he was already planning to shave it off. But his eyes were clear, the puffiness and bleariness of previous months gone. So was his nervousness. He now sat serenely on the sofa, regarding John with benevolence. The drug user's messiness of the flat was gone also – now, the flat was less cluttered, but much tidier, with most of the adornment consisting of religious books and musical instruments.

John's hair was longer, too, and he had grown a beard in India, which, like Brian, he would soon shave. But his mood was vaguely glum. He was that much glummer for being glum. Because he expected that by now, he would be joyous.

"You did finish the course?"

"Sure, George and I both did."

"Did you fall out with the Maharishi?"

"No, we got on just fine. It's…"

Brian leaned forward expectantly.

"It's…I thought I would be happy, you know? I thought I'd come to the end of this thing, and that waiting there, after all the meditation and teachings and all that, would be the Answer. I even thought maybe we would learn it on the last day or something. Then the Maharishi just sort of wished us well, and we were off. And I thought, here I am, the same person, with the same problems and all the same fears and all the same desires, and I haven't changed…"

"You have changed, John. You just don't know it yet. It's quite like planting a seed."

"I know that intellectually," John said. "But emotionally, I suppose –"he gave an embarrassed chuckle – "I thought I would have this sort of permanent grin on my face."

Brian smiled. "It's not like that, John. That's what I've come to learn. Like you at first I thought I should never be unhappy again, or angry, or anything negative. But we live in an imperfect world, and we'll always be imperfect, though we can always draw closer and closer to perfection. The key is to keep moving forward. Loving God is a struggle, and the Maharishi isn't going to have some perfect answer, and no other person is either. But the way it works is, no effort, no rewards." He took a sip of water. "It's a long period of discipline even to get to the stage of enlightenment the sages and saints can reach."

"That's the problem, Brian," John said. "You know me – discipline is not my thing."

"Don't sell yourself short, John," said Brian. "But I know what you mean."

"What do you do when it gets tough, then – when you start doubting?"

Into the wee hours of the morning, John Lennon and Brian Jones talked about faith, enlightenment, and the hardships on the road to wisdom.

When he finally said goodnight and left to go home to Weybridge, John was sadder but wiser. He came to realize that he had known all along, deep down, that Brian was right – salvation could come at once, but understanding of that salvation, enlightenment or "higher consciousness," could not, for if it did our minds would not be able to receive it. The path he had set out on was not a false one, but it was going to be a lot longer and tougher than even a retreat in the foothills of the Himalayas would put him in a position to realize – it would, in fact, have to go on his whole life.

The more he thought about it, the more he realized that he needed with him someone whose desire to reach enlightenment would match his own, someone who would understand his quest and stand with him in it.

April 4, 1968

The way Sam Cooke remembered it, he had just taken off his jacket and was sitting down on the bed when it suddenly flooded his mind – the memory that was so vivid it nearly caused him to lose his balance and fall to the floor.

It wasn't the first time he remembered that day, of course – far from it. The awful events of the night of December 10-11, 1964, were forever etched into his mind. His entire life since then, in a way, had pivoted on his guilt and shame over his actions that night. But in that moment, sitting on the bed in the motel room, the remembrance suddenly became real – so real he felt it was directly in front of him, as if he were at the motel again, watching the whole ugly drama unfold.

Sam had arrived that night at Martoni's, a favorite hangout in Hollywood. There, after having a few drinks and holding court in the manner of a major star on a roll, he picked up an office receptionist named Elisa Boyer. Sam considered himself happily married to his wife Barbara, but that never had meant that he was unwilling to take advantage of the opportunities that presented themselves to a big star.

He took her briefly to another bar, PJ's, then left about closing time. He then drove her to a motel, the Hacienda, on Figueroa Boulevard in a seedy neighborhood near the Los Angeles airport, arriving shortly before 3 a.m.

Elisa then fled the room, taking all of Sam's clothes except his sport jacket and shoes. She later said that Sam had acted roughly toward her, but Sam was sure that she had intended all along only to rob him. Sam then showed up at the door of the hotel office, where the manager, Bertha Lee Franklin, encountered him. Sam angrily banged on the door, demanding to know where Elisa had gone. Elisa was not there, but Sam believed she had gone inside the office. He broke open the door, and raced through the office, finally grabbing and shaking Ms. Franklin. She went for the gun she kept handy for just this sort of attack, and as she and Sam struggled, fired twice into the ceiling before he knocked the gun away. Then she grabbed a stick, and using it as a club, struck him in the head.

Sam staggered from the office, dazed from the blow. He had suffered a concussion, and his left cheekbone was broken. His skin was broken too, and blood came from the wound. As he stumbled into the parking lot, the police arrived, after the hotel owner, who had been on the phone with Ms. Franklin when Sam broke in, called them. Upon seeing his condition, the police promptly summoned an ambulance. Sam was taken to Centinela Hospital, where he was treated for his injuries and released soon after.[59]

Sam survived the beating, and his career survived what could have been a very serious scandal – Allen Klein, still a few years away from his relationship with the Rolling Stones, had made sure of that. Cooke's saintly image was in total contrast to his behavior that night, and had Klein not paid both Ms. Boyer and Ms. Franklin hefty sums to remain quiet, the scandal could easily have destroyed him.

But, while Klein's money had ensured the burial of the truth, the stain on Sam Cooke's soul, and the burning of his conscience, was not so easily assuaged. He had, after all, hardly been cynical about his faith when he began singing with the Soul Stirrers – his Christian belief was sincere and heartfelt. And he knew that nothing he had done that night was justifiable in any way according to the faith to which he was so devoted.

Over the years, though, as he came to believe afterward, he had gradually become seduced by fame and wealth and the power that went with those things. He had left his gospel group, the Soul Stirrers, to become a pop singing star. Then he had become more and more enraptured with the luxuries and adulation that accrued to him as a pop star that, in time, he lost his perspective. He had flown into a blind rage that night when Elisa Boyer dared suggest that he – *he! Sam Cooke! Doesn't she know who I am?* – not only wouldn't have her but might have been set up for theft in the first place. His selfishness had led him into a fury of violence that could easily have ended with the loss of his life – indeed, Ms. Franklin had told him point-blank that if she had it to do over again, this time she'd make sure she shot him dead.

After the incident, Sam dropped out of the public eye for a while. He went through a long period of introspection, thinking deeply and praying for guidance, deciding what things really mattered to him, how he could possibly do sufficient penance before his Lord, and how he could turn his life back in the right direction, back toward the service of others. In time, he came to devote himself to the twin and interrelated causes of his church and the civil rights movement. He became one of the most powerful and devoted supporters of Dr. Martin Luther King, frequently traveling with him and using his star power not for himself but to help bring attention to the causes King had charged himself with championing.

It wasn't until the latter part of 1967 that Sam Cooke felt ready to return to the recording studio. His new music knitted his spiritual and public concerns together more fully than ever before, bringing his soulful voice to songs of overcoming struggles both personal and public, with no clear line between the two. The resulting album, *Prodigal Son*, was released in early 1968, along with its first single, the powerful, moving ballad "You'll Know."

But he still placed his service to Martin Luther King and his work on behalf of the poor and the downtrodden ahead of all other concerns. And so it was that in early April 1968, when King asked him to accompany him to Memphis on a trip in support of the city's striking sanitation workers, Cooke readily agreed.

In the early evening of April 4, at the Lorraine Motel on Mulberry Street in Memphis, King, who had spoken the night before, was preparing to go with several of his friends, including Cooke, to the home of Memphis minister Billy Kyles to have dinner. About 6:01 pm, Kyles and King stepped out onto the third-floor walkway outside of King's room, exchanging a few remarks with the civil rights workers, including Andrew Young, in the parking lot below. Cooke, meanwhile, was in King's room, Room 306. He hoped to briefly review a few notes with Dr. King before they left for dinner.

As Sam sat down on the bed, he was suddenly, for whatever reason he could not explain, overcome by the vivid memory of that horrible night when he had nearly lost his life.

It disappeared as quickly as it came, but it left the singer deeply troubled. Getting up, almost staggering, he lurched toward the door. He hoped his spiritual mentor could give him some words of comfort, and he called out, "Dr. King!"

Hearing Sam Cooke's voice, Martin Luther King turned his head – just as, from the bathroom window of a nearby rooming house, James Earl Ray squeezed the trigger on his rifle.

The sudden turn of King's head and body in response to Cooke's cry caused his assassin to miss with the first shot, the bullet – apparently aimed at his chest – instead slamming into the wall. Ray then hastily fired a second shot, which apparently went wild – the slug was never found – while Cooke, racing to the balcony at the sound of the shot, pushed King down flat. At the same time, an undercover policeman who had been accompanying the group summoned backup and the men in the parking lot yelled and pointed toward the rooming house from which the shots had been fired.[60]

Ray ran out of the rooming house and onto Main Street, just in time to come face to face with a police car responding to the undercover's call. An officer called out, "Hey, you!" and Ray panicked. He fired a shot at the police car before fleeing on foot. The shot shattered the windshield, spraying the cops inside with broken glass, and wounding one in the shoulder.

If it was true, as some later charged, that the Memphis police did not do enough to protect Dr. King and would have allowed Ray to escape, Ray had just erased that possibility. He was now not only the attempted assassin of Martin Luther King, he was also a would-be cop killer, and he could expect no mercy from the police. Apprehended four blocks away, he already had a black eye by the time he arrived at the jail. He would eventually plead guilty to both crimes and be sentenced to life in prison.[61]

Martin Luther King, meanwhile, was taken to St. Joseph's Hospital in Memphis, just to be certain. He was released after being treated for the minor injuries he received when Cooke pushed him down to protect him.

Arriving back at the motel, King heard the news that rioting over his attempted killing was feared. He contacted reporters and prepared a statement for the media, and a message to be sent to President Kennedy, calling on the rioters not to give in to violence. "Hatred cannot be overcome with hatred," he said. "Violence cannot be thwarted with violence." Kennedy later publicly thanked King for helping to defuse what could otherwise have been an extremely violent situation.[62]

King returned to Atlanta soon after, but then went to Washington, D.C., to give a speech at the Lincoln Memorial, the site of his legendary "I have a dream" oration, elaborating further on the attempt on his life.

A crowd of some 250,000 poured into the Mall to hear the speech, and at the President's order, Secret Service protection was provided to ensure that the near-tragedy in Memphis would not be repeated. King spoke fervently, urging his supporters not to give in to the urge to violence. "My voice is not stilled," he said, paraphrasing the Book of Exodus, "and my natural force is undimmed." The judgment of God, he said, would be the "mighty hand" that will bring justice to those "who seek to do harm to us and to our cause."

"Let the truth that is on our side, the truth of righteousness, be your voice," he said as the crowd roared. "Let not your love be stilled as it is stilled in the hearts of those filled with hate, who turn against us with weapons. For mightier than all the guns and all the swords and all the weapons forged by the hand of man is the sacred truth of God, that the spirit of man that He created is to live in freedom!"

King's attempted assassination and his April 1968 speech had the effect of reviving his influence in the black community, which had been on the wane for a while. Many leaders in the community, having grown impatient with King's gradual, nonviolent approach, had come to embrace more radical ideas. Malcolm X had been shot to death in 1965, but his more radical, confrontational approach to the problems of the black community had evolved into the increasingly violent rhetoric of black leaders like Stokely Carmichael, Eldridge Cleaver, and Huey Newton.

Instead, his incredible moral courage and determination to continue on the path of nonviolence, even after his own life had been threatened, not only restored his standing but made him seem more awe-inspiring than ever. As singer Sly Stone put it later in 1968, "Any idiot can be brave with a gun. Dr. King is brave with his heart and soul."

Sam Cooke, meanwhile, credited divine intervention with that moment on April 4, 1968 that may well have saved the life of Dr. King. "If I did anything," he said, "I acted as a channel for the Lord." Divine reward may nevertheless have come Sam's way shortly afterward, when "You'll Know" rose to the Number One position on the *Billboard* charts.

CHAPTER SEVEN: ALL TOGETHER NOW

April 14, 1968

John Lennon and Paul McCartney were back in America. For John, it was his first visit since the end of that final Beatles tour.

They had flown there with Buddy on April 9 to formally announce the startup of Apple Corps. For John, it had been a frenetic round of press conferences, interviews, discussions. He and Paul had a long TV interview on *The Tonight Show*. Johnny Carson, the regular host, wasn't there that night, and as a substitute there was some guy named Joe Garagiola. John couldn't remember how to pronounce his name. A baseball player or footballer or something like that. John couldn't keep track of American sports, and it was fairly clear Garagiola wasn't particularly interested in the Beatles or Apple. John couldn't wait to leave the studio. He was never comfortable doing interviews with people who patently didn't understand him and didn't care to try.

After the show, the little trio and their entourage – Ron Kass, the new head of the Apple records division, and Dennis O'Dell, the new Apple Films head, among them – took trains to New York for the next round of interviews. These were, for the most part, no more enlightening. John was getting bored.

Dennis, in the lobby of the Plaza Hotel with John after yet another interminable chat, suggested they go out on the town. Maybe find some girls. John shrugged. He wasn't really in the mood.

He and Paul were the two "bachelor Beatles." Ringo was the first of the group to tie the knot, marrying Maureen Cox back in

1965. Then the next year, George married Patti Boyd, although with George's constant meditation, that marriage was already feeling the strain. *Serves him right*, John thought with a laugh.

The closest he'd ever gotten to a long-term relationship was back in Liverpool, in his art school days. There had been a girl there, Cynthia Powell. They'd dated for a while, and it had started to seem pretty serious. But then the Beatles had gone off to Hamburg, and word had gotten back to her about John's philandering. He still thought Allan Williams, their first manager, who these days was back in Liverpool whining about how he'd "given the Beatles away," was the one who'd tipped her off. [63]

In the end, what mattered was that she had tearfully told John that she never wanted to see him again. She went back to Hoylake, and he never saw her again.

Unlike Paul, he hadn't had a steady girlfriend through the Beatle years. Jane Asher, Paul's romantic partner for so long – though, John knew, that was now on the rocks too – was exactly the type of girl who turned him off. Posh, a touch of snobbishness, of class superiority. Paul was a social climber – he wanted to be like those people. That sort of cliquish, condescending person just irritated John.

So he had stumbled along for years, his name linked to a variety of women – some, like designer Mary Quant and Twiggy, the model, famous in their own right – but no one had been *the* woman. None had been the one he dreamed of: An artist, who would understand him on his own wavelength. Not someone who was looking for something from him because he was a Beatle. Someone who was enough like him to complete him. Someone who could share with him his quest for enlightenment, and who might finally hold the key to the happiness he had sought since childhood.

He was tired of the pursuits, tired of the conquests. He was too famous to really need to pull birds; they just fell into his lap without a challenge. But he didn't see marriage as a real proposition either, the way even Paul did. His parents' marriage had fallen apart. Marriage was a crock. And anyway, who would he ever *want* to marry?

And Dennis wanted to "find girls." He sighed in exasperation.

"Look, we're in the art capital of the world," John said. "Isn't there something...artistic we can do?"

Dennis nodded thoughtfully. "Why don't we try to go to see an independent film or two down in Greenwich Village somewhere? I can arrange – "

"Don't arrange," John said with a smile. "I don't want them to clear out the theater for me. I'll wear a disguise if I have to."[64]

Meanwhile, on the tour, Buddy Holly, once a shy guy who had developed public speaking skills as a side benefit of his career, had them on impeccable display as he discussed the various divisions of Apple and raised the issue of other artists submitting work. "Because these fellows are the Beatles," he said, "we're aware that everyone with an idea out there probably imagines that he can just send it to us and we'll immediately support it. We're looking for good work, but please understand that we will not be able to use everything that is submitted."

It sounded harsh, but John and Paul both realized, it had to be said – otherwise, Buddy had assured them, they would be buried in an avalanche of demo tapes, film screenplays, manuscripts, and nutty proposals. Buddy had already made it clear to the hangers-on at Wigmore Street that no one without actual business inside the Apple offices would have to remain outside.[65]

John combed his hair a little differently before leaving the hotel, and substituted a pair of dark prescription sunglasses for his trademark round wire-frame National Health glasses, but otherwise made little effort to wear a disguise as such. Like most celebrities, he had long since figured out the secret to not being noticed: Be inconspicuous. Celebrity types wanted attention, as a rule, so they never failed to leave the house looking flamboyant. By simply dressing and acting in a way that wouldn't call attention to himself, he could generally avoid the massive crowds that would gather at the discovery of a Beatle in their midst.

The theater was on a dingy block of Bleecker Street. The entrance was a decaying, dirty wooden frame in green trim, with a hand-painted signboard greeting visitors. The sign said an independent film festival was in progress. The film being shown was called *Convergence*, "written and directed by May Ling." A side note said the director would be waiting in the lobby of the theater and would welcome comments on the film.

The stoned-looking hippie selling tickets at the box office didn't bat an eye at John. He and Dennis found seats in the back, in a near-empty row, the upholstery dingy and faded. John, sliding down in his seat, took off his dark glasses, put on his more familiar round wire-frame ones, and stared at the screen.

The film was the story of a 14-year-old Puerto Rican boy, living in Spanish Harlem, named Manuel, who suddenly discovers that he has been given the power to "fix one thing" in the lives of each person he encounters. How he decides to use this power – what things he decides to "fix" – were the point of May's funny, gentle, yet deeply moving film, shot mostly on the streets of lower Manhattan and Brooklyn. Although it used a bit of psychedelic imagery, it found its transcendence instead in the beauty of the everyday world, especially in the simplest things, and how Manuel finds the deepest and truest beauty within them. The film was not explicitly spiritual – except in the few scenes where *Revelations of Divine Love* showed up - yet May's strong sense of faith deeply imbued the script, and especially the twist ending. At a time when so much avant-garde art was negative – Western artists writhing in repulsion at the war in Vietnam and the betrayal of the leftist promise that it embodied, as exemplified by Yoko Ono's recently notorious "White Death" exhibit in Paris, sponsored by Roman Polanski – here was a film that presented genuine love and hope, that took the message of the "Summer of Love" and tried to extend and point the way for mankind to live it, even in a small way.

John was bedazzled.

Before the lights came up, before Dennis could say anything, John scrambled from his seat, racing to the lobby, eager to share his excitement with the director. Dennis tried to catch him to remind him that he still had his regular glasses on.

John raced into the lobby – to find a stunningly beautiful Asian woman, wearing a black pullover and white miniskirt, staring fixedly at the heads in the back of the theater.

"Hello," John blurted out, suddenly taken aback by the attractive woman. "Are you the director? Fantastic film. Really great."

The woman turned and audibly gasped. "Are you....John Lennon?"

He suddenly remembered his glasses. "Yes, but don't hold that against me." She chuckled, nervously. Her eyes had a wistful quality, but they danced too. John began to feel light-headed. "I'd like to talk about the film."

She hesitated for just a second – then grabbed his right hand. "Come on," she said. "That crowd will be all over you. We can talk in here," she said, pulling John into a tiny alcove, shutting the door behind her. Dennis just barely spied the couple disappearing into the alcove – good thing, too, he thought with a laugh, or I'd have been looking for John all night.

When John left, an hour later, it was with a long kiss and a tight embrace and May's promise to come to London as soon as she could.

May 29, 1968

The Beatles had reconvened at Abbey Road's Studio Three to begin work on their next album. Maybe the Maharishi hadn't made them enlightened Buddhas, but there had no shortage of inspiration. They had enough music available for a double album.

The first track they attempted was "Revolution," written by John as a slow, acoustic number. It was a putdown of the kind of political radicals who were becoming increasingly discredited by the events in Vietnam. John, roaring with leonine indignation, sneered at those who thought the world could be changed by "carrying pictures of Chairman Mao," referring to the Communist dictator in Manchuria (or "North China," or "Red China," or "the People's Republic of China," as it was variously called).

Eighteen takes were taped, the final one being roughly ten minutes long, the last six of which were a jam that descended into screams of "All right!" and, in the end, sheer white noise. After that last take, John had an idea: Why not take those last six minutes and build upon them to make an aural collage of various tapes, voices, sound effects and whatever else? Having dabbled in avant-garde experiments for the past year or so, Paul was open to the idea. But the basic part of "Revolution" was the song on the agenda the next day, as the band added overdubs to the now four-minute-plus track.

On day three of the sessions, there was a visitor to Abbey Road. John, for the first time, brought his new love, May Ling, to the studio to meet the other Beatles.

John had stayed in New York longer than expected – Paul and the rest of the entourage had flown back without him. He didn't let on, and they were a bit puzzled why he had wanted to stay behind – but then John had always seemed to like New York.

What he really liked, though, were the two weeks he spent with May, barely out of each other's sight for a minute, the passion of new love overwhelming them both. It seemed beyond even "love at first sight" – both of them felt as if they had been struck by lightning.

For John – depressed, anxious, feeling "so suicidal" according to one of his new songs – May was like a ray of sunlight, penetrating the darkness of drugs and fame, of pressures, of the emptiness of his life – the sense that he had come so far only to find that he had come nowhere, and that he had turned to the Maharishi expecting instant enlightenment, only to discover how far he had to go yet. But May made him feel like it was still worth trying – that, indeed, answers remained to be found, that he hadn't yet exhausted all the possibilities – that he had barely begun to dig into them.

May's feelings were clear from her actions. Having only just met John, she nevertheless had dropped everything behind in New York and moved to London, to be close to him, to be near him. It wasn't his celebrity. She was unimpressed with famous people per se. It was the force of his personality, his gentleness, his warmth, the brilliance of his mind and the depth of his love.

So she had flown to London. *Convergence* had finished its brief run in New York, and she quickly made a deal with a British independent film distributor as an excuse to come to England to see John. She had joined him her first night there at Weybridge, and they held each other tenderly, for long minutes, saying nothing, taking in one another's presence.

John already knew. He had met *her* at last. She was beautiful, and brilliant, and an artist – they could stay up long into the night talking art and making love. Maybe, someday, there would even be a baby, a beautiful child, a replica of their love. At last, he was sure, he could be happy.

Cordial, charming as always, she smiled and laughed her way around the group. But John thought he noticed something else. A twinkle, a light, in the eyes of Paul McCartney. Paul, the "pretty one," the one who always got all the girls, was checking his new girlfriend out, right in front of him, shamelessly.

Paul sat down next to her, chatting her up - or so John thought. Actually, Paul was just making pleasant conversation. He'd never make a move on John's girl. Especially not one who clearly meant so much to John. He couldn't do that. Not to his best friend.

But with Paul's voice purring, and May smiling demurely, John felt the rage rising in his throat. Always, it seemed, Paul had to step in his way, whether it was by stealing the show onstage, or by trying to write better songs, or by making himself the toast of London's art scene, or by being the ladies' man of the group...and with the woman who had consumed every thought in John's head for the last few weeks....

Finally, John got up in a rage, and stomped upstairs to the control room. To the shock of engineer Geoff Emerick, he seized a mixing board and toppled it over.

He ran upstairs, out the front door and into the darkness outside the studios, sucking in the cool London air. Ignoring the usual array of fans clustered in front of the gate, none of whom noticed him, he walked around to the back of the building, sitting down against the back wall in a sulk.

A few minutes later, a figure was standing over him.

"What was that about?"

John looked up at May. He could see the anger in her eyes, but there was genuine concern there too. These were the eyes that were so beautiful, so real, and he could see the love, and the worry, behind them.

Like a misbehaving schoolboy, John self-consciously pulled his legs toward himself and looked down at the ground.

"John, if you're going to get that mad just from me talking to someone...."

"I didn't," he lied.

"Yes, you did, and you made an fool of yourself. John, I came here, across the ocean, for you. Doesn't that tell you how I feel? I love you, and I'm not going to walk off with the first Beatle I see." This brought a reluctant, tiny smile to John's lips. "But please don't act like a jackass again," she added over her shoulder as she headed back toward the front.

John sheepishly reentered the studio a few minutes later. Emerick had by then set the mixing board back up – fortunately, it was still working. Emerick shook his head and waved his hand in a gesture of irritation.

The other three Beatles stared with blank expressions at John as he walked back down the stairs. His eyes met those of May, who by now was sitting on a stool, near the soundproofing baffles that partially concealed Ringo's drum set. She held a hand close to her face – she had obviously been crying, though she had done her best to conceal it.

John sat down at the piano, and gently began picking out a tune. He didn't face her. He stared straight down at the keyboard, watching his own fingers. Playing gently, he wandered into the melody of one of his India songs, "Child of Nature." He'd written it after one of the Maharishi's lectures on the unity of all natural things.

Still staring straight down at the keyboard, he quietly began to murmur new lyrics to the song, singing to May, telling her that he hadn't meant to hurt her and was sorry.

May began tearing up again, realizing that this was John's version of an apology. "It's all right," she said. Then she turned up her New York accent. "Just don't be a jackass again."[66]

That brought the laugh needed to lighten the mood, and the band resumed work. May remained as far out of the way as she could. When she left that night with John, all was well once again – but, she decided, all things considered, it might be best if she didn't hang around the Abbey Road studios with John. She knew he would insist otherwise – she knew him so well already – but she could be stubborn, too.

By the end of the first week, sessions for the new album were proceeding slowly, but none of the Beatles was unhappy with the pace. The group had only worked on a few songs, mostly "Revolution." More often, they were breaking into impromptu jam sessions that consumed much of the night. After the experimentation of the *Sgt. Pepper* days, and the release of India, they were beginning to rediscover the fun of simply playing together as the tight and versatile unit they were, able to pluck sounds from almost any genre and make them their own. Besides, Apple now served as insulating layer against EMI, isolating them somewhat from pressure to finish the new album quickly before all the vibes had fallen into place. And after the annoyance of *Sgt. Pepper*, the Beatles were determined that EMI would never push them around again.

Almost every night, Brian Jones showed up, plugged in his guitar, and played with the boys. He had become a fixture around Abbey Road, so much so that Geoff Emerick and George Martin merely nodded whenever he walked in.[67]

He hadn't played like this in years. Not since those early days, when things started to go wrong with the Stones, and the booze and the drugs had kicked in, and his focus went out the window. Mick Jagger had accused him of being ill-suited for fame, but that wasn't it. It was the isolation from the rest of the band that had upset him. He could play with anyone, but he wanted to be part of a band. A band of brothers, a group forming a collective soul when they played.

Now he had his focus back. The temptations were strong, but his determination was stronger. There were still nights when he woke up shaking, in a cold sweat, unsure if he could handle another day without a drink. But he held on, and his meditation exercises calmed him more and more. Besides, like George Harrison, he was in love with the Lord now.

"Surrender yourself to a higher power"; Brian often thought with a laugh these days when thinking about the Alcoholics Anonymous step. Surrender? It was the easiest thing he ever had to do. Staying the course was the hard part. Feeling the love of the higher power, the guiding hand helping him along, was as natural as breathing.

His own breathing was deep now; not the lethargic breathing of the alcoholic, but the full, deep breaths he had come to learn in meditation. When he wasn't meditating, he was playing his guitar, or indulging in a few small hobbies – he had an old love of model trains, cars and ships, and he had revived that, buying a kit from a hobby shop for the *Flying Scotsman* locomotive and building it. The intricate work, the cutting of the tiny parts, holding them gently with tweezers, gluing them together....focusing his mind on something other than another drink...it was helping him hold it together.

These days, when he heard himself play, he sounded better than ever before. Part of it was how focused he was, and part of it was how much he was just sitting in his flat and playing his guitar. But the bluesy, occasionally jazz-like clarity he had brought to the Rolling Stones in the past was now something greater than before. He was scaling musical walls, touching edges he had never touched. He could coax sounds and notes and phrases and melodies from the guitar he could never achieve before, for all his talent, and he could do so without losing any of his edge or sharpness.

The Rolling Stones didn't know what to make of it, and he really didn't care. He hardly cared what happened next. Let the Stones fire him, if it came to that. He was having too much fun now, playing the guitar and reveling in the simple joy of regaining his life. If he had to spend the rest of his life busking on street corners – if that was the penance God wanted him to pay for his years of dissolution – so be it. Never had he been so happy, and nothing he had cared about before had come close.

John Lennon likewise found himself enjoying the Beatles more than ever these days. If enlightenment wasn't going to come overnight, he had come to take greater joy in the circumstances of his own life, including the band. However unexpected it may have been that May would so rapidly walk into his life, he was filled with a joy unlike anything he ever felt.

Everything seemed right, and even the studio, even the Beatles, even the notion of facing the band and making yet more music – an idea which he had approached with ambivalence just a year ago – seemed to take on a new glow. He loved May, and he loved the Beatles, and best of all, the Beatles and Buddy Holly loved her too.

May urged John to use his newly-rekindled joy in making music with the Beatles as a creative spark. She was sure that John's artistic sensibility would inspire her film work. But as far as music was concerned, she believed firmly that John's best interests lay with the group. In her mind, she likened the Beatles to an artists' collective, like those she had known in the Village – the Beatles were the world's greatest collective of musical artists. She insisted to John that he, Paul, George and Ringo's individual talents coming together creating something stronger than any one of them could create individually.

She now insisted to John not only that his work with the group was important artistically, but that the Beatles should consider returning to live performances.

John smiled, but let out a moan. "Not in front of the screamers again," he said. "And the bloody death threats."

"It won't be like it was two years ago," she declared. "The mop-top days are over. The world knows you're artists now."

"They still think we're idiots."

"The older generation does, but the fans don't."

"Well, what about the death threats? Some madman said he would blow up the plane on the last Beatles tour in '66."

May inhaled heavily. She was still getting used to the world of celebrity. Death threats were something new to her, especially death threats based on who you were.

"Listen," she said. "If someone is going to try to get you, it won't matter if you are on a stage, or hiding at home, or in a studio or whatever – if someone wants to kill us badly enough, they'll kill us." She stood and walked to the window. "You shouldn't let that keep you from your audience."[68]

June 8, 1968

Another long jam session over, John set his guitar aside, and sat down in the floor in the midst of the other Beatles. Ringo remained seated behind his drums, Paul sat down on a stool, George climbed atop an amplifier – they understood that John had something to say. And indeed he did. He broached the subject he and May had been discussing - the return of the Beatles to live performances. What, he wondered, did the others think?

Paul was thrilled to hear the very notion coming out of John's mouth. He suppressed a smile, saying only, "I think it would be great." *Wouldn't do to get too giddy – let's not scare John off of this.*

George's first instinct was to say no. But he looked around the studio, at the bright white walls, then back at John and Paul, both looking at him with earnest eyes. He already knew what Paul thought, but he was surprised to hear the idea coming from John. *He has to want to do this*, George thought, *or he wouldn't have brought it up at all.*

Already, he could hear the fans saying, "It's George's fault. He's the stick in the mud. We'd be able to see the Beatles if –" Then, he thought, *why am I so worried about this? The sound won't be perfect, the gigs might be awful, we might be overrun with weirdos. In the end, what does it matter in the greater scheme of things?*

Be here now, he thought, echoing a piece of Hindu teaching. *Be in the moment.* "I'm in if everyone else is."

Ringo was happy to join with George, making the vote unanimous. He simply stated his usual amiability, his easygoing willingness to go along with whatever the group wanted. Privately, though, it was more - he missed the camaraderie of the road. He wanted it back.

As the notion began to gel, the Beatles began to delve into their many questions around the idea.

One of the biggest was: What are we going to play?

"We could do a few older numbers," Ringo suggested. "Maybe 'Hard Day's Night,' maybe 'Help!'" –

"If we do that one," John jumped in, "we should slow it down. Roy Orbison-style. How it should have been in the first place." John had long been disappointed in the Beatles' rendition of "Help!", feeling that the song was turned into an uptempo number for commercial reasons, which dampened its melancholy message.

"'Ticket to Ride,'" said George. "Or something we haven't done before on a live show – you know what's a good one…" And with that, he began playing the intro to "Every Little Thing," a relatively obscure track from late 1964's *Beatles for Sale* album.

"But what about *Pepper*?" urged Paul. "What about *Revolver*? We can't just do all old stuff."

John nodded. "They'll all want to hear the newer music. They'll want to hear what we do with it onstage."

Paul scratched his head. "See, the problem is…on the last tour, we couldn't get that sound on the show, you know? We did 'Paperback Writer,' but the track had that massive reverb on the vocal" - he imitated the sound – "and there was no way to do that onstage. I mean, we can't just do all the 'yeah yeah yeah' stuff and ignore all the work from the last two years. But we also have to do it right – we can't get it exactly like on the record, but at least we can do something closer."

"Not just guitars and drums," said John. "We need something else. If we had a Mellotron on stage, we could probably do 'Penny Lane' or 'All You Need Is Love' – we can set up the Mellotron to imitate the horns on the one and the strings on the other, or at least some approximation of it."

"But then who plays it?" said George. "If you play it, we lose a guitar. If Paul plays it, we either lose the bass, or you or I play the bass and we lose a guitar anyway. It's going to sound tinny either way."

"That's what I mean," said Paul, nodding. "The sound isn't as full. We don't want to come out and then have all the newest stuff sound crap on stage. The fans are going to expect more than that."

Ringo – in the quiet way he often had of cutting to the heart of a problem – intoned, "We need at least five musicians on stage."

The others nodded assent. But that led into another discussion – who? Of course, they could bring along a session player or two. But that would add the problem of unreliability – since session men would by definition be musicians-for-hire, the sound of the live show might not be consistent from show to show, a notion that rankled the group's two perfectionists, Paul and George, in particular.

George at last made a comment that summed up everyone's thoughts: "It really has to be something we do within the group. If we can't do it within the group, what's the point?"

John's answer to that – quietly spoken, but with a firmness in his voice that gently reminded everyone that he was the founder and, ultimately, still leader of the world's most famous rock band – was, "Maybe it's time to expand the group."

It was as if John had broken a opaque-glass window that everyone had been trying to peer through. *Expand the Beatles? Change the most successful lineup in history? Add a member?* But they had all been on the precipice of thinking about it. John simply made it OK for them to think about it some more.

They talked long into the night about the pros and cons of adding another member – including how to divide the group's earnings - and of what characteristics that hypothetical member should possess ("Maybe we should bring back Pete Best," John quipped sardonically at one point). Two things were clear, by the time the group broke for home with the sun coming up: the proposed fifth Beatle – who would be brought on as a full member, with one fifth of future earnings but no share in recordings already issued – had to be a multi-instrumentalist rather than a virtuoso on just one instrument, and ideally he should be someone the Beatles already knew and liked and would fit in with them.[69]

John arrived home at Weybridge, with May. She tumbled into bed with him. They were sharing a bed now, despite her misgivings. She hadn't lived like this in a while, not since she'd found that Julian of Norwich book, the one that had rekindled her faith, that made her excited about being a Catholic for the first time since she was twelve years old. She knew the rules. But she also knew that she was in love. And she knew that this was real. This was different. She lived in New York, worked in film, was an attractive woman – she got propositioned almost daily. She'd been with men before. But this was different – so different. She knew already that John was the One.

Most nights he would have been eager to make love with her. But the lengthy conversation with the Beatles had been draining. Exhausted, he fell into a deep slumber, and she soon joined him.

His sleep was soon awakened, however, by the insistent sound of the telephone ringing. May picked up the line, and sleepily muttered, "Hello?" then handed the receiver to John, saying, "It's Paul."

At the other end of the line, on Cavendish Avenue, a much more alert Paul McCartney – who minutes earlier had sat down with a snack, when he suddenly was hit with a flash of inspiration – paced back and forth. He heard John's half-asleep voice come on the line.

"John," Paul practically shouted, "Brian – he's it!"

John, still half-asleep, didn't understand at first. "Brian....you mean Eppy?"

"Not Brian *Epstein*," said Paul. "Brian *Jones*."

Now it was John's turn to suddenly sit upright. "I was thinking the same thing, but I was afraid to ask you three."

Brian Jones again showed up at Abbey Road three days later and ran through another jam with the Beatles. Afterward, as he sat down outside the studio, John and Paul came out to sit next to him. They made eye contact and nodded almost imperceptibly.

"This is great, isn't it?" he said to Brian.

"Smashing," Brian says. "I haven't enjoyed playing music this much since I don't know when. The Stones are like a bloody office job now."

John and Paul exchanged another look, and John nodded ever so slightly. Then he said, carefully, "Well, in that case...what do you think about joining up with us permanently?"

Brian laughed, thinking John was joking – but then Paul spoke. "We mean it, Brian," he said. "We've talked about it and we'd like to ask you to come in. We want to make music with you and have you be a part of the group. That's all of us - George and Ringo, too."

As both John and Paul broke into smiles, Brian realized that this entire train of conversation had been pre-arranged. It was nevertheless true – he was being asked to join the Beatles. He was dumbfounded.

"Can...can I ring you later?" said Brian. "I'll have to give it some thought. Can I give you my decision in a day or two?"

"Sure," said John. "We know it's a big change. Don't leave us hanging, though. We've decided we need a fifth member, and we want it to be you, but we'll need to make other arrangements if you spurn us." John stretched the word "spurn" into a long, drawn-out Liverpudlian – "*speeeeeeeern* us" – as a joke. He knew this was a very heavy moment for Brian and hoped to lighten the mood.

Brian went home with his head spinning. It was not every day that one was personally invited to join the most popular group on earth. On the other hand, for how unpleasant the Rolling Stones had become, he had been the founder of that band and had invested a great deal of emotional capital in it. He decided not to answer John at first, but in the meantime to go to Olympic the next day, where the Stones were working on their next album, to see what it felt like – to give the Stones one more chance.

CHAPTER EIGHT: ACROSS THE UNIVERSE

June 12, 1968

The sessions for the new Rolling Stones album, *Beggars' Banquet*, had gone on mostly without Brian. He'd shown up now and then, and when he liked something, he added to it. A soft blues called "No Expectations" had been greatly enhanced by the slide guitar line he'd played. He'd overdubbed a harsh, buzzing tamboura on a muddled protest song called "Street Fighting Man," that seemed to admonish the Stones' generation for not being more radical – a sentiment that was already badly out of step with the times. But for the most part, the Stones had been working as a quartet. Keith Richards complained in the studio about Brian's absence, since it forced him to do most of the work, but privately hoped he could be coaxed back. For everything that had happened between them, he still had a great fondness for Brian, and he was impressed by how Brian had turned his life around.

So, on the evening of June 12, everyone looked up with genuine surprise when Brian strolled nonchalantly into the studio holding a Gretsch guitar.

The hellos were awkward, and the silence that followed them even more so. Then Brian cleared his throat.

"I've written a song. It's a blues number. I think it would fit in well with the sound of this disc. I'd like to play it – maybe we can use it."[70]

Keith saw a chance to try to mend fences. He took his cigarette out of his mouth and looked up at Brian. His hands fell into his lap in a gesture of welcome. "Sure, Brian, let's hear it," he offered.

But before Brian could react, Mick shoved a microphone stand aside and marched up to him. "Piss off, Brian! You know fucking well we've got enough songs for the album already. Why don't you plug in your fucking guitar and do some work for a change?"

In that one second, years of memories rushed through Brian's head. All the betrayals. All the humiliations. The way Mick and the others had repeatedly made fun of him in the vans and limos between shows. The refusal to allow him to take part in songwriting, or to credit him properly when he did take part. The denial of a chance to speak during interviews and the general treatment of him like an unwanted stepchild. Keith stealing the woman he had loved. And, now it had come to this – Mick standing in front of Brian and talking down to him like a child. After Brian had founded the Rolling Stones, named the Rolling Stones, and led them through the tough early days when it would have been easy to give up on the band....

He wasn't even angry. He just felt sad. He stared at Mick for a long moment, long enough that the other Stones began to flinch awkwardly, long enough that Mick looked in every other direction but at Brian. He said not another word, but simply turned and walked quietly out of the studio. Then he returned to his Kings Road flat.

Stepping inside his flat, he let out a sigh, less of sadness now than resolution. He picked up the phone. He was still holding the Gretsch guitar and fumbled with it as he dialed John Lennon's phone number.

Meanwhile, after a few moments of silence, the Stones got back to work. The silence betrayed their misgivings, but no one was prepared to say a word about what had happened. None of the band wanted to confront each other.

They were not surprised when they continued working the next day, and Brian still didn't show up. What they didn't know was that Brian was at that moment at the Apple offices on Wigmore Street, signing contracts and paperwork, and having a celebratory round of drinks (club soda, in Brian's case) with John, Paul, George, Ringo, Buddy Holly, Ron Kass, Derek Taylor and Peter Brown.

When Brian didn't return to Olympic for the second day following his row with Mick, some began to wonder if they should contact him, although Mick insisted Brian was just "having one of his snits." Besides, he argued, it was hardly as if Brian had been around for most of the recording sessions, so why care now?

But Keith was worried, so to relax him, Mick's girlfriend Marianne Faithfull was finally dispatched to phone Brian at his flat. She reached him at home, and when she asked what was going on, got the answer, "Tell them I've quit."

Bill Wyman, Brian's best friend in the Stones, immediately phoned Brian back, with the other band members listening in on an extension. Brian confirmed to Bill that he had indeed decided to leave the Rolling Stones, and in fact had already that morning phoned a few friendly journalists to make his announcement public.

After a long pause, Bill said, "You could have at least told us yourself, Brian." Brian hastily assured Bill that he meant no insult to either him or Charlie Watts, but that he didn't have the stomach for another moment like the last one, and that he really didn't have anything to say to Mick or Keith.

By the time Brian's announcement hit the papers, the Stones had issued a terse one of their own, saying they wished Brian well and would search for a replacement for him, and would finish the new album as a quartet in the meantime.[71]

The Stones were not entirely surprised by Brian's departure. But they were completely bowled over by the news that they received as they gathered in the studio on the 16th to put the finishing touches on *Beggars' Banquet*.

Mick charged angrily into the studio. He held aloft a copy of the *Daily Mail*. "He's joined the bloody Beatles!" Mick said. He flung the paper to the floor. Sure enough, a front-page story in that day's *Daily Mail* was titled "Brian Joins Beatles" and was built around an Apple press release:

"We would like to welcome Brian Jones, formerly of the Rolling Stones, as a full member of the Beatles. We look forward to all of the great music we will be making with him. We are now five and the five are one. All you need is love. John, Paul, George, and Ringo."

June 28, 1968

Brian Jones joined the Beatles one year after the Summer of Love, but the momentum of a new age for rock music did not yet seem blunted. The change not only in the sounds, but in the culture behind them, was illustrated in the new issue of *Life* magazine, in an especially perceptive article by Shana Alexander titled "The New Rock."

Various "underground" publications, like Paul Williams' *Crawdaddy* in Boston, had sprouted over the past two years and were attempting to provide, for the first time, a fair analysis both of the growing artistry of rock music and of the phenomenon of the so-called counterculture: the peace-and-love trappings of the "flower children" that rejected the competitive and materialistic world of their parents' generation in favor of seeking a new way of life based on love, sharing and community.

Alexander's piece, which included a lengthy interview with members of the Grateful Dead, came as close as any mainstream publication had to correctly identifying the spirit of the counterculture circa 1968:

"This is not a political movement. Asked who they will vote for in the fall, some of those present giggle, and one says, 'the Maharishi.' It's more of a thought movement, an attempt to change the current accepted way of thinking, understanding and relating to the world around us. That reference to the Maharishi isn't an idle one – this is a generation of seekers, of people looking for a deeper meaning to life. They say they do not want to reject their religious traditions – they want to deepen them.

"Nor do the young people in the communes of Haight-Ashbury and Greenwich Village and scores of locations around the country have any quarrel with an America at peace, no grievances against their homeland; indeed, Stars and Stripes motifs are popular with these kids. What they want, they say, is to create a world where mankind lives up to its ideals, where peace and love are not just words, where the Golden Rule replaces the rule of the jungle and dog-eat-dog. 'And where it's fun,' adds band member Phil Lesh with a laugh. 'We're just trying to create a new type of life,' band leader Jerry Garcia chimes in. 'A life where people live in harmony with one another and with the world.'[72]

And there was much that was exciting in the new rock. One of the summer of '68's best releases was the new Doors album, *The Celebration of the Lizard*. After their stunning self-titled first album, the Doors had fallen victim to a classic case of "sophomore slump," releasing a second album, *Strange Days*, that was like the first one but not as good. But any fears that the band might be starting to fail were put to rest with their tough, chilling, spacey new disc, forever after regarded as the band's masterpiece.[73]

But some in the music biz were not in tune with the zeitgeist of peace and love. Allen Klein, the Rolling Stones' new manager, decided Brian Jones' departure was a golden opportunity to cash in. Klein had always yearned to manage the Beatles, but had been severely rebuffed by Brian Epstein, who refused even to shake Klein's hand when they were introduced. Klein resigned himself, after Buddy Holly's landing of the job Klein wanted, to never having the Beatles. But within days of Jones' departure from the Stones, Klein sued him for breach of contract – and also named the Beatles and Apple as defendants in the lawsuit, alleging they had encouraged the breach. The fact that Mick Jagger had hinted as early as 1965 at removing Brian from the group was beside the point. The point was clearly made by Klein in a bad pun to a subordinate: "There's a nice, big, juicy apple we can take a bite of."[74]

The problems besetting the Stones had not abated. The planned release of *Beggars' Banquet* was delayed due to a dispute with Decca Records over the album cover. The intended cover depicted a toilet stall covered with graffiti, which Decca found vulgar. The cover did not depict anything obscene, and many of the graffiti messages were inside jokes scrawled by the Stones and their friends and employees, but the record company flatly refused to release the album until the Stones changed the cover design. Preparing a new cover ended up holding up the release of the album for some four months. Keith Richards was particularly irritated by the change of album covers, but didn't tell the other band members why. Just before the photo shoot, he had gone into the stall and scrawled one last graffiti message on the wall: "So long, you Welsh bastard, I'll miss you."[75]

July 1, 1968

The now-five-member Beatles, though cocooned in the studio hard at work on the new album, found time to circulate in the public eye. John Lennon and May Ling went public with their romance for the first time at the London opening of *Convergence*. This new version of the film was enhanced with new footage which May had shot after arriving in London.

She'd wanted to work John into the film somehow, but couldn't find a way to get him into the story. "Maybe I should just stroll about nude," he said. He and May laughed – but then he suddenly stopped laughing, warming to the idea. "That's fantastic! Let's both do it!"

"Stroll around nude? Out of the question."

"Come on, love," John urged playfully. "It could be great art. A statement of freedom. Show the world that beautiful body."

"But it's not great art," she insisted. "It's just being nude. Nude for the sake of nude isn't art or freedom or anything like that. It's just...nude. It's like using your body to sell cornflakes. If being nude is part of the story, then fine, but if it's just nude for the sake of nude, I don't consider that great art, John." John knew that tone of voice well – it was the same one he used when making a decision for the Beatles. The line his new love had drawn was clear: this was her arena, and here she would make the decisions. The notion of a nude scene in the movie was dismissed as quickly as it had arisen.[76]

John celebrated the film opening by introducing May to the press, who were quickly and universally charmed by her wit and personality. The public consensus was that the most uncompromising of the Beatles had found, just possibly, the perfect soulmate.[77]

At the conclusion of the show, he released fifty white balloons into the London skies with the words: "I declare these balloons high."

August 29, 1968

When the Beatles started recording their album, the working title had been *A Doll's House*, after the famous play by Henrik Ibsen. But as the sessions progressed, once Brian joined, the Beatles felt that the title should reflect their situation as a band. So it was decided to simply title the album *The Beatles* and issue it with a plain white cover, with only their embossed name and a serial number unique to each copy, to signify a "new beginning" for the Fab Four – now the "Fab Four Plus One."

The "new" Beatles made their first public appearance by playing an impromptu concert on the roof of Apple Corps' new offices on Savile Row in London. Paul excited the news media to a frenzy of speculation by saying afterward that the Beatles wanted to get into the feel of performing live again in expectation of actual concert performances "sometime next year." The group brought traffic to a stop and onlookers clambering onto adjacent roofs as they tore through a brief set consisting of oldies, including, as a welcome to Brian, Robert Johnson's blues classic "I Believe I'll Dust My Broom." May Ling and Paul McCartney's new girlfriend, Linda Eastman, were standing by with film cameras to record the show. (Linda, a photographer when she met Paul, had quickly struck up a close friendship with May, who offered to teach her the ropes of filmmaking.) Their film would be aired that fall in both Britain and the United States as a TV special, and one day – under the title *The Beatles Live on the Rooftop 1968* – would become a mainstay of video rental stores.[78]

The rooftop concert was followed by a more formal live appearance on the David Frost show, to promote the release of the first single from the new lineup, "Hey Jude"/"Revolution," with audience members clambering onstage to join the group for the long coda and fadeout of the former song. The Beatles then followed up their David Frost appearance by flying to Los Angeles to appear on the *Tonight Show*, their first live TV appearance in over two years in the United States. Johnny Carson announced the group in his opening monologue, paying special attention to the recent addition of Brian Jones. "When Mick Jagger heard he [Jones] was leaving, his jaw dropped so far his lips nearly beat him to death," Johnny said. The joke got a weak laugh, and Johnny went into his "bad vaudeville performer" bit, saying with mock nervousness, "you see...he's, er, got these big lips...and..." Then, in one of the show's running gags, the house band struck up "Tea for Two" and Johnny briefly tap-danced like a failing vaudeville performer about to be pelted with tomatoes.

The Beatles stormed through "Revolution," then gathered at the desk next to Johnny – John, Brian and Ringo taking chairs, Paul leaning over from above, and George sitting cross-legged on the floor – to be interviewed by the host. Johnny concentrated as best he could on Brian, but the newest Beatle was understandably nervous and a bit tight-lipped, and John and Paul were soon jumping in, competing with each other for the best witticisms. John had caustic words for the Stones, saying, "They didn't want Brian in their band, and now they don't want him in ours, but he's made our band better, so they were the ones who were daft about it." Paul added, "They're worse off now. Brian's great, man. He can play just about anything. I can't believe the Stones didn't know what to do with him."

The Beatles didn't make a special point of denouncing the Maharishi, but they did say they were moving on. Johnny asked, "What led you to put so much faith in him?" John, sensing a putdown, shrugged and said, "We made a mistake. We're human." Johnny said, "No, of course, but I wonder, was there something in particular that drew you to him..." Paul jumped in, saying, "Well, he was charming, you know, and very happy and friendly, and he really does have a good relaxation technique. The problem is when you're looking for something more." Brian then added, "You can't find from a man the things that you need to go above man to find." Spiritual words, but nondenominational enough to get a round of applause from the audience and a nod from Johnny.

John got considerably more animated when the host asked about his new love. "May is fantastic," John gushed. "She's a brilliant artist, and has real understanding. She's got a depth to her that's not like any woman I've known, ever." The other Beatles quickly chimed in with assent, Paul saying, "She's a lovely person" and George adding, "She gives off good vibes – good vibrations, like the Beach Boys song."

The show ended with the Beatles' performance of "Hey Jude," with the members of the house band and studio audience joining the Beatles onstage for the "na na na" section.[79]

CHAPTER NINE: FLYING

October 25, 1968

When the new Beatles double album was released, with its plain, white minimalist cover with only the name of the group embossed on the front, it was called from the first day the "White Album."

The track "Revolution #9" was perhaps the most revolutionary - a pure, avant-garde musique concrete work, inspired partly by May but also by Paul's avant-garde flirtations over the previous two years. John and Paul worked together on it, culling a big pile of sound effects tapes, including nonsensical mutterings from all five Beatles that faded in and out at various points, mostly John and George, but a few from the others as well:

Paul: "The little man stood on the roof with his bat playing cricket..."

Brian: "A hairy beast comes up out of the ground and frightens all the little children..."

Ringo: "Each Thursday he would come back and leave a pat of butter next to the door..."[80]

Brian staked out his debut presence as a Beatle in emphatic fashion, bringing – along with his first Beatles composition, "Walking Alone Blues," the same song he had offered to play to the Rolling Stones at Olympic Studios – the palette of musical colors he had added to the Rolling Stones' music. He added a searing lead guitar to George's "While My Guitar Gently Weeps" and a wailing bluesy slide guitar to John's "Yer Blues," a saxophone to Paul's "Ob-La-Di, Ob-La-Da" and a beautiful sitar line to "Across the Universe," which George meshed with a wah-wah guitar; from the very first, the two guitarists found their styles sympathetic and wove a unique sound from them. [81]

Despite the triumph of the album, the Fab Four Plus One found themselves in courtrooms for much of the autumn, which was the chief reason they decided to wait until the next year to return to the concert stage. The Rolling Stones' suit against the Beatles and Apple was settled out of court for a sum which was undisclosed, but later revealed to be about a quarter of a million pounds.

The suit had won the Stones and Allen Klein some cash, but it had greatly damaged their credibility with rock fans in general. Brian Jones' defection to the Beatles was viewed sympathetically by most of the rock audience, especially after his outstanding performances on the White Album. It was obvious that he was unhappy in the Stones and wanted to leave, and the Stones never convincingly argued that he should not have done so. Fans concluded that greed could be the only motivation for the Stones to then turn around and file a lawsuit over Brian's departure. It was seen as petty and avaricious, and the "alternative" press slammed them universally for it.

That same month, *Beggars Banquet* finally came out. Compared with previous releases, sales were sluggish. It was soon apparent just how much the perception of the Stones' attack on the Beatles had affected their standing with the rock audience.

During the interlude leading up to the album's release, the Rolling Stones suffered yet another embarrassment. Eric Clapton, for a while touted in the press as Brian's replacement, revealed in December that he had indeed negotiated with the band but had turned them down. He cited his friendship with George Harrison, evoking the ugly lawsuit, and also said "If they didn't have room for Brian Jones' songs, there's no reason to think they'll have room for mine."

January 30, 1969

The Stones lawsuit finally settled, the Beatles regrouped at Abbey Road Studios to begin work on a new album. These sessions were set to be their swan song at the studio where they had laid the groundwork for their immense success. Their new state-of-the-art Apple Studios in the Apple headquarters building on Savile Row was still under construction, and wasn't expected to be ready until later in the year.[82]

Prior to the sessions, Paul McCartney had had the idea of filming the Beatles working on the album, but this idea was scotched in favor of filming the live concert performances the band was planning for that year. May Ling and Linda Eastman were to be co-directors of the concert film.[83]

The first session involved a run-through of various oldies and new songs, such as John's "Jealous Guy" – the song he had sung to May that night back in July, though in the end he set it aside as he felt it was not yet complete - Brian's "Family," Paul's "Let it Be," and George's "I Me Mine."[84] The second session on January 31 was spent mostly on jams and more oldies, as well as more new songs: John's "I Dig a Pony" and "Don't Let Me Down," John and Paul's "I've Got a Feeling," and George's "Let It Down." The traditional Liverpool folk song "Maggie Mae," the tale of a prostitute who robbed a local sailor, was also given a run-through, but the resulting tape would remain unreleased for many years.

The next session on February 5 produced a long jam, entitled "Dig It" on the tape box. It was left aside, mostly because the Beatles didn't see much use from it: the phrase "dig it" took center attention, with various ad-libs and asides shouted by John. Two more concrete songs were given run-throughs: Paul's "On Our Way Home" (later retitled "Two of Us") and George's "Hear Me Lord."

On February 6, the Beatles ran through just one song, Paul's ballad "The Long and Winding Road." Even in its spare piano form, "The Long and Winding Road" was seen as the strongest song introduced during the sessions so far, with John and Brian arguing for it to be the closing track on the current album.

George was not present at the session to give his opinion on "The Long and Winding Road." He had his tonsils removed on February 7, leading the Beatles to halt work on the new album for two weeks. George would remain in the hospital until February 15, which would give him time to recover well enough for the first serious sessions.

February 17, 1969

As he sat hunched over his guitar in the familiar confines of the Abbey Road studio , George Harrison could feel his frustration growing.

Over the years, his songwriting prowess had grown immensely. From his early stabs like "You Like Me Too Much" and "I Need You," George had blossomed into a major songwriting force, as his contributions to the White Album demonstrated. And along with his growing skills came a growing output.

But the quota to which John and Paul had assigned him in 1965 – two songs per album – remained the same, and there didn't seem to be any other outlet for his music than the Beatles' albums. So a huge backlog of unrecorded songs had been piling up. George tried not to let it bother him, but he felt as though his voice were being stifled. Would anyone ever get to hear his music?

The sessions for the new album underlined the problem. George would again get only two songs per album. There was no possibility of that allotment getting any higher, now that Ringo was writing the occasional song as well, and now that Brian had joined the group – his own creative stifling being part of the reason why he left the Rolling Stones. The bond that had developed between George and Brian, the two guitarists, was too great for George to resent Brian's contributions, but George still felt he was writing songs that had nowhere to go.

During the past two days, he had brought two more songs to the sessions, along with the previously-heard "Hear Me Lord." That song had already been vetoed. Another new number, "Let It Down," was not yet finished and did not impress the others. A third new number, "All Things Must Pass," was stronger but still got a thumbs-down from Paul. "That title sounds like death," he bluntly told George. "We ought to have something upbeat – we've got Brian and we're going back out on tour."

"It's not about death, it's about the cycle of life." George snapped back. "It's about a new beginning – that's what's going on with us, right? It's about bad times passing away, not good times. Listen to the words, man." Paul sat, nonplussed, for a moment, then quietly said, "All right, let's get on with it." They ran through the song again, but Paul still said no, and John did not argue the point in favor of George.

After having two of his songs rejected and another unfairly criticized, George was in no mood for a fresh lecture from Paul. But the Beatles began working on one of Paul's new songs, "I've Got a Feeling," and Paul, ever the perfectionist, was soon berating George, who wasn't producing the guitar sound exactly the way Paul wanted it.

"I'll play it however you want me to play it, or I won't play it at all if that's what you want," George seethed. Paul told him he was being difficult, at which point George muttered a curt "I'm off" and walked out.

Arriving home with a headache, he went to bed. Waking up a few hours later, he wrote a song about the experience – "Wah-Wah." The "wah-wah" of the title referred to the headache he left the studio with – "you've given me a headache, Paul." Upon completing the song, George sighed to himself. "Another one that won't get on the album."

Brian phoned George the day after the walkout, after giving him time to cool off. Perhaps better than anyone else, he understood George's frustrations.

"I hate knowing that I had a row with Paul," George said. "Especially in front of everyone like that. But it drives me crazy."

"Paul didn't mean it that way."

"I know," said George, "but I mean, I'm writing all these songs – there's so many, there's songs I haven't even played for the group – and no one gets to hear them. I feel like I'm making all this music and no one will ever hear it. I know John and Paul just want their space, and I dig that, but –"

"There has to be a way," said Brian. "John and Paul are quite reasonable. Believe me, it was much worse in the Stones, where you couldn't get a song in at all, or if you did they would take credit for it and put their names on it. There's got to be a way to resolve this."

"We can work it out," said George with a laugh.

Brian laughed as well. "Better than 'Get Off of My Cloud.'"

As it happened, while Brian Jones was talking to George, Buddy Holly was talking about George with the rest of the group. He had an idea – suggested to him by an offhand remark John had made a while back about "conceptual art" – that he hoped could resolve George's dilemma. George agreed to come to the studio later that week for a discussion with the rest of the group and Holly.

"I don't think there's any way it can be fair to John and Paul to give you more space on Beatles records," Buddy said. "That would only be taking space away from them." George bristled.

"But maybe, if it wasn't the Beatles," Buddy continued. "Maybe a group with no permanent members…"

George, annoyed, asked, "What are you talking about?"

But John chimed in, immediately picking up the thread of Buddy's idea. "Like, a side project for George? A conceptual group?"

"Yeah, that's what I had in mind," Buddy said. "Obviously you guys have to make this decision for yourselves; I can't make it for you. But consider this: George would continue to get space for two songs on Beatles records, Brian gets one, Richie [Ringo] gets one if he writes one.

"At the same time, we set up a 'conceptual' group, as John put it just now. It would be led by George, and it would have a floating membership."

Now John, picking up Buddy's wavelength and excited by it, was helping him elaborate his idea. "George, think of it - it would be you and whoever is in the studio with you. Whoever you wanted to work with you on the album – Brian could be on it, too, and Richie."

"Exactly," Buddy said. "George, you can use this side project to release albums on Apple. They would be your albums and not Beatles albums. So you wouldn't have to fight for space with John and Paul. You can release all the songs you want and make the music you want to make without having to fight the Beatles for it."

Paul, to George's surprise, was also enthusiastic about the idea. He said, "You could ask me or John to play on it if you want, George, but if we did it would be under your direction. This would be your baby." Paul wanted badly to make things right with George. Brian was right – he felt terrible about provoking George's walkout.

Over the next week, George discussed his objections and fears with Buddy and the group. He worried that his side project albums would be regarded as an "inferior" work of art next to the Beatles. Buddy assured him that would not be the case. "We won't regard it as a novelty or inferior item in any way," he said. "We'll put the same promotional machinery and the same work behind it as we do for any Beatles album."

One by one, George's fears were overcome, and by March, he had rejoined the group and recommitted himself to the upcoming album and tour, with the promise that Apple would swing behind his new project as soon as he decided to get it underway. George believed that Brian and Ringo would soon need songwriting outlets as well, and invited them to participate. Both eagerly assented. George politely told John and Paul that he would probably use other musicians for the rest of the lineup.

"They aren't offended, are they?" Brian asked.

"Who knows?" George said. "But if I let them in they might take over subtly."

He had even come up with a name for the "conceptual" group: Mangalam. The Sanskrit word meant "happiness," but it also meant "auspiciousness" – portending good fortune. George wanted his new conceptual group to be happy and successful.[85]

Sessions for the new Beatles album now proceeded smoothly, interrupted only by two social occasions: a pair of weddings.

On April 12, at the Marylebone Registry Office in London, James Paul McCartney wed Linda Louise Eastman. The huge crush of reporters and sobbing female fans outside was held to a minimum by the absence of the other Beatles. "We wanted to come," John told a reporter the following day, "but there were enough people there already – it was a circus. It would have been even worse if the rest of us had shown up." The other Beatles compensated for not attending by having lavish gifts sent to the newlyweds. Meanwhile, Sgt. Norman Pilcher of the London Drug Squad, who had let it be known among his colleagues that he thought it would be "quite a laugh" to stage a raid on one of the "longhairs" that evening as an embarrassment on the McCartneys' wedding day, received a stern warning from higher authorities that the Beatles, MBE, were to be left alone. Arresting Mick Jagger and Keith Richards was one thing, toying with the Beatles quite another, and none of them had yet been arrested on drug charges. George and Patti Harrison spent a quiet evening at home in Esher, entirely unaware until some years later, when Pilcher was finally himself prosecuted for tampering with evidence, what he had had in mind for them that night.[86]

Sixteen days later, John and May flew to New York. There, in a private civil ceremony on a Long Island cliff overlooking the Atlantic Ocean, John Winston Lennon and May Ling were married. "The sun came up just as [the ceremony] began," John said on the way to the airport back to England. "It was very beautiful."

As with Paul's wedding, none of the other Beatles were present – not because of any rancor but simply because they were unable to take the time away from working on the album. But Paul and Linda, George and Patti, Ringo and Maureen, and Brian and girlfriend Suki Potier all sent extravagant gifts to the newlyweds. May's parents did attend, and as a special surprise to John, May had his Aunt Mimi flown across the Atlantic from England so she could be present. Mimi shed copious tears as John and May took their vows.[87]

To the disappointment of some who imagined that John and May would use the occasion of their wedding to make a public statement of some sort, the couple flew to the Caribbean for a brief, secluded honeymoon before returning to London so that

John could resume work on the Beatles' new album.[88] John and May did, however, send an acorn to each of the major world leaders, asking them to plant them as a symbol of world peace. Chairman Mao did not respond, and neither did the Soviet leadership. But President Hubert Humphrey[89] and British Prime Minister Harold Wilson thanked John, as did leaders in India and throughout Europe.

May 11, 1969

At the Spahn Ranch, out in the desert near Los Angeles, a strange and chilling man named Charles Manson had, over the past few months, grown deeply confused by recent events. At the ranch, where he lived with his "Family," he played the Beatles' White Album over and over, puzzling over its messages.

He knew – the LSD had taught him – that he was Jesus Christ, and that his horrific childhood and the years in jail were but a prelude to his anointing and calling to his mission. The Beatles, too, he knew were the angels promised in the Bible's Revelation of John (The Apocalypse), come to send him messages, instructions on what he was to do next. But lately, the messages had grown confusing.

The White Album's penultimate track was titled "Revolution #9." Clearly, that must refer to Chapter 9 of the Revelation of John in the Bible, which reads in part: *"The appearance of the locusts was like that of horses ready for battle. On their heads they wore what looked like crowns of gold; their faces were like human faces, and they had hair like women's hair. Their teeth were like lions' teeth, and they had chests like iron breastplates. The sound of their wings was the sound of many horse-drawn chariots racing into battle. They had tails like scorpions, with stingers; with their tails they had the power to harm people for five months."* (Rev. 9:7-10, NAB)

Obviously, the long-haired angels were the Beatles. But why was there suddenly a new angel, the one named Brian? The Beatles were four – now they were five? Obviously there was something here he was meant to understand – but what? Did he perhaps miss something in the instructions? Over and over, he listened to the sound effects and muttered conversation of "Revolution #9," digging for clues.

Then suddenly, as he heard the new angel say something about a "hairy beast that comes up out of the ground and frightens all the little children," the answer struck Charlie between the eyes. That's it! He – Charlie – is the hairy beast the new angel Brian is talking about! So, Charlie reasoned, I come up out of the ground and frighten all the children...the angels MUST be telling me that I am to die and rise from the dead once again. This, then, must be the event that will trigger Helter Skelter – the Apocalypse (the title of Paul's song obviously a reference to that event).

Manson told the news to his followers, the loosely-knit group of runaways and abandoned kids he called the "Family." Most of them broke into sobs. But, insisted Manson, the instructions of the angels could not be denied.

The Family held an elaborate, day-long ceremony the next day, during which Manson had sex with as many of the girls as he could summon up the stamina for, one last time. At nightfall, he climbed atop a small mound, next to which his followers, on his instructions, had dug a makeshift grave. He placed a .45

pistol against his temple as his "Family" members sobbed and cried "Goodbye, Charlie!" With a grin, he reassured them: "Don't worry, man! I'll be back in three days!" Then he pulled the trigger.

As prearranged, the "Family" buried Manson's body, then dutifully took up by the graveside to await his return after three days.

It took about a week or so for it to fully sink in to the "Family" that Manson wasn't, in fact, coming back. Without Manson's hypnotic, Svengali-like presence, the members of the "Family," particularly the girls, began to realize that they had been functioning as nothing more than a harem for a lunatic. One by one they drifted away, most hitching rides back to Los Angeles, some telling each other that it was a good thing at least that "no one got hurt." The last follower, an innocent-looking girl named Lynette Fromme (known as "Squeaky" to the Family), and the most loyal of Charlie's flock, stayed the longest, nearly starving to death before she finally left. A few weeks later, Manson's body was dug up at the site and cremated like any homeless drifter's.[90]

May 22, 1969

Back in London, the Beatles, unaware of the gruesome events near Los Angeles, completed their new album. Originally it was to be titled *Get Back*, as a nod to its "back to basics" approach. But toward the end of the sessions, Paul McCartney began to have second thoughts about the title he had dreamed up, fearing that it might suggest the Beatles were going backwards, rather than back to basics. John then suggested *Let It Be*, after another of Paul's songs. "People thought it meant 'let it be' in the sense of 'leave it alone,'" said John, "but I took it to mean 'let it happen' or 'let it become' – you know, we've begun to learn how to change ourselves and our world, now let's let it be."

"Family" was another strong Brian Jones contribution, not bluesy this time, more like a folk song, like Donovan's music but with more of an edge. George's "I Me Mine" railed against self-centeredness at all levels, while his "For You Blue" was simply a jaunty love song. Paul's "Get Back" and "Let it Be" underpinned the theme of the album, while "One After 909," an early Lennon-McCartney tune the duo had resurrected, brought home the "back to basics" concept. Paul's "Two of Us" was not about him and John, as some fans thought, but about him and Linda; still, it celebrated togetherness – echoed by "I've Got a Feeling," which combined unfinished Paul and John songs. "I Dig a Pony" was inspired, surreal nonsense, while "Don't Let Me Down" was an aching plea to May: two sides of John Lennon. Also released from these sessions was another George number, "Old Brown Shoe," as the flip side of the single "Get Back."[91]

Two days after the album's release, the long-delayed film *Yellow Submarine,* the first official full-length feature from Apple Films, at long last held its London premiere, with the Beatles attending. The animated work had been produced by King Features, who had contracted to produce a film based on the Beatles' music in 1967. The story, inspired by a 3 am phone call from John Lennon to one of the film's producers ("Wouldn't it be great if Ringo were followed down the street by a yellow submarine?") depicted the Beatles boarding the Yellow Submarine to rescue a peace-and-love paradise called Pepperland from the onslaught of negative forces called the Red

Meanies (taken by many to be a reference to the Soviet Union). The film was nearing completion in the late spring of 1968 when, to the dismay of the producers, the Beatles added Brian Jones to the group. King Features then had a portion of the script rewritten, to work an animated Brian into the movie, with the original four Beatles finding Brian in the Sea of Holes and welcoming him into the Yellow Submarine. The soundtrack album, consisting of *Sgt. Pepper/Magical Mystery Tour*-era rejects, was released in August on Apple. Side Two consisted of incidental music from the movie, arranged by George Martin. Side One included, along with "Yellow Submarine" and "All You Need Is Love" (the moral of the film), the outtakes "Only a Northern Song," "All Together Now", "Hey Bulldog", and "It's All Too Much." While the Beatles didn't appear to contribute much to the film, aside from a filmed sequence at the end, the movie nonetheless was dazzling visually and had a certain sweetness that penetrated the psychedelic veneer. Brian Jones told a reporter at the premiere, "I was happy that, instead of killing off the villains or something like that, they're invited to join everyone else at the end, once they've reformed, and they all become one."[92]

Buddy Holly also announced shortly afterward that Northern Songs, the music publishing company formed early in the Beatles' career to publish the songs of Lennon and McCartney, had been purchased by Apple. Dick James, the Beatles' longtime publishing partner, had decided to sell his shares. Holly acted quickly, thwarting an attempt by British media magnate Sir Lew Grade to obtain the valuable catalogue. With the Beatles now in control of their own publishing, Holly announced that Northern

Songs would be folded into Apple Music over the course of the year.[93]

CHAPTER TEN: MAGICAL MYSTERY TOUR

June 2, 1969

The crowds that had swarmed the *Yellow Submarine* premiere for a glimpse at the Beatles were as nothing compared to the international pandemonium that descended on America and Britain as the initial sets of tickets went on sale for the first Beatles concert tour in three years. Madison Square Garden, the site of the opening show in the States, sold out in two hours. Fans waited as long as four days for the box office to open, and dozens lost shoes or eyeglasses in the chaos when it did.

The Madison Square Garden show was scheduled for July 3, with 19 dates across the United States to follow. The tour would end with a free show. Fortuitously, May Ling's parents owned a farm near Watkins Glen, New York, accessible to a number of nearby railroad passenger lines and highways, which seemed an ideal location for an outdoor free festival. As soon as the free show was announced, fans – over a month in advance – began streaming toward upstate New York. A separate group of promoters who had been planning a rock festival to be held near Bob Dylan's home in Woodstock decided against holding their concert, realizing they couldn't possibly compete with the crowds who would head to the Beatles' show – which, as it happened, was scheduled for the same weekend the Woodstock promoters had hoped to use.[94]

On June 14, the heart of London was brought to a virtual standstill as an estimated crowd of 250,000 flocked to Hyde Park for the event of the summer: the return of the Beatles to the concert stage.

Crowds swarmed throughout the park itself and neighboring Knightsbridge, making it virtually impossible for traffic to get through. Harrods, in fact, later unsuccessfully filed suit against Apple for disrupting their business that Saturday. The crowd was well-behaved, though, and nothing untoward took place.

The opening set was provided by Jethro Tull, still relative unknowns, and without much of a chance of attracting the attention of a crowd impatiently awaiting the return of the Beatles. Still, Ian Anderson, his face all but buried behind his long mane of curly hair and beard, dressed in a shabby raincoat that gave him the look of a hobo, gave it his all, perching on one leg, whirling his flute manically, gesticulating and bugging his eyes out, and gradually making so much of a spectacle of himself that at least some of the fans were compelled to watch, then listen, and finally to give their resounding approval.

Buddy Holly nodded with a thin smile as he watched backstage. He remembered the Diamonds, and how they had produced an overwrought version of the Gladiolas' "Little Darlin'" back in 1957, intending to ridicule the song – only to have it become a hit, because in rock and roll, the more outrageous you were, the better. *This band*, Holly thought, *is nothing if not outrageous.*

The following set, though, by Traffic, seemed interminable. Steve Winwood was eager to put on a good show, but the subtleties of Traffic's music were lost, especially after Jethro Tull's over-the-top act. Besides, the fans were beginning to get restless, and had little patience for lengthy jazzy excursions. Traffic weren't booed off the stage – the crowd was too well-behaved for that – but the response was decidedly tepid. Paul

McCartney, halfway through their set, waved Buddy Holly back toward the dressing rooms. "Let's not use them again," he said. Holly rolled his eyes and nodded.

After a space of about a half an hour, the road crew – twenty men, for things had now gotten much bigger than in the old days, when Mal Evans and Neil Aspinall used to set up and break down the band's equipment themselves – had finished setting up the stage for the climactic act of the afternoon. With the sun shining brightly over Hyde Park, the Beatles took the stage.

For this, the first show of the legendary 1969 tour, their appearance would become as iconic as their matching collarless jackets had once been. John wore a white cotton shirt and white cotton pants, his long hair flowing down to his shoulders, a day or two's worth of beard growing on his face. His eyes were wide, behind his wire-frame glasses – the first time he had ever worn them onstage – and carried a musical smile, so much more welcoming than the squint he had so often affected during the Beatlemania days, when he had been afraid to wear his glasses in public, and his nearsighted squinting so often came across as a hostile glare.

Paul had on a blue shirt and black jacket thrown over it, his collar open wide, and black pants, and he whooped with joy as he strutted to the microphone holding his Hofner violin bass, which he had pulled out of mothballs. His signature instrument, he had discovered, had still had the set list taped to the back of it from the 1966 tour. A much longer set list was taped there now.

George had on a denim shirt and jeans, and wore a bandanna cowboy-style around his neck. His initial apprehension gave way to a wide smile as he heard the crowd's roar, and he stepped to the microphone and, almost inaudibly, said "Hare Krishna."

Ringo was the most formal of the five, telling a reporter later on, "It was a show – I felt I should dress up." He wore a white shirt and black blazer, but added a psychedelic multicolored cravat, and took his place behind the drums with a relaxed air, clearly happy that the return to the road didn't appear to mean a return to the days of racing in flight from screaming crowds.

Brian, in a purple tie-dyed shirt, white trousers, and white hat – a getup he would replace with an American-flag shirt for the U.S. leg of the tour – was clearly the most nervous, trying his best to smile but with the color gone from his face. He was about to make his debut in front of hundreds of thousands as a Beatle.

He had meditated before taking the stage, after fighting hard against the almost overwhelming urge to have a drink. It had forced him up out of his chair backstage, and he had slammed his fists into the wall. Then he thought, "Fuck me, I hope I didn't just damage my hands." And that thought made him even more rattled in turn.

Buddy Holly had come in when he heard the noise. "Are you all right?"

"Terrible," said Brian. "Bloody terrible."

"Take a deep breath, Brian," Holly said. "Remember your exercises."

Brian, quivering, began his breathing exercises, reciting a prayer in his mind to keep himself focused. Slowly, his hands stopped shaking. Calming, he sat back down onto a divan, falling into his exercises, letting his mind relax, the desperate need for a drink fading into the background as he focused hard upon the prayer.

As Buddy left, Brian pulled himself into a lotus position, meditating until the call came to take the stage.

Now he was getting nervous again, but it was too late for anything other than to go out on the stage and...be a Beatle.

The crowd roared and screamed, surging forward, but without the manic energy of the Beatlemania days; instead, they seemed more like disciples pushing forward for a look at their prophets. Many in the front, John realized, were staring up at them with literally open-mouthed awe, as if they expected a blessing. This prompted him to walk to the mike and, with a shrug, say, "We're just going to play music, you know - we're not going to part the Red Sea or anything."

Still, this was the avatars' first show since the mop top days. Expectations understandably ran high, especially in the wake of all the Beatles had created since 1966. But unlike the last time they performed, there were no screaming girls tearing at them, and concert technology advances since 1966 meant the audience would actually be able to hear them now. This wasn't Beatlemania – it was something that had transcended Beatlemania.

It would have been easy for the Beatles to disappoint, but they were determined not to do so. Not certain what sort of "happening" would be worthy of the event, the band – in the "get back" spirit of their new album – finally decided to dispense with any attempts at elaboration beyond that required musically – they would just go out and play their songs. But they had rehearsed exhaustively, for two weeks straight before the show, to make sure they sounded tight and professional. The result was described by Nick Kent in *New Musical Express*: "They didn't float down from the clouds like deities. They didn't perform magic tricks. They just did what they do best - came out and performed their music. In the end, that was all the magic that was needed."

The Beatles opened with a medley of "Sgt. Pepper's Lonely Hearts Club Band" and "With a Little Help from My Friends," with Brian adding orchestral sounds on a Mellotron and Paul changing the next-to-last line of the former song from "Billy Shears" to "Ringo Starr" to lead into Ringo's lead vocal. Three tracks from the new album followed: "I Dig a Pony," "Get Back," and "Two of Us." They then reached back to 1965 for "Nowhere Man" and "We Can Work It Out."

Brian's guitar and John's scream led them into "Revolution," followed by "She Said She Said" and "Day Tripper." George got his first star turn with "While My Guitar Gently Weeps," with Brian's wailing guitar solo, followed by two more White Album tracks, "Happiness Is a Warm Gun" and "Blackbird," the latter performed on acoustic guitars by all four guitarists to accompany Paul's vocal, with Ringo adding subtle percussion. They used the same arrangement for "Yesterday." Then they donned their electrics again for "I've Got a Feeling," a medley of John's "Yer Blues" and Brian's "Walking Alone Blues," and "Helter Skelter." The pace became gentler with "Dear Prudence" and "Every Little Thing," after which John sat down at the keyboards for "Lucy in the Sky with Diamonds." Then came "Norwegian Wood" and "Across the Universe," with first George and then Brian playing the same sitar, trading it from one to the other between songs as if it were a sacred object. "Don't Let Me Down" followed, then "Lady Madonna" and "Penny Lane."

John's original intent for "Help!" was fulfilled, as the Beatles slowed it down and played it as a Roy Orbison-like ballad. They wrapped up with "Ticket to Ride," "Let It Be" and "All You Need Is Love." For the encore, the group reached back to their moptop days for three numbers: "I Saw Her Standing There," "Please Please Me," and "A Hard Day's Night," before finally ending the proceedings with a long, audience-participation-oriented version of "Hey Jude." With just minor variations, the Beatles would play the same set throughout the tour.

More than a few fans - particularly those fortified by "electric Kool-Aid" - came away from the concert declaring that they'd "seen God." Even many of those who hadn't felt the joy of the show that profoundly, though, regarded it as the greatest experience of their lives.

June 20, 1969

While the spring and summer were a series of triumphs for the Beatles, the Rolling Stones' failing fortunes seemed to be unrelenting.

After months of embarrassment, including the Eric Clapton debacle, the Stones had finally found a replacement for Brian Jones, a young guitarist named Mick Taylor. The newest Stone offered talent along with the apparent willingness to shut his mouth and take orders, a trait Mick Jagger found appealing. The band had commenced recording a new album to be released in time for Mick's film schedule - he was playing the title role in the film *Ned Kelly*, the story of the well-known Australian outlaw, and was jetting back and forth to Australia for the filming. Mick was determined that the Stones should tour that year, too. With the tremendous amount of attention being lavished on the Beatles, Mick wanted nothing more than to steal some of their thunder. After all, it had been three years since the Stones had toured the States as well, but unlike with the Beatles, and for that matter Bob Dylan, no one seemed in a hurry to welcome them back. Keith Richards, for his part, was sure that unless the Stones toured that year, regardless of what the Beatles were doing or not doing, they'd be finished as a band.

Nonetheless, Mick found himself once again competing with the Beatles anyway. The new Stones album, titled off one of the album tracks, was called *Let It Bleed* – just in time for a new Beatles album called *Let It Be*.

Brian's departure had hardly ended the bickering within the group, which had grown exponentially between Mick and Keith.[95] So fractious was the tone in the studio that much of the album was recorded with studio musicians. On tracks where the Stones all appeared, they often weren't playing together; rather, they overdubbed their individual parts onto the basic track, all the better to avoid seeing one another and getting into another shouting match. Mick Taylor played well on the album, but was intensely nervous at stepping into Brian's shoes, and his nervousness showed. The two best tracks, "Gimme Shelter" and "You Can't Always Get What You Want," framed the album, but on other tracks the Stones simply went back to recording blues covers. A long number titled "Midnight Rambler" was dropped from the album after Mick and Keith disagreed over its arrangement.[96] On another track, "You Got the Silver," Mick's voice was accidentally erased, and he was unavailable to re-record it, having already left to begin filming. A disgusted Keith Richards dubbed his own voice instead, his first recorded lead vocal.

A frustrated Mick Jagger lashed out at the Beatles in an interview in the Sunday *Times*: "I think the Beatles are a bit sad, really...I've never really been impressed with them as performers. They make great records, but I've never liked them on the stage. We were always a lot better at doing live shows...I can't imagine Brian's really happy there. Brian's a blues player. He can't be happy playing all that poppy stuff, all that sort of frothy music..."

Brian, contacted for a response, said only, "If I were happy in the Stones, doesn't it seem that I'd still be with them?"

July 3, 1969

The center of midtown Manhattan came to a standstill with activity focused on Madison Square Garden, as, for the first time since 1966, the Beatles (again preceded by opening act Jethro Tull, now joined by the new trio of Crosby, Stills and Nash, made up of refugees from the Byrds, the Hollies and Buffalo Springfield, with a folk-country sound) took the concert stage in America.

May's and Linda's camera crews were busily filming away, and many of the scenes outside the Madison Square Garden venue that afternoon would become iconic: the hippie girl saying, "This night is going to be like every Christmas you've ever seen, every Fourth of July, every holiday you can imagine;" the long-haired grad student expounding on the Beatles' "cultural significance;" the oily-haired, middle-aged man who stormed past and said, "Bunch of long-haired creeps - bring back Vic Damone!"

The concert went amazingly smoothly, even better than the Hyde Park show. The Beatles had Buddy Holly to thank for that. Even with all the work of running Apple, he had devoted a great deal of time to the details of the tour. Neil Aspinall, the Beatles' longtime road manager, and roadie Mal Evans handled all the equipment themselves on the last tour in 1966. For the 1969 tour, Neil oversaw all the tour arrangements, while Mal was in charge of a small army of about 30 people including lighting crew, sound crew, stage setup, and the Beatles' musical instruments.

Additionally, concert promoters flocked to the Beatles' assistance - Bill Graham, Lou Adler, Sid Bernstein - to give advice and help, particularly in organizing the August 16 free show and in lining up acts to make it a true rock festival. The city of Watkins Glen was initially reluctant to allow the show, but May Ling, through her family, was able to direct Buddy Holly to the appropriate palms to grease.

The August 9 issue of *Crawdaddy* featured the Beatles on the cover, with the headline "Magical Mystery Tour." Inside was Greil Marcus's extensive coverage of the Madison Square Garden show and Michael Lydon's of the Hyde Park show, along with a special treat for readers: an extensive interview with John Lennon, conducted by Ben Fong-Torres.[97] The articles were glowing, and John was in a fine mood throughout the interview, the only discordant note coming when he laid into Mick Jagger in return for last month's comments, accusing him of copying the Beatles throughout the Stones' career and asserting that the

Stones had never been in the same class as the Beatles: "The best thing about the Stones was Brian, and now he's in our band."

August 17, 1969

What had started as a free concert to close the Beatles' tour had, by the time it was staged at Watkins Glen, been expanded into a three-day extravaganza.

Roads were jammed with traffic for miles in every direction as an estimated crowd of almost half a million descended on the field two miles outside of the little town. The railroads serving the town ran a series of special passenger trains from New York City to help handle the crowds. Nonetheless, thanks to the hard work of Buddy Holly, Neil Aspinall and their many assistants, and their anticipation of the huge crowds, sanitary facilities were adequate and food and medical supplies plentiful, with the food ranging from the conventional (area restaurants made a killing on the festival) to the offbeat (Wavy Gravy's Hog Farm commune undertook the work of making "breakfast in bed for 400,000.")[98]

Best of all, the weather stayed good the whole weekend, with hardly a cloud in the sky.[99]

A bevy of stars had been assembled by the various promoters working on the festival. Some didn't make it. The Doors, their membership in flux at the time, make a later-regretted decision to turn it down.[100] Iron Butterfly, the makers of the psychedelic trash classic *In-A-Gadda-Da-Vida,* who were trapped in an airport, made special requests to have helicopters sent just for them, and were told what to do with their requests. But the rest was an amazing array: folk singer Richie Havens; English folk innovators the Incredible String Band; bubblegum pop band

Tommy James and the Shondells; the good-old-fashioned rock and roll of Paul Revere and the Raiders; the psychedelia-mixed-with-jazz-mixed-with-salsa of Santana; Sam and Dave; Jethro Tull; Canned Heat (whose song "Going Up the Country" became an unofficial anthem of the festival); Janis Joplin; funk pioneers Sly and the Family Stone; the artsy Moody Blues; the "Godfather of Soul," James Brown; the Grateful Dead; the roots-rock of Creedence Clearwater Revival; the Who; the Jefferson Airplane; the gravelly-voiced soul singer Joe Cocker; hard-rockers Led Zeppelin; the Kinks, Country Joe and the Fish; the Band; Crosby, Stills and Nash; the Beach Boys; Jimi Hendrix; Bob Dylan – in short, "everybody who was anybody," and as wide a gamut of performers and styles as had ever been assembled.[101] The Beatles, of course, closed the festival, headlining on Sunday night, the audience surging toward the stage and joining in on the final numbers.

The Beatles' tour wrapped up with the Festival, but the heady air of Watkins Glen resulted in a few days of further celebration in New York City. John Lennon and May Ling, taking a few days off after the triumphant close of the tour, found themselves out for a drink with Jimi Hendrix. Hendrix gushed over the "groovy scene" at Watkins Glen and thanked John profusely, both for inviting him, and for not making a big deal over Hendrix's not performing with the Jimi Hendrix Experience, his longtime backup band, at the festival.

John was puzzled. Jimi laughed.

"Dig it, man," he said, "it's nothing against Noel and Mitch – they're great players – but I just want to try something different. It's the same groove all the time, and I want to do something different, maybe get into a jazz thing, play with Miles Davis, or do something funky, maybe mix what I'm doing up with James Brown or Sly...There's lots of ideas I have, but they just keep fucking with me."

"Who keeps fucking with you?" John asked.

"The record company," Jimi replied. "Reprise. And the management company. They just want to keep digging the gravy train, you know? Jimi is their gravy train and they want that gravy train to keep coming in. Like when the Beach Boys did *Smile*, right – Capitol didn't want it because they just wanted the gravy train, even though the Beach Boys didn't want to do surf music any more – that's why I said 'You'll never hear surf music again' at Monterey, man, because I knew the Beach Boys were digging the thing they were doing...." He trailed off.[102]

John and May both nodded sympathetically. Jimi was rambling, but John knew only too well what he meant. May jumped in. "They're not letting you do what you want to do," she said. "No artist can do his best work that way."

"They're running me ragged," Jimi said. "Just keep going out and doing shows with the Experience – that's the only fucking thing they want. Noel's got his thing now, the Fat Mattress, and he wants to do his stuff, but the record company doesn't want to hear about it. 'Fuck that, man, just get out there and play some more' – that's all I'm getting. I don't know how much longer I can keep doing this shit."

John didn't give it a second thought. "Come over to Apple," he said. May nodded vigorously.

Jimi laughed again. "Oh, man, I'm still on my contract."

"Then buy them out," John said excitedly. "Borrow the money against your future royalties on Apple if you have to. But come to our label, and you'll be your own man. We're not going to push anyone around or make anyone do stuff they don't want to do."

Jimi said, "Oh man, one label, another label…."

"It'll be different," John insisted. "I swear it will. When we started Apple, we wanted everyone – all our friends – to come on to it. It was meant to be a place where we could all do our own thing. It's just that whole fucking business with the Rolling Stones upset all that. But we can still do it."

Jimi leaned forward, rubbing his eyes. "So you're saying I'd get to do what I want to do," he said.

"Sure," John said. "When we came out with Apple I wanted to say 'Just tell us you have a dream and we'll give you so much money and send you off.' That's how bloody naïve I was," he said with a laugh. "Buddy pointed out to me that every wanker in the world would be sending us garbage if I said that. But what I meant was, somebody who wants to do something different – we're not going to tell them 'No, it has to be commercial' or 'No, stick to what you did that gave you hits' or all that stuff that *we* used to get told to us. Anyone who is on our label is going to get freedom. Tour when you want to, and make the records you want to, and don't worry about the gravy train. And sod your managers if they don't like it."

Jimi's lips widened into a thin smile, the intriguing thought building on his face.[103]

CHAPTER ELEVEN: OH MY LOVE

September 3, 1969

After their American sweep, the Beatles returned to their homeland to begin the European leg of their worldwide tour with a show at Wembley. Twelve more dates in the British Isles followed, including a return to Liverpool. The group then traveled to the continent, playing shows in Paris, Munich, Hamburg, Milan, Vienna, Berlin, Stockholm, Copenhagen, Warsaw, Prague[104] and Athens. Then came a long flight to Japan, for the beginning of the final set of shows: Tokyo, Kyoto and Osaka, Shanghai and Peiping,[105] and then a trip to India to perform in New Delhi. "We're shunning the Philippines," John cracked pointedly, referring to the Beatles' near-beating there in 1966 after supposedly ignoring a dinner invitation from Imelda Marcos.

The European and Asian legs of the tour consumed most of the rest of 1969 and proved a fitting way for the group to close out the decade of the Sixties, which the Beatles had done so much to define. It was almost an afterthought when the Beatles flew back to Los Angeles for one last gig on the way home – an appearance on *The Dick Cavett Show* on December 5.[106]

Cavett topped rival Johnny Carson in the ratings for the first time the night of the Beatles' appearance. The band, high in spirits after a tour that removed all the bad taste of their unpleasant 1966 tour from their mouths, were in an appropriately festive mood. They sang a humorous medley of Christmas carols, before launching into "Come Together," a new song written by John, intended for the next album.

When Cavett pointed out that the Beatles appeared on the *Tonight Show* the last time they did a TV spot in the States, John answered that while "that man [Carson] is a nice enough fellow, you seem to know more about rock and that. You're a bit more funky." The avuncular host got a laugh when he answered, "Well, I've never really thought of myself as *funky*, but thank you anyway."

Cavett asked the Beatles what plans they had for the upcoming few weeks off before they began recording their next album.

John Lennon announced, for the first time publicly, that May was pregnant. Paul ("not to steal John's thunder") revealed that Linda was also pregnant, with her and Paul's first child, joining Linda's daughter from a previous marriage.

George excitedly explained his upcoming side project, Mangalam, and said he would be going back into the studio once the Beatles' album was done to work on the first album by his "conceptual" group.

Brian told Cavett he had recently bought a new home – Cotchford Farm, the former country home of *Winnie the Pooh* author A.A. Milne – but over the course of the tour had broken up with his girlfriend, Suki Potier, "so I don't have any babies on the way like John and Paul." He planned mostly to oversee some building work on the house, but would also be joining George in the studio to work on the Mangalam album. Cavett offered his condolences over Brian's breakup with Suki, but it was clear from Brian's nonchalant attitude that she was not the woman he was waiting for.

Ringo got the biggest laugh of the evening with his plans: "I'm probably just going to fly down to Tahiti, lie on the beach and loaf."

While John and Paul flew back home, George, Brian and Ringo stayed behind in Los Angeles for a few days, to film a brief cameo appearance on the hit TV show *Rowan & Martin's Laugh-In*.[107] The appearance itself was nothing spectacular. But from the moment the three Beatles arrived on the set, Brian was asking everyone in sight about "that bird in the bikini with all the words painted on her" – Goldie Hawn. "I couldn't take my eyes off her," he said. As it happened, Goldie was just getting over a broken engagement of her own. Throughout the day or two of filming, the two were constantly in each other's company. By the time Brian left for London, rumors were buzzing about a romance between the actress-comedienne and the Beatle – and indeed, Brian and Goldie were on the phone daily from that moment until the series finished the season and she was able to join him in London.[108]

September 25, 1969

The Rolling Stones watched the events of the summer of 1969 unfold with increasing dismay.

Keith Richards, at least, was eager to get back into the studio, after months of delay caused by Mick's film schedule first on *Ned Kelly* and then on *Performance* – with neither film, as it happened, making much of a splash, though *Performance* did eventually become something of a cult favorite. But the series of bad decisions and erratic acts coming from Mick Jagger over the past few years had done much to upset the Rolling Stones' career, and Keith had grown increasingly distant from him.

The latest event to drive another wedge between the two Stones had occurred after the release of *Let It Bleed*. One of the tracks was a rocking number titled "Honky Tonk Women," based on a guitar riff Keith had come up with. With Mick Taylor, Brian Jones' replacement, not fully a member of the band at the time of the recording, the Stones had cut the song with a visitor: Dick Taylor, bassist for the Pretty Things and one-time bassist for the fledgling Rolling Stones. Dick had played rhythm guitar, and Keith later overdubbed another lead guitar line. It was a hot, fantastic rocker. Keith was sure it was the hit single the Stones so desperately needed.

But Mick Jagger blocked the release of this version as a single. He somehow got it into his head that Dick Taylor would demand royalties or possibly sue the Stones. Instead, and without telling the other Stones, he and Allen Klein got Decca Records to substitute a country run-through of the song the Stones had recorded as a joke, that they called the "Country Honk" version. That version, and not the rocking one, was released as a single. It was so awful that most radio stations flipped the single over and played the B-side, "You Can't Always Get What You Want," taking that song to Number 21 on the charts – a minor hit, but hardly the smash the Stones needed. Keith was furious.[109]

Meanwhile, as Keith watched Brian Jones' success with the Beatles, he convinced himself more and more that it was Mick's fault that Brian left the band, and that it had been unnecessary, minimizing his own role ("Anita? She's just a chick! That cat and I go way back; we could have worked it out," he told a reporter).

A furious and sullen Richards had barely spoken to Jagger throughout the sessions for the album. The band finished the record and –at long last - prepared for a U.S. tour later that summer. But Richards had already decided to find someone else to manage his affairs individually - he no longer trusted Allen Klein.

Significantly, Keith also decided against giving one of his latest songs, "Wild Horses," to the group, believing that Jagger couldn't sing it. Since Keith Richards was no one's idea of a singer, that could only mean he was starting to think about having someone else sing his songs.[110]

The band spent a merciful few weeks out of one another's presence after the album came out, but regrouped in late August to begin rehearsals for the tour, with the first show set for August 26 at Madison Square Garden – the same venue where the Beatles had launched their comeback.

Rehearsals no sooner had begun than they became just as tense, if not worse, than the sessions for the album, with Jagger and Richards frequently descending into shouting matches and nearly coming to blows a few times. Richards let it be known that he had made overtures to Peter Grant, Led Zeppelin's manager, about taking over the Stones' management - or at least, Richards'.[111]

Literally on the eve of the tour, Mick Taylor, deeply stressed by the bickering and tension – not at all what he had in mind when he signed on with the Rolling Stones - suddenly threw down his guitar in mid-rehearsal and announced that he couldn't take it anymore - he was quitting.[112] Klein flew into a rage, but there was little he could do. Taylor, unlike Brian Jones, had been brought into the Stones as an employee rather than a full partner, which meant he had the right to leave whenever he wanted, with no fear of legal repercussions. It was far too late to do anything about canceling or rescheduling the tour. A series of frantic phone calls around London quickly turned up, as the only guitarist available (or willing) to fill in for Taylor on such short notice, Robert Fripp of King Crimson.[113] He was hurriedly tapped to fill in temporarily on guitar, but the band had virtually no time to rehearse with him.

Mick Jagger had also arranged to have the tour filmed. The film was set up to build to a climactic free concert, as with the Beatles' tour. Richards objected, stating that once again it made the Stones appear to be copying the Beatles, but he was overruled.

The Stones held a press conference in New York at the beginning of their tour, just prior to the Garden show. Jagger had hoped for an insouciant exchange with the media. Instead, he was hammered by questions about the lawsuit, Taylor's and Jones' departures, the Beatles, and rumors of arguments within the Stones. As Jagger stumbled over his answers, Richards, embarrassed, visibly seethed next to him.[114]

The opening night's concert at Madison Square Garden set the tone for the rest of the tour. Ticket sales were disappointing, with *Let It Bleed* doing poorly in the charts, and the single stalled. The performance was sloppy and erratic, because the band was under-rehearsed due to Taylor's departure and Fripp's last-minute addition. Fripp, although a very talented guitarist, played in a more classically-influenced style and was thus a poor fit for the Stones. As bad performance followed bad performance on the tour, Keith Richards' mood grew more and more sour.

The Stones tour limped toward the final show, scheduled for September 25, with the intention being to hold a free concert in San Francisco, as an appropriately exciting climax to the tour and film. The concert had been scheduled for Golden Gate Park, but at the last minute, the city of San Francisco, citing traffic and security issues, withdrew the permit for the concert.

The Stones' tour manager, Sam Cutler, then rearranged the concert site to Sears Point racetrack near the city. However, at the last minute, the owner of Sears Point, fearing liability issues, backed out. With less than 48 hours to go, Cutler hastily met with the owner of the Altamont Speedway in Livermore. Cutler was sure he had a deal. But then Allen Klein interfered. He balked at the agreed-on fee, demanding a bigger cut for the Stones. When the parties could not agree on the price, the speedway owner withdrew. The Stones were left without a venue. They canceled the announced free concert.[115]

Radio stations were flooded with angry calls from Stones fans who had traveled to San Francisco for the free show and now felt burned. But far worse than the public relations blow was the financial blow. The Stones had planned to release a film of the tour and a live album. But given their sloppy performances on the tour, the band had already decided to abandon the live album. Now, because of the concert cancellation, the planned movie was without a climax, and it too would have to be abandoned.[116] Given the amount of money spent on the filming, coupled with the poor ticket sales, this meant the Stones would take a financial bath on the tour.

For Keith, this news was the last straw. He flew back to London alone.

The day after his arrival, Keith Richards, like his bandmate over two years earlier, phoned a few friendly journalists and announced that he was quitting the Rolling Stones. This time, there would be no new guitarist. Mick Jagger told the press two days later that Keith "could not be replaced." The Rolling Stones, the band that four years earlier had seemed poised to challenge the Beatles themselves, had split up.[117]

December 31, 1969

The Sixties were coming to their end, and John Lennon, the man whose band had done so much to shape the popular culture of the decade, and the love of his life, May Ling Lennon, decided it was time to celebrate the end of the era and the beginning of the 1970s – a time when John and May looked forward to deepening love, for each other, and around the world. The darkness of the Soviet war in Vietnam still hung over the world's peace, but that peace had not been broken, and the Lennons decided it was time for the couple to invite each and every one of their friends, as many as they could remember, to a New Year's Eve celebration at their new country house, Tittenhurst Park. Dozens of friends and acquaintances, almost a who's who of Sixties London, showed up to help the happy couple ring in the new decade.

One of those guests was Keith Richards. He was invited at John Lennon's insistence – "for auld lang syne, for old times' sake," John told him. Keith was reluctant at first – the ugly final year of the Stones and their breakup still hung heavily over him. But in the end he came, with a specific mission in mind: to try to repair his friendship with Brian Jones. Keith harbored no illusions that Brian would abandon his new career with the Beatles, and he wouldn't even presume to ask. But for some reason he could not fully comprehend, the Stones' breakup had left him with a great need to put things in his life in order, and the first item on the agenda was to end once and for all the issues between himself and Brian.

Keith complimented Brian profusely on his work with the Beatles over the past two years. He told him it was great to see him cleaned up and looking so good. Brian thanked Keith, and said in return that he was sorry about the Stones' breakup. "Cor, I'll bet you're sorry to see that happen to Mick," Keith retorted, and Brian laughed. In the course of a long conversation, tentative at first but gradually warming and including many reminiscences about the Stones' early days, Keith apologized about Anita - "You know I never, ever meant to hurt you, man" - and Brian said, "Forget it, it's in the past. And I think I've found someone anyway."

"That's great! Who?"

"An American actress," Brian said. "Goldie Hawn."

"Blonde, like all your other birds?" Keith said with a laugh.

Brian smiled benevolently and nodded. "But she's real."

Keith patted his ex-bandmate on the shoulder. "I'm happy for you, man. And I really am sorry about everything that went down between us."

"What are you going to do without the Stones?

"Don't know yet. But something'll happen."

Keith, the burden of making peace with Brian now off his shoulders, made the rounds of the guests at the party. As the night wore on, and drinks were consumed, Keith found himself sitting at a table with singer Rod Stewart and guitarist Ron Wood.

Like Keith, they'd had a turbulent year. The saga began in February, indirectly, when Pete Quaife gave his notice to the Kinks that he was quitting as their bass player. Quaife had grown increasingly disgusted with the preferential star treatment given Ray Davies. Furthermore, Quaife believed that the various multimedia productions Davies was involved in, which were to include the Kinks, were not only detrimental to the band but reduced them to being virtual sidemen. Quaife was persuaded to stay until the end of the band's spring and summer tour, ultimately hanging around until September ("the worst six months of my life," he later asserted). By the time Quaife left, two other British bands were disintegrating: Steve Marriott had decided to leave the Small Faces to form Humble Pie, and the Jeff Beck Group, including vocalist Stewart and guitarist Wood, had split up.

Stewart and Wood were recruited to replace Marriott in the Faces (who, in deference to the new members' taller physical stature, dropped the "Small" from their name). However, a few rehearsals convinced bass guitarist Ronnie Lane that he would have little in common musically with the new members, and he decided to leave the Faces as well.[118] Having been courted by Ray Davies for weeks, he finally agreed to join the Kinks in

October, during the sessions for *Arthur (Or the Decline and Fall of the British Empire)*. Lane in turn quickly persuaded Faces keyboardist Ian McLagan to join him as the Kinks' keyboard player. Stewart, Wood and drummer Kenney Jones found themselves without a group, and disbanded the Faces without having ever played a live gig, and with only a few raw tracks laid down in the studio.[119]

As the drinking and carousing continued into the wee hours at John Lennon's party, Keith Richards, Ron Wood, and Rod Stewart had come to the realization that they were very much kindred spirits.

"Fuck it," Rod said, his words slurring. "We should form a new band."

Ron chuckled, but Keith leaned forward seriously. "That's exactly what we should do!" he exclaimed.

"You're barmy," said Rod.

"No," Keith said, "it's perfect. It's like – it's meant to be. Me and Ronnie on guitar, you singing – it's just bloody perfect!"

Now Ron Wood became serious. "You really mean it?"

Keith nodded. "I can ask Bill and Charlie to join us – I don't think they're doing anything yet. We're still friends, and they're pissed off at Jagger too. I'm sure they'll come on."

Rod whistled. "Fuck me! Bill Wyman and Charlie Watts! The greatest rhythm section out there!" Now his eyes grew wide with interest, too, and he slid to the edge of his seat.

The conversation now grew more serious, as the three musicians discussed with enthusiasm the future of their new band.

"What are we going to call it?" Keith asked.

Rod said, "I don't know, but we should start recording right away. Start recording first and worry about the name later. We want to make sure it works. Look how fast the Faces fell apart – we didn't even have time to put out a bloody 'Best of Faces' album!" he said, breaking into a laugh.

Ron smacked him on the arm. "That's the name! 'Best of Faces'!"

The wide smiles around the table were confirmation that the new name was perfect; as Ron Wood would say later, "It describes us to a tee – the five ugliest blokes in the world, but we get laid more than anyone else."[120]

January 22, 1970

"Morning, Mother," John said, as May stepped into the kitchen, where he was pouring himself a cup of tea. The winter sun poured through the south French doors, brightening the little kitchen nook at Tittenhurst where John and May liked to have breakfast.

"Morning, Dad," she shot back, her face curving into a smile. She sat down at the breakfast table. John set down his tea and hustled over, pouring her a glass of orange juice. She took the glass and sipped it lightly.

"How are you feeling today?" he asked.

"Not so bad," she said. "A little nausea when I woke up, but it went away." She took another sip. "I may take my camera out and do some filming on the grounds today."

He frowned slightly. "Don't overexert yourself."

She laughed. "You're such a den mother."

"Den *father*," he corrected. "I'm going to be a daddy, in case you haven't heard." He walked over to May and clasped her hand. "I love you so much."

"I love you too, John," she said.

Almost involuntarily, her hand went up to the ever-present crucifix around her neck. "Thanking Him for bringing us together?" John whispered. Her smile broadened, but she said nothing. Their lips met gently.

Then John stepped back. "I've got a present for you," he said. He went swiftly out into the study, then returned, triumphantly holding aloft a pot of white chrysanthemums. "I had these brought in for you."

"You're too good to me, John."

He wasn't going to the studio that day, though the Beatles were working on a new album. He had told the others he planned to take the day off. "I'm going to just sit all day and be with May and me baby."

He had found his ideal woman, and now she was going to have his child. He couldn't be happier.

CHAPTER TWELVE: AWAITING ON YOU ALL

April 6, 1970

The Beatles, their triumphant year of touring behind them, were now ready with a new masterpiece. The album was recorded largely at the group's new studio at Apple on Savile Row, but in honor of the EMI studios that had been the home of their work all through the Sixties, they decided to title the new album *Abbey Road*.[121]

The album included a collection of individual songs on Side One and a "pop symphony" made up of shorter songs on Side Two, like John's "Mean Mr. Mustard" and Paul's "She Came in Through the Bathroom Window." The "symphony" was largely Paul McCartney's work, and Lennon was a bit dismissive of it, describing his own songs as "bits of crap I wrote in India." But the medley took on a rhythm and series of moods all its own, rising to "The End," a final track which featured a round of guitar solos from Paul, John, Brian and George (in that order) and ended with a benediction from Paul.

John was prouder of his work on the first side, including the slow burn of "Come Together" and the anguished pleas of "I Want You (She's So Heavy)," another ode to May. The real surprise, though, was the strength of George's two contributions, the love song "Something" and the joyous and optimistic "Here Comes the Sun." Two of the most memorable songs on the album, they helped stoke anticipation for what George would unveil when he began recording with his Mangalam project. So strong were George's songs that "Something" was selected for the album's single, with "Come Together" on the B-side. Ringo turned in a fine contribution also, with a jaunty country-flavored tune titled "Octopus's Garden." Brian, for his part, was so impressed by the quality of the other Beatles' contributions that – his own insecurities as a member not yet fully conquered – he decided to wait awhile before offering another song to the Beatles.

Abbey Road was instantly hailed as one of the Beatles' best albums and a fine start to the new decade. Out of the album, though, came one of the more bizarre events in Beatle history – an utterly unexpected, unaccountable rumor.

At university dorms across the country late in the spring of 1970, the new Beatles album could be heard playing up and down the halls. As with previous Beatles releases, college students sat up late into the night trying to divine the meanings of the song lyrics.

On the night of May 2, a DJ at Detroit radio station WKNR-FM, Russ Gibb, received an eerie phone call from a "Tom" at Eastern Michigan University, advising him to play certain Beatles records backwards, listen closely to the fadeouts of others, and look at the details of certain album covers, including the new one. From this phone call snowballed an amazing rumor that quickly spread nationwide - that Paul McCartney was dead.

The most widely-circulated version of the rumor held that Paul was killed in a car crash in November 1966 and replaced by an imposter, who fortunately also was a sound-alike. The Beatles decided to stay together but to subtly reveal the truth to their fans via "clues" inserted into their records and album covers. John Lennon, so the story went, took over the task of writing

McCartneyesque ballads like "Hey Jude." Brian Jones was added to the band to cover up the deficiencies in the imposter's musical abilities.

One set of "clues" was to be found on the cover of the new album, *Abbey Road*. The cover scene, it was said, depicted the Beatles leaving a cemetery, with John (all in white) as the preacher, Ringo (wearing a suit) as the undertaker, Brian (wearing a gray cloak) as the Grim Reaper, and George (wearing denim) as the gravedigger. "Paul" was out of step with the others, and held a cigarette in his right hand, whereas the real McCartney was a southpaw. A Volkswagen parked nearby gave his age on its license plate – "28 IF" he had lived.

Other clues abounded on *Magical Mystery Tour* and the White Album. The repeated phrase "number nine" on "Revolution #9" became "turn me on dead man" when the White Album was spun in reverse. A piece of gibberish spliced between "I'm So Tired" and "Blackbird" on the same album turned into a voice that sounded like John's and seemingly said "Paul is dead man, miss him, miss him." John supposedly muttered "I buried Paul" at the end of "Strawberry Fields Forever." And, of course, there was Brian's line about "a hairy beast that comes up out of the ground and frightens all the little children" on "Revolution #9."

Gibb kept the rumor hot as long as he could, fending off call after befuddled call from fans who insisted that they just saw the real Paul McCartney on the Beatles' tour. As the rumor finally started to dissipate, Gibb said, "I've never really thought about whether Paul's actually dead or not. I've been too busy looking for clues." But before the rumor would disappear, it would engage the attention of the world's media, even making the cover of *Life* magazine.[122]

Paul certainly appeared live and well at the premiere that May of *Get Back: The Beatles in Concert*, the film directed by May Ling Lennon and Linda McCartney of the Beatles' 1969 tour. A live album with the same title was being mixed at Apple and would be released in November.

Two months after the movie premiere, on July 8, May and John received a long-awaited gift, one that meant much more to them both than any movie could.

They had wanted a baby right from the start. But somehow, at first, they couldn't conceive. There were a few times in the spring of 1969 when May appeared to be pregnant, and they had excitedly consulted a doctor, and…disappointment.

John had begun to fear that it was his fault. Maybe, he thought, he'd messed up his system too much with drugs to enable him to produce viable sperm. An English doctor – who regarded John's long hair with disgust and condescension – had suggested as much. John had no use for that doctor and didn't return to him, but the question had continued to nag at him.

Then, that summer, in the midst of the Beatles' tour, he had consulted a Chinese doctor in Chicago. "No drugs, eat right, one year you have baby," he had insisted to John. And now, one year later, they had a son.[123]

He was christened Sean Ling Lennon, taking part of both of his parents' names.[124]

When John called the other Beatles to tell them the happy news, Paul said with a laugh, "We beat you to the punch." He and Linda were in Scotland, celebrating the birth of their first child, a daughter, Mary. Another McCartney daughter, Stella, and a son, James, would eventually follow.

With both John and Paul tending to new babies, it was left to Brian Jones – appearing in public with Goldie Hawn for the first time - to represent the Beatles at the August 14 premiere of *Watkins Glen*, the second Apple film directed by May Ling Lennon and Linda McCartney and drawn from the previous year's tour. The film documented the tour's climactic festival and focused mostly on the other performers. With Buddy Holly obtaining appropriate clearances from the other artists' labels, Apple issued a soundtrack album as well.[125]

May 23, 1970

In the wee hours of the morning, as most of London slept, George Harrison, Brian Jones, and Ringo Starr, joined by a group of musicians ranging from guitarist Eric Clapton, to keyboardist Gary Wright, to a crack horn section, gathered at Apple Studios to record the first Mangalam album.

Since Mangalam was George's baby, he contributed the bulk of the material, drawn from the backlog of songs he had accumulated over the past few years. Ringo had no songs to contribute to the album, but he offered to play drums. Brian did have some songs, but he graciously decided to let the debut album be entirely George's, while offering to play guitar, keyboards, or whatever else George needed.

First up was "Hear Me Lord," the song rejected for *Let It Be*. Ten basic takes were made, with all the musicians gelling together almost from the start, as if they had been playing together for years. But two days later, George's side project was almost derailed.

George, perched atop a stool in the middle of the studio and huddled over an acoustic guitar, ran through a new song for the assembled players, another spiritual tune entitled "My Sweet Lord." It was one, he thought, that had hit potential. It was inspired and uplifting.

After he finished, however, Brian Jones stared at him, a blank look on his face. Then, ever so quietly, he said, "You know that's 'He's So Fine,' don't you?"

George's languid eyes suddenly widened. "No…it…it isn't," he said, stuttering in shock. "It's from 'O Happy Day.' An old gospel number….the Edwin Hawkins Singers had a hit with it last summer, and I thought…." Then suddenly defensive: "I didn't take anyone's song – it's an old folk gospel thing, not something with a copyright…."

"I'm not disputing where you got it from," Brian said. "Probably 'He's So Fine' is based on 'O Happy Day' too. But you got really close to the 'He's So Fine' melody. You could be sued. The publisher could come after you."

George sat silently for a moment, then said quietly, "All right, let's work on something else." The session resumed with work on another song, "I'd Have You Anytime." Nonetheless, when George left Apple Studios after the session, the possibility that Brian raised continued to bother him. Was "My Sweet Lord" a copy of "He's So Fine"?

The next day, George phoned John Lennon, played him the demo of "My Sweet Lord" over the phone, and asked what he thought.

"Brian's right," said John. "It's too close."

George was nonplussed. "I didn't even realize...."

"Look, it's nothing to nick a tune - everyone does it sometimes. There's only seven notes. They're going to get reused now and again. But you've got to change it just enough so it's not exactly the same."

Now simply embarrassed, George spent the next week reworking "My Sweet Lord," trying various arrangements, to see if he can save it from the cutting room floor or himself from a lawsuit.

By the following Monday, June 1, George had managed to alter the melody of "My Sweet Lord" enough so that if the publishers of "He's So Fine" ever decided to sue, he'd prevail in court. "My Sweet Lord" was recorded on June 3, with overdubbing of vocals on June 4.[126]

Mangalam, released on August 5, fulfilled both George Harrison's hopes and those of his fans. Those who hadn't been paying attention to the growth in George's songwriting skill, even as displayed on *Abbey Road*, were taken completely by surprise by the majestic scope of his work. The revised "My Sweet Lord", released as a single, was a surprise hit, reaching Number One on the charts in both Britain and the United States, which thrilled George to no end. John Lennon complimented his bandmate in tongue-in-cheek fashion, telling an interviewer that for how often he heard George singing "my Lord" on the radio these days, that surely must mean there is a God.[127]

John wasn't sure what, exactly, he thought about that.

October 24, 1970

John lay on a small bed in a twilit room in Tittenhurst. May, lying next to him, was dozing off and on, with Sean sound asleep in a crib by her side. The room was simply decorated, almost all in white, with a large vase of white chrysanthemums on a white table.

He leafed through the latest issue of *Life* magazine. A voracious reader, he read the big American publications as much as the British ones.

He stopped as an article caught his eye: "The Counterculture Goes to Church." It was written by Shana Alexander, who had written the magazine's previous exploration of the hippie movement two years earlier.[128]

"[The young generation] has grown up in a world that's wealthy and comfortable enough," she wrote, "a world where people are tremendously good at following rules, as much out of convention as conviction, at least. But it can seem a cold world. Love of money trumps all, and love for thy neighbor falls by the wayside. Technocratic answers – whether discredited ones like Nazism or Communism, or the latest scientific advance, or the 'new, improved' products touted on TV day in and day out as the answers to all our ills – leave so many people empty and unfulfilled at best – and in piles of dead bodies at worst. Just ask the Vietnamese.

"'People walk through their lives like zombies,' says Duane Pederson, founder of a growing nationwide 'Jesus People' hippie movement. 'So many people decide they're going to follow the rules, but they follow them out of inertia, or love of order, or because everyone else is doing it. People are isolated from one another, from other people that they sit next to every day.'

"So this younger generation – wanting something more – began experimenting, casting aside conventions, abandoning forms in the hope of finding truth beyond form. The hair got longer, in imitation of the Beatles, and then longer still. Drugs came in, and free love, and communal living.

"It has taken a few years for the counterculture to begin to sense that these experiments lead to a dead end, to a desiccation that is worse than the conventional world they tried to escape – the addiction, the motherless children, the failure to produce any real human connection or genuine feeling. The experiments have been less a liberation than a slow death.

"So they have begun turning back, slowly, painfully, groping their way toward – faith.

"Once again, they followed the Beatles. The Fab Four, soon to become Five, had embraced the Maharishi, so their followers found a plethora of gurus as well – some innocent, some malevolent, sadly taking advantage of the spiritual yearnings of their adherents.

"But there are those, like Janice Owens of Denver, Colorado – who until last summer was living in a commune in California, but chose this summer to have a traditional Presbyterian wedding – who have begun to think that maybe, just maybe, the traditional faiths hold answers after all, despite what the smart set says." The article went on to describe Janice's wedding and her decision to have one.

John chuckled. "Crap," he said. "Everything they write about us is always crap."

"What is?" said May, awakening. John passed her the magazine, and she read the article, as he gently stroked her hair.

"You see?" he said as she finished. "No matter what young people do, they think it's because of the Beatles."

"Well, the media need some way to make sense of what they're seeing," May said. "But this woman does have some points."

John was skeptical. "Like what?"

"Well, we saw it on the tour," she said. "Both of us. We even noticed it. The whole generation is looking for something. They're seeking, John."

"We all are," he said. "I haven't got any answers."

She turned to stare at him. She had a *way* of staring at him. It wasn't accusatory; far too gentle to be called that. Yet there was something about her gentle eyes that seemed to pull John out of himself.

"I mean, I'm not an atheist or anything," he said. "There were times I used to think that, but even when I was a kid, I would go into trances, you know, trance out into alpha…I mean, when I started doing acid, it just felt like reality to me, you know what I mean? It's like, when I did acid, that was the real world, and the trips felt like all those visions I had since I was a kid, when that sort of reality goes away, and it's like you're through the looking glass. It would seem like that's the real world, and it's rich and full of energy, and it contains all truth and all being and all points connect with each other, and everything's joined, and it's this single, serene, unmoved Whole…you know?" May nodded.

John went on. "So it's like I've seen the face of God…they all think I'm against God, because of that thing I said about the

Beatles being bigger than Jesus. I've spent four years explaining that shite. I always tell the news people that the Beatles are on the side of God, but they never believe me."

May pulled her feet under her. "Well, I'm sure you've wondered just why you're so famous," she said.

"All the time. But if there's a God, a God who's like a person, what does he want from me? I don't know how to find him."

"You know what the kerygma of the Catholic Church says?"

"The what?"

She laughed. "The kerygma," she repeated. "The proclamation, the preaching – the central teaching. That all people are saved and that salvation is a free gift from God – you don't do anything to earn it. You just believe in and love God and follow Him."

John scratched his head and gave May a sly smile. "That's not what we were told in Sunday school."

"I know it isn't," she said. "Sunday school teachers are lousy a lot of the time. But it's not complicated. Everything is well with God."

"'All shall be well, and all shall be well, and all manner of things shall be well,'" said John, quoting Julian of Norwich's most famous line.

May laughed. "You know me too well."

"Fortunately, that's true," he said. He took her hand gently, and they exchanged a soft and tender kiss.

He leaned back, then sighed and shook his head. "I go back and forth, though."

"Well...pray anyway. Even if you're not sure it's doing any good, pray anyway. Act as if you believe. See what happens."

"If you say it, it must be right," he said, and kissed her again.

December 10, 1970

At the end of the year, *Crawdaddy* featured a front-page article that asked, "Is Rock Dead?" The article was actually a series of essays, written by a group of some of the top rock journalists.[129]

The gist of the introductory essay, written by Paul Williams, was that the excitement and sense of wide-open opportunity that had characterized Sixties rock was fading. The walls were beginning to close in again as the rock scene matured, and as a sense of what was "possible" began to replace the free-spirited experimentalism of the passing decade. No party can last forever, he mused, so it was perhaps unrealistic to expect the sheer exuberance of the Sixties to go on nonstop. Still, some contributors were put off by what seemed to be a constriction of the zeitgeist. And a growing feeling of rising darkness in the world, underlined by the ongoing Soviet war in Vietnam, began to undercut the hope that peace and love would prevail. In reviewing the year's albums, the writers said that sense of vague disillusionment was perhaps captured best by Creedence Clearwater Revival, in albums like 1970's *Willy and the Poorboys*. Likewise, Neil Young's *After the Gold Rush* reflected this sensibility down to its very title.

But the quality of the music remained high, and some contributors, in rebuttal, insisted that rock was not dying so much as maturing – taking the lessons, both musical and spiritual, that had been learned during the past decade and applying them toward a deepening spirituality in song lyrics, coupled with a growing sophistication in musical artistry that drew from the best of what had come before. It was more a refinement than a loss of nerve.

Along with the Beatles' *Abbey Road*, particularly strong entries that year came from two of rock's greatest artists. Bob Dylan, in the spring of 1969, had heralded his own "back to basics" approach with *John Wesley Harding*, where he accompanied his poetry with a muted guitar and piano, bass and drums, played by Nashville session pros instead of his usual Band (who had gone on to be a successful act in their own right).[130] The proceedings had a country feel, which helped point Dylan's next direction. Then, in 1970 – after a few months of mutual admiration from Dylan and country star Johnny Cash – the duo teamed up to produce the stunning *Nashville Skyline*, the country-duet album many fans had dreamed of. The album came across as a broad, sweeping portrait of America circa 1970, with intimate love songs like "Lay Lady Lay" set against wide-open-sky epics like "On the Third Day."[131]

Jimi Hendrix, meanwhile, released his first album on his new label, Apple – *The First Rays of the New Rising Sun*. Saved from his punishing tour schedule, and permitted the opportunity by his association with Apple to experiment both with the funky sounds of Band of Gypsies and the jazz sounds of Miles Davis, who played on the album, Hendrix took his music into spaces even he had never before climbed, jettisoning the last of the dated acid-rock sound that was beginning to saddle him and moving his guitar-playing brilliance into areas of unexplored improvisation. "Music like this *has not existed before on this planet*," wrote Lester Bangs in one of the many breathless reviews.[132] Miles took the cue from the experience of playing with Jimi to reinvent the jazz-rock genre on his own *Bitches Brew*.

The Doors essayed a remarkable return to form in 1970. The band had released three strong albums, culminating in 1968's classic *The Celebration of the Lizard*, before original bass player Doug Lubahn left the band after months of putting up with Jim Morrison's drinking and chronic lateness for gigs. Lubahn quit shortly after a canceled show in Miami in March 1969, where Morrison was apparently too drunk to take the stage, and according to Lubahn, said "something about wanting to take his cock out."[133] The band subsequently completed the album *The Soft Parade* as a four-piece, attempting to make up for the lack of a bass player by augmenting their sound with strings and horns. This attempt backfired, and only muddied the Doors' sound instead. Besides, after the gritty poetry of *Lizard*, Morrison's lyrics on *Soft Parade* sounded pedestrian at best.

Fans feared this might be the end of the band, but Morrison took steps in late 1969 and early 1970 to curb his drinking. The Doors enlisted Marc Benno as their new bass guitarist and recorded their powerful 1970 comeback album, *Morrison Hotel*, to rave reviews and a general sense of recovery of the band's momentum.[134]

Other strong entries were turned in by the Kinks, with their tirade against greed in the record industry, *Lola Versus Powerman and the Moneygoround*; by the Beach Boys, with *Sunflower*; by Derek and the Dominoes, Eric Clapton's new group, with the searing double album *Layla and Other Assorted Love Songs*; by Van Morrison with *Moondance*; by Sam Cooke with *Angel*; and by Ritchie Valens with his sad, sweet collection titled *Canciones*.[135]

The Who, meanwhile, marked time in 1970 with *Live at Leeds*. Despite having had, to date, two Number One hits and several top tens, a record of success which had enabled them to ease back on what could have been a frenetic tour schedule in 1967-69, their album releases had been somewhat uneven.[136] It was true that they had begun by 1967 to come up with both the time to finish their albums fully and the money to record properly, now that Pete Townshend's guitar-smashing had been dropped from their stage act after the climactic set at Monterey in June 1967. But 1966's *Substitute,* 1967's *Happy Jack* and 1968's *Magic Bus* had all been cobbled together by their record company from various singles, B-sides, and unreleased tracks that were in the can, and each had a disjointed feel.[137]

Still, 1966's *A Quick One* had in a backhanded way benefited from the band's then-still-grueling tour schedule. Stuck for new material to close a ten-minute gap in the album's playing time, Pete Townshend had, at the urging of Kit Lambert, used the opportunity to write the band's first "mini-opera," "A Quick One While He's Away", which gave the album its title.

The band's three best LP's to date were 1965's *My Generation*, 1967's *The Who Sell Out* and the recent "rock opera" *Tommy*. The first was the only one of the three recorded "on the run" – with the others, the more relaxed tour schedule allowed the band time to follow through on the album's concepts. *The Who Sell Out* was based on pop radio, particularly the "pirate radio" stations that had operated off the British coast from 1964 to 1967 – mock commercials linked the album's songs. The band in fact had originally wanted to sell ad space on the album, but found no takers besides Coca-Cola. So the band made up their own ads, interspersing them between the songs, which included one of the band's greatest ever, their second Number One hit, "I Can See for Miles."

The Who had announced plans in 1968 to compose a "rock opera" as a full-length project, and were quite dismayed when the Pretty Things beat them to the punch with their widely acclaimed LP *S.F. Sorrow*. "We didn't get to be the first out of the gate," Townshend later told *Crawdaddy*. "But it turned out to be a blessing in disguise. Since we didn't have to be first, we could take a bit longer and focus on making *Tommy* a better and stronger LP. We got an extra month out of it before the album's release [in July 1969] and used that time to really tighten up and crystallize the story. So, thanks to Phil May and Dick Taylor for fucking us up!" (The Pretty Things' *Parachute,* meanwhile, was another of 1970's crop of strong albums.)

The Who now turned their attention to their next project, another "rock opera" – the one the world would come to know as *Lifehouse*.

The *Crawdaddy* article went on: "Meanwhile, it seems, the Beatles have settled into a kind of stasis, following the triumphs of their comeback tour and *Abbey Road*, and Brian Jones' successful integration into the band. Lennon and McCartney seem to be more involved these days with marriage and children than with songwriting. You can't help thinking that they must see this change in their lives as a deliverance. The hip London clubs have grown stale; the old faces are either gone or sad, like partygoers who don't know the party is over, and the new ones

promise no excitement that has not already been experienced. Rumor has it that George Harrison's marriage is crumbling, but Brian Jones is a virtual aerial commuter as he flies back and forth to Los Angeles to be with his new love, Goldie Hawn. And Ringo is appearing in films, and has expressed aspirations to direct – something he can no doubt consult May Ling about."
Ringo had in fact surprised many fans by being the second Beatle, after George, to release a solo album. During the sessions for the Mangalam album, he'd met Pete Drake, a legendary Nashville session musician whom George had hired to play steel guitar on some tracks. While on a session break, Ringo had confided to Drake his dream of making his own album of country music, a genre he loved. Drake promised Ringo that in return for just two weeks of the Beatle's time, he could concoct an album for him using his array of contacts among Nashville's musicians and songwriters. The result was *Beaucoups of Blues,* a low-key but pretty album that gave Beatles fans a chance to hear him in an unusual musical setting.

The greatest activity around the Beatles in late 1970 has more to do with Apple than with the group. Buddy Holly continued working diligently at Apple, following the signing of Jimi Hendrix with Janis Joplin, whose first album for Apple, *Pearl*, was released to wide critical acclaim in January 1971, and new acts James Taylor and Deep Purple. Holly also saw to it that plenty of the profits coming from the records division were used to help support the Apple Foundation for the Arts.[138]

The Foundation had gradually come to expand its mission since the company's first months. By now, it was sponsoring arts and music programs for poor children worldwide and contributing to scholarship and educational funds. It had also begun working to steer young people away from drugs and toward spiritual answers to their problems instead. In April 1970, this effort was underlined with the creation of the Life Spiritual Center, which promoted spiritual work "regardless of denomination," allowing adherents to work with the Foundation in doing all manner of good deeds. The Life Spiritual Center's main criterion for approving a request was, "Does what you want to do spread love in the world?"   The LSC within a few years became a popular destination for grant applications even from mainstream churches.[139]

CHAPTER THIRTEEN: DON'T LET ME DOWN

February 2, 1971

While acts like the Who focused on rock operas, the Beatles returned to work with a set of mostly softer, low-key songs when they convened at Apple Studios to begin work on their next album.

Mostly softer, because the most difficult track to record proved to be one of the most harrowing songs John Lennon ever wrote, a bitter description of coming off drug addiction – "Cold Turkey." The lyrics told of the excruciating pain of heroin withdrawal in no uncertain terms, ending with literal screams from John – little imagination was needed to picture the junkie in the song thrashing in a sweat-drenched hospital bed. To match the intensity of the lyrics, John wanted a very dirty, primitive rock sound. The basic problem: the Beatles were too good. Having played together so long, the Beatles were by 1971 such consummate professionals that they actually found it hard to sound as grungy as John wanted for the record. John repeatedly urged the others to "think Hamburg," and at one point even brought in some records by the Stooges, the MC5 and the Velvet Underground to suggest the sound he wanted. Finally, after numerous takes, the Beatles produced a harsh, rough version, beginning and ending with screeching feedback from John's, George's and Brian's guitars, that John deemed perfect. For years afterward, alternate takes of "Cold Turkey" leaked out, becoming staples of bootleg Beatles albums.[140]

The rest of the album was considerably more expansive, even George's lament "Isn't It a Pity," a meditation on how hard it can be for people to show love to one another.[141] John elsewhere essayed a tender ode to May with "Oh My Love," and sang of immediate consequences on "Instant Karma," while nonetheless proclaiming universal love over massed pianos simultaneously played by himself, Brian, and, in overdub, Paul. John was so pleased with the recording that he insisted that the song be made the title track of the album.[142]

Also included was "Jealous Guy," the song of apology John had begun writing that night in 1968, at the White Album sessions, when his tantrum had embarrassed May. The song that had started out in India as "Child of Nature" now was sweetened with a string section, offsetting John's yearning lead vocal.[143]

Paul's contributions were also a bit somnolent, including a sort of urban "Eleanor Rigby" tale of a lonely secretary in "Another Day," a soft number called "Junk" (originally a reject from the White Album), and a charming if nondescript ode to Linda called "Every Night." However, Paul closed the album with one of his most achingly powerful love songs, "Maybe I'm Amazed," which was picked as the first single.[144]

George's lengthy "Isn't It a Pity" left limited space on the album for another of his songs, so – his need for a secondary songwriting outlet now fulfilled by Mangalam – he graciously gave up a spot on the album to Brian, who brought in an earnest if modest song about pollution and the environment, "Something Worth Knowing."

Instant Karma, coming after *Abbey Road,* seemed a more relaxed effort, partly because of its laid-back tone – the title track, "Another Day," and "Cold Turkey" were the only uptempo songs – and partly because, aside from perhaps the title track and "Isn't It a Pity," it aimed for no grand philosophical statements, instead choosing to make its point through simple love songs.

Instant Karma was soon joined by additional Apple releases. Jimi Hendrix issued his second Apple album, *Sky Bridge*, produced by Paul McCartney. Best of Faces' second album, *Every Picture Tells a Story*, was released that summer to critical acclaim and great commercial success. (The self-titled first album, released in 1970, had been little more than a warm-up for the first "real" album.) The general consensus was summed up by a review in *Crawdaddy* that described the new band's sound as "the Rolling Stones with a heart." The group's efforts were rewarded with Number One hits for both the album and its lead single, "Maggie May"/"Wild Horses."[145]

On September 18, Best of Faces played a sold-out gig at New York's Madison Square Garden, in the midst of their hugely successful debut tour. As the band took the stage for the encore, Keith Richards announced, "We'd like to introduce an old friend – and a Beatle." The crowd erupted in an ecstatic roar as Brian Jones took the stage. Brian joined Best of Faces on guitar as they tore through two old Stones hits, "Jumpin' Jack Flash" and "Satisfaction." Afterward, Brian emphasized to reporters that it was a one-time thing only – the Rolling Stones were not re-forming, and he had no intention of leaving the Beatles. Still, he said, "it's good to know that Keith and I are mates again."

Buddy Holly also signed a new act to Apple that fall, a performer who had one British hit to his credit but was nevertheless a cult item at that point, and not an especially admired one at that – David Bowie. It would be another year or so before the world at large realized what a coup Holly had scored.[146]

August 25, 1971

After almost a year of work, the Who completed and released their second rock opera – *Lifehouse*. It told a futuristic tale of a society where music had been banned. A world government controlled most of the world's population, who lived underground, by using "experience suits" (a sort of early vision of virtual reality on Pete Townshend's part) to keep them entertained and docile. The government told everyone that the world's surface was too polluted to live on, and it had been abandoned to renegade hippies and other unwanted castoffs. Bobby, an electronics wizard, discovers the lost art of rock music from a spiritual guide called "Baba O'Riley." Fleeing the government's police, he escapes to the surface, to find that the pollution has dissipated and the hippies are living free and happily – he meets a group who travels around in a van, and falls in love with their daughter, Mary.

Commandeering an old concert hall, Bobby names it the Lifehouse and uses his electronics wizardry to break into the experience suit circuitry. A rock band begins playing there, and the hippies on the surface gather, Watkins Glen-style. Bobby uses the experience suit circuitry to invade the minds of the rest of the world's population, bringing them the music, and they begin to tune in electronically. The souls of the experience suit wearers, the audience and the band become more and more linked and more and more in harmony as the music continues to play. The souls of each person combine to help create the music, which is reflected back at each person.

At the end, the government's security forces find the Lifehouse, come in and shoot Bobby – but his body disappears before hitting the floor. The troops look around – to find that the Lifehouse, the area outside and in fact all the world except themselves and the government people are gone. The world's population became so harmonious in the music that they actually left their physical bodies behind. The government troops and the government have the world under their complete control at last – but they are alone on a world without light, a world reduced literally to hell. The rest of the world's billions have joined each other, the universe and God in total harmony.

Pete Townshend originally toyed with the idea of filming *Lifehouse*, even suggesting, much to the Who's dismay, that they literally carry out the plot of the film by renting a hall in London and playing continuously for everyone who showed up until the harmony depicted in the story emerged. But a talk with Jimi Hendrix about the concept convinced Townshend that no movie could approximate the pictures the audience members would create in their heads "if you get the music right."[147]

December 4, 1971

Ringo had released his second solo album, but this one was much stranger than the first. *Beaucoups of Blues* had fight right into Ringo's style – even in the Beatles, he often leaned country when taking one of his rare vocal turns, as on "Don't Pass Me By" or "Octopus's Garden." But *Sentimental Journey* was a true oddity – a collection of old standards like "Stardust" and "Love Is a Many-Splendored Thing" that Ringo had recorded with a lavish orchestral backing. His only explanation for confused fans and music press was that he wanted to make the album as a gift to his mother.[148]

Shortly after the release of Ringo's album, in a ceremony in Los Angeles, Lewis Brian Hopkin Jones and Goldie Jean Hawn were married. Unlike some previous Beatle weddings, this one turned into a media circus. John and May were unable to travel, as May was pregnant and nearing term again, but the other Beatles attended, along with all the members of Best of Faces, Jimi Hendrix, Buddy Holly, and a slew of Hollywood friends and acquaintances of Goldie.

John and May's daughter was born on January 12, 1972, and after his beloved late mother, John insisted on naming her Julia.[149]

January 28, 1972

Throughout 1971, while Best of Faces' first album and debut tour rose to smashing success, the rock audience puzzled over the mysterious lack of activity from Mick Jagger. The former Rolling Stones lead singer had remained secluded throughout the entire time since the Stones' breakup, giving no interviews and feeding ever more speculation about what he was up to the longer he remained quiet.

Finally, ending the enigmatic silence, he unleashed a solo album, *The Mick Jagger Album*. The record was an instant hit, rising swiftly up the album charts – but then it tumbled down the charts even more swiftly. Anticipation had turned rapidly into disappointment.

    Mick Jagger's solo debut turned out to be a classic example of how the greatest rock bands are usually more than the sum of their parts. In the context of the Rolling Stones, Mick's slurred vocal delivery had worked, and his technical limitations as a singer had not mattered. But without that very specific niche, his disadvantages as a singer bubbled to the surface. Several attempts at ballads were marred by his inability to hold a long note convincingly well. A stab at country music entitled "Dead Flowers" was ruined by a mock-hillbilly accent that was so overwrought it became ridiculous. Furthermore, without Keith Richards as a foil, Mick had written fewer songs, falling back instead on doing cover versions of recent glam-rock hits like T. Rex's "Bang a Gong" and David Bowie's "Oh! You Pretty Things." This tactic backfired, making Jagger appear to be jumping on the glam-rock bandwagon.[150]

    Perhaps because the gap between what was expected and what was released was so great, the leading rock critics savaged the album. Greil Marcus wrote in *Crawdaddy*: "Dylan once wrote a song called 'It Takes a Lot to Laugh, It Takes a Train to Cry'. I don't know about the train, but the first line must have been a premonition of Mick Jagger's new album." Boston's Jon Landau wrote in *The Real Paper*: "I used to be one of the Stones' biggest supporters. But that was when they were the Stones...Jagger's album suggests that he is desperately craving irrelevance." *Creem* magazine's *enfant terrible,* Lester Bangs, chimed in: "LORD NO, this is the unholy nightmare...This album makes you WANT TO DIE."

March 7, 1972

Walking through the front door of the main house at the Tittenhurst Park estate, John Lennon was in a deeply contemplative mood. He had spent nearly an hour outside, just wandering the grounds and sitting by the lake he had put in when he bought the house, and he was feeling quite serene.

Suddenly, he was startled out of his reverie by a piercing sound. It was an all-too-familiar one – Julia, his baby daughter, crying again. Grumbling under his breath, he headed toward the nursery.

Unlike Sean, who was relatively quiet, Julia had turned out to be a fussy baby. Constantly, it seemed, she was crying – for her bottle, for a change of nappies, for what seemed like no reason at all much of the time, at least as far as John was concerned. Furthermore, her crying would often provoke Sean – now getting into his "terrible twos" – into a screaming tantrum of his own.

He walked into the nursery, and now the noise was accompanied by that ugly odor. The nappies again. He was unsurprised to find that it was May who was changing Julia.

Wrinkling his nose at the smell, John said, tentatively, "You know, love – we could hire someone to do this. A nanny, or something...."

Finishing with the new diaper and picking up Julia to soothe her cries, May gave John a blank look. "I'm bonding with my daughter," she said. "With *our* daughter."

Waving his hand in front of his nose, John said, "Look, I know it's important to bond, and all that, but...you can get some help, you know, for the...dirty parts...."

Now May turned up an eyebrow. "There are no 'dirty parts,' John," she said. "It's all part of raising your baby. I don't want someone else to do that for us. I'm her mother."

"I know...but...."

"John, if you don't want to help," she said, "don't help."

He quietly exited the room, and returned to the fresh air outside.

What's wrong with me?, he wondered. May had been the best thing that had ever happened to him – better than the Beatles, even. He had no doubt of that. He loved her. That hadn't changed a bit.

But lately...it didn't feel the same. It had been so exciting at first, in the rush of their love. Now May was irritable, and the house was full of dirty nappies and crying children.

He'd asked to be with her, and make a family with her. This is what he had wanted. So why was it making him so...well, not "unhappy"; he wasn't sure what he meant, what the right word was...but it wasn't the same. This is what I wanted, he reflected – shouldn't I be happy now, at last?

Even when the exhaustion of being a new mother wasn't draining May, she just didn't seem like her old self. She used to be so inspiring, so full of philosophical wisdom. It wasn't just screwing, John mused, although she was easily the most exciting woman he'd ever met. In the early days, three or four years ago, they would sit for hours cross-legged on the floor, just talking – about life, about God, about art, about music, about the human condition, about anything at all – sometimes all night. Now, May was buried in the dirty nappies she insisted on taking care of herself, and she didn't seem to have time for any of the things that he used to so enjoy about being with her. Now he felt like he was alone most of the time while May tended to the kids like a mother hen. He had found a truly unique woman, and he never thought life with her would get so…ordinary.

May had told him to pray, as if he really meant it. He did, from time to time, not as often as he told her he did, but sometimes. If it was helping, though, he couldn't tell. He wasn't going to go crazy for any one thing, like May had been lately, getting more and more into her Catholic stuff. So he gave it the occasional shot, yet he still didn't feel any commitment. No great rush of spiritual revelation had he received.

"Paul has like two hundred fucking kids and he's happy," thought John as he sat down on the front steps of the house, shaking his head. "Wonder what he's going to do with them this year."

The Beatles were planning another tour. It had been three years since the 1969 tour – ironically, the same interval that had passed between their 1966 "retirement" and their 1969 "comeback" – but this interval didn't seem so long, partly because the Beatles had eased into a more relaxed work schedule, partly because they knew that, sooner or later, they would hit the road again – and, just as importantly, so did their fans.

They would go around the world again and play a long series of dates on various continents. But while the question before the last tour was about what music they would play, this time they had stumbled over a different question: *where* to play.

Paul had brought up *that* idea again, the one he had brought up when they began discussing the 1969 tour: playing small venues, perhaps surprise performances under an alias, in order to get back in touch with their audience. John still thought it was a bit like going back into the past, but having performed live in 1969, he was now felt comfortable in front of audiences again, something he'd lost in 1966 amid the crazed Beatlemania and the death threats. Maybe Paul did have a point. Then again, they couldn't do an entire tour like that. George had put his foot down, and Ringo even more emphatically: they weren't going to go back out on tour unless the Beatles made money on the tour, which would require them to play large venues. Brian had the fifth vote, but he didn't feel it was his place to make waves, although privately he was intrigued by Paul's idea.

As they had done so many times before, the Beatles had asked Buddy Holly to step in. And he had provided an answer. Soon it would be implemented. The Fabs would be back on tour again.

Not a moment too soon, thought John. He had once dreaded the idea of going back out on the road. Now he was looking forward to it. A break from crying babies and dirty nappies. Maybe he could convince May to come along – bring the children if she must, but then they'd have no choice to hire someone to look after them, and then once she got used to the idea....

John suddenly got up and ran back inside the house, ignoring May and Julia, who by now had quieted down, and racing for the telephone. He called Paul. He wanted to get the band together and rehearse. The tour was coming soon. The Beatles needed to be ready.

May 15, 1972

Apple Records continued its string of successes with the first British Number One and the first American chart hit (Number 16 in the *Billboard* listings) for David Bowie, with his single "All the Young Dudes." Bowie later revealed that he nearly gave the anthemic song away to the band Mott the Hoople, until a paternal talk from Buddy Holly and Paul McCartney convinced him to record it himself instead.[151]

Best of Faces continued the success of the previous year with their 1972 album *Exile on Main Street*. Initial fears on the part of the group that issuing a double album so soon into their career would be a commercially unwise move were assuaged by the success of *Every Picture Tells a Story*. The group had already won a huge fan base, particularly among former Rolling Stones fans who embraced the new group as the replacement for the old one. The new album continued the bluesy-yet-sentimental sounds of the previous one, and won Best of Faces their second gold album.[152]

June 3, 1972

The new Beatles LP, *Ram*, had been hurriedly completed, over sessions in March and April, to be ready in time for the tour.[153] Work had been proceeding on and off since January. Paul had hoped that he could persuade his fellow Beatles to come up to his farm in Scotland, where he had installed a new recording studio, and finish the album there. But the pressures of getting the record out in time for the tour were too great for anyone else to want to take a chance on an untried recording facility. Paul tried not to be too disappointed, although a song he had recorded at his new studio – a paean to the Scottish countryside called "Heart of the Country" – virtually as a solo track would be included on the album, with overdubs added by John, George, and Brian in the Apple Studio in London.[154]

Still, given how quickly it was recorded, *Ram* turned out to be a surprisingly cohesive album, and livelier than the relatively gentle *Instant Karma*. Paul both opened and closed the album: the opening track was an uptempo number titled "Too Many People," the closing number an elaborate, Beach Boys-like production titled "The Back Seat of My Car" that ended with four-part harmony sung by John, Paul, George, and Brian. The lyrics of "Too Many People," along with Paul's fourth contribution, "Uncle Albert/Admiral Halsey," had an obscurantist cast that puzzled some listeners, but both songs were exhilarating nonetheless.[155]

George's "All Things Must Pass" had been brought back from its 1969 oblivion – it no longer sounded negative, now that the group itself was no longer in danger, but rather a reflection on changes in life in general.[156] John had graciously pulled back some of his allotted space to allow more room for George, and the "quiet Beatle" had three songs on *Ram* as a result – a rousing hymn called "What Is Life" that opened side two, and the warm, subtly insistent, charming "Ballad of Sir Frankie Crisp," named after the original builder of George's Friar Park estate, complete with a country-style pedal steel guitar overdubbed by Brian, a song that welcomed listeners to open themselves to the Inner Light.[157]

Brian himself relinquished a spot to Ringo, who brought in the strongest song he had written to date, "It Don't Come Easy."

The Beatles worked especially hard on Ringo's song, with John and Paul overdubbing several layers of background vocals, George adding one of his tastiest guitar solos, and Brian arranging a horn section.[158]

John's three contributions included a tribute to the late Brian Epstein titled "Brother Sam," which he had begun writing back during the White Album sessions but didn't finish until that spring, and two new numbers.[159] His tone remained upbeat, even humorous, but it was starting to take on a bit of an edge. "Crippled Inside" was a sprightly song, driven by a dobro played by Brian and John's ragtime-style piano playing, but the lyrics talked about wearing a mask to hide one's inner distress. "It's So Hard" was a straight blues number, and while it didn't descend to the level of despair of 1968's "Yer Blues," it still evoked life's difficulties.[160]

But one week after the release of the album, life for the Beatles was going smoothly. They opened their 1972 world tour with – of all things – a one-week residency at the Las Vegas Hilton, the site of Elvis Presley's triumphant return to the concert stage in 1969 – the same year the Beatles had made their comeback to live performances.

Elvis had been performing regularly at the Hilton (the International until 1971) but was now also committed to a return to Hollywood, having finally scored big in the movies with roles in *Butch Cassidy and the Sundance Kid* and the recent cop dramas *Dirty Harry* and *The French Connection*. All those years of cheesy Hollywood musicals, it seemed, had finally paid off.[161] Elvis' schedule had left Hilton owner Kirk Kerkorian with space to fill – and into the breach stepped the Beatles.

When the Fabs arrived in Las Vegas on June 8, two days before the first show, they held a press conference at the Hilton. One of the first questions, from the reporter for the *Los Angeles Times,* was an obvious one: why Vegas? Why had the Beatles chosen to open their tour in a relatively small concert room in the nation's gambling capital?

"We're the big payout," George answered, and John threw in, "The Beatles – it's the new floor show." The laughter all around, for a moment, recalled those first Beatles press conferences of 1964, the lads answering questions with sharp but good-humored cracks.

"We thought it would be a laugh," said Paul. "You know, we're in good company here, with Frankie and Sammy and all the rest."

"And the magic shows and the nude dancing girls," added Brian, for another laugh.

"Do you have any fear of following in Elvis' footsteps?" asked another reporter.

"We've been following in Elvis' footsteps all our lives," said Ringo. "He's the greatest. We're just going to do our thing."

The week of shows – a rousing success, in contrast to the Beatles' previous appearance at the Sahara in 1964, which had received an ambivalent response from the Las Vegas gambling crowd – was followed by a much larger show at the Forum in Los Angeles. This in turn was followed by two shows in San Francisco: a show at a small club in the Mission District followed by two nights at the much bigger Winterland Ballroom.

And thus the pattern was set for the entire tour – a lengthy series of shows that would consume the rest of the summer and into the fall, taking the Beatles across the United States and Canada, back to Britain and Europe, and once again to the United States for another leg. This was the solution worked out by Buddy Holly, who once again had acted to broker a compromise within the group, this time between Paul's desire to play small venues and George and Ringo's insistence on playing large shows. The tour schedule would alternate between big venues – including Madison Square Garden in New York and a return to the Watkins Glen site, scene of the 1969 festival, for another one-day outdoor extravaganza – to shows at relatively tiny concert halls like the Bottom Line, a rock club in Manhattan, and a small performing arts center in Dayton, Ohio.

The Beatles had once again blazed a new path. Conventional wisdom called for performers to start out playing small venues, like clubs, then gradually progress to bigger and bigger venues as their careers advanced. But the Beatles had now gotten so big that they ran the risk of alienating their audience entirely. So they had turned the formula on its head: they would vary their concert tour between the big shows that would bring in money and give large audiences a chance to see and hear them and smaller venues that would give those lucky enough to get in a chance to hear the band perform up close and personal. The profits from the big shows helped defray the cost of the smaller ones (which seldom took in enough "gate" to make a profit).

Once the Beatles had established the precedent, other big rock groups followed suit. Concert tours became a smorgasbord of big and little shows, with opportunities to see the bands outside of large stadiums and arenas. Some acts, like Pink Floyd, had begun using extravagant special effects, which did not work well, or at all, in smaller venues; but these acts would get around that problem by rehearsing both a "large venue" and a "small venue" show, and then performing the one that was appropriate to the venue.

Opening acts, over the course of the Beatles' tour, ranged from Stevie Wonder to T. Rex to Deep Purple to Badfinger at the larger venues, to relative unknowns at the smaller venues, who benefited enormously from the chance to open for the most famous name in rock. One of those, opening for the Beatles in Atlantic City, was a virtually unknown performer by the name of Bruce Springsteen.

When the second American leg of the tour resumed in early September, Paul finally got to live out his fantasy in full.[162]

On Thursday, September 7, the staff at the student union at the University of Pittsburgh were stunned when none other than Buddy Holly and Paul McCartney casually walked into their office. They were even more stunned when the pair nonchalantly asked whether the Beatles might not play a show at the student union the following night.

The show was entirely unannounced, but the student union quickly became packed. Yet the audience did not encroach upon the Beatles personally – never rushed the stage, didn't try to touch the musicians – instead sitting as close as possible, seemingly too astonished at the presence of the likes of John Lennon and Ringo Starr in their student union to do anything but watch and listen. The band loved the shows and loved being so close – two girls, shivering, were invited onstage to sing background vocals on "Here Comes the Sun," and the whole audience ended up singing along with "Hey Jude."

A few days later, on Tuesday the 12th, a few hours to the east at Penn State University, the usual array of sunbathers, Frisbee-throwers, and meditating hippies was enjoying the late summer sunshine on the HUB lawn, the grassy area outside the student union. Some became mildly interested when representatives of the University's student concert committee, acting very close-mouthed, began setting up an impromptu concert stage facing the lawn just outside the building.

But their mild interest turned to gape-mouthed astonishment as, without any announcement at all, the figures of John Lennon, Paul McCartney, George Harrison, Brian Jones and Ringo Starr strode from inside the building and mounted the concert stage – Paul hefting his bass, John and George quietly tuning their guitars, Brian sitting down behind a keyboard, Ringo giving the drums a few test thumps as he took his place behind the kit. When they were ready, John, grinning, said, "Hello and thank you all for coming…." Then counted "one, two, one-two-three-four" into the opening number, "Come Together."

By the time they got to the third number, College Avenue, down the slope of the HUB lawn from the HUB building itself, was blocked to traffic by hundreds of students converging on the lawn from every direction – emptying the shops along College Avenue, streaming down from the apartments and fraternity houses beyond, racing huffing and puffing from the East Halls dorms and the Rec Center, as news of the Beatles' sudden surprise performance swept the campus like a prairie fire.

The Beatles managed to play a third surprise show at Syracuse University in upstate New York on Thursday, but as they traveled to the next target, Colgate University in Hamilton, for a show on Saturday night, the jig was up – the rumor mill had gone into overdrive, the unmarked rented bus the Beatles had been using for travel had been identified, and as they arrived, they were trailed by vans full of reporters and TV cameras. Still, John told reporters outside the recreation center at Colgate, "It was great fun while it lasted."

John had forgotten how much fun touring could be. Paul was right – it was a gas playing for audiences up close like that again. Now it was like the REAL old days – the days back in Hamburg, before the Beatles became *THE BEATLES*, when it was just raw energy and excitement. Even on the bigger shows, he was having a ball. The audiences were thrilled to see their heroes, but they didn't act insane now. Perhaps they'd matured, but whatever the cause, it wasn't like the crazed hysteria of the Beatlemania years at all. Just great fun playing for fans who really wanted to hear the music.

And then there were the perks.

There'd been girls, and booze, and drugs, back during those Beatlemania tours, of course – plenty of each. But they'd had to be discreet then. No way could the Fab Four, the darlings of the silver screen and Top Forty radio, let their teenybopper fans know about their shenanigans. But now, they could let their hair down. They could do whatever they wanted, with anything and anyone they wanted, just with a snap of their superstar fingers. By 1972, it was assumed in at least some fan circles that a rock and roll tour represented a rolling free-for-all party that never had to stop.

George and Brian stayed out of it. Each would retire back to his hotel room after the show, order up some room service, and spend the night reading, or meditating, or playing the guitar. George left Patti at home – they were on the outs anyway – but Goldie joined Brian in Los Angeles, traveling with them for a few shows, the two of them clearly beaming in one another's presence. Their love delighted John, and he respected Brian too much to try to tempt him into joining the parties on the road. Brian had seen enough of that in the Rolling Stones, and as far as he was concerned, he was done with it. He'd barely survived it.

Paul, to John's annoyance, was being something of a wet blanket. He'd brought along not only Linda but the kids. They trailed after him from show to hotel and hotel to show, and the buses and trains and planes along the way, charming when they wanted to be, but occasionally making with that piercing wail that John had come to dread in his own home. Paul seemed happy enough, pulling out a guitar whenever he got a chance and singing silly songs to the kids – and every now and then John would look at him a bit wistfully and wish he could adjust to being a new dad as readily as Paul had, though the feeling would evaporate as quickly as it came.

So it was up to John and Ringo, and their roadies and entourage, to fly the party flag. Ringo had left his wife, Maureen, at home, with their kids; like George, he'd been having marital problems. But Ringo loved nothing so much as a good party, and he reveled in the atmosphere of being on the road.

May had come along briefly at first, reluctantly leaving Julia and Sean at home in the care of a babysitter. But she'd abandoned the tour after the first few shows and gone back to England. John missed her, but he couldn't deny that he was having a better time without her around.

So the partying coalesced around John and Ringo and the road crew. They got more and more aggressive as the tour went on. Ringo and John took to having "Guinness fights," seeing who could drink the most beer without passing out.

Neither of them ever showed up drunk for a show – they didn't even seem to be plagued with hangovers. But Buddy Holly, for one, was starting to worry. One night, about halfway through the second leg of the tour, he made a point of sitting next to John on the chartered flight that was taking the Beatles to their next gig.

After making some small talk, he tentatively queried: "Have you been in touch with May?"

"Sure," said John. "I call her all the time. Easier than her trying to call a traveling circus flea like me."

Another pause. "Maybe she could come back out on the tour with us."

"So I can change diapers like Paul? Or pray all the time like Brian?"

Buddy sighed. "John, that's just part of being a father. My kids..."

"Aren't with you, are they?" John snapped. "Bloody hell, Buddy, I'm not neglecting me kids. I'm just having some fun, you know? We did nothing but work in the studio for so long I forgot how great the road can be. I'm just having a laugh with it, and I wish you and May and everyone would get off my back!"

"You're drinking a lot," Buddy said.

"Have I been late for a show? Or messed up during one?" John said.

"No."

"Then what's the problem?"

"Just keep it...under control, is all."

"Fine, I'll remember that," John said with sarcasm.

Buddy got up and walked to the restroom, not wanting to antagonize John further. John settled back in his chair. His right hand reached into the pocket of his jacket, and he fingered the small plastic bag inside it. If he was getting this much grief over some drinks, he thought, *it's a good thing nobody has told Buddy about the coke. Or, for that matter, about the groupies the roadies have been bringing back to the hotel rooms every night.*

CHAPTER FOURTEEN: BAND ON THE RUN

October 12, 1972

While the Beatles tour was garnering mass acclaim and positive reviews, and dominating the alternative press, Mick Jagger entered Olympic Studios in London, the site of some of the Rolling Stones' previous triumphs, to try to recover from the debacle of his first solo album. The record that materialized, though, *Another Taste of Mick Jagger*, did little to boost the former Stones singer's sagging reputation. Although it did at least rock harder than that disastrous first album, it was even more obviously and blatantly an attempt to rip off the glam-rock scene. The public, having been burned by the first album, rewarded Jagger's mediocre effort accordingly: the album stalled in the American charts at Number 46.

When Jagger hastily recorded a third album, *Mick the III*, released in January 1973, it proved to be his most dismal flop yet, stopping at Number 154 on the LP charts. It had now been only a year since Reprise had made a considerable publicity fuss over their signing of Jagger as a solo artist and the release of his first solo LP. By early 1973, he found himself dropped from the label. Reprise deleted his three albums from their catalog in 1975, ironically making *The Mick Jagger Album* a much-sought-after relic. Later in 1973, Jagger finally fell out with Allen Klein, and he and Jagger ended up suing each other. The same year, Mick's new wife, Bianca, whom he had married in 1971, and who had quickly tired of Jagger once he could no longer support her jet-set tastes, filed for divorce.[163]

November 11, 1972

It was so small, May nearly missed it.

She noticed it in the hallway, lying on the floor near Julia's room. The daylight had only just begun streaming through the tall windows of Tittenhurst Park's main house. She'd gotten up early, to check on her daughter, as she so often did. She walked quietly down the hallway, hoping not to disturb the kids – or her husband.

John had come home drunk again late last night. He hadn't said anything, but muttered under his breath and collapsed on the sofa. He wasn't violent, at least not to her or the children. But that was small comfort. Whether he was violent to anyone else, she had no idea.

It had all happened so suddenly. She had finally recognized that John did not want to be involved with the day-to-day tasks of raising the children and had agreed to hire a nanny. But she still wanted to be involved, which had frustrated John, who, so he said, had wanted her around more. That had caused another argument, driving the wedge, the one she felt growing between herself and John, in further. She felt the distance between them growing, but she didn't know how to fix things, and that made her afraid.

All so suddenly. Up until Julia was born, he'd been a wonderful man. But being a father brought out a side of him she hadn't ever seen before. It wasn't just his complaints about having to take care of the kids. It was as if being a father had triggered some kind of unpleasant memories. She knew the story of John's horrible childhood, of course – how his father had left the family to go to sea, how his parents had divorced when he was five, how his mother was too flighty to take care of him and left him in the care of his aunt – all the world seemingly knew the story by now, after Hunter Davies had written that Beatles biography back around the time she met John. She was sympathetic, but every now and then it scared her – she would see a sort of odd resentment in John's eyes. Somehow being a father had brought back some part of those memories, it seemed. John, normally so open, absolutely refused to talk about it.

So she had prayed for him, and she kept praying, after the Beatles tour started and he developed a taste for the lifestyle of a rock star on the road. She had accompanied him at first but went home when the party atmosphere made her feel uncomfortable. She had hoped he would get out of his system whatever he needed to get out on the tour.

But whatever it was, he hadn't gotten it out at all. He'd instead kept partying when he got back to London. He'd gotten a massive taste of a life he had left behind, it seemed, and decided he'd liked it. Now he was coming home drunk, after spending the night in the company of young stars like Marc Bolan of T. Rex, at the London clubs he had once eschewed. As if that wasn't enough, she was sure he was doing drugs again, cocaine or worse. He had told her once upon a time that when he met her, all desire to lead that kind of life had blown away like dust. That seemed like centuries ago.

But the one thing she'd been sure of had been John's fidelity. Then she saw it.

It was small but glittery in the early morning light, standing out against the white carpet. Puzzled, she picked it up. She examined it. Then, realizing what it was, she turned it over and over, looking at it again and again, hoping that there could be some explanation, something that would allow her to ignore what she was holding in her fingers.

It was a hotel room key.

John hadn't been out of town since the tour. And she certainly hadn't. There was no reason John would have someone else's key. Or rather, there was one likely reason.

She walked slowly, trembling, to the living room, where a groggy, disheveled John Lennon, still wearing what he wore to the club the night before, was waking up.

His clothes were a mess, and his hair was dirty and greasy – this from a man she had come to know in the early days as being fastidious about how his shirts were tucked in. He smelled vaguely of booze, or vomit. She barely noticed the smell, though. She stood over him, her face drawn and pale.

John, struggling out of his stupor, looked up at her. He quietly whispered her name, then said, "Love, what's...."

"Is this yours?" Her voice was hoarse.

"What?"

She thrust the hotel key under his nose.

The shocked look on his face already told her all she needed to know. He fumbled for an explanation. "I...uh...that's not...I had that for one of the roadies, he...."

Her eyes began filling with tears. "What roadie? You're not on tour anymore. Don't lie to me, John."

He turned away from her gaze. He hung his head, not answering.

She pulled his face toward hers with her hand, so that he was forced to look into her eyes. "Did you sleep with another woman?"

He hesitated, and that alone told her the truth.

They said little over the next three days, John shamefacedly fleeing the room whenever May appeared. Then, in the early evening, May quietly approached him in the sitting room at Tittenhurst.

"I would like for you to leave," she said in a hushed tone.

"What?"

May smelled alcohol on his breath. It was nine in the morning.

"I want you to live somewhere else for a while."

John looked down at the floor. "Is it…over?

She sighed, and her eyes again began to fill with tears. "I don't know," she said. "But I can't be with you if you're going to play rock star games. I'm not a groupie. I won't let you treat me like one."

John started to try to answer, but his mouth hung open wordlessly. There was nothing he could say. Glumly, he walked upstairs and began packing his bags.

The following afternoon, he left for Los Angeles. On the long flight, he gazed up at the ceiling of the cabin.

"All right, God," he thought silently, "May always tells me I should be praying to you like you're there. So here's my prayer." He coughed, and looked up again glumly. "Please don't let me lose her. Please convince her to let me come home."

January 22, 1973

"Sit down, dear boy. Make yourself at home."

John Lennon collapsed, smiling, into the sofa, across from Keith Moon.

"Have yourself a brandy," Moon added with a flourish. He had already consumed half a dozen himself, and he was just getting started. He loved playing the host. Especially to a fellow heavy drinker.

The Who's madcap drummer was staying at the Beverly Hills Hilton. His own marriage had ended in divorce, due to his heavy alcohol and drug use, and he'd been staying away from England as much as the Who's schedule allowed him. When unpleasant topics, like his failed marriage, came up, Keith preferred to change the subject: humor was the order of the day, and Keith made sure he and everyone else around him was in a constant state of laughter. No matter how forced.

John Lennon hadn't known Keith Moon particularly well until two months ago, when he'd landed in Los Angeles. But lately, he, Keith and songwriter Harry Nilsson had been almost constantly in one another's company. John was now hanging out with the most notorious drinkers in the rock music industry.

The party had not stopped with the end of the 1972 tour after all. John had found a way to keep it going.

In fact, it was a bigger party than ever. Keith and Harry knew how to do it right. Girls every night. Chauffeured limos. Porterhouse steaks. And a never-ending flow of Courvoisier, Dom Perignon, and expensive wines. Not to mention the cocaine.

"What was I thinking?" he would say on more than one night in a slurred voice, sitting across a table from Keith and Harry, and his bandmate Ringo, who flew out in early February to join the party, and the kind of assorted hangers-on with no names and barely recognizable faces who always seemed to show up whenever a rock star was being free and loose with the cash and the booze kept coming. "What was I thinking getting married? What have I been missing?" Then he would muse for a second. "If only May and I could have had it like this…"

By March, they were making the tabloids. John and the gang showed up at a Smothers Brothers show at the Troubadour. John, blindingly drunk, heckled the main act, and was photographed coming out of the restroom with a tampon stuck to his forehead, the kind of joke that seems funny the night before. (A waitress, annoyed at John's antics, told him off. "Don't you know who I am?" he drunkenly snapped, attempting to bring up the celebrity artillery. "Yes," she said. "You're an asshole with a tampon on his forehead.")

John was waking up in a tangle of groupies every night – and not just the third-rate ones that would service the road crew on the tour. Keith's personal gofers, who became John's personal gofers, saw to it that they got the pick of the crop. The skies were sunny in Los Angeles, the ocean was beautiful, and the fun went on and on.[164]

So, John wondered, *why the hell am I so damned lonely?*

April 24, 1973

Paul McCartney was being interviewed by *Newsweek,* at the hotel in New Orleans where the Beatles were staying. As ever when he dealt with the press, the group's natural public-relations man was charming and engaging, by turns funny, self-deprecating, and warmly human, even as he sought to gin up excitement around the news that the Beatles were back in the studio working on a new album. But when the topic turned to John and his recent escapades, Paul uncharacteristically found himself having to put on a brave face.

He admitted that John was doing "a bit more drinking" than in the old days and that he'd "gotten into a few scrapes," but he insisted that there was nothing wrong with John. "[John] is very professional," he said. "I mean, he's been making music for how many years now. He never comes into the studio out of it or messed up, really. He's bringing in some of his best work. His songs are great, and he was great on the tour."

But Paul was beginning to realize that coming to New Orleans had been a mistake. The hope was that, rather than flying John back to England, with uncertain results, it would be easier on him if the Beatles flew to America instead to start work on their next album. Besides, it would be in keeping with his intention to have the group try recording in different locations.[165]

Paul had quietly suggested to George and Brian that it would be better to get John (and Ringo) away from Los Angeles and the ongoing party there. Both had readily agreed. But then Paul made the tactical error of picking New Orleans as a place to record. He was intrigued by the city's musical history, extending back to the birth of jazz and including some of the first rock and roll records. Paul thought it would be mind-blowing to record a new Beatles album in the legendary J&M studios, where Fats Domino and Lee Dorsey had cut their first sides. Maybe, Paul fantasized, the Beatles could pick up on the local vibe – maybe even get some of the local musicians to make guest shots on the album.

But it turned out that the party atmosphere of New Orleans, which carried on even though Paul had been careful to wait until after Mardi Gras to regroup the band there, was exactly the wrong place to bring John Lennon in the spring of 1973. In between sessions, John would make a beeline for Bourbon Street, there to spend hours at the bars and clubs getting drunk out of his gourd. Just like in Los Angeles, he was soon the hit of the town. But a darker side was beginning to emerge. Geoff Emerick, the Beatles' longtime engineer who had tagged along to New Orleans with them, remembered later, "One drink and he was a great deal of fun. Three drinks and he started getting violent. Four drinks and he started saying, 'I don't know where the Beatles are going next…I don't know what else there is left to do.' Six drinks and it was 'If there's a God how come he didn't answer when I asked for him.' Eight drinks and it was 'Why did she leave me?'"

Though John, as Paul stated, was still functioning at a high rate in the studio, the rest of the group – particularly Brian, who had the experience to know – began to notice that he was starting to take on the false glow of alcoholism. More and more often, his cheery demeanor in the studio was accompanied by slurred words and gestures. Worst of all, before the end of the sessions, he would begin dipping into bottles of champagne and brandy between takes, violating a longtime Beatles sanction on being out of it in any way while recording.

And while Paul had told *Newsweek* that John was bringing "some of his best work" to the sessions, only two of John's songs surfaced on the album. John had always been the edgiest of the Beatles, but that edginess had before been tempered with sweetness and humor, so it had come across as provocative but not abrasive. But now John seemed chillingly serious, and his new songs wavered between maudlin self-pity and an acid fury against the deity (and by extension, the wife who was devoted to that deity) who, he now growled to anyone who would listen, had deserted him.

The self-pity showed up in the song that became the album's penultimate track, "Nobody Loves You (When You're Down and Out)," a song that John had absurdly suggested he might submit to Frank Sinatra for possible recording, that accused virtually everyone around John of being hustlers, their only interest in him being based on his stardom.[166] It was hard for Paul not to think, as he added his bass guitar to John's song, that John might well have felt that way about the hangers-on who partied with him. Maybe even Keith Moon and Harry Nilsson, though they surely felt that way about their own entourage. Maybe even Paul himself.

The other song to make it onto the album was "Imagine," a pleasant piano ballad that John initially told Paul represented "what I hope for the world."[167] But upon a close listen, the vision John was presenting had a dark side. He was as eager to denounce religion as he was to promote the idea of humanity living in oneness and peace, and the world he envisioned in the song was in the end darkly nihilistic. Paul was unnerved. He was as aware of anyone of the growing spiritual movement among the younger generation – a movement whose birth the Beatles had helped to midwife. Now John seemed to be abruptly turning on the group's more spiritual fans, a notion that made Paul uncomfortable and led to an argument between himself and John when he suggested that perhaps John might consider changing some of the lyrics ("All you care about is selling fucking records," John had slurred). The message was not lost on the song's hearers, even within the group itself – "Imagine" was recorded as a trio of John on piano, Paul on bass, and Ringo on drums, with George and Brian both refusing to play on the song.

They would have been even more appalled had Paul allowed them to hear "I Found Out," a song John brought into the studio that Paul firmly rejected for the album. Over a sharp, jagged guitar line, John snarled out a litany of deprecations and insults against believers in general and the Beatles' fans in particular.[168]

"What the hell was that?" Paul said.

"It's how I feel," said John. "I'm writing songs how I feel. You should try it sometime."

Paul ignored the insult, but he was becoming frustrated. "John," he said, "why put down our fans like that?"

"Because they're fools," he said. "Just like I was. There's no fucking God."

"Look," Paul began, "I know all this is about May...."

"FUCK MAY!" John snapped, flinging his guitar aside. "And fuck you too!"

A half a bottle of brandy later, he had calmed down and was behaving cheerily toward Paul. "Fuck it," he said. "Keep the song off the album if you want. Doesn't matter."

In the end, the Beatles did not record the song. The album came to be dominated by Paul's songs – but even in some of those he was obviously reflecting on the group's situation with their troubled founder. The album was titled after the opening track, "Band on the Run" – a subtle comment on both the Beatles' current behind-the-scenes situation and on Paul's yearning for the group to break out of it, to fly away, to escape and find freedom.[169]

As the sessions progressed, John contributed less and less to the album. He had initially played a mean piano on "Nineteen Hundred and Eighty-Five," the apocalyptic Paul track that closed the album. He'd added strong guitar and vocals to Paul's "Jet" (another flight-and-escape metaphor) and a shimmering Hammond organ to "Let Me Roll It."[170] But he appeared less and less on the tracks recorded later. His acoustic guitar strumming in the coda section of "Band on the Run" was doubled by George and Brian, and the latter had added the colorful synthesizer that swept over the song's middle section. Brian likewise supported John's acoustic guitar on the George's "Give Me Love (Give Me Peace on Earth)," an earnest and beautiful song that hoped for a better world steeped in God's spirit – the very opposite of John's "Imagine."[171] Brian played the harmonica on "Apple Scruffs," George's funny and warm tribute to the fans who for years had gathered outside the Beatles' studios and offices. On the last three songs recorded, John didn't appear at all: not on "Has Anybody Seen My Baby," Brian's contribution, a churning Creedence-like rocker;[172] not on Paul's "Live and Let Die," which Paul had composed for the James Bond movie of the same name;[173] not on "Photograph," Ringo's homespun lyric about a lover with nothing left to show for his failed romance but an old snapshot that George turned into a musical extravaganza.[174] Ringo, in particular, was hurt by the lack of John's presence.

(Unlike John, though, he was sober every day for the Beatles' recording sessions.)

Once the album was released in July, John almost immediately took a train back to Los Angeles, where he resumed his drinking. By this point, his bandmates had become so frustrated with him they were almost happy to see him go. The question that wouldn't go away, though, is what the Beatles could possibly do after this, given the state of mind of John Lennon.

CHAPTER FIFTEEN: COLD TURKEY

October 11, 1973

The flickering light on the screen provided the only illumination in the editing booth. Just three persons stared intently at the images on it – the footage shot that day, in the eerie confines of the Oregon State Hospital and its environs in Salem, Oregon. Some footage was shot outside, and the rain that fell off and on, so typical for this time of year in Oregon, only enhanced the dismal look that the director sought for the scenes.

The three onlookers were the cinematographer; a highly-rated up-and-coming actor, Jack Nicholson, who was the main character in the movie being shot, playing the role of McMurphy; and the director, an attractive woman whom the world had come to know as May Ling Lennon, but who these days had reverted to calling herself simply May Ling.

May had come a long way from the days when she shot movies in the streets of New York with a do-it-yourself crew using handheld cameras. Now she had a full production crew and a budget of $4 million, as well as some of the most respected actors in the movie business, for her current production, her first major Hollywood film.

Film star Kirk Douglas had for some years been trying to get a studio interested in making a film of Ken Kesey's psychedelic, symbolic novel *One Flew Over the Cuckoo's Nest*. Set in a mental asylum, the novel had widely been considered impossible to translate to film. But Douglas had pressed for it, and his efforts had come to the attention of friends of May's, who in turn brought it to her attention. Eager to prove herself – and to show that she wasn't dependent on her estranged husband – she had quickly agreed not only to direct but to co-produce the project with Douglas. Pointedly, the production would be handled by United Artists – not Apple Films.[175]

She'd invited her star, Jack Nicholson, in to view the day's shooting because she wanted to bolster his confidence. He'd been reluctant to take the starring role of McMurphy – the criminal who is sent to the mental asylum and becomes a rallying point of resistance to "the system" – because he was unsure he could do it justice. But May had been very happy with his work and wanted him to see it.

Jack, sitting hunched over in the tiny editing booth, was indeed pleased with his performance. And with the film in general.

He leaned over to whisper to May: "This is fantastic. You're doing a great job."

"For a woman, right?" she whispered back, with a cynical look out of the corner of her eye.

"No, for anyone," Jack insisted. "This is a movie no one thought could be made, but you're making it."

Despite herself, a smile played across May's lips. "Everyone thought Kesey's novel was too acid-drenched to film," she whispered back. She paused. "There's always a way."

Jack regarded her for a moment as she stared intently at the screen. "Speaking of being drenched in drugs," he whispered with a hint of a smirk, "how is John these days?"

May's slight smile turned quickly to a frown. "I'm not really in contact with John much," she said.

"I didn't think so," he said. He cleared his throat.

May looked back at the screen, studying the images, looking for the best footage. "Cut that last five seconds," she directed the cinematographer. "Bad background stuff."

Jack leaned in again. "So…" he said.

"So?"

"Are you divorcing him?"

May shot him a look, then turned back to the screen. "I'm Catholic," she said. "We don't believe in divorce."

"I thought it wasn't a church marriage."

"It wasn't."

"Then what…."

Now her voice raised above a whisper. "Jack," she said. "Are you trying to talk me into letting you fuck me?"

The cinematographer leaned in closer to the screen, now trying not to hear the conversation happening inches away, which was making him distinctly uncomfortable.

"No, no," Nicholson insisted, speaking aloud now also. "I just want to know what's going on."

"What's going on is that the man I fell in love with has turned into a drunken asshole, and I don't want to talk about it."

"All right, all right," Jack said. "I'm sorry. I didn't mean to upset you."

"You didn't upset me. But shut up and watch the footage." She finally allowed herself a tiny smile.

For at least five more minutes, not a sound was heard in the booth other than those coming from the editing screen. May glanced at her watch. The nanny should be bringing Sean and Julia around soon. She hadn't worked since Sean was born, but once she'd kicked John out, she'd decided she would have to return to work or else lose her mind. She'd tried to function as both mother and film director, but the film work had eaten up her time, and she'd had to hire a nanny to care for the children after all. "Congratulations, John," she thought with derision. "At least you won *that* argument."

November 9, 1973

Four months after the Beatles' *Band on the Run* came out, Best of Faces, whose mix of good-time rock 'n' roll, "morning-after" regrets, and heartfelt poignancy had turned out to be a winning formula, continued their streak with their fourth album for Apple, *Ooh La La*.[176]

The title track – a mandolin-and-guitar-driven essay on the topics of aging and wisdom – was written by Kinks bassist Ronnie Lane, with an assist from Ron Wood. The Kinks were in the midst of a period where they disappeared from the public eye somewhat as Ray Davies devoted his talents to a series of insular concept albums even his most loyal fans found difficult to understand. Lane knew the Kinks would be unable to use his song in this context, so he gave it away to Best of Faces after completing it with Wood. His gesture helped erase any lingering bad feelings from his brief stint with Wood and Rod Stewart back in 1969, and he, along with the group, was rewarded with their second Number One single.

Around the same time, the Who released their latest album – and third rock opera – *Quadrophenia*. The album was generally well received, despite the complaints of some listeners that the music was drenched in synthesizers.

The day after *Quadrophenia*'s release, following several months of litigation, a settlement was reached between the Who and their former manager, Kit Lambert. Lead singer Roger Daltrey had initiated the lawsuit against Lambert after learning through an independent audit that over $1 million in royalties had not been remitted to the band. Lambert's sloppy business practices, rather than any deliberate dishonesty, were to blame. Still, Daltrey convinced the Who to dispense with Lambert and hire Bill Curbishley to manage them instead.

Ironically, this perhaps suited Lambert. He was a fantastic promoter and idea generator but had a lackluster approach to running a going concern. He had frankly become a bit bored with the Who, now that they were so successful they no longer needed his over-the-top promotional wizardry, though Pete Townshend still valued him as a sounding board for ideas. The Who's parting of the ways with their manager was as amicable as possible considering the circumstances, but it still left Lambert in need of something to do.

Shortly afterward, to somewhat less fanfare, the BBC debuted a new program: *Mick Jagger and Friends*. The former Rolling Stones singer was the "presenter" for a light-hearted talk show that ran for three years. However, attempts to revive his music career continued to fail, including his ill-fated 1976 attempt to ride the disco craze, "I Wanna Dance Dance Dance (All the Time Time Time)."

February 2, 1974

John Lennon lay on his back on the sofa in the little West Hollywood apartment he was now renting, his eyes darting back and forth, as he read intently the book with its black cover and large white letters spelling out the title, *The Primal Scream*.

Dr. Arthur Janov, the author of the book, had sent prepublication copies back in 1970 to a number of celebrities, including John, hoping to draw attention to his "primal therapy." May had picked up the book, leafed through it, and tossed it aside, telling John it was "a bunch of bullshit."

But it was now four years later, and May was gone. John knew why. He just didn't know why he kept drinking and doing drugs. It wasn't fun anymore.

Taking a walk through West Hollywood the previous day, to clear his head and try to get sober for at least a day or two, John had wandered into a bookstore. Sitting on a shelf he saw a used copy of *The Primal Scream*. He remembered the book and May's curt dismissal of it. But hadn't May dismissed him, too?

Now, hours later, he found himself thoroughly engrossed. Dr. Janov's ideas made everything perfectly clear. Now he finally understood.

Dr. Janov argued that neuroses and addictions – like John's out-of-control drinking – were the result of the pain of childhood traumas. He argued that persons repress their unmet childhood needs and desires by burying them deep in their psyches. But the unmet needs keep pressing for satisfaction, so one starts building up various "defenses" against them. These can include anything from neurotic behavior to substance abuse to following various surrogate parent figures. Dr. Janov argued that belief in God was nothing more than an attempt at finding a "substitute daddy" by patients who had not received enough fatherly love in childhood.

John smirked as he read those words. So, the God that May had put such faith in – the God that had abandoned him when he wanted May to take him back – was just a substitute for Freddie Lennon, the father who had abandoned John in childhood and only contacted him when he became a world-famous Beatle, or Julia, the mother who had left him with her sister instead of raising him herself. Maybe May herself had been just another substitute.

Dr. Janov's "primal therapy" called for patients to reenact their disturbing childhood experiences. It wouldn't do to simply talk the problems out, he argued, because intellectual talk only engaged the cerebral cortex, which is not the part of the brain where deep emotions are stored. He urged his patients to express the pain of the reenacted experiences by unrestrained, spontaneous screaming – hence the book's title – or even violence. Dr. Janov insisted that by releasing this pain, patients could once again feel their emotions honestly and would no longer be affected by addictions.

Lennon didn't know, but in the few years since the book was published, primal therapy had already become controversial, with many psychologists arguing that it produced minimal results. Two former trainee therapists at Dr. Janov's center, Joseph Hart and Richard Corriere, had in 1973 abandoned him and struck out on their own. Their patients followed them, and they later argued that at least 40 percent were faking their "primals." Others questioned the idea that simply re-experiencing pain could lead to the removal of the defenses against that pain.

But John was sold. It seemed so perfectly clear to him – his parents had abandoned him, and he'd spent years trying to find a substitute – Brian Epstein, Buddy Holly, May Ling, the Maharishi, God. He'd not been able to find one, and that's why he was drunk all the time. That had to be it.

He no sooner finished the book than he began looking for Dr. Janov's phone number.[177]

May 20, 1974

The Who's former manager, Kit Lambert, left London behind that spring and moved to the sunny climes of Marina del Rey. He had put his break with the band behind him, and was seeking a new project to excite his interest, when an article in the *Los Angeles Times* on the growth of cable television caught his eye. It seemed that not only were people willing to pay for cable television, they were willing to pay extra to see uncut movies on the new Home Box Office (HBO) channel. A brainstorm struck Lambert's fertile imagination: What if there was a 24-hour cable channel devoted to pop music? There could be concerts, interviews, promo films (the term "video" having yet to be popularized)... he could barely wait to begin making phone calls.[178]

Within a few days, Lambert had arranged a meeting with Don Kirshner. Kirshner, who first made his fortune running the Brill Building stable of songwriters in the early 1960s, had ties to both the music and TV industries. He was involved in the creation of *The Monkees* and was by then hosting his own late-night syndicated series, *Don Kirshner's Rock Concert*, which featured performances by artists not normally seen on television.

Kirshner seemed more than a bit out of place as the host of a TV show, but he was a hard-nosed businessman who knew a good idea when he heard it. And Lambert's idea – which he had by now dubbed "The Music Channel" – sounded like a very good idea indeed. He signed on to a partnership deal with the former Who manager to develop the network, the Music Channel LLP.

By July, Kirshner and Lambert were able to secure their first wave of funding, through a combination of Kirshner's planning and Lambert's cajolery. Buddy Holly of Apple, Clive Davis of Columbia, David Geffen, and a number of other record company executives were among those who invested in the new venture, seeing the obvious promotional value of a rock music cable channel.[179]

June 12, 1974

The John Lennon sitting and talking to the small group of reporters did indeed seem different from the one the world had known for so long. He even seemed different from the drunken John of the last year and a half.

But "different" didn't necessarily translate to "better." John insisted that he was "more aware" than he had ever been. But his very demeanor was unnerving.

John had always been known for his biting, sarcastic tongue, but most often his sharper comments were dropped in the middle of an interview in which his warmer side would also come out. He didn't put up with people who didn't bother to learn anything about him or were condescending, but with a friendly reporter, he would be more humane, giving earnest and thoughtful answers to questions. And always, the renowned John

Lennon sense of humor would shine through, softening the blow of his edgier comments. John always seemed honest, often bluntly so, but never mean or vicious.

But, despite John's insistence to the reporters at the mini-press-conference at Apple's Los Angeles office that he "was never more together" than now, he now gave the impression of a thoroughly unpleasant person – so much so, in fact, that at least a few wondered if the drunk of last year wouldn't have been a better interview subject.

John had called the mini-press-conference with a few handpicked reporters to announce the release of his solo album, titled simply *John Lennon*, that he had recorded in L.A. during the spring. But he also wanted to talk about Primal Scream Therapy, to explain what it was, and how it had changed his life. The reporters were only moderately interested, and Lennon began snapping at them, saying that "you can't understand the album until you know what primal screaming is all about."

His behavior matched the change in his demeanor. He had always had a hard stare, but now he glared angrily at one person after another. His voice was rough and had a bitter tone. He sounded constantly angry and impatient. Even his appearance was different: he'd cropped his famously long hair to a severely short cut. Asked why, he declared, "Long hair is just another drug. It's another thing you do to keep yourself away from reality. I'm back to reality now."

"I'm done with all the crutches," he said. "I'm done with all the things that you use to pretend reality doesn't exist, whether it's drugs, sex, or God or whatever. No more bullshit. I'm free now, and I don't need anything else."

John said that he used the sparsest of instrumentation on the album because he wanted to convey his new-found sense of freedom. "Just like you fill your minds with some kind of dope so you can't feel what's real, we pile on all these instruments. But for this I did just the piano and the guitar. That's all I needed." Most of the songs featured only a muted bass guitar and drums – played by Ringo – accompanying John. He went on to describe several violent arguments with the album's producer, Phil Spector, who wanted to add string accompaniments to a few tracks, including "Scared" and "How?" "I don't need no icing," John snarled.[180]

"What sort of things would you describe as dulling reality?" one reporter, earnestly trying to understand what John was talking about, asked. "Is it just drugs, or other things?"

"It's everything!" John shot back. "Everything you do to try to shut out how your parents didn't love you. That's true about most of the parents out there." Leaning in to the reporter, he extended an index finger toward her cup of coffee. "Probably yours, since you're doing it too."

The reporters, less than blown away by the "new John," began directing questions away from the concept of primal screaming. The more questions they asked that had nothing to do with the album or the therapy, the more irritated Lennon became. One reporter finally asked, "Does the solo album mean you are leaving the Beatles?"

"No," John growled. "But I'm going to be honest if I'm in the Beatles. No more bullshit."

"'If?'" the reporter persisted.

"What does it fucking matter?" he almost shouted. "If you're depending on the Beatles, that's just another drug too. *Live in fucking reality!*"

With regard to the topic of May Ling, the newly "honest" John refused to answer any questions at all. "Listen to the fucking album," was all he would say. "It'll tell you all you need to know." The truth of that statement was undeniable. John's feelings were on raw display on the new record, more so than on any music he'd ever made.

John took his listeners on a harrowing journey through his past, his childhood, his marriage, his disappointments and letdowns, and his most naked emotions, presented in a way no celebrity of his stature had ever dared. The tolling of funeral bells opened the record, heralding "Mother," where John recounted his childhood abandonment and howled in pain. The result was similar to "Cold Turkey," except that on the earlier record John's howling had been affected, an attempt to imitate the sound of a junkie in withdrawal – here, it was coming directly from his soul. Alternately, he tried to console himself over losing May, and beat himself up over his failures. "Love" recalled many a Beatles love song, but this time the emotion of love was presented as naked, open need. For all his protestations about honesty, he saw fit to include "Now and Then," a song that all but begged May not to leave him – ignoring the fact that she was already gone. The most chilling moment of all, perhaps, was "My Mummy's Dead," the album's brief closer, sung to the painfully childlike tune of "Three Blind Mice."[181]

The record was not very pleasant, but it was deeply compelling.

August 25, 1974

John Lennon sat at the kitchen table in the new apartment he had taken in West Hollywood. He had cleared out of the old one because he wanted to get away from all the booze and drugs that the old place evoked. The new one was sparsely furnished. The kitchen table and two chairs were among the few accoutrements. John had barely anything in the fridge and hadn't yet turned on the stove. The bedroom had just a bed and a single small dresser. The one appliance that was on incessantly was the television, which John had positioned so that he could watch it from either the kitchen or the living room. A few books, including Dr. Janov's, were propped up on a small bookcase separating the kitchen from the living room.

The television was playing some entertainment-related thing on the news. Possibly Rona Barrett, the Hollywood gossip columnist, but he was distracted. He was instead staring at the pack of cigarettes on the table. He'd walked out and purchased them that morning. He hadn't lit one. He assured himself that he didn't need crutches like that anymore. But his hands were shaking.

His attention suddenly turned to the screen when he heard his name mentioned. It was indeed Rona Barrett.

"....the head Beatle is said to be washed up these days," she confided in her nasal voice. "He's hardly doing anything for the Beatles and dropping hints that he's not going to work with them anymore. And that rough new record of his is tanking."

The record wasn't exactly "tanking," but by the Beatles' standards, it was only having a modest impact on the charts.

Buddy Holly, hearing the rough mixes, had, like Phil Spector before him, begged John to sweeten the music up a bit and take some of the edge off of it. John's answer was to repeat his standard mantra these days: "No more bullshit."

"....while he's going down, the woman he's now separated from is going up. May Ling's directorial debut on the United Artists hit *One Flew Over the Cuckoo's Nest* is the talk of the summer. The film has more than earned back its budget, and the word around Tinseltown is already talking Oscar both for the talented May and for her stars, Jack Nicholson and Louise Fletcher. It's hard for this reporter to believe that a successful lady like her will want to stay saddled to...." John flicked off the TV.

He sat back down at the table. His hands were now shaking even more.

Finally, in a single motion, he pulled a cigarette from the pack and lit it.

He leaned back in his chair, and his gaze fell upon Dr. Janov's book.

"Didn't work, Arthur," he muttered. "Didn't work."

CHAPTER SIXTEEN: THE ART OF DYING

September 19, 1974

Buddy Holly felt like he no longer recognized the person he was seeing.

There was John Lennon, stumbling about the Apple offices, back in England for a few days before returning to his Los Angeles haven. His clothes were disheveled, something John never used to allow, so meticulous a dresser was he even during his hippie days. His hair, now growing out again, was matted and greasy. He wore a grin, and laughed wildly, almost manically, but it was a hollow laugh. But what really struck Holly that night were the eyes. John's eyes were deep yellow, jaundiced, like the victim of a severe case of hepatitis. That, in fact, was John's excuse for the way his eyes looked – that he had suffered a bout of hepatitis.

But Holly wasn't stupid. He recognized the jaundiced yellow of the heavy cocaine user in those eyes.

"Come on, man," John barked. "I need some cash. Let me get into the account."

"No," Holly said firmly. "Forget it, John."

"I just need it for a business thing…." His voice trailed off.

"What business thing? You wouldn't handle the business if we paid you to. I'm not giving you money to buy coke."

John froze. His icy glare hit Holly hard. "It's not for coke."

"The hell it isn't." Holly glared back at John.

"You're fired!" John said. "Some manager! You're supposed to do what I say!"

Holly replied coolly, "I'm the group's manager. I'll wait and see what the other four say before I decide I'm fired."

With that, John, in a fury, put his foot through a television that Holly kept in his office. He staggered out of the room, his foot bleeding.

It wasn't until Holly stepped out into the hallway a short time later that he realized just how much John was bleeding. A slick trail of red blood led from Holly's door down the hallway and down a staircase.

Holly quickly summoned Neil Aspinall from his office, and the two of them followed the line of blood out of the hallway and into the Savile Row sidewalk. The blood was clearly gushing from John's leg. *He must have cut a major artery kicking that TV,* Holly thought. *And he probably didn't even notice.*

They caught up with him a few blocks later. He'd left the trail of blood along Savile Row for over a block. It led Holly and Aspinall to where he had collapsed, on a doorstep. He lay unconscious, drool seeping from his mouth, his glasses askew. Dark blood spurted from John's leg with every heartbeat.

An ambulance was summoned, and John was taken to the nearest hospital, where the doctors reported that had his wound gone unattended for any length of time, John might well have died. In the event, he was weaned off the drugs while in the hospital, and three days later proclaimed to Buddy Holly his willingness to return to work with the Beatles as soon as possible.

But within a few more days he fell back into what were by now becoming once again his regular habits. All the Beatles were concerned about John, most particularly Brian, who had insisted to Holly that the group should do whatever it took to get John into rehab. Now, after the incident in Buddy's office, the other Beatles, even a most reluctant Paul, came to agree with Brian. Whether they could "get" John into rehab was the question, though. But there was one glimmer of possibility: the new Gladys Presley Center, a rehab center in Memphis that Elvis, after coming out of rehab himself, had founded and named after his beloved mother.[182] Maybe the cachet of Elvis' name could do what the Beatles couldn't.

October 11, 1974

The sun flickered through the curtains of the West Hollywood apartment, the Los Angeles heat already beginning to simmer though the sun had barely just come up. John sat alone at the kitchen table with a cup of tea, stirring it aimlessly.

He was now 34 years old. He had ruined his marriage. He had made a big public deal about the "therapy" offered by Dr. Arthur Janov – even made an album based on it, where he denounced most of what he used to believe – only to discover that the "therapy" left him defenseless when the pain came back. So he had reenacted his childhood pain. So what? He already knew his mother had abandoned him, and his father. He already knew he had been lonely as a child and felt unloved. In the end, Dr. Janov didn't tell him anything he didn't already know about himself. Screaming a whole lot and experiencing it and crying like a little baby had helped for a while. But when the misery started coming back, what good was it? He'd let go of everything, of everyone, because Janov had convinced him that everyone and everything around him had represented an emotional crutch of one kind or another. That was supposed to help him. But now he was just alone with his pain.

He had just a short while ago summoned an Apple employee to help him bundle another girl from his apartment without his having to confront her. Another empty night of sex. Already half-drunk as the day began, he mumbled, "I guess this is it now. One slut after another."

He stood up and hobbled to the window, his foot still partially bandaged from his injury the previous month, pulling the curtains aside. The sunshine bit into his eyes. It felt like it was accusing him. He picked up a bottle of brandy from the counter and took a slug.

He slid the window open and climbed out onto the balcony of the third-floor apartment, overlooking Norton Avenue, just off Santa Monica Boulevard.

He wasn't expecting anyone today. His drinking buddies had long since moved on. He'd had a falling-out with Keith Moon, and another with Harry Nilsson. And he wasn't on speaking terms with the other Beatles either, not since that big argument where they tried to convince him to go the "Gladys Center" as he sneeringly called it. He wondered if they even wanted him back. "Maybe they'll just form another band without me," he mused, staring out over the balcony. He took another hit from the brandy bottle. "Paul will write all the songs, George and Brian will play guitar, and they'll airbrush me off the fucking album covers."

The only people he seemed to be in touch with these days were either Apple employees, who had no choice but to answer his summons, or drug dealers, or groupies, or the various leeches and lowlifes that wandered in and out of his life. One such had stolen his favorite appliance, his TV, two days ago. Now he didn't even have that anymore.

He climbed up onto the railing of the balcony. He took another drink from the bottle.

He stared out over the Los Angeles landscape. May was out there somewhere, he knew. Her film career was taking off. Directing a hit movie had made her a prized commodity in Hollywood. He had heard about the many offers she was getting these days. Surely some of them would be romantic as well as business offers. He'd messed it up, and now she was gone…she'd surely divorce him someday soon, the papers might come any day – he kept waiting for a process server to appear at the door.

He stared down at the sidewalk below, bringing both legs to the outside of the railing.

Presently he saw a hummingbird dive below into the bushes, its wings buzzing as it sought nectar among the flowers. It flew straight down.

"I'm going down too," John thought as he watched the bird. "Going straight down." It would be so easy. Just to fall straight down, to keep on going straight down…no pain…never even notice….

He let go of the balcony railing.

A few minutes later, a woman, going for her morning jog along Norton, stopped and screamed. She broke into a run, racing inside a storefront on Santa Monica.

"It's John Lennon!" she screamed. "Somebody call an ambulance! John Lennon's lying on the sidewalk! In a pool of blood!"

John sat by a cool stream. The water was rushing gently over the rocks. Down in the water he could see tiny minnows skittering among the pebbles.

A soft breeze blew through the reeds next to the water. As he looked around, he saw that the meadow gave way to a forest a short distance beyond the stream.

The sun was shining, with just a few clouds in the sky. But the air around was pleasant, and there was no intensity of heat. Birds were chirping as they flew amid the tall grasses that rose just above the stream.

John reckoned the time to be about noon, so he couldn't tell which way was east or west. He couldn't quite remember how he had gotten here.

Then he noticed something he hadn't at first. His glasses were missing.

Yet he was able to see clearly. For the first time in so long he could not remember, he could see the whole horizon all around and everything in it, without need of the glasses he had worn for so long.

He looked down at himself. The dirty T-shirt and jeans he last remembered wearing were gone. Instead, he wore what seemed to be a white cotton shirt and trousers. Sandals were on his feet. He could feel his hair tousling in the wind. It felt full, but as if it was freshly washed. The dankness and greasiness he had gotten used to were gone.

So were the odors. The smell of unwashed clothes, unwashed body, alcohol, vomit – the stench of the last two years of his life – had disappeared like the dew. Instead, everything smelled rich and fresh. He marveled for a few moments, picking up the scents. As he did so, he was dazzled. It seemed as though he were experiencing dozens of scents, more than he had ever known before – the sweetness of the grass, the richness of roses from somewhere, a plethora of plant aromas, and even the smell of some nearby animals, whose scent was nevertheless pleasing.

"Well, that takes care of smelling and seeing," he thought to himself – the first conscious thoughts he had had. "Wonder what tasting is like." He reached down into the stream, cupping his hand, and pulled up a handful of water. Sipping it, it seemed as though it was the clearest, freshest taste he had ever known. Just plain water, and yet his whole body tingled and felt refreshed.

"I don't know where I am," he finally decided. "But it's time to find out." He stood and began walking toward the line of trees that enclosed the meadow.

Paul was at his farmhouse in Scotland, the cold autumn winds whipping across the ocean. He was playing a game in the kitchen with his young son, James. Stella and Mary had gone outside to play. Heather, as always, was sitting in her room, sullenly avoiding everyone. She had become a worry for both Paul and Linda.

The telephone rang, and Linda picked it up. "Oh my God!" she gasped.

Paul looked up. "What is it?"

Linda's eyes filled with tears.

As John walked toward the trees, the grass felt cool around his feet. His whole body felt refreshed and recharged. The lethargy of alcoholism felt gone altogether. He jumped in the air, excited, and then began running toward the trees.

He broke into laughter, and ran faster, making his way through the tall grass to the trees. His whole body felt unbelievably light. He wasn't in the least fatigued from his run. He felt as though he could run hundreds of miles.

Brian was meditating on the sun porch of his Cotchford Farm home. He went out there frequently, several times a day. Goldie sometimes didn't know what to make of it, but she usually reacted with a shrug.

But not today. "I think you'd better come to the phone," she said in a raspy voice, interrupting Brian's mantra.

Now John was walking amid the trees. The sunlight fell in dappled patterns on the ground. It didn't seem dark, though – the forest was suffused with a glowing light. It seemed not eerie but warm and welcoming. Birds were chirruping as they flitted from branch to branch. Ripe fruit hung from some of the trees, rich reds, oranges, blues, purples – brighter and deeper colors than he could ever remember seeing.

LSD was like the real world in Technicolor, he had once told a reporter. Wherever he was, it was so deep and rich that the experiences he had known from his drug use seemed dull gray in comparison.

Everything around him felt warm and loving. There was no decay in this forest, no rotting branches, no fallen leaves, no dying trees, no undergrowth, no bugs except those that scrambled peacefully – joyously, almost – across the ground. It was as serene a place as he had ever known.

"This can't be the world," he thought. "Where am I?"

Then he remembered.

George was working in his garden. It was late in the year, past the gardening season, but he always found some work to do. Gardening was refreshing for George. He felt the combination of manual labor and serenity to be restorative. And on his Friar Park estate, at Henley, near London, he had plenty of work to do.

Today he was pruning dead branches from some of the trees, silently chanting "Hare Krishna" as he did so. He watched intently each branch as he snapped it free and it tumbled to the ground. He hadn't decided to get up on the ladder just yet – he was focusing on the smaller trees, nearest the ground.

He heard a shout. He turned to see his new love, Olivia Arias, waving to him from the porch. For a moment, he was about to wave back, till he noticed that she was summoning him – and that, even from a distance, she looked distraught.

John continued on through the forest, a little more purposefully now. It had come back to him: the balcony, the booze, the sudden rush of air as he plunged toward the sidewalk. Now, he was sure, this must be something other than the world he knew. He must be in the afterlife.

The gentle wind played through the trees, pushing tufts of leaves about. He walked on, for what seemed like hours, although he had no real sense of time. Everything seemed to be happening "right now." He didn't think of the time by the stream and his time now walking through the forest as distinct; there was no "past" or "future." It all seemed to be happening at once.

And when he thought about his life, he seemed to see it all at once: his childhood; his father and mother abandoning him; happy games in Strawberry Fields; getting to know his mother again, and then that terrible night when she was hit and killed crossing the street; his leather jacket and the tough, sullen demeanor he threw out in art school, when he wanted no one close to him, no one to penetrate his hide, nothing to hurt him again; Paul, and playing their guitars together in the front room at Menlove Avenue; Hamburg and the long hours and the uppers and the prostitutes; the sweat thick on the walls of the Cavern; Beatlemania and the hordes of screaming girls, fun and exciting at first, exhausting later, mind-crushing after a while; the thousand LSD trips; the Maharishi; May....

May.

And the children.

Suddenly a massive wind kicked up, blasting John in the face, blowing back his hair. He could hear the leaves and branches thrashing, but he could not see, could not open his eyes. He grabbed hold of a nearby tree for support, then fell back against the tree.

The intense wind lasted only briefly – but when it cleared, a bemused John found himself once again at the edge of the forest, where he had been surrounded by it before. He looked out to see an open clearing, with rocky uplands – looking, he noted with a trace of wry humor, not unlike the countryside around Paul's beloved Scottish farm.

A light wind played over the grass, but the air felt colder than before, more like the misty Scottish highlands as well. He took a few steps forward, then saw a large white rock. He felt compelled to see what was on the other side of the rock. He stepped around the rock, and there he saw the little man.

He was sitting at the stubby bottom of the rock, whittling and humming a tune that John recognized as an Irish folk song. He was short, about four feet tall, but not tiny. His clothes were simple, like those of a farmer from some older time in history, and he had white hair and a white beard.

He had been walking through the forest, he knew not for how long – for eternity – and he hadn't seen another person. He'd started thinking that maybe George was right, and when you die your ego dies and your spirit is absorbed into the cosmic consciousness – only he had too big an ego to absorb. Now he saw this man – an old man with a beard, just like in some Sunday school class from when he was six years old, but not up in the sky, and dressed in the clothes of a farmer. And an Irishman, apparently, no less.

"You're not God, are you?" he asked.

The old man kept whittling, but a tiny chuckle escaped his lips. "No, lad," he said. "Too small for that, as you can see."

"That's good," John replied. "I'd have been ready to ask for me prayers back if you're what I came across."

The man's right eyebrow rose slightly. "That mouth of yours, lad," he said. "You'd do well to watch it. It's gotten you in trouble before, you know."

"I know," he said, a bit glumly. The remembrance of his "bigger than Jesus" comment once again flitted through his head, and it felt salty and bitter. Then he brightened again. "Well, if you're Irish, you must understand about blarney and having a temper and that," he said.

"That I do, lad, that I do," he said.

John looked up at the mountains, then back at the little man, who carried on with his whittling. "So what happens now?"

"What do you mean?"

"Where do I go now?"

"Well, that would be up to you, now wouldn't it?"

John bristled. "How would I know where to go next? I don't even know how I got here or where I am."

The man said nothing, but carried on whittling.

John, in frustration, walked to the edge of what had now come into focus as a cliff. He could see mists draped along the valley below, between the mountains in the distance, which seemed to have grown. Some pockets of the valley looked in the distance like the place he had first found himself in – bright and filled with sun. Others looked darker, gloomier.

When he turned back toward the old man, he drew back in surprise. A single tear had rolled down from the man's eye and traced its way across his wind-beaten face to his white beard.

"Why are you crying?" John said.

"For you, lad," the old man said, his voice softer than before.

"Why?"

For the first time, the old man's eyes met John's. "*You did not love.*"

Ringo had picked up the phone himself at his Los Angeles residence, from which lately he worked on his acting gigs and other assorted projects, biding his time until he heard from John again, counting the hours, but happy it was not him, happy he had kicked the worst of his drinking habit – happy it was not he who was threatening the future of the Beatles, because while John was irreplaceable, there was little doubt they would find another drummer if worst came to worst.

He broke into sobs when he heard the news, but decided at once to meet the other Beatles at the Los Angeles airport when they arrived. Paul was already aboard a flight from London. He would soon be followed by George and Brian, who met him at Heathrow Airport.

"What do you mean, I didn't love?"

"Think about it," the man said.

"I was a most loving man! I gave nothing but love to the whole world!" John said indignantly. "Even when the world did nothing for me, I...."

"'Did nothing for you'? Is that really true?"

John said nothing in response, glaring at the man instead.

"Do what I say, lad," the man said. "Think about it."

With that, it seemed, the very sky filled with projections – a kaleidoscope of images, a massive flood, names and faces and places pouring in front of him: the events of his life.

Stunned, he watched closely.

Spread before him were his many indiscretions – the girls in art school, the girls in Hamburg. Cynthia Powell, who he had long since forgotten about, but who cried over him for days when they broke up, once she had found out he had slept with other girls during the Hamburg jaunts. The dozens of groupies, of hangers-on, of girls here and there around London, attracted by the fame and fortune and charisma of the Beatles, of the chance of being close to one of them, even for a little while, of taking home some of the power that seemed to flow and emanate from the group. He had taken his fill of each and not looked back.

Then there were his friends, some of whom he had hurt badly: Pete Best, the Beatles' original drummer, who wound up in a bakery, forgotten by the group; or the Maharishi, who had watched with puzzlement and sadness as John had stalked off. John had thought the man was ripping him off, that he only wanted his money. But he knew now that the Maharishi was sincere, that whatever the limitations of his path, he had only wanted to help. He had wanted to love John, and John had turned away.

That began to reveal itself as the pattern of his life. After his wounding by his mother and father, he had craved love, but on his terms. He feared getting hurt again and would either cling tightly to those he loved, smothering them, or alternatively he would spurn them, rejecting their love, his deep affection turning to icy cold scorn overnight.

But no one had he hurt more than May, Sean, and Julia. He had spent so much time inside a bottle, trying to numb his own pain over losing them. But it had been only his own pain he had cared about. He knew he had been foolish and selfish to turn away from May the way he had done. But he had never stopped to consider how really deeply they had been hurt. Now he felt their pain, crushing him in waves, slamming against him like shocks of electricity. He lost his footing and fell to the ground, moaning. All this is what those he loved had felt, he knew, and he had caused it – he alone.

He did not love.

He had tried to spread love around the world, and so many millions knew the word Love from his lips, indeed felt the only connection to Love they had ever known through the music of the Beatles. Yet he had not loved those closest to him. Not in the deepest, truest, most real way. Not in the way that really mattered, where he let them mean more to him than he did.

Even the fans, he thought. I came to regard them as a burden, an annoyance, a frustration – when it was a blessing to be able to bring love to so many. For all the times he had been loving to his fans, there were also times – too many times – where he had not been so.

He cried, breaking into deep sobs. "I want to love!" he rasped.

He heard the little man's voice again. "I thought you wanted to be happy, lad."

"I don't care if I'm happy!" John rasped through his sobs. "I just want to love! Please! Let me love!"

John all at once felt the pain, sharp and deep and intense, throughout his body. He wanted to scream but felt too weak to do so. A white light hovered overhead.

The pain was not searing, but deep, as if his entire body were out of joint. It was excruciating.

He gasped again, choking. He heard voices. Frantic voices, like people shouting.

Then he felt hands gripping his arms and legs. He was lying in a prone position, he realized. He could hear more garbled shouting but couldn't make out the words.

He felt a burst of air coming into his lungs from...a breathing tube?

The white light overhead gradually began to resolve itself. Fluorescent lights. There was indeed a breathing tube in his mouth, and he began to notice other tubes, around him, attached to him.

He was lying in a hospital bed.

He now saw that the voices he heard had belonged to doctors and nurses. He was alive.

He felt a hand grip his right hand.

He turned his head, ever so slightly, and saw May Ling's face.

CHAPTER SEVENTEEN: ALL THINGS MUST PASS

January 31, 1975

At 8:00 pm Eastern Time, the new cable network flickered to life on those television sets tuned to it in five markets. The first image was of a sophisticated-looking Kit Lambert, sitting in an easy chair and sipping a glass of champagne. "Ladies and gentlemen," he said with a quiet, wry smile, "It's time for some rock 'n' roll." With that, the Music Channel was up and running.

The new channel featured a mixed bag of programming. Don Kirshner had moved his *Rock Concert* show to the new network, and had successfully convinced the producers of *The Midnight Special*, another live concert program, to create a version of the show to be aired on the new channel. In addition, *The King Biscuit Flour Hour*, a staple of radio which featured live concert performances, debuted a TV version to be aired on Friday nights.

Along with live concert footage, the channel showcased interviews, documentaries on famous bands (including a new program called *Behind the Music*), rock movies, rock-related movies (like *The Man Who Fell to Earth*, starring David Bowie), and assorted "underground" programs and cult films.

The channel featured a number of the increasingly popular promo films that would come to be called "videos" but eschewed adopting a radio-like "rotation" format. Instead, variety was the key, with current music mixed with "blasts from the past," and with slots devoted to as many different genres as possible. The "blasts from the past" included reruns of classic series like

Shindig and *Hullabaloo,* Britain's *Ready Steady Go, Top of the Pops,* and *Old Grey Whistle Test,* and Germany's *Beat Club.*[183]

Kirshner and Lambert hired a number of hip young producers to work on programming for the network, who insisted that the network take on the task of introducing new, untried bands and off-the-wall performers like Frank Zappa who at that time didn't normally get on network TV. In response, Kirshner reluctantly conceded the wee hours of the morning to a single such program which covered the 12 pm to 6 am time slot on weekends, called *Night Flight.*[184]

The network also secured rights to the long-running syndicated hit *Soul Train.* Dick Clark's flagship, *American Bandstand*, remained on ABC for the time being, but in a contract dispute seven years later, Clark finally moved his venerable show to the Music Channel, eventually retiring as host in 1987 (to be replaced by Rick Dees).[185]

February 28, 1975

Paul McCartney was quiet and pensive as he sat looking out the window on the flight from London to New York, the first time he had been back to see John since Christmas. He had avoided a few autograph seekers at the airport and endured the knowing stares of others in the first-class cabin. A flight attendant offered him a drink, but he politely declined. He was too preoccupied to want anything.

He was flying by himself today. Linda had offered to go with him to New York, but Paul had insisted that she stay home with the kids. He smiled thinking of it. Linda was always so willing to be helpful.

He tugged at his shirt, and rested his hand on his chin, staring out the window. He was so used to looking out of airplane windows, he reflected. So many times had he flown across the Atlantic since that first trip in 1964, when he and the others had nervously awaited their reception in America, only to be delighted upon their landing with thousands of screaming fans at the airport in New York. It had been so long, such a long journey. Back in the little house in Allerton, Liverpool, he knew that someday he would fly in an airplane – he had had that confidence. That seemed a thousand years ago.

The conversation that was about to happen was not something he was anticipating with joy. He didn't know what to expect. Only to expect the unexpected. It had always been that way with John.

Three and a half months had gone by since the day he had gotten that horrible phone call.

He and the others had rushed to Los Angeles. Paul had not been surprised to see the other Beatles. But he had been surprised to see May. She was as surprised as he was that she was there.

Two years had gone by since the love of her life had slept with another woman. She had thrown him out and refused to let him come home, and in response, it seemed, he had doubled down on the callous and selfish behavior that had caused her to throw him in the first place. She had suffered, but Sean and Julia had suffered more.

Her Catholic faith didn't allow for divorce, but she did see a way out. Since John had insisted on a civil ceremony back in 1969, in the eyes of the Church they technically weren't really married. So, she had decided with great reluctance, the time had come to cut the cord with John, find someone new, and marry for real. She had instructed her lawyer to begin divorce proceedings just two days before John's suicide attempt. John hadn't even known.

Her career had grown by leaps and bounds. She had proven herself in Hollywood with the massive success of *Cuckoo's Nest* and was now beginning work on two more movies. She had the wherewithal she needed to strike out on her own. No one could possibly suggest that she was hanging on to John for his money. Besides, he had spent so much of it, on alcohol and drugs.

But her career was time-consuming. And, with their father gone, she was determined that Sean and Julia should at least have their mother, so she spent as much time with them as she could. So she hadn't had time to meet anyone else.

Besides, the more John deteriorated, the harder the prospect of approaching him about a divorce had seemed. How could she talk to him about a divorce or about the children or indeed anything when he was drunk or high all the time?

Their conversations had grown fewer and fewer, mostly by her choice. By the last few months, she had contacted him only when an issue needed to be resolved regarding the children. Every conversation with John ended up one of two ways: with him in sullen anger, grunting and snapping at her over the phone, barely saying a word; or with him in drunken incoherence pleading with her to come back. Either way was like having her heart pulled out through her throat. At times, she wondered whether she had ever really loved him in the first place.

Then, in Los Angeles, the news came over the radio about John's suicide attempt. Before she realized what she was doing, she was halfway out the door, telling her secretary that she was on her way to the hospital.

And in that moment, she knew the answer to her question. You don't rush to the bedside of someone you don't love.

John had fallen about thirty feet. He had suffered massive internal injuries, and a concussion which had left him in a coma. His right leg had caught part of a lower balcony railing as he fell, which ironically may have slowed him down enough to save his life. But his knee had been badly damaged by the trauma, to the point where he would now walk with a permanent limp.

He had been in a coma for three days, the world awaiting with bated breath, hoping, praying. Telegrams, flowers, cards, had poured in by the truckload to the hospital in Los Angeles – by the literal truckload, so many that the hospital had to hire space at a nearby warehouse. A special switchboard had to be set up to field the incoming phone calls, from fans begging for news, sending their wishes, or just crying, and from the press, eager for updates almost to the second on John's condition.

When John finally came out of his coma, one of the first congratulatory calls he received, to his amazement, was from President Ronald Reagan, who was also in a hospital, in Washington – he had been the victim of an assassination attempt at the hands of Arthur Bremer. Reagan had been on the receiving end of just as much, if not more, attention from the world, and nearly as many prayers and good wishes, fewer than John thanks only to the knowledge that his wounds were not life-threatening. Indeed, between the shooting of the President of the United

States and near-suicide of a member of the Beatles, the world had paid attention to little else, it seemed, the last few days. Reagan had been in a jovial mood both before and after his surgery – saying of his surgeons, "I hope they're Republicans" – but he was genuinely and surprisingly concerned for the well-being of John Lennon. He repeatedly asked after him and made a point of telling his staff to ensure that John's family and loved ones received his best wishes.[186]

When John was reported stable by the hospital, Reagan called with his congratulations. Aware that the press would be covering the call, Reagan repeated his joke from a few days earlier: "I'm glad the doctors who worked on you were Republicans as well, John."

John weakly replied, "As long as they weren't Beatle-haters."

The good news of John's recovery spread around the world, along with prayers and songs of gratitude, culminating on Friday, October 25, with a spontaneous peaceful march in Central Park in New York, joined by tens of thousands, who handed out flowers like it was 1967 all over again and sang, until some of the wealthy folk in Upper East Side apartments complained to police. An even bigger march followed the next day in Hyde Park in London.

The relief over John's condition came easier than repairing his broken marriage. May Ling may have rushed to John's side, but they remained awkward around one another at first. The damage had been great, and it couldn't be cured overnight. Although Julia was still too young to understand what had happened, Sean in particular had lost much of his trust in his father, and John had no way of knowing if he could win it back.

But he had not forgotten what he had asked for: the chance to love, to give love for real, and to give it to those closest to him. He told only a few people about what he had seen. He wasn't sure whether it had been a glimpse of the afterlife, or whether it had just been a comatose dream, although at least one of his doctors told him that it was impossible for his brain to allow for functional dreaming so close to death. He was determined, regardless, to do what he said he would do.

The first step was to wean himself off drugs and alcohol once and for all, and toward that end, as soon as he was healthy enough to travel, he booked himself directly into the Gladys Presley Center for a regimen of rehabilitation that would last until just after the New Year. It was by no means easy, even given the advantage conferred by being in the hospital. He hadn't been able to get cocaine, obviously, so at least he didn't have that clouding his system anymore. But getting off the alcohol was considerably harder. On not a few nights in the Presley Center he lost his composure and broke down in tears when the ache for a brandy had become overwhelming.

By the time John was released from the Presley Center, May had arranged for him, her, and the children to move into the Dakota building on the Upper West Side in New York. She decided to relocate her production company to the Big Apple, reckoning that New York, being halfway between Los Angeles and London, would be easier for John's visitors and John himself to handle – and would get John away from the city where he had nearly died.

The members of the press who gathered at Grand Central Terminal in New York on January 5, 1975 to witness John's arrival in New York were shocked to see just how bad Lennon's injuries had been, especially when he emerged from the railroad car in a wheelchair. Nevertheless, he was in good spirits, better than he had been when speaking to the press for ages. "New York's a happening place," he joked when asked about his planned convalescence there.

Physical therapy had followed, John gradually learning to walk again. He slowly and painfully graduated from wheelchair to walker to cane. His doctors feared he might have lost some dexterity in his nervous system, threatening his ability to work as a musician again – to sing, to play the guitar, to play the piano. John feared that possibility himself, so greatly that at first he dared not try to sing, and wouldn't touch any of his instruments.

So he did something he hadn't done for a long time, in fact had never truly done before at all. He prayed - genuinely. He gave thanks for everything that had happened so far – his life had been restored to him – but asked for one more thing: that he could be a musician again.

He and May tiptoed around each other, their conversations terse and clipped. Things were even worse with the children. Sean and Julia were sullen and spoke little to John. As they played in the other rooms of the suite, he would sometimes listen from the kitchen, quietly crying – wanting desperately to go into the room and play with his children, despite knowing that everything would instantly turn stilted and awkward if he did. He felt sick when he remembered his whining about Julia's dirty diapers and crying jags.

But slowly, he and May spoke more and more easily. A few light comments here, a few jokes there. They slept in separate beds, a contingency necessitated by John's physical condition, but also because May was still not ready to share a bed with John again.

At least the alcohol and drugs were gone. And though John was sadder, and quieter, the spark she had known had not gone out. Before long, she began finding messages scattered around the apartments, scrawled in John's hand, left for her – "You are the rest of the universe." "Thank you for surviving me." Not the desperate pleas of the drunken John on the telephone, but simple messages of love – given freely without any expectation of receiving anything back.

Then, one day in early February when he had moved up to walking with a cane, he quietly made his way out of the apartment and went for a stroll – a difficult one, but a stroll nonetheless – through the streets of the Upper West Side near the Dakota. Finding a florist shop, he went inside.

He spent a few minutes looking at the lavish displays of roses. Then, with a smile, he asked, "Do you have white chrysanthemums?"

Later, after returning to the apartment with the flowers, John sat at the piano. He stared at the keyboard for a long time. May watched him secretly from a side door.

After an interval that seemed like hours, he placed his right index finger on middle C. Then he formed a chord with his right hand. He began playing, quietly, tentatively at first, then gradually warming up.

His hands worked the way they were supposed to.

Warming to his task, he began to move through a variety of styles, a slow country tune at first, then something more bluesy, then finally working himself up into a rock and roll rhythm, until finally he pounded at the piano like Little Richard.

To his sudden embarrassment, May entered laughing and clapping. "I didn't know you were listening," he said.

She kissed John on the cheek. Then their lips met, and they kissed again, and again, for a long time.

The frostiness between John and kids was harder to overcome. He still wasn't sure if his children would ever trust him fully again. He knew that they might not, but he also knew that he would not let them down again. Whether or not they reciprocated was beside the point. He would be their father no matter what.

Paul McCartney ascended the elevator at the Dakota, pensively regarded the detailing of the old wooden interior. An odd place for John to live, he thought, all this history all around. John didn't like the deadening hand of the past and much preferred things that were new.

On the other hand, Paul thought, John was a sentimentalist, to a degree few people realized. He had even asked Aunt Mimi to send him his old Quarry Bank school tie to his digs in New York – a school John told each and every person that he hated. *Maybe this place reminds him of Liverpool*, thought Paul.

They exchanged pleasantries, Paul warmly exclaiming how well John looked. It wasn't the first time Paul had seen John since he had recovered from his coma. He had, in fact, been in fairly frequent touch with him, although broaching the subject of the Beatles never seemed appropriate, and John never brought it up. Paul, Linda and the children had made a visit to the Presley Center at Christmas, bringing gifts for John, May, and the children, and it had been a warm and wonderful few days, the couples happily enjoying the holiday. At the end, John had thanked Paul for "not bringing any Beatles talk with you."

Now that day had finally come. They both knew it.

After making small talk over tea for a brief while, Paul finally spoke the dreaded words. "I want to talk about the Beatles," he said.

John didn't answer, but he steeled himself. This could turn into an argument.

Paul stood and walked to the window, looking out at the traffic on Central Park West. "You know the group means a lot to me," he said.

"Yeah, it means a lot to me too," John answered. *But it means more to Paul,* John thought. *That's his life. The Beatles are everything to Paul.*

Paul sat down, and stared into his tea. John waited for an imprecation. He was ready for the fight. Paul would surely demand they get back to work. John would not do anything that would cause him to abandon May again.

What Paul said next startled John.

"But you mean more to me than the Beatles," Paul said. "You're my best friend. And I almost lost you."

The look on John's face softened, but he remained silent.

"I almost lost you more than once," Paul continued. "Not just when you nearly…died. I almost lost you over everything that was happening…"

"You mean me being out of me fucking head on drugs and booze and not giving a fuck about anyone or anything?" John said. A slight smile came to his lips.

"Yeah," Paul said with a slight, nervous laugh.

Paul stood up again, and walked once more to the window.

"I don't want to lose you," Paul said. "More than that, I don't want to be the reason you're lost. I don't want the Beatles to be the reason you're lost."

John wanted to jump up and reassure Paul, but he knew he couldn't. Paul was right. The Beatles had been John's means for much of his life of trying to fill the hole in his soul left behind by his parents. But that hole could no longer be filled by the group – and trying to do so had been slowly killing John.

Paul again sat back down. He was pacing, John realized. "The thing is – I think maybe, you know, the time has come to…let it go."

"Let what go?"

"The group."

"You mean we should end it? End the Beatles?"

"Yeah."

A cold chill came down John's back. This was, after all, the group he had founded back in 1957, when they were the Quarry Men and lucky to get a job playing a church fete. He had often thought over the past months about not coming back to the Beatles. But now that the reality was here, the shock of actually pulling the plug was profound indeed.

Then he looked across at Paul's face. Paul looked devastated, near tears. But he also looked earnest and hopeful. He wanted this for John. He wanted John to say yes.

John felt a sudden catch in his throat. Paul was doing this for him. He surely hated the idea of ending the Beatles. Yet he had decided to make this sacrifice for John.

Choking up, John rasped, "The others...."

Paul cut in quickly. "I've already talked this over with George and Richie and Brian," he said. "They're in agreement with this."

Now, even as he wiped away a tear, a smile came to John's face. "Cheeky, Paul," he scolded. "Macca the weaver of schemes once again."

Paul laughed, "Yes, that's me, the master manipulator," he said.

John took a sip from his tea. "So what are the others going to do?"

"Brian wants to get into record production. Richie wants to do more movie roles. George says he'll probably just do a lot of gardening."

"And you'll make five albums a year," John retorted. Paul now laughed openly.

"Then you like the idea?'

John paused. The end of the Beatles. He was prepared to fight for it, but now that it was here....

Suddenly, he got to his feet.

"You know," he said, "we can't end it just now. The last album we did was a bummer. Two years ago and I didn't give a crap. And we haven't done a tour since '72. Kids have graduated from college and stuff since then."

Paul stood up too, his eyes widening with surprise.

John hobbled around the table, taking his turn at staring out the window. Paul waited expectantly.

Finally, John set down his teacup, placed both hands on the table, and smiled widely. "I say we do one last album. Make it a really good one, like in the old days – everybody brings in their best stuff and we give it 100 percent. And we'll do a last tour with it – go around the world, like in the old days, give them all one last big Beatles show."

Paul smiled broadly. "Take the Beatles out with a bang?" He thought for a second, then added, tentatively, still worried about John's situation: "Do you want to record it here in New York?"

John thought for a minute, then said, "No." Then he elaborated, excitedly. "We go back to our roots to do it. Back to the old place."

"Apple?"

"Older, Paulie," John said. "Let's do it at Abbey Road. Where we started it all." Paul laughed again. John really was a sentimentalist, however tough he tried to appear.

Paul mused for a moment, still smiling. "We ought to make it a double album," he said.

"We've done that before," John said. "Last great album from the great and holy and wonderful Beatles *should* be a double bloody album, don't you think?"

CHAPTER EIGHTEEN: LETTING GO

March 6, 1975

Gathered in front of the microphones, for the press conference, the Beatles shuffled around a bit. They had done this far too many times to be nervous, but they all knew they were about to drop a bombshell. Paul smiled congenially, and so did John, but George, Brian and Ringo all carefully examined the rafters around them.

Buddy Holly asked the news media to "Please quiet down – we're about to begin." The voices and assorted noises of moving chairs and scratching pens died down, and the bright lights illuminated the podium in the conference room at the Apple offices where the Beatles prepared their "special announcement." John spoke first on behalf of the whole group.

While they thoroughly enjoyed making music, and loved their fans, he said, they believed they had taken the concept of the Beatles as far as it could possibly go. "It's turned into a routine. Album, tour, album, tour." Not to mention the fact that the touring had a lot to do with that downward spiral that nearly took him out entirely back in October. He and the others had concluded that it was time to devote more of their personal time to their families.

So – in an act unprecedented in rock – the five members announced that they had decided to "retire" the Beatles. They weren't splitting up, John made clear, as the others began to chime in. They had every intention to continue to work together in leading Apple, and to participate in one another's solo projects – "in twos, threes, maybe fours," George Harrison joked. But they would not continue to make new albums or tour on a regular schedule.

John announced that they were currently making one more foray into the studio as a group, where they were recording a final album, to be released in the summer. Completion of the album would be followed by a worldwide farewell tour. After that, they intended to focus largely on solo projects, or simply spend their time with their families.

Despite their "retirement," though, Paul also insisted, they would perform occasionally as the Beatles from time to time, for special occasions or when the mood struck them – just not according to a set schedule. "Don't worry if you haven't ever seen us live," Paul McCartney assured the fans. "We're not going away. We'll be coming round."

John Lennon, his old friend, couldn't help but suppress a chuckle at that comment. *Paul is Paul*, he thought.

He looked around at his old pals, who he was closer to than ever, even as they let the band go; and to his wife, standing off camera to the side, who had come back to him, who had forgiven his betrayals. And he couldn't suppress a broad smile.

Finally – he knew for sure now – he was happy.

June 5, 1975

Record stores worldwide had trouble keeping up with the sales of *Goodnight Vienna*.[187] On its release date, so rapidly was the final new Beatles album selling that record stores were simply opening up boxes and selling copies directly from the boxes, without even bothering to put them on the racks.

The Beatles closed their career with a double album widely acclaimed as one of their finest LPs ever, almost as varied as the White Album and filled with emotions poignant and hopeful, sad and joyous, and optimistic and loving. The title was derived from a song John wrote for Ringo to sing on the album: a Liverpool expression meaning, approximately, "let's get out of here," and a perfect tongue-in-cheek way for the Beatles to take a final bow.

Paul kicked off both sides one and three of the album, with two versions of a song that explored the definitions of the word "stars." In the opening track, "Venus and Mars," the "stars" were celebrities, rock stars – and, sure enough, the song burst into "Rock Show," Paul's celebration of live rock and roll, with a built-in promise that the Beatles would play Madison Square Garden and the Hollywood Bowl in the course of their last tour. When the reprise of the song resurfaced at the beginning of side three, the "stars" were now of the astronomical variety, in the Beatles' sole dabble into science fiction. *Venus and Mars*, in fact, had been the working title for the album, until John brought in "Goodnight Vienna."[188]

The "Venus and Mars" reprise was succeeded in turn by the song that was perhaps the biggest and best surprise on the album. With "Walk Away Dreaming," Brian Jones, long respected for his skills as a musician and arranger, finally came into full flower as a songwriter. A high-energy rocker with a majestic sweep, "Walk Away Dreaming" was as strong as any of John's, Paul's, or George's contributions to the album, or indeed any of their albums – Brian had written a Beatles song as classic as any other.

The song was so good, in fact, that it was picked for a single release by the group. Brian was to be on the A-side of a Beatles single! Paul mentioned it casually one day in the studio as they approved the final mix of the track – "that one should come out on 45" – but it deeply moved Brian. He went off to an anteroom, sat down, and mused. For so long in the Rolling Stones he had wanted to be the center of attention, or at least to be recognized as a key part of the group. His reward had been ostracism from the Stones. He had wanted a sexy, desirable girlfriend, and his reward had been Anita's betrayal. But then he'd decided he wanted God more than any of those things, and gave up on all that – and his reward had been not only God, but a true and happy marriage, and real recognition for his musical talent. *Funny how that works,* he thought. But, like John Lennon, he could now say he was genuinely happy.

Paul contributed a number of love songs, including the deeply romantic "My Love." But he also experimented a bit. "Bluebird," which continued the theme of flight as a metaphor for freedom that Paul had used on *Band on the Run*, was built on jazzy-sounding diminished-seventh chords. "Picasso' Last Words (Drink to Me)" was chopped up and mixed, to emulate the painter's style, and included snippets of songs from both the new album and *Band on the Run*. "Junior's Farm" and "Letting Go" were straight-up rockers, the latter with a soul-like horn section added.[189]

George contributed a straightforward love song, "You," and a sardonic self-portrait, "Dark Horse," along with the gentle "Be Here Now," a deep philosophical rumination that stood with the finest of his spiritual songs.[190]

John's "Mind Games" was a complete contrast to the iconoclasm and nihilism of the *John Lennon* album, a deeply spiritual piece driven by Brian's uplifting slide guitar that called on the listener to express genuine love – not the selfish craving of John's last album but real love, given with an overflowing heart.[191]

Some of John's songs, to no one's surprise, were inspired by May and traced both their difficulties and their reconciliation. "What You Got," riding Paul's funky bass guitar line, reached back to the time of their separation, with John begging May to take him back. The string-heavy "#9 Dream" and "Bless You," the latter of which employed the same sort of jazzy chords used for "Bluebird," were both paeans to May, wishing her well without any expectation of reciprocation. "One Day at a Time" evoked their efforts to rebuild their marriage. John's other two contributions, "Whatever Gets You Thru the Night" and "Intuition," were both songs of acceptance, of open hands in contrast to the closed fist he had displayed on his solo album, and John hadn't sounded so joyous in years.[192]

Paul had one more contribution, "Mull of Kintyre," a gentle ballad, done up like a folk song, about his Scottish farm retreat. John persuaded the group that the song should close the album. "I'm going home to my family after the tour," he said. "Paul's going home to his, and to his farm." John wanted to explicitly emulate the ending of J.R.R. Tolkien's *Lord of the Rings,* wherein Sam Gamgee – after all the world-saving adventures, and after seeing Frodo off on his journey over the sea – returned home to his hobbit hole and simply announced that he was back. By putting "Mull of Kintyre" at the end of the album, John said, the Beatles would be saying the same thing: "We've done our bit, now it's time to go home."[193]

Even as they rode off into the sunset, then, the Beatles set one final precedent. Some had wondered for a while how rock and roll and its stars, with their emphasis on youth, would manage to age gracefully. The notion of "retiring" voluntarily from the scene became an increasingly popular one, and helped aging rock bands avoid the spectacle of spending year after year schlepping around concert halls, releasing album after indifferent album, and generally making themselves look pathetic. The Beatles' voluntary retirement helped clear the music scene for the emerging sounds of disco and "New Wave," and the music scene would continue to refresh itself in the same way every ten years or so afterward.

Paul decided that the placement of "Mull of Kintyre" at the end of the album required a bit of extra authenticity, so the Beatles hired the Campbeltown Pipe Band, from the village nearest Paul's farm, to play bagpipes along with them. Brian Jones managed to wheedle his way in and added his own bagpipe, adding one more notch to the amazing array of instruments he had played over the years on first Rolling Stones and then Beatles records.

Still, they wouldn't be the Beatles without classic Beatles humor, and the very last track on the album, as it turned out, was a brief snippet of the band playing their version of the closing theme to *Crossroads,* one of Britain's most popular soap operas.[194]

Goodnight Vienna was the Beatles' best-selling LP of all time, beating out even such previous contenders as *Sgt. Pepper*, partly because it was the announced final Beatles album but also very much on merit. The album produced three Number One singles – "Mind Games," "My Love," and "Walk Away Dreaming." It was one of the group's most critically acclaimed albums and won the Grammy for 1975's Album of the Year.

The Beatles Farewell Tour began with a performance in, fittingly enough, Liverpool on June 21. The group spent the better part of the next year on the road, playing throughout Britain, Europe and Asia, taking a few weeks off, then making a triumphant 30-show return to the United States in the summer of 1976 that would wrap up with a final concert in New York, carried live on the Music Channel. The group's final tour was criticized by some in the emerging "New Wave" scene as being a self-congratulatory exercise, and an easy way to fill their own pockets. But even most New Wave fans felt it was only fitting that the group that had rewritten not only the book, but the entire library, on popular music give itself an appropriate sendoff.

This time around, though, one thing was very different from 1972 – drug dealers and sellers of alcohol were strictly banned, a rule that was enforced even among the road crew. All the Beatles stayed clean and sober for every show. And May and the children traveled with John as much as they could throughout the tour, with May stopping off only when the needs of her film production business required it. They beamed in one another's presence. It was like they were on their honeymoon all over again.

CHAPTER NINETEEN: ALL YOU NEED IS LOVE

June 13, 1985

"It's nine a.m. in London, it's four a.m. in Philadelphia, and around the world, it's time for Live Aid!" announced BBC DJ Richard Skinner, to open the Saturday morning Live Aid show at Wembley Stadium in London. He was speaking to the first of the estimated audience of 3.5 billion who would watch at one point or another that memorable weekend, that *Crawdaddy* would describe on the cover of its next issue as "The Day the World Rocked."

The whole worldwide Live Aid extravaganza had been started by Bob Geldof, the leader of the New Wave group the Boomtown Rats. One evening last September, he'd been watching the BBC news. The British network ran a special report on the famine gripping Manchuria in the wake of the collapse of the Communist government there. Graphic images splayed across the TV screen of starving children and mothers desperately trying to find a few grains of rice; of swarms of hungry Chinese people descending on the meager rations arriving by truck; of governmental bureaucrats, lost in procedures, who could not or would not get help to the suffering masses.[195]

Overcome and in tears, Geldof began writing a song about the catastrophe – a protest song, one that evoked the approaching Christmas season. His first instinct, of course, was to record "Do They Know It's Christmas" with his band, and from the first he thought of donating the receipts of the single to the Chinese aid effort. But then he began to reason: how much good would that do? There was no guarantee the record would be a hit. And even if it were – it would raise, at most, a few thousand pounds? That would be a pittance compared to the vast sums that were obviously needed.

I can't do this myself, he decided. I must involve others. As many people as possible. He contacted Midge Ure of the band Ultravox, and together they hatched the idea of an all-star group, to be promoted under the name "Band Aid," to record the song and release it as a charity single.

Geldof began calling his friends and contacts in the music industry – focusing without apology on enlisting the biggest names he could get, in order to maximize sales of the single. Many of the most popular British and Irish performers of the time were persuaded to give their time free – here Geldof's soon-to-be-famous skill at cajoling performers into helping with the cause first showed itself. Because of the short time frame – Geldof wanted the single out in time for Christmas – the number of performers available was limited, but the lineup assembled was nonetheless startling.

The single was recorded and mixed in one marathon session on November 25, 1984. Along with Geldof and Ure, the session included: David Bowie; Peter Gabriel; Paul Young; Jim Kerr of Simple Minds; Jody Watley; Keren Woodward of Bananarama; Paul Weller of the Jam; George Michael of Wham!; Sting of the Police; and the members of U2, Spandau Ballet, Duran Duran, Heaven 17, Kool and the Gang, Tears for Fears, Status Quo, Culture Club, Frankie Goes to Hollywood and Big Country.

The record was a sizable hit, reaching Number One in Britain and Number 13 in the United States. But it was only the beginning.

The Band Aid single was barely released when calypso great Harry Belafonte wondered why American artists were not making a similar effort. Together with fundraiser Ken Kragen, he began assembling a group of American singers to make their own benefit single. Belafonte and Kragen, like Geldof, found the music community most eager to help, and Michael Jackson and Lionel Richie were asked to write an appropriate song. They finished "We Are the World" on the night before the recording session, on January 21, 1985, for what was soon dubbed "USA for China."[196]

The sessions brought out an even more amazing array of stars. Particularly noteworthy performances were given by Stevie Wonder, Bruce Springsteen, Bob Dylan, Ray Charles, and, on the song's middle eight, the brief trio of Jennifer Warner, Sam Cooke and Cyndi Lauper.[197]

The obvious next step was to produce a *We Are the World* album, including both the British and American benefit singles, as well as tracks contributed by participating artists. Both the album and the single were smash hits, reaching Number One on the American charts.

Geldof, meanwhile, was working hard to coordinate his relief efforts with all the others out there. "I didn't want us competing with each other, stepping on each other's toes," he later said. "The more money going to buy food for China, the better – who cares who got the credit for raising it?"

Toward that end, Geldof's Band Aid organization – soon renamed "Live Aid," in anticipation of the benefit concert Geldof and Ure were already planning – offered to act as a clearinghouse coordinating relief efforts among the myriad charitable groups already working to raise funds for China. The response was overwhelming. Geldof was actively involved in all aspects of the work, determined to ensure that overhead remained as low as possible and that no one siphoned money off for any reason.

When Live Aid announced that its next step would be a benefit concert, the list of performers wanting to participate grew rapidly. By the time "We Are the World" topped the charts in April, the concerts had been expanded into a set of two shows, scheduled over two days, in London and Philadelphia. The concerts would be linked by a satellite broadcast and aired on television networks worldwide, so that all around the world people would be able to see the shows. Throughout the concerts phone banks would be set up to enable viewers at home to make donations.

The concerts had already grown from a single charitable event into the most colossal musical performance that had ever been planned. And still events continued to gain momentum.

First, it occurred to Geldof and Ure that the concerts shouldn't be confined to Britain and the United States. Accordingly, concert events were arranged for the weeks leading up to the two main shows, scheduled for July 13-14, for venues throughout Europe, Russia, Asia, and even some African and South American states. Only most of the Middle East, still clinging together as a bloc despite the fall of the Soviet Union six years earlier, stubbornly refused to participate – but even there, Israel would allow the broadcast and stage local concerts.[198]

Then, some of the church organizations participating in the relief effort mentioned to Geldof that local parishes, in the spirit of "using music to do good" the Live Aid events had generated, were staging special choir performances to help raise funds at their churches in the weeks before the July shows. That's when it dawned on Bob: why should only rock performers participate? What kind of response would Live Aid get if it approached jazz musicians, country musicians, classical, folk, you name it?[199]

Again, Geldof found the answer was an overwhelming yes. An almost crazy explosion of scheduled performances, beginning at the start of May, marked the calendars of cities large and small throughout the world. There was the "Country Aid" show scheduled for June 29-30 in Nashville and featuring a dazzling array of country stars. There was "Swingers' Aid" in Las Vegas, with pop singers like Mel Torme, Steve Lawrence and Eydie Gorme, and a reunion of the "Rat Pack," and with Johnny Carson as master of ceremonies. There were jazz shows, blues shows, folk shows. There was a special performance of the New York Philharmonic conducted by Leonard Bernstein at the Metropolitan Opera. Scranton, Pennsylvania, even held a "Polka Aid" show. Although the phone banks were not opened up until the climactic July shows, the Music Channel, in the United States, and its various offshoots carried video of many of the performances.

Performers unable to get a spot on any of the bigger shows organized smaller ones, in smaller venues and smaller cities, until it seemed, for a while in the late spring and early summer of

1985, that just about everyone who could carry a tune or play an instrument was devoting at least a little time to getting on a stage and trying to raise some money to help curb the famine in China. They were joined by comedians, too – a "Comic Relief" show was organized in Los Angeles, and comics also showed up at the music concerts to introduce the bands.[200]

In the bargain, music fans in 1985 – regardless of their tastes – had the chance to see thousands of fine, outstanding live performances. For rock fans, the two shows on the second weekend in July were possibly the greatest two days in the history of live rock music.[201]

First onstage were the Coldstream Guards, to play the Royal Salute and British national anthem as Prince Charles and Princess Diana – greeted by Bob Geldof – took their seats. Then followed a benediction, delivered by the Archbishop of Canterbury, who was joined onstage by representatives of the Catholic, Lutheran, Methodist, Jewish, Hindu, and Buddhist faiths as well – the Buddhist monk coming from Shenyang in the famine-stricken land.[202]

Throughout the shows, every hour or so an appeal to the viewers to donate funds was repeated – Geldof was adamant that the point of the shows not be missed. Due to the many names on the lineup, sets were generally limited to three songs each.

About three hours into the London show, at 7 am East Coast time, the Philadelphia show at JFK Stadium opened, and the audience watching at home saw the performances flip back and forth from one continent to another until the close of the London show. This would be repeated on Sunday as well.

The Saturday show in London was dominated by New Wave acts, including Graham Parker, the Psychedelic Furs, Rockpile, Big Country, Blondie, Cyndi Lauper and others – most especially, of course, the Boomtown Rats, with Bob Geldof declaring that that day was the greatest of his life. The evening was closed by Genesis, who reunited with former lead singer Peter Gabriel in one of the weekend's many memorable band reunions, and by the Bee Gees, who returned to the mid-70s with their disco flair.[203]

The Philadelphia show on Saturday was more varied, ranging from the funk of George Clinton to the heavy-metal crunch of Black Sabbath (reunited with singer Ozzy Osbourne) to the country sound of Willie Nelson to the mainstream rock and roll of Bob Seger, the New Wave sounds of the Talking Heads, and the classic mid-Sixties sound of the Four Seasons. Pop-rock band Journey got the crowd singing much of their 1982 hit "Don't Stop Believin'."[204]

The first of a series of big surprises was the set by Janis Joplin, who had virtually retired from the music business. After her 1971 hit album *Pearl,* Janis' musical career had slowly faded. She hadn't had a hit in almost two years when, in 1975, she received a great boost from, of all things, an appearance on the country music and comedy show *Hee Haw,* where Janis sang a stunning version of the Hank Williams classic "I'm So Lonesome I Could Cry." At the end of the show, she was welcomed by Buck Owens, who related to the audience a 1968 incident in which Janis had visited him backstage and gushed her admiration, only to have him throw her out and call her a "dirty hippie." Janis had tears in her eyes as Buck apologized before the TV audience, telling her, "That was the worst thing I could have said, and it's completely untrue. You are a fine talent and a fine lady."

More telling for her career, her performance in a few of the comedy sketches was so good that her manager decided to begin pitching her to Hollywood for acting gigs. She got her big break about a year after the *Hee Haw* gig, when she was cast as "Red Hot Mama" in the comedy flick *Smokey and the Bandit*. From that point on, she quickly became Hollywood's go-to girl when a brassy Southern lady was required. Live Aid was her first live performance in nearly ten years.

After a warmly-received set by a reunited Simon and Garfunkel, a huge roar welcomed the also-reunited Doors. After completing their 1971 album *L.A. Woman,* Jim Morrison had moved to Paris. The band followed him there later in the year and recorded what became their final album, *Oeuvre le Chien.* The Doors announced their breakup in 1972, Jim Morrison explaining that making music had become uninteresting and that he wanted to do other things. He had worked mostly as a writer since then, completing his 1976 novel *An American Prayer* and writing columns and articles for numerous publications including the *New Yorker, Crawdaddy* and *Esquire.* Now he performed live with the Doors for the first time in 13 years, leading them through a set that culminated in their now-classic "L.A. Woman."[205]

Two soul legends followed the Doors: Stevie Wonder and Sam Cooke. Then the night sky was lit up by a series of 1950s founding fathers. Fats Domino sang three of his biggest hits, followed by the Everly Brothers. An even more ecstatic roar than the one that greeted Jim Morrison was bestowed on Buddy

Holly, who hadn't performed live since 1960, but was urged to take the stage once again, for this special day, by his Beatle clients. Holly, accompanied by the Everlys, sang his two biggest hits, "That'll Be the Day" and "All My Hopes and Dreams."[206]

Two Fifties legends appeared together: Chuck Berry and Little Richard. The "Georgia Peach" greeted the audience by saying, "Bless you all for coming! Bless you all for what you're doing here tonight...now let's play some rock 'n' roll!" Each sang three of their classic songs, accompanied by an all-star band of Fifties and Sixties talent.[207]

The Beach Boys closed the first night in Philadelphia, drawing another huge roar from the crowd as Dennis Wilson, who had entered drug rehabilitation nearly two years before, rejoined the band for the first time since then, his brother Brian, with tears in his eyes, nearly crushing him in a bear hug.[208]

The stages went silent, and the crowds dissipated, but the excitement remained high. The Music Channel ran footage of other Live Aid performances all through the night. Meanwhile, audience members who had purchased tickets for both night's performances made their way to motels, camped out in vans, or just stayed up all night.

The Sunday performances, in contrast to Saturday's, began at the same time – even though that meant the London show would go well into Monday morning.

Up first in Philadelphia, appropriately enough for a Sunday morning, was a gospel performance by the New Testament Baptist Church Choir. Then the parade of rock 'n' roll founders that had closed Saturday night continued with a set by Roy

Orbison. Darlene Love was joined onstage by Linda Ronstadt for a double performance, which included an unforgettable duet on Love's 1963 hit "Today I Met the Boy I'm Gonna Marry." Other classic duets followed: Kenny Rogers and Dolly Parton, Carole King and Carly Simon, Kenny Loggins and Stevie Nicks. These were interspersed around another widely varied program that included funk stars War, New Wave band the B-52's, and soul greats Al Green and Aretha Franklin. Teddy Pendergrass, another soul star who had been in a near-fatal car accident, came onstage in a wheelchair, and with tears in his eyes received the roaring approval of the fans as he sang "Reach Out and Touch." Michael Jackson joined his brothers onstage to sing both his recent smashes and some Jackson Five classics.[209]

As night fell, Bob Dylan appeared before the curtain to perform three numbers. At one point, Dylan thought of saying something about giving some of the money to American farmers, then decided against it. That wasn't the reason for this concert. That could wait for another night.[210]

Only the King of Rock 'n' Roll could have closed such a night in Philadelphia, and Elvis never looked better, opening a seven-song set that started with "Suspicious Minds" and ended with "Jailhouse Rock." Then, most of the two day's performers joined him onstage, where as a group they belted out "We Are the World."

The London show on Sunday started with a single song, "He Ain't Heavy, He's My Brother," performed by the reunited Hollies (sans Graham Nash, who was performing in the United States with Crosby, Stills and Nash). Donovan took the stage next, and to a cry from someone in the audience of "I thought you were dead!" he answered crisply, "Not yet!" With only an acoustic guitar, he sang three of his Sixties hits.[211]

Following a morning and afternoon program that included some of the biggest music names of the Seventies, U2 enhanced their reputation as one of the best and most inspiring live bands of the Eighties, playing a fourteen-minute-long version of their hit "Bad." During the song, lead singer Bono noticed a girl being crushed against the barriers near the front of the stage who was unable to signal the security guards. As the band kept playing the song, he jumped off the front of the stage, made his way to the barriers and rescued the girl, then brought her on stage, where he danced with her before finishing the song.

The Kinks appeared with a stellar set, opening with their 1972 hit "Celluloid Heroes," followed by 1966's "Sunny Afternoon," before rocking things up considerably more with a medley of "You Really Got Me" and "All Day and All of the Night."[212]

Queen's performance was absolutely their finest moment, and went down as one of the greatest performances in rock history, with lead singer Freddie Mercury leading the crowd on "Radio Ga-Ga" and "We Will Rock You."

David Bowie, up next, drew another huge response at the end of his four-song set when, introducing "Heroes" – the song he had written in 1977 after observing a young couple in East Berlin fighting for the freedom to love one another – he dedicated the song to the two young Germans he had seen that day, to his son, to "all our children, and all the children of the world."

The Who were up next, but unfortunately, a technical problem caused a brief interruption of the sound during their opening number, "My Generation." This prompted Keith Moon to declare, tongue-in-cheek, at the end of the song, "Two billion people watching and it's the 'Oo that get the bad microphones!" Their performance was ragged, but powerful, and at the end of "Won't Get Fooled Again," Pete Townshend smashed his guitar, and Keith Moon kicked over his drum set, to another thunderous roar from the crowd.

It was a moment of triumph for Moon. Like John Lennon before him, he'd gone into rehab at the Gladys Presley Center, but not before the Who told him flatly at the end of their 1975 tour that unless he straightened out, he was fired from the band – a move suggested to Pete Townshend by Brian Jones. Keith's problems were partly psychological and required nearly a year of psychiatric treatment before he was ultimately able to rejoin the Who. Fortunately, although a little of his dexterity was gone due to his advancing age and the abuse he'd heaped on his body, the Live Aid concert showed that he hadn't lost his famous sense of humor. He'd already begun to parlay that particular talent into a comedic film career, working with British comedian Rowan Atkinson.[213]

The appearance of Best of Faces was not a surprise, but the rumor mills again had been grinding, this time as to whether either of the former Rolling Stones besides Brian Jones – singer Mick Jagger or guitarist Mick Taylor – would join them onstage. But Jagger was not there. Once his career had hit rock bottom at the end of the 1970s, he had found religion, and was now living a simple life as a Trappist monk in Belgium. He had performed earlier in the Live Aid concerts, appearing at Brussels, almost unrecognizable in robes and shaved head. But he declined to perform any old Rolling Stones songs, doing only hymns instead.[214]

However, Rod Stewart, Keith Richards, Ron Wood, Bill Wyman and Charlie Watts were indeed joined by Mick Taylor as they tore through three of their classics: "Maggie May," "Tumblin' Dice" and "Reason to Believe." Then Tina Turner joined them onstage to sing "Hot Legs" with Rod.[215]

By then it was nearly dawn in London, and the crowd was exhausted. Still, there was one more band to see. And no one wanted to miss them.

The Beatles had promised to perform at various one-off events, but as it happened this was the first time they had performed together since their voluntary "retirement" at the end of the 1975-76 farewell tour. But their records had remained popular. Apple, thanks to Buddy Holly, gained control of the Beatles' back catalog at the end of 1975. All the group's albums were reissued in their original British versions worldwide. Because of the way records had been marketed in the Sixties, many of their hit singles hadn't been album tracks in Britain. So, to collect their greatest non-album hits, Apple also issued a three-record set called *The Audition,* the title referring to a joke John had made at the close of the "rooftop concert" in 1968. Apple had subsequently put out three live albums: *The Beatles in America,* from the farewell tour; *The Beatles at the Hollywood Bowl,* live shows from 1964 and 1965; and *The Beatles Live at the Star Club, Hamburg, Germany, 1962.* A *Live at the BBC* album was also pending in 1985.[216]

John's prediction had been right: Paul was the most active solo Beatle, releasing eight albums by 1985. George had eased into a more relaxed schedule, releasing only four. Ringo surprised everyone with his debut solo album in 1977, though his output had been uneven since then. Brian, now finally respected as a songwriter, released four albums, including one blues and one jazz album all featuring his original compositions, and was rumored to be working on a classical piece as well as traveling to Africa and other locations to record "world music" to be released to audiences who had no idea of the world's vast array of music. He'd also become one of the most sought-after record producers around, working on albums ranging from New Wavers like Blondie and Elvis Costello to the Electric Light Orchestra and even Stevie Wonder.

John had done the least work of all, for it was much more important to him to be with May and his son and daughter. He'd finally given May something she'd always wanted: a real church wedding, on October 8, 1977, the day before his 37th birthday. And in preparation for the wedding, he'd taken a step that no one could have expected just three years earlier: he was baptized as a Catholic. He told anyone who asked that his family and prayer made him happier now than all his years as a Beatle ever had, that he was fulfilled now in a way that even making music could not ever fulfill. He was happier, too, than Janov's therapy could have ever made him. For it wasn't enough simply to remember, he had come to believe. One had to forgive.

It was hard work repairing his damaged marriage, but he'd committed himself wholeheartedly to it. He was determined to win back May's trust. So they made no immediate moves, staying at the Dakota for a few more years, until 1981, when he finally returned to England, selling Tittenhurst and its unpleasant memories and buying a new place in Sussex – not far, as it happened, from one of Paul's new "country" homes – but maintaining a residence in Long Island as well.

Still, he was moved to make music from time to time. In 1978, he'd done an album of oldies titled *Rock 'n' Roll* – which, along with the *Hollywood Bowl* album, fit right in to the "back to basics" New Wave aesthetic. In 1981, he'd made a duet album with Brian Wilson, *West 119th and Menlove*. And just last year, he'd released *Skywriting by Word of Mouth,* with some of his best songs since the Beatle days.[217]

It was on the way home from the sessions on the duet album with Brian Wilson on the night of December 8, 1980, that he had had that weird premonition in the car, on the way back to the Dakota, that something didn't seem right. He'd ignored it at first – but then remembered what Brian had said not long before, the thing Buddy Holly had reminded him, about listening to that "still, small voice." May had been right so often – this sounded like her kind of wisdom – so he asked her what she thought. "If you really feel like you're being told something," she said, "I would honor it." So, just as they were pulling up to the Dakota, he'd asked the driver to continue past and to instead head for a restaurant nearby in the Upper West Side for a late-night meal, from which they called home to check on the kids.

Meanwhile, a disturbed young man named Mark David Chapman, who had waited all night on 72nd Street and who seemed frustrated that Lennon had not returned to the Dakota, suddenly took off running. He later told police that he had decided to run back to Central Park and kill himself there. He nearly succeeded in that task anyway – heedless of the traffic in his agitation, he was struck by an oncoming car as he ran out onto Central Park West. He was knocked unconscious but suffered only relatively minor injuries; fortunately, the car's driver hit the brakes soon enough. But police investigating the incident found the gun on him. When he regained consciousness, they asked him about the gun – and his answer was, "I need to kill John Lennon." He was promptly committed to a psychiatric hospital.

John was sanguine to the press when he learned of the gunman's presence – "Guess I had a better night than he did" – but privately he was in awe: Brian, and Buddy, and May, had been right, once again.

Five years later, he still hadn't forgotten the memory of that night. It was another lesson learned.

May, of course, came back to Apple, continuing her stellar career both as a film director and as the head of the Apple Films division. A row of Oscars now lined a shelf outside her office in London.

The "Fab Four plus one" by 1985 had clearly aged when seen up close, but betrayed no sign of slowing down as they took their places. John and George hadn't had their hair so short since 1964 (aside from John's severe crop in 1974) – quite a change for the two who had always had the longest hair of the "longhairs." More importantly, a beaming John, even as he walked with his now-permanent limp, looked as exuberant as he had on the farewell tour.

As he stepped toward the microphone, May Ling sprinted from the backstage area to his side. The crowd cheered wildly for a full five minutes as John and May embraced and kissed, the other Beatles looking on with benevolent smiles. One last tuning of their guitars, and they were ready.

In one more memorable moment for Live Aid, the sun popped over the London skyline just as John began the opening lines of "Come Together." The rising sun was greeted by George's "Here Comes the Sun."

Each of the Beatles would sing one song that morning, and Ringo's number was "With a Little Help from My Friends," the *Sgt. Pepper* song that evoked reaching out to one another for a helping hand. Brian then sang his soaring 1977 hit "Walk Away Dreaming," and the awe the song invoked was felt by more than one person that weekend.

Finally, Paul closed the Beatles' set with his 1969 plea to "Let It Be." The world has learned a little bit about love, the song seemed to say, now it was time to let it blossom.

With the Beatles still onstage, Bob Geldof came out, accompanied by David Bowie, Pete Townshend and Rod Stewart, declaring, "If you're gonna cock up, you might as well cock up in front of two billion people."[218] But then he made an announcement that brought the final lengthy cheer of the evening: preliminary figures reported by the accountants were showing that the dozens of shows, the contributions from the churches and religious organizations, capped by the final show, had indeed raised enough money, coupled with aid from world governments and all the other private donations, to ensure that the famine in China would be stopped in its tracks.

The London performers then returned to the stage to sing the final song of the Live Aid concert, "Do They Know It's Christmas."

After the final applause died down, as the crowd began filtering out into the growing sunshine of north London, the road crew began taking down the equipment. Most of the performers filtered backstage, where they would rest or have small celebrations before leaving Wembley – it would take a while to clear the stadium, and leaving in such ostentatious means as a helicopter or a limousine would have seemed crass in light of the weekend's cause.

John Lennon briefly walked out to the side of the backstage area, watching the roadies disassembling the cords, disconnecting the amplifiers, putting away Ringo's drum kit. Then he gazed out over the lip of the slowly emptying stadium seats, toward the London skyline, beginning to arise to another day.

Suddenly he noticed someone at his side. He looked to his right to see his thirteen-year-old daughter, Julia. She was a lovely girl, clearly on her way to becoming a beautiful woman, and John smiled as he thought of how much she reminded him of her mother.

"It's been a good day, hasn't it?" she said.

John nodded. "Yeah," he said. "Not bad at all."

APPENDIX A: World Events 1941-85

Josef Stalin's suicide on June 30, 1941 threw the Soviet government into disarray at a deeply critical moment of the Second World War. Even as the German armies plunged deep into western Russia, the sudden vacuum at the top of the government provoked an immediate power struggle, with secret police head Lavrenti Beria, Foreign Minister Vyacheslav Molotov, and a number of Red Army generals and Politburo apparatchiks among those contending for power. Molotov finally managed to thwart his opponents and emerged as the new General Secretary, but only at the end of three weeks' worth of maneuvering. As a result, the Soviet Union's armies and air units were less than thoroughly organized to combat the German onslaught. The Russians eventually recovered, but not in time to prevent the fall of both Moscow and Leningrad (St. Petersburg) to the onrushing Nazis in the fall of 1941. Molotov's new government regrouped in Kuibyshev (Samara), and the front finally stabilized along a line running south from near Gorky (Nizhny Novgorod) roughly along the Oka River, but the Soviet Union had taken a severe beating and still threatened to collapse. These were the darkest days of the war, as the Japanese in December attacked Pearl Harbor and the British territories in Asia, bringing both Japan and the United States into the war.[219]

The Soviets managed to defeat a major German offensive in the south at Stalingrad (Volgograd) in late 1942 as well as another attempt to cross the Volga at Saratov in 1943[220], but they were a long way from being able to resume the offensive, and did not in fact do so until late in 1943. Most of the spring of 1944 was taken up with the massive and bloody struggle to recover Moscow. Thus, by the time the Western Allies landed at Normandy on June 6, 1944, the Red Army was still a long distance from even the prewar border of Poland.[221]

Stalin's suicide also had ripple effects further west. The failure of nerve of the leader of the socialist movement, in contrast to the resolute stand of Winston Churchill in Britain, had the effect of throwing Communist party members elsewhere in the world into disrepute. In occupied France, for example, the Communist party was eclipsed as the center of resistance to the Nazis by Charles de Gaulle's Free French movement, operating from England. By 1944, enough former French military personnel had managed to slip out of the country and regroup in England that de Gaulle was able to join the Normandy invasion at the head of a virtually reconstituted, and formidable, French Army, rearmed with American weapons and equipment.[222]

The new Soviet government had Stalin's ruthlessness but not his propaganda skills, and they soon found themselves having difficulty in gaining the diplomatic upper hand with the West. Whereas Stalin, for all his bloodthirstiness, could pose as a genial "Uncle Joe" to Allied diplomats, Molotov had a coldly intellectual, condescending demeanor that was off-putting to nearly everyone who encountered him. Molotov's inability to connect with others was apparent in the summit talks between himself, Churchill and President Franklin Roosevelt held at Teheran in 1943. He was unable to make a persuasive case for revising the borders of Poland, or for annexing the Baltic States and Finland, as Stalin had wished; Churchill pointed out that the boundaries of those countries had been agreed to by the Soviet

Union in treaties in 1921 and that the states in question had done nothing to abrogate those treaties. Britain had entered the war to defend Poland, he pointed out, and he would not accept any major revisions to Poland's borders; at the most, the Soviet Union could pick up some small pieces of territory (he agreed as well that Vilnius and Memel would go to Lithuania and that Danzig, or Gdansk, would become permanently Polish along with a small slice of German territory to its east). But the Baltic States and Finland must remain independent, and Poland must retain "substantially" its 1939 borders, and neither Churchill nor FDR would be budged from this position.[223] Molotov also attempted to pressure the Western Allies into moving up the opening of a second front in France into 1943, to relieve German pressure on the Soviet Union; but Churchill and FDR both pointed out that the Red Army was not advancing either. Molotov said with irritation, "We are not yet ready." FDR replied, "Why then do you ask us to move before we are ready?"

The Western Allies did clear the Axis armies out of North Africa by mid-1943. They occupied Sicily and then landed in Italy as Mussolini was overthrown and the Italians surrendered. However, the Germans immediately occupied Italy. At that point, Hitler ordered the arrest of Pope Pius XII as part of his campaign to gain control over (and ultimately eliminate) the various Christian churches in the New Order of Nazi-occupied Europe. But an intelligence officer in the SS, a devout Catholic who was uncomfortable with the notion of arresting the Pope, made contact with elements of Abwehr (German Army intelligence) who were plotting against Hitler. The Abwehr men in turned warned the Vatican. The Pope and a few cardinals were spirited out of Rome and through the Italian countryside, racing ahead of the SS in a Hollywood-worthy saga (and indeed Hollywood would make a movie about the event in 1952). Escaping Italy in an innocuous-looking fishing boat, the Pope was taken to a British submarine which had been contacted by the Italian resistance. The submarine took the Pope to England, and from there he boarded a ship to the United States, where he set up a temporary Vatican-in-exile in St. Patrick's Cathedral in New York (the Catholic Church today refers to this time as the "Second Babylonian Exile"). Once there, the Pope issued a papal bull excommunicating Hitler and other Catholics in Germany's leadership, and declaring anathema any Germans who cooperated with them. There was no immediate effect on the German war effort, other than the immediate arrest of hundreds of Catholic priests and the defiling of the Vatican, including the placing of an ugly concrete swastika in St. Peter's Square (removed when Rome was taken by the Allies in June 1944). But it's impossible to know how much the attacks on the Church sapped the will to fight among German Catholics, though after the war many of them said that, to the extent they fought on, they did so out of fear of retaliation rather than loyalty.[224]

The Western Allies, including the rebuilt French Army, had by September 1944 broken out of their beachhead at Normandy, liberated most of France, and advanced practically to Germany's western border. Here they stalled, as the retreating Germans had destroyed the French railway system, and the Allies needed time to repair the lines to bring their supplies forward. The Allies attempted to use trucks to compensate, but they were unable to adequately supply the armies. (General George Patton would later regard it as significant that trucks were unable to meet his logistics needs and that the railroads were necessary.)[225]

At that point, Hitler shocked his generals by declaring that he planned to go over to the offensive in Russia, driving the Red Army back. He reasoned that another defeat at this point would demoralize the Red Army and cause the overthrow of Molotov and the final collapse of Russia, after which he could turn west and deal with the Western Allies. When it was pointed out that the Western Allies, at Germany's border, constituted the more immediate threat, Hitler declared that Germany's "West Wall" defenses, built before the war, would stop cold any Allied offensive, at least long enough for Germany's new "wonder weapons" like the V-2 rockets to turn the tide of the war.[226]

So the Russians, who by this point had advanced in the center of their front to around Orsha, were thrown back by an unexpected German counteroffensive, which succeeded in advancing almost to Smolensk. The counterattack punched a huge bulge into the Soviet front line, leading the Western Allies to dub the onslaught "the Battle of the Bulge." But the effort did not succeed in provoking the fall of the Soviet Union; all it did was squander Germany's last remaining offensive strength. It did, however, further delay – by months – the Soviets' advance into Eastern Europe.

Meanwhile, in the West, an argument had broken out between the British commander, Field Marshal Bernard Montgomery, and Patton over the next offensive action to take. Montgomery wanted to drop the British First Airborne Division into the Dutch town of Arnhem in order to seize the bridges over the Rhine there. British armored divisions would then advance north and link up with the paratroopers, and the way into north Germany would be open. Patton wanted to push east through the Ardennes – he believed that the West Wall had long been denuded of its heavy guns, sent to Russia instead, and would therefore present no obstacle – and cross the Rhine around Mainz. The Allied supreme commander, General Dwight Eisenhower, rather than picking between the two hotheaded generals, decided that the Allies had sufficient resources to carry out both plans simultaneously – which would prevent the Germans from concentrating against either one.[227]

The two assaults began on October 15, 1944, with the airborne drop into Arnhem. The Germans had so stripped the region of tanks for their assault against the Russians that they did not have enough armor to thwart the unexpected British offensive, and Montgomery succeeded in taking the Arnhem bridges. Patton, meanwhile, was right about the West Wall; he broke through easily and quickly advanced to the Rhine. By early November – even as the Germans were still advancing against the Soviets – the whole Western Front had crumbled, and the Allies were into Germany proper.

Eisenhower now summoned his generals to brief them on a plan quickly drawn up to exploit the German collapse. Montgomery and the British would continue their advance, securing the Ruhr and then pushing east, sweeping around Berlin from the north. Omar Bradley and his American forces, with the support of the French, would advance northeastward from France, aiming to cross the Elbe, take Leipzig, and wheel around Berlin from the south to link up with Montgomery and thereby surround the German capital. Patton was chagrined that he would not be part of the final assault on Berlin, but Eisenhower pulled him aside and told him he had a special objective in mind for him: he was to race across southern Germany, cutting off any possibility of the Nazis retreating into the Alps to carry on a guerrilla fight there; then, Eisenhower said, "get as far into Czechoslovakia and Poland as you can." Whatever Molotov had said, the Western Allies understood that the best way to secure Poland's borders would be with boots on the ground. Furthermore, Roosevelt had quietly suggested to Eisenhower that he didn't trust Molotov and that if the Russians got to Poland first, they would almost certainly attempt to establish a Soviet puppet state.[228]

Patton carried out his mission spectacularly. By Christmas, with the Russians still having advanced only to Minsk after resuming the offensive, he had liberated Prague and most of Czechoslovakia and wheeled northward to take Lwow in southeastern Poland. He would finally meet the advancing Red Army at Brest-Litovsk in eastern Poland. The Soviets managed to occupy a corner of northeast Poland (which they kept permanently, incorporating it into the Soviet Union) but got no further. The Russians were forced to settle for occupying the Baltic States and Finland – where Communist governments were quickly installed – and the East Prussia region of Germany, which had been awarded to them as an occupation zone in the second summit meeting, at Yalta, held December 28, 1944 to January 9, 1945. But they got no other part of Germany or Poland and none of Czechoslovakia. They were more successful further south, occupying Romania, Hungary, and Bulgaria in January, and meeting up with Communist leader Josip Broz Tito who had driven the Germans from Yugoslavia, but the British managed to land troops to secure the surrender of the Germans in Greece.

As the Allies advanced into eastern Poland, paramilitary units in the Polish capital, Warsaw, rose in revolt against the Germans. The Americans quickly organized a drop of the 101st Airborne Division into the Polish capital to help hold the city against the Germans. But bad weather then closed in, preventing the resupply of the beleaguered Allied forces for nearly two weeks.[229] At one point, a German commander sent a message to General McAuliffe, the commander of the 101st, demanding his surrender; McAuliffe scrawled back a single-word reply: "Nuts!"[230] Finally the weather broke, and the Allied air forces – who by this time had virtually destroyed the Luftwaffe – resupplied Warsaw's defenders until Patton's tanks were finally able to reach the Polish capital.

The final assault on the capital of Nazi Germany began three days before Christmas, with Berlin now utterly cut off. Although Allied bombers and artillery devastated the city, the Germans fought bitterly, and the Americans and British each suffered some 200,000 casualties – more than the Americans lost in every other engagement of the war – in taking the city. The siege lasted until the end of February, by which time the Soviets were securing their control of southeastern Europe, other German forces elsewhere were being mopped up, and numerous German commanders were ignoring Hitler's orders and surrendering on their own. Finally, on March 2, with American units just blocks from the Reich Chancellery and his bunker, Hitler killed himself.

The Germans formally surrendered one week later, on March 9, ending the war in Europe.[231]

The third summit conference among the Allied leaders was originally to have been held in April, but Roosevelt's death on April 12 forced a postponement until May 22.[232] Still, when the conference opened in Potsdam in defeated Germany, the new American president, Harry Truman, found Molotov no easier to deal with than had FDR, and Molotov's hopes of either manipulating or intimidating him were soon dashed. The Allies made some preliminary agreements regarding the end of the war. It was agreed that Poland would have its 1937 borders with the exceptions of the "panhandle" region in the far northeast annexed by the Soviet Union and the Vilnius region, given to Lithuania, and that Germany would cede Danzig and a piece of East Prussia to Poland. The occupation zones were agreed upon: the Soviets in East Prussia, the Americans in eastern Germany between the Elbe River and the Polish border (surrounding Berlin), the British in northwestern Germany and the French in southwestern Germany.[233] Berlin was likewise divided into four occupation zones, with the Soviets gaining much of the eastern half of the city. (The flight of Germans from this zone would soon prove such an embarrassment to Moscow that in 1953 they erected the notorious Berlin Wall, encircling East Berlin and making a virtual prison out of the Soviet zone.)[234] But on other matters, agreement fell apart. No agreement could be reached on the future government of postwar Germany or on reparations, and the Soviets refused to recognize the governments in Poland and Czechoslovakia that had been installed by the Western Allies. Most significantly, Molotov refused to commit to entering the war against Japan as the United States had requested at both Teheran and Yalta, saying only that "the Soviet Union will act in accordance with its interests."[235]

As it happened, the development of the atomic bomb removed the need for Soviet intervention in the Japanese war anyway, but Molotov nonetheless declared war on Japan following the drop of the first bomb on Hiroshima on August 6. A second bomb was dropped on Nagasaki on August 9, and Japan formally surrendered five days later, but that didn't stop the Soviets from occupying Manchuria, the northeastern region of China that had been under Japanese occupation since 1931. The United States hastily landed troops in Korea to ensure that that peninsula (under Japanese rule since 1910) would be secured, and Truman adamantly refused to allow the Soviets a zone of occupation in Japan itself; clearly, the Truman administration already had come to distrust the Soviets.[236] With Japan's surrender, the Chinese civil war broke out again, with Chiang Kai-shek's Kuomintang driving the Communists under Mao Zedong out of their bases in northwestern China. Mao fled to Manchuria, where the Soviets promptly set him up in the provincial capital of Shenyang (Mukden) as the leader of the so-called "People's Republic of China." Some Americans, including the military liaison to Chiang, General Joseph Stilwell, argued against providing military aid to Chiang, but Truman no longer trusted Molotov and feared that his support for Mao was a bid to seize all of China. The war raged into 1947, with successes and reverses on both sides, until a ceasefire agreement in July 1947 divided both Manchuria and Sinkiang (called the "People's Republic of East Turkestan") from China proper. The Soviets attempted to do the same in Tibet, but were thwarted by British intervention. (It was during this Chinese war in 1946 that a wealthy Shanghai merchant who was the father of May Ling, future wife of Beatle John Lennon, fled China to bring his family to New York to live.)[237]

The Americans and British at this point might have thought they were winning the scramble with Communism for the shape of the postwar world. But before the end of 1947, the Soviets pulled off a series of amazing coups that would alter the entire shape of the postwar world, even at home in America and England.

The Labour government of Clement Attlee, which had succeeded Churchill in the British elections of July 1945, now moved to grant independence to India. Mahatma Gandhi, the Indian independence leader, prepared to set up a British-style democracy. But Mohammed Ali Jinnah, the Muslim leader, declared that the Muslims of India must have their own country, separate from the Hindu-dominated India. Gandhi reluctantly agreed to the partition of India into two states, India and Pakistan.

But almost no one was prepared when Pakistan, just two days after independence, suddenly signed a very binding treaty of alliance with the Soviet Union.[238]

Then, in the succeeding weeks of 1947 and into 1948, a wave of uprisings and coups swept the Middle East, each one more disastrous than the next from the standpoint of the West. It transpired that immediately after the war, Soviet agents had made contact with various Muslim leaders in the Middle East, many of whom had for years resented British domination in the region and Jewish immigration into Palestine and who had been pro-Nazi during the war. Now some of these same leaders turned on their Western-allied governments. In Iran, Mohammed Mossadegh, a member of the Iranian parliament, led a coup against the Shah; once Mossadegh took power, he too signed a treaty with Moscow, and Soviet troops promptly entered Iran for "protection" as British oil company officials were expelled.[239] In Iraq, Syria, Jordan, Egypt, and Libya, royal governments were overthrown by "nationalists" who soon proved to have strong Soviet ties. In Turkey, the Turkish Socialist party – despite Russia's longstanding enmity toward Turkey – ousted President Ismet Inonu and called for Soviet "assistance." Even in Saudi Arabia, the heartland of the Islamic religion, the royal government was forced to give way to a new group of secular leaders who had Soviet ties.[240]

The alliances were gathered together on May 1, 1948 – a major Communist holiday – with the signing of the Treaty of Helsinki, the so-called "Helsinki Pact," which formally bound together as allies the Soviet Union, Finland, Estonia, Latvia, Lithuania, East Germany, Hungary, Romania, Bulgaria, Turkey, Syria, Iraq, Iran, Saudi Arabia, Jordan, Egypt, Libya, Afghanistan, Pakistan, East Turkestan, Mongolia, and Manchuria. Vietnam and Indonesia joined upon gaining independence later that year, once their new leaders, Ho Chi Minh and Sukarno respectively, "came out" as Communists.[241]

Yugoslavia refused to join, but this was cold comfort to the West – which quickly formed the NATO and PITO (Pacific and Indian Treaty Organization) alliances in retaliation.[242] The Soviets had more than made up for their failure to establish

Communist satellites in Poland and China. They had fulfilled the longstanding Russian dreams of gaining control of warm-water ports on the Mediterranean Sea and Indian Ocean and of obtaining at least a part of India.

Even worse, the Soviets now controlled the majority of projected future oil supplies. The United States was still the leading producer of oil in the world, with large supplies also in Canada and parts of Latin America and Africa. But America's oil supplies were known and finite, at least given the technology of the time; whereas in the newly-Soviet-dominated Middle East, new petroleum resources were now just being tapped, resources that could potentially exceed the world's known oil deposits. Now those resources were in the hands of the Soviet Union, with the Helsinki Pact nations refusing to sell their oil to the West. These resources, coupled with those of Romania, Indonesia, and the Soviet Union's own oil fields, put the Kremlin in possession of potentially a majority of the world's future reserves. Analysts soon were speaking in shock and horror of an "Oil Gap" between the Soviet bloc and the West.

Worse, it came to light over the summer of 1948 that American diplomacy and British intelligence had been compromised in the months leading up to the Soviet's virtual takeover of the Middle East. A high official in the State Department, Alger Hiss, was found to have been a Soviet agent. Likewise, the notorious "Cambridge Spy Ring" consisting of Kim Philby, Donald Maclean, Guy Burgess, and Anthony Blunt (along with possibly others), Soviet agents since the 1930s, had infiltrated the highest echelons of British intelligence. The effect of these spy rings was to focus American and British intelligence on China to the exclusion of burgeoning events in the Middle East until it was too late for the West to take action. Hiss was sentenced to death for treason, and so were the Cambridge Four, but the embarrassment to both governments was acute.[243] The final straw was the successful detonation of a Soviet nuclear weapon in September 1948 – partially the result of information provided by Soviet spies who had infiltrated the American nuclear program.[244]

In Britain, the Attlee government fell in October 1948. Ernest Bevin served as prime minister until elections were held, in April 1949, at which time the Labour government was ousted. The Labour party would not again form a British government until the 1960s under Harold Wilson.[245]

In America, the Republican Party decided to forego both Thomas E. Dewey, the favorite of the party's moderates, and Robert Taft, beloved of conservatives, and persuaded General Dwight Eisenhower, the hero of the European war, to run. Truman subsequently lost the general election in a landslide to Eisenhower.[246] The Republicans also retained control of both houses of Congress, and a new senator from California, Richard Nixon, took the lead on exposing Communist spies and propagandists, an effort made more credible by the Hiss conviction. He was assisted in this effort by Wisconsin Senator Joseph McCarthy, but Nixon remained the key figure in this endeavor. Nixon's efforts were considered heavy-handed by some, but he seldom went after anyone who was not likely to be truly involved with the Soviet Union, as opposed to simply a dissenter. As a result, his work was never discredited, and those who were prosecuted, such as the "Hollywood Ten," did not find many souls willing to go out on a limb to redeem them in subsequent years. The Hollywood Ten are remembered as Soviet propagandists to this day.[247]

In the years since the war, Eisenhower had come to place increased reliance on many of the military men who had served during the war, including two whom others accused of instability – Douglas MacArthur, now serving as viceroy of occupied Japan; and George Patton, his valued tank commander in Europe, who had narrowly survived a jeep near-accident in Germany shortly after the end of the war. Both men soon became among Eisenhower's key advisers – and both urged Eisenhower to take drastic steps to address the "Oil Gap."

First, the exploration of oil was stepped up, and new deposits were found, including in Alaska, off the Gulf Coast, and off the coasts of both Great Britain and Norway.

Second, wherever possible, conservation of oil came into play, as restrictions on production from existing wells reduced the supply and drove up the price of the commodity. Automobiles became smaller and more fuel-efficient; Ford's Edsel failed not primarily because it was ugly (though it was) but because it was the last of the "gas guzzlers," a type of car that had become obsolete in the face of the new compacts. Likewise, with petroleum being the main source of plastic, America and the West never developed a "throwaway" society. Plastic was far too dear to be molded into picnic forks that would be used once and thrown away. When the use of plastics was necessary, they were generally melted down and recycled when discarded.[248]

Alternatives to oil were tapped whenever possible. Coal received a new lease on life, being used not only for energy but in conversion to plastics and to diesel fuel in lieu of petroleum. (This, of course, was music to the ears of coal-mining communities ranging from Scranton, Pennsylvania, to Elkins, West Virginia, to Carbondale, Illinois, to the newer mines out west, all of which were soon enjoying a new era of prosperity.)[249] Nuclear power plants mushroomed as scientists determined that the atom could be used in controlled reactions. Since communities were initially wary of having "little atom bombs" nearby, the Atomic Energy Commission was careful to strictly regulate the safety of plants, and the industry became known for its safety standards, with such plants as the Three Mile Island facility in Pennsylvania, winner of a four-time safety award in 1979 and touted as a model for nuclear safety.[250] The taming of the Tennessee River valley in the 1930s was also emulated elsewhere, as state governments moved to erect hydroelectric facilities wherever possible, which also translated to increased flood protection across the United States. Even sewage was pressed into service, as in the 1960s scientists determined that algae could be used to consume urban sewage, with the algae then being processed into diesel fuel. The railroads were encouraged to continue their experiments with using pulverized coal in steam turbines, bringing the steam locomotive into the modern era.[251]

Since railroads were obviously more amenable to both diesel power and to power provided by overhead wires connected to either nuclear or hydroelectric plants, the railroad industry also received a new lease on life. Eisenhower reluctantly decided he had to abandon his dream of a nationwide system of "Interstate" superhighways modeled on the German autobahn. (Patton, particularly, egged him on. When Eisenhower related a 1919 cross-country trip in which it had taken weeks to cross the country on muddy roads, Patton retorted, "Have you been out of the house, sir, since then? The US Highway system [the "shield" highways] already link every city in the country. Sure, they're not superhighways, but the states can build those at the local level in places where they need them." Patton also reminded Eisenhower of the bottlenecks that nearly stopped the Allied advance in Europe in 1944 and how trucks were unable to resolve the supply dilemma. When Ike asked whether an autobahn would have helped, Patton chuckled: "Ike, for God's sakes, the goddamn Nazis HAD the autobahn, and they lost the war!")[252]

Instead, a series of high-level meetings with railroad officials resulted in the Transportation Act of 1950. The Act created the Department of Transportation, which abolished the Interstate Commerce Commission, Civil Aeronautics Board, and an alphabet soup of smaller agencies, and created five agencies under the DOT: Federal Railroad Administration, Federal Highway Administration, Federal Aviation Administration, Federal Transit Administration, and Federal Maritime Administration. These agencies were to handle all necessary federal issues for their respective modes, ranging from funding to regulations to safety. In addition, the Transportation Act deregulated the railroads in terms of their ability to create rates, while creating a funding mechanism through the FRA by which passenger service would be assured to all communities in the United States exceeding a population of 10,000. The FTA likewise would provide funding for urban and suburban mass transit systems. This, it was hoped, would encourage individuals to leave the car at home at least some of the time. But the Act did allow the railroads much greater flexibility in deciding on schedules for individual trains. (Some conservatives balked at the funding measures, but the railroads successfully made the case that they were asking for no more than was being provided for the use of public highways. In any event, it was clear to most Americans that these measures were taken out of national necessity.)[253]

The Act retained the old ICC restrictions on railroad mergers, which were less common than might have been the case otherwise, but it did remove the old restrictions on allowing railroads to purchase trucking and airline companies. The latter proved especially important; the New York Central Railroad, for example, purchased Pan American Airways, and was soon integrating its passenger trains with flights, allowing passengers to travel seamlessly between the American interior and European capitals without even having to retrieve their luggage on the way. (Overseas air travel was helped by railroad ownership, in fact, since domestic travel on airlines remained very expensive – something that was done as a luxury, by celebrities like Frank Sinatra in the 1950s or the Beatles in the 1960s, rather than something that was commonplace, due to the high cost of aviation fuel.)

Labor laws also were relatively untouched by the Act, which meant that most freight trains still had four-man crews. This was necessary given the technology of the 1950s, but arguably became less so later on. Still, the railroads eventually would decide that if they must have four-man crews and the cabooses they required (both of which would have otherwise been phased out in the 1960s), they should at least earn their keep; beginning in the late 1950s, new cabooses were designed with air compressors that helped trigger the train's air brakes from the rear of the train, making braking smoother.[254] This and other innovations, along with deregulation, allowed the railroads to retain the lion's share of freight business into modern times.[255]

Passenger services, too, evolved over the years, with the railroads adopting innovations ranging from "auto trains" that allowed passengers to bring their cars along, to variations on meal service (family-style meals and "party nights" for college students both becoming popular), to new amenities beyond description. America's system of railroads and mass transit are to this day widely considered the best in the world.[256]

The most indirect effect of the "Oil Gap," but perhaps the most important in the long term, was in the area of research and development. The Eisenhower administration started the ball rolling by providing tax incentives for the implementation of new manufacturing methods that used less fuel. As companies in every industry looked for new and more efficient ways of doing things, research and development became a much more important part of the corporate culture than the three-martini lunch ever had been. This emphasis on R&D allowed America's seven big car companies, five large steel companies, electronics pioneers like Zenith and RCA, and others to remain ahead of the technological curve, which has kept American industry competitive and has kept America the world's leading manufacturer of just about everything right up to the present day.

Overseas, the government of India, shaken by the establishment of the Helsinki Pact, quickly spearheaded the signing of the PITO treaty along with Japan, Korea, Thailand, the Philippines, Australia and New Zealand. Elsewhere in Asia and Africa, NATO members like Britain and France created specific deadlines for independence for their colonies, working hard to establish both Western-style democracy and industrialized structures before they left, lest the Helsinki Pact gain any more ground. Not all of these efforts were immediately successful, but at least no new Asian or African nations after 1948 joined the Soviet alliance formally. In some cases, like in Malaysia and Kenya, Communist guerrillas did have to be defeated before full independence would be granted. The United States made a conscious effort to do the same in Latin America, replacing the exploitation of the past with mutually profitable investment in local industry that increased American popularity in the region and enabling the states of Latin America to thwart the few Communist uprisings that took place, like that of Fidel Castro in Cuba in the mid-1950s.[257]

The Soviet bloc remained deeply formidable well into the 1960s, with Molotov's successor, Nikita Khrushchev, promising the West, "We will bury you." In the Middle East, violence flared from time to time as the Soviet bloc states clashed with the new state of Israel, created as a Jewish homeland in the Holy Land and allied to the West. The Soviets threat seemed at its highest in 1957, when the satellite Sputnik achieved the first successful space flight, a black eye to the Americans.

But, over time, the internal weaknesses of the Soviet system began to set in. Ironically, the glut of oil the Soviets enjoyed, coupled with the inherent bureaucracy and lack of incentive of the Communist system, made their economy sluggish and eventually obsolete in the face of the nimbler economy the Americans had produced by successfully making oil a servant rather than a master. In the Middle East, dependence on the Soviet economy as the sole buyer of oil likewise created a certain somnolence, and the Middle Eastern states lagged behind the rest of the world in industrial development, though they were heavily armed by the Soviets.

The strains on the Soviet system became apparent in the 1960s with the war in Vietnam. Ho Chi Minh, the founder of the Communist state, died mysteriously in 1952.[258] He was succeeded by a line of Politburo members in Hanoi, none of whom had his charisma but all of whom were more prepared to use a heavier hand than he in converting the Vietnamese masses to "socialism." The forced collectivization of the farms brought death and misery to millions, but they also inspired hundreds of thousands of Vietnamese, with nothing to lose, to join a guerrilla movement, supported by the American CIA, aimed at overthrowing the Communist regime. These loosely-organized rebels, soon dubbed the "Viet Tu Do" ("Freedom Vietnamese"), were by the mid-1960s creating a serious threat to the Hanoi regime.[259] Moscow, using bases in friendly Manchuria and Indonesia, began intervening militarily in 1966 under Khrushchev's successor, Leonid Brezhnev. The bloody and brutal Vietnam War that resulted, with its horrifying atrocities, had the effect of discrediting the last remnants of Communist thinking in the West.

Meanwhile, the societies of the Middle East transformed themselves, focusing so thoroughly on the West and on the destruction of America and Europe, and the Christian and Jewish faiths, and especially Israel, that Islam itself began to lose serious claim to being a religion at all, instead taking on the characteristics of a totalitarian system, indistinguishable from the Communism it once abhorred but now apologized for, with simply a few rituals thrown in. Muslims outside the Middle East, disillusioned, began, at great personal risk, to convert to Christian or other faiths, or to establish a "Reform Islam" that interpreted the Koran radically differently from how it was being practiced in the Middle East.

Christian conversion would soon become a feature of life in the West too. The counterculture of the 1960s, and its quest, were symbolized by the Beatles. Initially they were eager simply to embrace a new and less materialistic way of life. Toward that end, they indulged at first in drugs and "free love." Over time, though, millions came up against the same limitations the Beatles had found. Then they turned to faith. Again, at first, they in many cases turned to esoteric Eastern faiths such as the Maharishi had preached to the Beatles. But over time, like May Ling – and, one day, John Lennon – they had turned toward more traditional denominations. The Catholic Church, its reputation enhanced by its heroic stance against the Nazis and by the efforts of the 1950s and 1960s, like the long-running TV show "Bill Frye the Religion Guy," to explain to kids that there is no real divide between religion and science, gained many new adherents. So did the various Protestant churches, the Orthodox churches, the Jewish faith, and the many new churches founded by individuals who believed in Christ but could not find a home among the more traditional faiths. By the 1980s, church attendance was swelling so high in almost every denomination that popular magazines were beginning to speak of a "Third Great Awakening" in the United States.

Eisenhower retired from office in 1956, still a popular president, and was succeeded by Thomas Dewey.[260] However, Dewey was unable to retain Eisenhower's popularity, being plagued with an economic downturn and with accusations that as a longtime isolationist he was uncomfortable with America's role in the Cold War. He narrowly lost in 1960 to the young Senator John F. Kennedy of Massachusetts.[261]

Kennedy served two terms, defeating Senator Barry Goldwater in 1964, despite accusations of connections to the Mafia, some members of whom were rumored to want to "take him out" after his younger brother Robert, as attorney general, began cracking down on the Mob. (Mafia connections would turn up in the oddest places in those days, as when a drifter named Lee Harvey Oswald, arrested in April 1963 after murdering right-wing activist General Edwin Walker in Texas, was found to have some friends who were Mobsters.)[262] His second term was marred somewhat by the ongoing struggle over civil rights, which threatened to turn violent until Martin Luther King made his historic address following the attempt on his life in 1968. Efforts to integrate black and white America have proceeded continually, if not without bumps along the way, since that time.

Kennedy nonetheless remained popular enough in 1968 to propel his second vice president, Hubert Humphrey, into office.[263] But Humphrey soon proved too liberal for the middle-of-the-road political path America had taken, and the economy experienced a significant downturn during his presidency. He lost in a landslide in 1972 to California Governor Ronald Reagan.[264] Humphrey had underestimated Reagan, and had challenged him to a television debate (the first since Kennedy had trounced Dewey doing the same in 1960).[265] This backfired badly; when Humphrey at one point went into a tirade, Reagan – an experienced Hollywood actor before entering politics – gave a slight head shake and replied, "There you go again." Reagan concluded the debate by asking a simple but devastating question: "Are you better off than you were four years ago?"[266]

Reagan, who won a second term against Jimmy Carter in 1976[267], presided over the beginning of the fall of the Soviet Union, an event inherited by his 1980 successor, Robert Kennedy (who defeated Reagan's vice president, Gerald Ford).[268] The strain of the slowing Soviet economy, its inability to keep up with the West, coupled to the increasingly frustrating Vietnam War, which the Soviet Union could not win for all the bombs it dropped and troops it committed, began to tear the very fabric of the Soviet empire apart. Brezhnev died in 1973[269] and was succeeded by Andrei Gromyko, who attempted to end the war "honorably" and reach some sort of accommodation with the West that would allow the resumption of trade. But the war ended in the worst possible way for the Soviet Union. Once Soviet troops were evacuated in 1975, the Hanoi regime hung on in wobbly fashion, but was finally overthrown by the Viet Tu Do in 1977.[270]

Gromyko died in 1977 under mysterious circumstances, but his replacement – after a few false starts – was Alexander

Yakovlev, a notorious dissenter within the ranks of the Politburo. It was hoped that Yakovlev's "new thinking" could produce the reforms necessary for the Soviet Union to survive. Yakovlev did introduce reforms, but they had an effect even he did not anticipate – they opened the floodgates for a populace eager to live in freedom.[271] The attempt to hold free elections in 1978, for example, only weakened the Kremlin's control without creating fundamental changes. The Red Army, once the pride of the nation, was no longer trustworthy after the bloody Vietnam War destroyed its morale, and therefore Moscow was in no position to contest as in 1979 the nations of the European wing of the Helsinki Pact began to agitate for freedom. Finland – whose capital gave its name to the "Helsinki Pact" – Latvia, Estonia, Lithuania, Romania, Hungary and Bulgaria over the course of 1979 threw off their Communist regimes, with no reaction from Moscow. East Germany's Communist rulers stepped down in the midst of a general strike late in the year, which also meant the end of the occupation of East Berlin, which was nominally part of the "German Democratic Republic," and the destruction of the Berlin Wall. East Germany would be reunified with Germany the following year, the capital of Karl-Marx-Stadt reverting to its old name of Konigsberg.[272]

The Soviet Union itself struggled into 1981, until Yakovlev proposed a new treaty with the restive Soviet republics that would give them more autonomy. Communist hardliners at this point arrested Yakovlev and attempted to install a new hardline government under Yuri Andropov. But the Red Army, in an ironic reversal of the 1917 Russian Revolution, refused to obey the orders of the Communist regime, leaving Andropov with no choice but to resign.[273] The Union of Soviet Socialist Republics crumbled, and by the end of 1981, a new government for the "Republic of Russia" had come to power under a nuclear physicist and well-known dissenter, Andrei Sakharov.[274] Although Ukraine voted in a referendum to stay with Sakharov[275], other republics left the Soviet Union, with Belarus voting to unite with Poland and Moldova voting to unite with Romania.[276] Armenia, in the Caucasus, voted for independence. Azerbaijan and the new republics in Central Asia, primarily Muslim, gained their independence but ominously did not abrogate the Helsinki Pact, choosing to join their Muslim neighbors as allies. The Middle East, heavily armed and hostile to the West, remained the greatest potential threat to peace in 1985.

    Manchuria held out a bit longer, though Mao Zedong had died in 1976. Hua Guofeng had initially succeeded Mao and pledged to follow in his footsteps. But he lasted only two years before being replaced by Deng Xiaoping, who – like Yakovlev in Moscow – attempted to reform the Communist system to allow it to survive. His efforts were in vain, though, especially after the fall of the Soviet Union, and he was ousted on February 19, 1984 by the hardline "Gang of Four," which attempted to reintroduce the repressive Communist rule that had claimed so many lives through the 1950s to the 1970s. But instead, protestors – a crowd growing to some 300,000 – virtually froze the capital, Shenyang. The Gang of Four then attempted to use troops to disperse the crowds, but the Manchurian troops – sensing the wave of freedom emanating from Russia, and many of them having been secretly converted to Christianity over the years by missionaries from China proper – followed the example of the Red Army and instead formed a protective cordon around the protestors. The Gang of Four fled the capital but were easily tracked down. At the Gang's would-be hiding place, the soldiers sent to track them found only Jiang Qing, Mao's widow, still alive. She swallowed a cyanide pill, proclaiming, "Long live Chairman Mao and the glorious people's revolution." The commanding officer at the scene muttered over her body, "Mao is dead, and now so are you."

Although a nationwide referendum in Manchuria held one week later voted overwhelmingly for reunification with China, Communist loyalists went out of their way to make a final, bloody act of vengeance. They purposely destroyed the country's irrigation systems and food distribution networks, setting on fire delivery trucks by the hundreds (Manchuria, like other Soviet bloc nations, had gotten used to the oil glut and had become utterly dependent on truck transport in a way that would have seemed absurd in the West) and destroying seed grain that was about to be planted. The resulting famine was beyond the ability of the Chinese government to deal with, and threatened to take the lives of some 100 million people – about half of Manchuria's entire population – by the end of the year. This was the famine that prompted the "Live Aid" concerts: a symbol of the ethos of faith in God and love for one another that, many hoped in the summer of 1985, would continue to grow throughout the world.

APPENDIX B: SELECTED DISCOGRAPHY

ALBUMS BY THE BEATLES

PLEASE PLEASE ME

Released March 1963, rereleased December 1975

Side One:
I Saw Her Standing There
Misery
Anna (Go to Him)
Chains
Boys
Ask Me Why
Please Please Me

Side Two:
Love Me Do
P.S. I Love You
Baby It's You
Do You Want to Know a Secret
A Taste of Honey
There's a Place
Twist and Shout

WITH THE BEATLES

Released November 1963 rereleased December 1975

Side One:
It Won't Be Long
All I've Got to Do
All My Loving
Don't Bother Me
Little Child
Till There Was You
Please Mr. Postman

Side Two:
Roll Over Beethoven
Hold Me Tight
You Really Got a Hold on Me
I Wanna Be Your Man
Devil in Her Heart
Not a Second Time
Money (That's What I Want)

A HARD DAY'S NIGHT

Released July 1964, rereleased December 1975

Side One:
A Hard Day's Night
I Should Have Known Better
If I Fell
I'm Happy Just to Dance With You
And I Love Her
Tell Me Why
Can't Buy Me Love

Side Two:
Anytime at All
I'll Cry Instead
Things We Said Today
When I Get Home
You Can't Do That
I'll Be Back

BEATLES FOR SALE

Released December 1964, rereleased December 1975

Side One:
No Reply
I'm a Loser
Baby's in Black
Rock and Roll Music
I'll Follow the Sun
Mr. Moonlight
Kansas City/Hey Hey Hey

Side Two:
Eight Days a Week
Words of Love
Honey Don't
Every Little Thing
I Don't Want to Spoil the Party
What You're Doing
Everybody's Trying to Be My Baby

HELP!

Released August 1965, rereleased December 1975

Side One:
Help!
The Night Before
You've Got to Hide Your Love Away
I Need You
Another Girl
You're Gonna Lose That Girl
Ticket to Ride

Side Two:
Act Naturally
It's Only Love
You Like Me Too Much
Tell Me What You See
I've Just Seen a Face
Yesterday
Dizzy Miss Lizzie

RUBBER SOUL

Released December 1965, rereleased December 1975

Side One:
Drive My Car
Norwegian Wood (This Bird Has Flown)
You Won't See Me
Nowhere Man
Think for Yourself
The Word
Michelle

Side Two:
What Goes On
Girl
I'm Looking Through You
In My Life
Wait
If I Needed Someone
Run for Your Life

REVOLVER

Released August 1966, rereleased December 1975

Side One:
Taxman
Eleanor Rigby
I'm Only Sleeping
Love You To
Here There and Everywhere
Yellow Submarine
She Said She Said

Side Two:
Good Day Sunshine
And Your Bird Can Sing
For No One
Dr. Robert
I Want to Tell You
Got to Get You Into My Life
Tomorrow Never Knows

SGT. PEPPER'S LONELY HEARTS CLUB BAND

Released June 1967

Side One:
Sgt. Pepper's Lonely Hearts Club Band
With a Little Help From My Friends
Lucy in the Sky With Diamonds
Getting Better
Fixing a Hole
Strawberry Fields Forever
Being for the Benefit of Mr. Kite!

Side Two:
Within You Without You
Penny Lane
Lovely Rita
Good Morning Good Morning
Sgt. Pepper's Lonely Hearts Club Band (reprise)
A Day in the Life

MAGICAL MYSTERY TOUR

Released March 1968

Side One:
Magical Mystery Tour
The Fool on the Hill
Flying
Blue Jay Way
Your Mother Should Know
I Am the Walrus

Side Two:
Hello Goodbye
When I'm 64
In the First Place
Baby You're a Rich Man
All You Need Is Love

THE BEATLES ("THE WHITE ALBUM")

Released October 1968

Side One:
Back in the USSR
Dear Prudence
Glass Onion
Ob-La-Di, Ob-La-Da
Wild Honey Pie
Birthday
While My Guitar Gently Weeps
Happiness Is a Warm Gun

Side Two:
Martha My Dear
I'm So Tired
Blackbird
Not Guilty
Rocky Raccoon
Don't Pass Me By
Why Don't We Do It in the Road
I Will
Julia

Side Three:
Revolution
Yer Blues
Mother Nature's Son
Walking Alone Blues
Sexy Sadie
Helter Skelter
Long Long Long

Side Four:
Across the Universe
Honey Pie
Savoy Truffle
Cry Baby Cry
Revolution #9
Good Night

LET IT BE

Released June 1969

Side One:
Two of Us
I Dig a Pony
Family
I Me Mine
Let It Be
Get Back

Side Two:
I've Got a Feeling
One After 909
Don't Let Me Down
For You Blue
The Long and Winding Road

YELLOW SUBMARINE

Released August 1969

Side One:
Yellow Submarine
Only a Northern Song
All Together Now
Hey Bulldog
It's All Too Much
All You Need Is Love

Side Two:
Pepperland
Sea of Time
Sea of Holes
Sea of Monsters
March of the Meanies
Yellow Submarine in Pepperland

GET BACK: THE BEATLES IN CONCERT

Released November 1969

Side One:
Sgt. Pepper's Lonely Hearts Club Band
With a Little Help From My Friends
Two of Us
Nowhere Man
We Can Work It Out
Get Back

Side Two:
Revolution
She Said She Said
Day Tripper
While My Guitar Gently Weeps
Blackbird
Yesterday

Side Three:
Yer Blues/Walking Alone Blues
Dear Prudence
Across the Universe
Help!
Lucy in the Sky With Diamonds

Side Four:
Don't Let Me Down
Every Little Thing
All You Need Is Love
Hey Jude

ABBEY ROAD

Released March 1970

Side One:
Come Together
Something
Maxwell's Silver Hammer
Oh! Darling
Octopus's Garden
I Want You (She's So Heavy)

Side Two:
Here Comes the Sun
Because
You Never Give Me Your Money
Sun King
Mean Mr. Mustard
Polythene Pam
She Came in Through the Bathroom Window
Golden Slumbers
Carry That Weight
The End

INSTANT KARMA

Released April 1971

Side One:
Instant Karma (We All Shine On)
Another Day
Jealous Guy
Junk
Isn't It a Pity

Side Two:
Cold Turkey
Oh My Love
Something Worth Knowing
Every Night
Maybe I'm Amazed

RAM

Released May 1972

Side One:
Too Many People
Crippled Inside
Ram On
Brother Sam
Uncle Albert/Admiral Halsey
All Things Must Pass

Side Two:
What Is Life?
Heart of the Country
It Don't Come Easy
The Ballad of Sir Frankie Crisp (Let It Roll)
It's So Hard
The Back Seat of My Car

BAND ON THE RUN

Released July 1973

Side One:
Band on the Run
Jet
Has Anybody Seen My Baby
Imagine
Let Me Roll It

Side Two:
Give Me Love (Give Me Peace on Earth)
Apple Scruffs
Live and Let Die
Photograph
Nobody Loves You When You're Down and Out
Nineteen Hundred and Eighty-Five

GOODNIGHT VIENNA

Released June 1975

Side One:
Venus and Mars
Rock Show
Love in Song
What You Got
Be Here Now
Picasso's Last Words (Drink to Me)

Side Two:
Mind Games
No Words
One Day at a Time
Junior's Farm
My Love
You

Side Three:
Venus and Mars (reprise)
Walk Away Dreaming
Bluebird
Whatever Gets You Thru the Night
Dark Horse
Letting Go

Side Four:
#9 Dream
Bless You
(It's All Da-Da Down To) Goodnight Vienna
Intuition
Mull of Kintyre
Crossroads Theme

THE AUDITION

Released November 1975

Side One:
My Bonnie
Ain't She Sweet
Cry for a Shadow
Love Me Do (45 version)
From Me to You
Thank You Girl
I'll Get You
She Loves You

Side Two:
I Want to Hold Your Hand
This Boy
I Call Your Name
Long Tall Sally
Slow Down
Matchbox
Sie Liebt Dich
Komm, Gib Mir Deine Hand

Side Three:
I Feel Fine
She's a Woman
Leave My Kitten Alone
Yes It Is
Bad Boy
If You've Got Trouble
That Means a Lot

Side Four:
I'm Down
We Can Work It Out
Day Tripper
Norwegian Wood (alternate take)
Paperback Writer
Rain
Nowhere Man (live in Japan 1966)

Side Five:
Across the Universe (alternate take)
Lady Madonna
The Inner Light
Hey Jude

Side Six:
What's the New Mary Jane
Old Brown Shoe
Dear Boy
C Moon
You Know My Name (Look Up the Number)

THE BEATLES IN AMERICA

Released November 1976

Side One:
Venus and Mars/Rock Show
What You Got
Jet
Dark Horse
Bless You
Let Me Roll It

Side Two:
Maybe I'm Amazed
Instant Karma
Letting Go
Live and Let Die
Mind Games
It Don't Come Easy

Side Three:
No Reply
I've Just Seen a Face
You've Got to Hide Your Love Away
Come Together
It's So Hard
My Love

Side Four:
Jealous Guy
Here Comes the Sun
In My Life
Give Me Love
Photograph
The Long and Winding Road

Side Five:
Walk Away Dreaming
While My Guitar Gently Weeps
Brother Sam
Blackbird
Yesterday
Julia

Side Six:
Lady Madonna
Band on the Run
A Hard Day's Night
I Saw Her Standing There
I Want to Hold Your Hand
She Loves You

THE BEATLES AT THE HOLLYWOOD BOWL 1964-65

Released November 1979

Side One:
Twist and Shout
She's a Woman
Dizzy Miss Lizzie
Ticket to Ride
Can't Buy Me Love
Things We Said Today
Roll Over Beethoven

Side Two:
Boys
A Hard Day's Night
Help!
All My Loving
She Loves You
Long Tall Sally

ALBUMS BY JOHN LENNON

JOHN LENNON

Released June 1974

Side One:
Mother
Hold On (John)
Now and Then
Scared
Isolation

Side Two:
Remember
Love
Well Well Well
Look at Me
How?
My Mummy's Dead

ROCK 'N' ROLL

Released August 1978

Side One:
Be-Bop-a-Lula
Stand By Me
Rip It Up/Ready Teddy
You Can't Catch Me
Ain't That a Shame
Do You Wanna Dance
Sweet Little Sixteen

Side Two:
Slippin' and Slidin'
Peggy Sue
Bring It on Home to Me/Send Me Some Lovin'
Bony Moronie
Ya Ya
Just Because

WEST 119TH AND MENLOVE (with Brian Wilson)

Released March 1981

Side One:
Free as a Bird
H.E.L.P. Is on the Way
Tight AS
Everybody Wants to Live
You Are Here
Still I Dream of It

Side Two:
Games Two Can Play
Out the Blue
Lines
I Know (I Know)
Goin' On
Meat City

SKYWRITING BY WORD OF MOUTH

Released February 1984

Side One:
(Just Like) Starting Over
Cleanup Time
Nobody Told Me
Real Love
Help Me to Help Myself
Beautiful Boy (Beautiful Girl)

Side Two:
Watching the Wheels
Borrowed Time
Old Dirt Road
Woman
Grow Old With Me

ALBUMS BY PAUL MCCARTNEY

PAUL MCCARTNEY'S WILD LIFE

Released May 1976

Side One:
Let 'Em In
Get on the Right Thing
You Gave Me the Answer
Magneto and Titanium Man
Little Lamb Dragonfly

Side Two:
Silly Love Songs
Call Me Back Again
One More Kiss
When the Night
Treat Her Gently/Lonely Old People

RED ROSE SPEEDWAY

Released April 1977

Side One:
Big Barn Bed
Eat at Home
San Ferry Anne
Mrs. Vanderbilt
She's My Baby
Hi Hi Hi

Side Two:
Beware My Love
Tomorrow
Helen Wheels
Sally G
Listen to What the Man Said

LONDON TOWN

Released March 1978

Side One:
London Town
Café on the Left Bank
I'm Carrying
Backwards Traveler/Cuff Link
Girlfriend
I've Had Enough

Side Two:
With a Little Luck
Famous Groupies
Mamunia
Name and Address
Don't Let It Bring You Down
Warm and Beautiful

BACK TO THE EGG

Released May 1979

Side One:
Reception
Getting Closer
We're Open Tonight
Old Siam, Sir
Daytime Nighttime Suffering
Girls' School
Arrow Through Me

Side Two:
Goodnight Tonight
After the Ball/Million Miles
Winter Rose/Love Awake
So Glad to See You Here
Baby's Request

COMING UP

Released July 1980

Side One:
Coming Up
Front Parlour
Frozen Jap
All You Horse Riders
Blue Sway

Side Two:
Temporary Secretary
On the Way
Mr. H. Atom
You Know I'll Get You Baby
Summer Day's Song
Bogey Wobble

Side Three:
Darkroom
One of These Days
Secret Friend
Bogey Music

Side Four:
Check My Machine
Waterfalls
Nobody Knows

TUG OF WAR

Released April 1982

Side One:
Tug of War
Take It Away
Somebody Who Cares
What's That You're Doing

Side Two:
Ballroom Dancing
The Pound Is Sinking
Wanderlust
Get It
Be What You See
Dress Me Up as a Robber
Ebony and Ivory

PIPES OF PEACE

Released October 1983

Side One:
Pipes of Peace
Say Say Say
The Other Me
Keep Under Cover
So Bad

Side Two:
The Man
Sweetest Little Show
Average Person
Hey Hey
Tug of Peace
Through Our Love

GIVE MY REGARDS TO BROAD STREET

Released September 1985

Side One:
Stranglehold
Not Such a Bad Guy
No Values
Rainclouds
Goodnight Princess

Side Two:
Press
Good Times Coming/Feel the Sun
Talk More Talk
Angry
No More Lonely Nights

ALBUMS BY MANGALAM/GEORGE HARRISON

MANGALAM

Released August 1970

Side One:
I'd Have You Anytime
My Sweet Lord
Wah-Wah
Beware of Darkness
I Live for You

Side Two:
I Dig Love
Awaiting on You All
Dehra Dun
The Art of Dying
Hear Me Lord

LIVING IN THE MATERIAL WORLD (Mangalam)

Released November 1973

Side One:
Living in the Material World
The Light That Has Lighted the World
Don't Let Me Wait Too Long
Who Can See It
Chow Time
Run of the Mill

Side Two:
The Lord Loves the One (That Loves the Lord)
Behind That Locked Door
Try Some Buy Some
The Day the World Gets 'Round
That Is All

THIRTY-THREE AND A THIRD (George Harrison)

Released June 1976

Side One:
Woman Don't You Cry for Me
Dear One
Beautiful Girl
It's What You Value
See Yourself

Side Two:
Let It Down
True Love
Pure Smokey
Crackerbox Palace
It Is "He" (Jai Sri Krishna)

EXTRA TEXTURE - READ ALL ABOUT IT (George Harrison)

Released February 1979

Side One:
Love Comes to Everyone
The Answer's at the End
Simply Shady
So Sad
Blow Away

Side Two:
Faster
Dark Sweet Lady
Your Love Is Forever
Soft Touch
If You Believe

SOMEWHERE IN ENGLAND (George Harrison)

Released June 1981

Side One:
Hong Kong Blues
Unconsciousness Rules
Life Itself
Lay His Head
Baltimore Oriole

Side Two:
Writing's on the Wall
Flying Hour
Far East Man
Sat Singing
Learning How to Love You

GONE TROPPO (George Harrison)

Released February 1983

Side One:
Wake Up My Love
That's the Way It Goes
Soft-Hearted Hana
Greece
Gone Troppo

Side Two:
Mystical One
Unknown Delight
Baby Don't Run Away
Dream Away
Circles

ALBUMS BY RINGO STARR

BEAUCOUPS OF BLUES

Released October 1970

Side One:
Beaucoups of Blues
Love Don't Last Long
Fastest Growing Heartache in the West
Without Her
Woman of the Night
I'd Be Talking All the Time

Side Two:
$15 Draw
Wine, Women and Loud Happy Songs
I Wouldn't Have You Any Other Way
Loser's Lounge
Waiting
Coochy Coochy

SENTIMENTAL JOURNEY

Released November 1971

Side One:
Sentimental Journey
Night and Day
Whispering Grass (Don't Tell the Trees)
Bye Bye Blackbird
I'm a Fool to Care
Stardust

Side Two:
Blue, Turning Grey Over You
Love Is a Many-Splendored Thing
Dream
You Always Hurt the One You Love
Have I Told You Lately That I Love You
Let the Rest of the World Go By

RINGO!

Released June 1977

Side One:
I'm the Greatest
Have You Seen My Baby
Back Off Boogaloo
Sunshine Life for Me (Sail Away Raymond)
You're Sixteen

Side Two:
Oh My My
Step Lightly
Six O'Clock
Devil Woman
You and Me (Babe)

RINGO'S ROTOGRAVURE

Released November 1978

Side One:
A Dose of Rock 'n' Roll
Occapella
Pure Gold
The No-No Song
Husbands and Wives

Side Two:
Cookin' (In the Kitchen of Love)
I'll Still Love You
This Be Called a Song
Only You (And You Alone)
Easy for Me
Las Brisas
Spooky Weirdness

BAD BOY

Released March 1980

Side One:
Who Needs a Heart
Bad Boy
Lipstick Traces
Heart on My Sleeve
You Don't Know Me at All

Side Two:
Hard Times
All by Myself
Call Me
Old Time Relovin'
A Man Like Me

CAN'T FIGHT LIGHTNING

Released October 1981

Side One:
Private Property
Wrack My Brain
Drumming Is My Madness
Attention
Stop and Take the Time to Smell the Roses

Side Two:
Dead Giveaway
Monkey See - Monkey Do
Sure to Fall
You've Got a Nice Way
Lady Gaye

OLD WAVE

Released June 1983

Side One:
In My Car
Hopeless
Alibi
Be My Baby
Oo-Wee

Side Two:
Cryin'
Picture Show Life
As Far As We Can Go
Everybody's in a Hurry but Me
Going Down

ALBUMS BY BRIAN JONES

DON'T LOOK BACK

Released August 1977

Side One:
Thank You (For Being There)
Hard Time Living
Sparkle
Because of You
Windowpane

Side Two:
Circle of Friends
Which Way Home
I Knew It Would Happen
Normal Day
When He Comes

THE BRIAN JONES BLUES PROJECT

Released January 1979

Side One:
Cotchford Farm Blues
Gimme Some Time
Don't You Worry 'Bout Me
Tennessee
End This Game

Side Two:
Never Stop Lovin' You
Born Under a Bad Sign
New World Blues
Pride and Joy
Don't Let 'Em Drag You Down

MOTION OF LOVE

Released July 1982

Side One:
Motion of Love
Nuances
Another Time and Another Place
Everything Is Seen in Dreams

Side Two:
This is Not a Dance Song
Just Passing Through
Mastermind
Supernatural Train

THE FLYING GLOUCESTERMAN

Released January 1985

Side One:
High Wire
Love Thief
Green Flag
Twisted and Tangled
It's No Mystery

Side Two:
Engine Driver
Don't Say Goodbye
Safety in Numbers
Adorable
Live Your Love

SELECTED ALBUMS BY THE ROLLING STONES

THEIR MAJESTIES REQUEST

Released March 1968

Side One:
Sing This All Together
Citadel
In Another Land
2000 Man
Dandelion

Side Two:
She's a Rainbow
The Lantern
Gomper
2000 Light Years from Home
We Love You

LET IT BLEED

Released June 1969

Side One:
Gimme Shelter
Love in Vain
Honky Tonk Women (Country Honk)
Live With Me
Let It Bleed

Side Two:
Sweet Home Chicago
You Got the Silver
Lemon Squeezer
You Can't Always Get What You Want

SELECTED ALBUMS BY BEST OF FACES

EVERY PICTURE TELLS A STORY

Released August 1971

Side One:
Every Picture Tells a Story
Bad 'n' Ruin
Wild Horses
Had Me a Real Good Time
Amazing Grace
Mandolin Wind

Side Two:
Maggie May
Sister Morphine
Sweet Lady Mary
Reason to Believe

EXILE ON MAIN STREET

Released May 1972

Side One:
Stay With Me
Los Paraguayos
Shake Your Hip
True Blue
Tumblin' Dice

Side Two:
Italian Girls
Torn and Frayed
Miss Judy's Farm
Loving Cup

Side Three:
Happy
Ventilator Blues
I Just Wanna See His Face
I'd Rather Go Blind
That's All You Need

Side Four:
Interludings
You Wear It Well
Moonlight Mile
Shine a Light
Soul Survivor

OOH LA LA

Released November 1973

Side One:
Silicone Grown
If I'm on the Late Side
Coming Down Again
Ooh La La
Cindy Incidentally

Side Two:
Silver Train
Farewell
My Fault
Fly in the Ointment
Borstal Boys

IT'S ONLY ROCK 'N' ROLL

Released October 1974

Side One:
All in the Name of Rock 'n' Roll
Sweet Little Rock 'n' Roller
It's Only Rock 'n' Roll (But I Like It)
Bring It on Home to Me
Stone Cold Sober

Side Two:
Three Time Loser
Alright for an Hour
If You Really Want to Be My Friend
Luxury
Fingerprint File

A NIGHT ON THE TOWN

Released August 1976

Side One:
Hot Legs
Tonight's the Night
You're Insane
The Killing of Georgie (Parts 1 & 2)

Side Two:
Sailor
Born Loose
Fool for You
You Got a Nerve

BLONDES HAVE MORE FUN

Released June 1978

Side One:
Miss You
Ain't Love a Bitch
Blondes (Have More Fun)
The First Cut Is the Deepest
The Best Days of My Life

Side Two:
Far Away Eyes
Last Summer
Before They Make Me Run
Scarred and Scared
You're in My Heart

FOOLISH BEHAVIOUR

Released June 1980

Side One:
Dance
So Soon We Change
She Won't Dance With Me
Gimme Wings
My Girl

Side Two:
Oh God I Wish I Was Home Tonight
Passion
Foolish Behaviour
She's So Cold
Say It Ain't True

TONIGHT I'M YOURS

Released November 1981

Side One:
Start Me Up
Tonight I'm Yours
Hang Fire
Little T&A
Black Limousine

Side Two:
Young Turks
No Use in Crying
Jealous
Sonny
Never Give Up on a Dream

ALBUMS BY THE WHO

MY GENERATION

Released November 1965

Side One:
Out in the Street
I Don't Mind
The Good's Gone
La La La Lies
Much Too Much
My Generation

Side Two:
The Kids Are Alright
Please Please Please
It's Not True
A Legal Matter
The Ox

SUBSTITUTE

Released June 1966

Side One:
I Can't Explain
Leaving Here
Here 'Tis
Anytime You Want Me
Lubie (Come Back Home)
Shout and Shimmy

Side Two:
Substitute
Motoring
Anyway Anyhow Anywhere
I'm a Man
Daddy Rolling Stone
Circles

A QUICK ONE

Released December 1966

Side One:
Run Run Run
Boris the Spider
I Need You
Whiskey Man
Heat Wave
Cobwebs and Strange

Side Two:
Don't Look Away
See My Way
So Sad About Us
A Quick One While He's Away

HAPPY JACK

Released July 1967

Side One:
Disguises
In the City
Batman
Barbara Ann
Bucket T
Call Me Lightning
I'm a Boy

Side Two:
Happy Jack
I've Been Away
Man With the Money
Hall of the Mountain King
Doctor Doctor
Pictures of Lily

THE WHO SELL OUT

Released November 1967

Side One:
Armenia City in the Sky
Mary Anne With the Shaky Hands
Politician
Tattoo
Our Love Was, Is
I Can See for Miles

Side Two:
I Can't Reach You
Relax
Jaguar
Silas Stingy
Sunrise
Rael

MAGIC BUS

Released September 1968

Side One:
Glow Girl
Fortune Teller
Little Billy
Dr. Jekyll and Mr. Hyde
Girl's Eyes
Dogs

Side Two:
Faith in Something Bigger
Glittering Girl
Someone's Coming
Melancholia
Early Morning Cold Taxi
Magic Bus

TOMMY

Released May 1969

Side One:
Overture
It's a Boy
1921
Amazing Journey
Sparks
Eyesight to the Blind

Side Two:
Christmas
Cousin Kevin
The Acid Queen
Underture

Side Three:
Do You Think It's Alright?
Fiddle About
Pinball Wizard
There's a Doctor I've Found
Go to the Mirror
Tommy, Can You Hear Me
Smash the Mirror
Sensation

Side Four:
Miracle Cure
Sally Simpson
I'm Free
Welcome
Tommy's Holiday Camp
We're Not Gonna Take It

LIVE AT LEEDS

Released May 1970

Side One:
Young Man Blues
Substitute
Summertime Blues
Shakin' All Over

Side Two:
My Generation
Magic Bus

LIFEHOUSE

Released August 1971

Side One:
Baba 1: One Note
Baba O'Riley
Teenage Wasteland
Naked Eye
Baba 2: Universal Grid
Behind Blue Eyes

Side Three:
Put the Money Down
Time Is Passing
Too Much of Anything
Baba 4: Robert Shall Have His Vengeance on London Town
Getting in Tune
Let's See Action

Side Two:
Goin' Mobile
Now I'm a Farmer
Mary
Greyhound Girl
Baba 3: Revelation
Bargain

Side Four:
Pure and Easy
Won't Get Fooled Again
Baba O'Riley (reprise)
Baba 5: Lost Note/Bobby
Song Is Over

ODDS AND SODS

Released September 1972

Side One:
Join Together
When I Was a Boy
Postcard
Love Ain't for Keeping
My Wife
The Seeker

Side Two:
The Relay
We Close Tonight
Here for More
Heaven and Hell
Water
Long Live Rock

QUADROPHENIA

Released November 1973

Side One:
I Am the Sea
The Real Me
Four in One
Cut My Hair
The Punk Meets the Godfather

Side Two:
I'm One
The Dirty Jobs
Helpless Dancer
Get Out and Stay Out/Ace Face
I've Had Enough

Side Three:
5:15
Sea and Sand
Drowned
Bellboy

Side Four:
Doctor Jimmy (And Mister Jim)
The Rock
Love, Reign O'er Me

TOMMY (ORIGINAL MOTION PICTURE SOUNDTRACK)

Released December 1974

Side One:
Overture
It's a Boy (Pete Townshend, Vicki Brown)
Ernie's Holiday Camp (Keith Moon, Ann-Margret, David Bowie)
1951 (Ann-Margret, David Bowie)
Amazing Journey (Pete Townshend)
Christmas (Ann-Margret, David Bowie)
Eyesight to the Blind (Eric Clapton)

Side Two:
The Acid Queen (Tina Turner)
Do You Think It's Alright 1 (Ann-Margret, David Bowie)
Cousin Kevin (Paul Nicholas)
Do You Think It's Alright 2 (Ann-Margret, David Bowie)
Fiddle About (Keith Moon)
Do You Think It's Alright 3 (Ann-Margret, David Bowie)
Sparks
Extra, Extra (Simon Townshend)
Pinball Wizard (Elton John)

Side Three:
Champagne (Ann-Margret)
There's a Doctor I've Found (David Bowie)
Go to the Mirror (Rod Stewart, David Bowie, Ann-Margret)
Smash the Mirror (Ann-Margret)
Mother and Son (Ann-Margret, Roger Daltrey)
I'm Free (Roger Daltrey)
Sensation (Roger Daltrey)

Side Four:
Miracle Cure (Simon Townshend)
Sally Simpson (Pete Townshend)
Welcome (Roger Daltrey)
TV Studio (David Bowie, Ann-Margret)
Tommy's Holiday Camp (Keith Moon)
We're Not Gonna Take It (Roger Daltrey)

THE WHO BY NUMBERS

Released October 1975

Side One:
Slip Kid
However Much I Booze
Girl in a Suitcase
Dreaming from the Waist
Imagine a Man

Side Two:
Success Story
They Are All in Love
Blue, Red and Grey
How Many Friends
In a Hand or a Face

WHO ARE YOU

Released December 1977

Side One:
New Song
Keep Me Turning
905
Sister Disco
Jools and Jim

Side Two:
The Quiet One
Empty Glass
Love Is Coming Down
Who Are You

FACE DANCES

Released November 1979

Side One:
You Better You Bet
Don't Let Go the Coat
Cache Cache
Trick of the Light
Dance It Away

Side Two:
Face Dances
Misunderstood
Heart to Hang Onto
Let My Love Open the Door
Gonna Get Ya

THE KIDS ARE ALRIGHT (ORIGINAL MOTION PICTURE SOUNDTRACK)

Released June 1980

Side One:
My Generation
(*Smothers Brothers Comedy Hour*, 1967)
I Can't Explain (*Shindig*, 1965)
Anyway Anyhow Anywhere
(*Ready Steady Go!*, 1965)
Substitute (BBC, 1966)
Happy Jack (*Live at Leeds* outtake, 1970)
Young Man Blues (London Coliseum, 1970)

Side Two:
A Quick One While He's Away
(Monterey Pop Festival, 1967)
Sparks (Watkins Glen, 1969)
Pinball Wizard (Watkins Glen, 1969)
We're Not Gonna Take It
(Watkins Glen, 1969)

Side Three:
Baby Don't You Do It
(Cow Palace, San Francisco, 1971)
Bargain (Cow Palace, San Francisco, 1971)
Pure and Easy
(Forest Hills, San Francisco, 1972)
My Wife (Gaumont State Theatre,
Kilburn, London, 1975)
Baba O'Riley (Shepperton Film Studios, 1979)

Side Four:
Join Together
(Pontiac Silverdome, Michigan, 1975)
Roadrunner
(Pontiac Silverdome, Michigan, 1975)
My Generation Blues
(Pontiac Silverdome, Michigan, 1975)
Won't Get Fooled Again
(Shepperton Film Studios, 1979)

ALL THE BEST COWBOYS HAVE CHINESE EYES

Released June 1981

Side One:
Rough Boys
I Am an Animal
My Baby Gives It Away
You're So Clever
And I Moved

Side Two:
Keep on Working
Cat's in the Cupboard
A Little Is Enough
I Like Nightmares
Another Tricky Day

IT'S HARD

Released April 1983

Side One:
Stop Hurting People
The Sea Refuses No River
Dangerous
It's Hard
Eminence Front

Side Two:
Athena
Exquisitely Bored
It's in You
Somebody Saved Me
Slit Skirts

SELECTED ALBUMS BY OTHER ARTISTS

SMILE (The Beach Boys)

Released March 1967

Side One:
Our Prayer
Heroes and Villains
Vege-Tables
Do Ya Dig Worms
Child Is Father of the Man
Cabinessence

Side Two:
Good Vibrations
Wonderful
Barnyard/I'm in Great Shape
Wind Chimes
Mrs. O'Leary's Cow
Love to Say Da-Da
Surf's Up

WOODSTOCK (Bob Dylan)

Released December 1967

Side One:
Odds and Ends
Lo and Behold
This Wheel's on Fire
Million Dollar Bash
Please Mrs. Henry
Apple Suckling Tree
Tears of Rage

Side Two:
The Mighty Quinn (Quinn the Eskimo)
Yea! Heavy and a Bottle of Bread
Nothing Was Delivered
You Ain't Goin' Nowhere
Tiny Montgomery
Open the Door, Homer
I Shall Be Released

WILD HONEY (The Beach Boys)

Released February 1968

Side One:
Wild Honey
Aren't You Glad
With Me Tonight
Country Air
A Thing or Two
Getting Hungry

Side Two:
Darlin'
I'd Love Just Once to See You
Here Comes the Night
Let the Wind Blow
How She Boogalooed It
Whistle In

THE CELEBRATION OF THE LIZARD (The Doors)

Released July 1968

Side One:
Hello I Love You
Love Street
Waiting for the Sun
Summer's Almost Gone
Wintertime Love
We Could Be So Good Together

Side Two:
Spanish Caravan
My Wild Love
The Celebration of the Lizard

THE VILLAGE GREEN PRESERVATION SOCIETY (The Kinks)

Released November 1968

Side One:
The Village Green Preservation Society
Do You Remember, Walter
Picture Book
Johnny Thunder
Last of the Steam-Powered Trains
Big Sky
Sitting by the Riverside

Side Two:
She's Got Everything
There Is No Life Without Love
Mr. Songbird
Polly
Susannah's Still Alive
Days

Side Three:
Autumn Almanac
Berkeley Mews
Did You See His Name
Plastic Man
King Kong
Mindless Child of Motherhood
Wonderboy
Misty Water

Side Four:
Animal Farm
Village Green
Starstruck
Phenomenal Cat
All of My Friends Were There
Wicked Annabella
Monica
People Take Pictures of Each Other

REVERBERATION (The Beach Boys)

Released January 1969

Side One:
We're Together Again
Friends
Busy Doin' Nothing
She's Goin' Bald
Can't Wait Too Long
Lonely Days
Do It Again

Side Two:
When a Man Needs a Woman
I Went to Sleep
Wake the World
Passing By
Fall Breaks and Back to Winter
Little Pad
Meant for You

Side Three:
I Can Hear Music
A Time to Live in Dreams
Be With Me
Anna Lee the Healer
Transcendental Meditation
Be Here in the Morning
Bluebirds Over the Mountain

Side Four:
Little Bird
All I Want to Do
The Nearest Faraway Place
Breakaway
Celebrate the News
Be Still
Time to Get Alone

MORRISON HOTEL (The Doors)

Released September 1970

Side One:
Roadhouse Blues
Who Scared You
You Make Me Real
Peace Frog
Blue Sunday
Ship of Fools

Side Two:
Land Ho!
The Spy
Queen of the Highway
Indian Summer
Maggie M'Gill

THE FIRST RAYS OF THE NEW RISING SUN (Jimi Hendrix)

Released December 1970

Side One:
Dolly Dagger
Night Bird Flying
Room Full of Mirrors
Belly Button Window
Freedom

Side Two:
Ezy Rider
Astro Man
Drifting
Straight Ahead

Side Three:
Earth Blues
Izabella
Drifter's Escape
Beginnings
Angel

Side Four:
Stepping Stone
Bleeding Heart
New Rising Sun (Hey Baby)
In from the Storm

SELF-PORTRAIT (Bob Dylan)

Released April 1972

Side One:
Watching the River Flow
Clothes Line Saga
Wallflower
Only a Hobo
Bring Me a Little Water
I'm Not There

Side Two:
Down in the Flood (Crash on the Levee)
George Jackson
Tomorrow Is a Long Time
Song to Woody
When I Paint My Masterpiece

APPENDIX C: PERFORMANCES AT LIVE AID

Wembley Stadium, London - July 13, 1985

Coldstream Guards	Royal Salute
	God Save the Queen
Status Quo	Rockin' All Over the World
	Caroline
	Don't Waste My Time
The Style Council	You're the Best Thing
	Big Boss Groove
	Internationalists
	Walls Come Tumbling Down
The Boomtown Rats	I Don't Like Mondays
	Drag Me Down
	Elephant's Graveyard
Adam and the Ants	Viva La Rock
	Stand and Deliver
Ultravox	Reap the Wild Wind
	Dancing With Tears in My Eyes
	One Small Day
	Vienna
Spandau Ballet	Only When You Leave
	Virgin
	True
Elvis Costello	All You Need Is Love
Sade	Why Can't We Live Together
	Your Love Is King
	Is It a Crime
The Police	Roxanne
	Message in a Bottle
	Every Breath You Take

Graham Parker	Heat Treatment
	Howlin' Wind
	Discovering Japan
The Psychedelic Furs	Love My Way
	Heaven
	Pretty in Pink
Rockpile	Cruel to Be Kind
	Girls Talk
	I Hear You Knocking
Big Country	In a Big Country
	Wonderland
Blondie	Dreaming
	The Tide Is High
	Rapture
Cyndi Lauper	Money Changes Everything
	Girls Just Want to Have Fun
	Time After Time
Genesis/Peter Gabriel	In the Air Tonight
	Solsbury Hill
	Shock the Monkey
The Bee Gees	Stayin' Alive
	Nights on Broadway
	How Deep Is Your Love
	If I Can't Have You

JFK Stadium, Philadelphia - July 13, 1985

Joan Baez	Amazing Grace
Kris Krisofferson	All I Really Want to Do
The Four Tops	Shake Me, Wake Me
	Bernadette
	It's the Same Old Song
	Reach Out I'll Be There
	I Can't Help Myself
Black Sabbath	Children of the Grave
	Iron Man
	Paranoid
George Clinton	One Nation Under a Groove
	Tear the Roof Off the Sucker (Give Up the Funk)
	Why Should I Dog You Out
Journey	Any Way You Want It
	Lights
	Don't Stop Believin'
The Four Seasons	Sherry
	Walk Like a Man
	Who Loves You
	December 1963 (Oh What a Night)
Crosby, Stills and Nash	Southern Cross
	Teach Your Children
	Suite: Judy Blue Eyes
Judas Priest	Living After Midnight
	The Green Manalishi
	You Got Another Thing Comin'
Bob Seger	Rock and Roll Never Forgets
	Roll Me Away
	Night Moves
Willie Nelson	Blue Eyes Crying in the Rain
	On the Road Again
George Thorogood/	Who Do You Love
Bo Diddley	The Sky Is Crying
	Madison Blues

Simple Minds	Ghost Dancing
	Don't You (Forget About Me)
	Promised You a Miracle
The Pretenders	Time the Avenger
	Message of Love
	Stop Your Sobbing
	Back on the Chain Gang
	Middle of the Road
Santana	Brotherhood
	Primera Invasion
	Open Invitation
	By the Pool/Right Now
Talking Heads	Swamp
	Take Me to the River
	Burning Down the House
Van Halen	Everybody Wants Some
	Panama
	Jump
John Cougar Mellencamp	Small Town
	Jack and Diane
	Hurts So Good
Smokey Robinson	Cruisin'
	The Tracks of My Tears
	God Is Love
Ray Charles	Georgia on My Mind
	I Got a Woman
	What'd I Say
Foreigner	I Want to Know What Love Is
	Urgent
	Feels Like the First Time
The Band	Stage Fright
	Up on Cripple Creek
	The Weight
Janis Joplin	Me and Bobby McGee
	Piece of My Heart

Simon and Garfunkel	Loves Me Like a Rock
	The Boxer
	Bridge Over Troubled Water
The Doors	Roadhouse Blues
	Light My Fire
	People Are Strange
	L.A. Woman
Stevie Wonder	Higher Ground
	Sir Duke
	I Just Called to Say I Love You
	I Believe (When I Fall in Love It Will Be Forever)
Sam Cooke	You Send Me
	You'll Know
	A Change Is Gonna Come
Fats Domino	Blueberry Hill
	I'm Walkin'
	Ain't That a Shame
The Everly Brothers/ Buddy Holly	Bye Bye Love
	Wake Up Little Susie
	That'll Be the Day
	All My Hopes and Dreams
The Beach Boys	Don't Worry Baby
	Wouldn't It Be Nice
	Surf's Up
	Getcha Back
	Surfin' USA
	Good Vibrations

JFK Stadium, Philadelphia - July 14, 1985

New Testament Baptist Church Choir	Rough Side of the Mountain
	Will the Circle Be Unbroken
	Oh Happy Day
Roy Orbison	Only the Lonely
	Dream Baby
	Oh, Pretty Woman
Darlene Love/Linda Ronstadt	Then He Kissed Me
	To Know Him Is to Love Him
	Today I Met the Boy I'm Gonna Marry
Kenny Rogers/Dolly Parton	Lady
	Here You Come Again
	Islands in the Stream
Kool and the Gang	Cherish
	Joanna
	Jungle Boogie
Carole King/Carly Simon	I Feel the Earth Move
	Nobody Does It Better
	You're So Vain
	Will You Love Me Tomorrow
Al Green	Love and Happiness
	Call Me
	Let's Stay Together
War	The Cisco Kid
	Low Rider
	Why Can't We Be Friends
The B-52s	Planet Claire
	Private Idaho
	Rock Lobster
Fleetwood Mac	Rhiannon
	Dreams
	Don't Stop
Aretha Franklin	Angel
	Ain't No Way
	Rock Steady

Ashford & Simpson/Teddy Pendergrass	Solid
	Reach Out and Touch Somebody's Hand
Madonna	Holiday
	Into the Groove
	Love Makes the World Go Round
Tom Petty and the Heartbreakers	American Girl
	The Waiting
	Rebels
	Refugee
Kenny Loggins/Stevie Nicks	Celebrate Me Home
	Whenever I Call You Friend
The Cars	You Might Think
	Just What I Needed
	Heartbeat City
Neil Young	Sugar Mountain
	The Needle and the Damage Done
	Helpless
	Nothing Is Perfect
	Powderfinger
Prince	Raspberry Beret
	4 the Tears in Your Eyes
	Purple Rain
Eric Clapton	White Room
	Let It Rain
	Layla
Led Zeppelin	Rock and Roll
	Whole Lotta Love
	Fool in the Rain
Bruce Springsteen	Badlands
	Born to Run
	Drive All Night
Duran Duran	Hungry Like the Wolf
	New Moon on Monday
	Rio

Hall & Oates/The Temptations	Out of Touch
	Maneater
	Get Ready
	Ain't Too Proud to Beg
	The Way You Do the Things You Do
	My Girl
The Jackson Five	Wanna Be Startin' Something
	Beat It
	Billie Jean
	I Want You Back
	The Love You Save
	I'll Be There
Bob Dylan	Ballad of Hollis Brown
	When the Ship Comes In
	Blowin' in the Wind
Elvis Presley	Suspicious Minds
	The Wonder of You
	His Hand in Mine
	If I Can Dream
	Return to Sender
	Don't Be Cruel
	Jailhouse Rock
USA for China	We Are the World

Wembley Stadium, London - July 14, 1985

Donovan	Colours
	Catch the Wind
The Hollies	The Air That I Breathe
	He Ain't Heavy, He's My Brother
The Animals	Don't Let Me Be Misunderstood
	The House of the Rising Sun
	It's My Life
Three Dog Night	Mama Told Me Not to Come
	Celebrate
	Joy to the World
James Taylor	Fire and Rain
	You've Got a Friend
	Shower the People
Van Morrison	Domino
	Moondance
	Wild Night
The Electric Light Orchestra	Livin' Thing
	Strange Magic
	Shine a Little Love
Yes	Owner of a Lonely Heart
	Close to the Edge/Roundabout
Earth, Wind and Fire	Serpentine Fire
	Shining Star
	Singasong
Culture Club	Do You Really Want to Hurt Me
	Miss Me Blind
	Karma Chameleon
Howard Jones	Hide and Seek
Roxy Music	Sensation
	Boys and Girls
	Slave to Love
	Love is the Drug
Paul Young	Come Back and Stay
	Every Time You Go Away
U2	Sunday Bloody Sunday
	Bad
The Kinks	Celluloid Heroes
	Come Dancing
	You Really Got Me
	All Day and All of the Night

Queen	Bohemian Rhapsody
	Radio Ga-Ga
	Hammer to Fall
	Crazy Little Thing Called Love
	We Will Rock You
	We Are the Champions
David Bowie	Blue Jean
	Rebel Rebel
	Modern Love
	Heroes
The Who	My Generation
	Pinball Wizard
	Love, Reign O'er Me
	Won't Get Fooled Again
Elton John	Bennie and the Jets
(with Kiki Dee	Rocket Man
and George Michael)	Don't Go Breaking My Heart
	Don't Let the Sun Go Down on Me
Best of Faces	Maggie May
(with Tina Turner)	Tumblin' Dice
	Reason to Believe
	Hot Legs
The Beatles	Come Together
	Here Comes the Sun
	With a Little Help from My Friends
	Walk Away Dreaming
	Let It Be
Band Aid	Do They Know It's Christmas

AUTHOR'S NOTE AND ACKNOWLEDGEMENTS

This story is a work of fictional alternate history. It should not be taken as reflective of real history, nor should it be assumed that the characters in it bear any resemblance to the real-life people upon whom they are based (or that any fictional characters bear any intended resemblance to real persons). It's simply my take on one possible set of outcomes had the fortunes of history turned out differently. There are surely an infinite set of outcomes, of course, that could arise from the same set of circumstances. I can think of more than a few myself.

I am aware that there are other books out there that depict scenarios of the Beatles staying together. After all, the most popular alternate history ideas – what if the Confederacy had won the Civil War; what if John F. Kennedy's assassination was thwarted; what if Napoleon had won the Battle of Waterloo – are popular precisely because of their emotional impact. I purposely avoided reading any of those other books, because I didn't want to, even inadvertently, pick up another author's ideas. I'm sure that my approach to the question "what if the Beatles had stayed together" is different from other approaches, and that similarities between other books in this vein and my own are limited to items like the fact that several key characters are named John Lennon, Paul McCartney, George Harrison, and Ringo Starr.

    I didn't attempt to address every possible item that might have become better (according to any given definition of "better") in the world of *Walk Away Dreaming*. In reading this book you may have been hoping to see *Star Trek* complete its "five-year mission," say, or for Gimbel's department stores to survive. I would encourage you to apply your imagination to the world that *Walk Away Dreaming* lives in, and see if you can't invent such aspects of the world that might be different while remaining consistent with the story. Or, if you feel the world of *Walk Away Dreaming* is missing something, invent another alternate world. There are infinite numbers to choose from.

    My faith in God and my personal values inform this story. If I have any hope in your reading it beyond entertaining you, it's that it may inspire you: that you might see in a vision of how things might have turned out more happily in the past an inspiration to make things happier for all of us in the future.

    Many thanks to Mike Pacholek for the initial spark, and to Mike Kerrigan and Dan Haskins for urging me on.

Special thanks to Dave Renshaw both for his encouragement and for the insider's description of how the filmmaking process works.

Special thanks to my editor, L. Jagi Lamplighter, for making it all come together in the end. And thanks to Jeremiah Humphries for the cover design.

Paul Mendoza comes due for an extra helping of gratitude. I'd still be puttering around on the Internet with this idea without his helping me put it into action. He will recognize some of his ideas in this story as well, and I thank him for them.

Thank you to Father John Henderson for the spiritual guidance.

NOTES

[1] Stalin fled Moscow after the fall of Minsk, and brooded at his dacha for several days, but was coaxed back to the Kremlin by the remainder of the Soviet leadership. He quickly took to organizing the Soviet Union's war effort upon his return.

[2] The Beechcraft Bonanza was prone to losing its tail in poor weather conditions. On February 3, 1959, Peterson went straight down just after taking off from the airfield at Clear Lake. He, Buddy Holly, Richie Valens, and J.P. Richardson were all killed.

[3] The American rail system, particularly passenger trains, was in dire straits by 1966. Passenger service was dying rapidly.

[4] The war in Vietnam involved American, not Soviet, forces.

[5] Yoko Ono's *Ceiling Painting* featured the word "YES" when one looked through the spyglass. John Lennon later cited this positive message – in contrast to the negative messages then common in the avant-garde art world – as a key moment when he realized that he and Yoko thought alike.

[6] The meeting at the art gallery was the beginning of the love affair between John Lennon and Yoko Ono, which resulted in marriage in 1969; Lennon remained with Yoko, except for a period in 1973-74, until his death in 1980. Yoko did not recognize Lennon at first but later claimed it was because of his haircut and glasses. Roman Polanski visited Dunbar's gallery the following day and was impressed with Yoko's work.

[7] Mick Jagger was charged only with possession of amphetamines. Richards was charged only with allowing controlled substances to be used in his home. The relatively lesser charges helped in securing the two musicians' quick release from prison.

[8] "True Love Ways" and "It Doesn't Matter Anymore" were released posthumously after Holly's death. No record of "All My Hopes and Dreams" was noted in the HC Universe.

[9] Brian Epstein himself did the transatlantic arm-twisting that convinced Capitol to release "I Want to Hold Your Hand" in America.

[10] The Kinks' greatest record success in America was with "Tired of Waiting for You," which peaked at Number Six on the *Billboard* chart. "You Really Got Me" and "All Day and All of the Night" both peaked at Number Seven.

[11] The Kinks' managers didn't accompany them to the States for the tour, and the brawl took place, with the result that the Kinks were effectively banned from performing in the States until 1969. Their career never completely recovered.

[12] "Sunny Afternoon" reached Number 14 on the *Billboard* chart. It was the last Kinks single to make the U.S. charts until "Lola" late in 1969, in large part because the performance ban meant that the Kinks were hampered in promoting their record releases.

[13] The Who didn't perform in America until 1967. "Substitute" failed to chart at all in the States, though it was a hit in Britain.

[14] Brian Jones was arrested on May 10, 1967, the same day Mick Jagger and Keith Richards were arraigned. He was charged with possession of drugs after the police found marijuana, cocaine, and amphetamines in his apartment. He was initially sentenced to nine months in prison, but the sentence was subsequently reduced to probation. On May 21, 1968, he was again arrested, though he claimed that the drugs found in his apartment at that time were left by the previous tenant. Brian's drug arrests were cited by many as part of the downward spiral that would lead to his death on July 3, 1969.

[15] "Penny Lane" and "Strawberry Fields Forever" were issued as a 45 single in February 1967, months before the *Sgt. Pepper* album's June release. Neither song was included on the album.

[16] In part because of Brian Wilson's mental issues, the Beach Boys never completed *Smile* as originally intended. A number of tracks were issued on subsequent Beach Boys albums, and Wilson many years later completed a new version on his own, but the original LP was never released.

[17] "She's Leaving Home" and "When I'm 64" both appeared on *Sgt. Pepper*.

[18] Political leftist radicalism became almost part-and-parcel with the counterculture from about 1967 on.

[19] President John F. Kennedy was assassinated in Dallas, Texas, on November 22, 1963. His successor, Lyndon Johnson, signed the Civil Rights Act.

[20] The 1967 Detroit riot was an especially severe one.

[21] The Kinks did not appear at Monterey. "Dead End Street" failed to make the *Billboard* Top Forty.

[22] Neither the Lovin' Spoonful nor the Rascals appeared at Monterey.

[23] No Motown acts were present at Monterey.

[24] The Beach Boys reneged on an earlier commitment to appear at Monterey. That, coupled with the failure to complete *Smile*, caused the band to lose much of their "hipness" to the rock audience, who began to regard them as an oldies act.

[25] Love did not appear at Monterey.

[26] Neither Stevie Wonder nor Wilson Pickett appeared at Monterey.

[27] Moby Grape did not appear at Monterey.

[28] Cream, Procol Harum, and the Velvet Underground were not present at Monterey.

[29] Donovan did not appear at Monterey.

[30] The Yardbirds did not appear at Monterey.

[31] The Doors were overlooked in the planning for Monterey, in part because they were based in Los Angeles rather than San Francisco.

[32] The Who made their first important American appearance at Monterey, so the audience was unfamiliar at that point with their guitar-smashing stage ending. Jimi Hendrix both smashed and burned his guitar at the end of his set – a point of great consternation to the Who, leading them to insist on going on stage first to ensure that the audience knew that the guitar-smashing ending was the Who's idea.

[33] Bob Dylan was in seclusion at the time following a motorcycle accident in July 1966.

[34] The relatively small amount of drugs found, and the prison sentences initially imposed – three months for Jagger, a year for Richards- led a number of establishment figures to come to the Stones' defense, most notoriously the *Times*, which published an editorial titled "Who Breaks a Butterfly on a Wheel?"

[35] The sentences were overturned on appeal.

[36] Only the first single was recorded by the Who.

[37] "I Can See for Miles" reached Number Nine, the Who's biggest chart success in the States.

[38] Brian Jones' sad descent into drug and alcohol abuse continued unabated. In June 1969, he left the Rolling Stones, to which he was contributing little by that point. On July 3, he was found dead in the swimming pool of his home, Cotchford Farm.

[39] No record of May Ling whatsoever was noted in the HC Universe.

[40] Mao Zedong's Communist government was in control of China and was actively providing aid to the Communist North Vietnamese regime. Chiang Kai-shek's Kuomintang regime had been forced to flee to the island of Taiwan following the Communist victory in the civil war in China in 1949.

[41] The Beatles ignored all advice to employ professionals and insisted on filming *Magical Mystery Tour* themselves, following the Merry Pranksters' "psychedelic home-movie" format. The resulting film aired on December 26, 1967 on British television and was very poorly received.

[42] "Magic" Alex Mardas succeeded for at least two years in siphoning money from the Beatles for his various dubious projects. He didn't fully lose their favor until the expensive debacle of the Apple recording studio, which was completed in the spring of 1969 but turned out to be unusable.

[43] "Sexy Sadie" was written as an attack on the Maharishi Mahesh Yogi, with whom Lennon had fallen out.

[44] Mick Jagger and Keith Richards having been released from prison much earlier, the Stones quickly resumed work on the next album, which was completed by Christmas 1967.

[45] The stripper sequence is a particularly long – and rather dull – sequence in the *Magical Mystery Tour* film.

[46] The fact that the film has no plot is one of its problems.

[47] No sequence like this was noted in the *Magical Mystery Tour* film in the HC Universe.

[48] The album was released under the title *Their Satanic Majesties' Request*. Most reviewers disliked the album, accusing the Stones of copying the Beatles' *Sgt. Pepper*.

[49] Although Bob Dylan recorded with the Band through much of 1967, no album was released. Some of the songs were re-recorded for *Bob Dylan's Greatest Hits Vol. 2* in 1971; the original recordings, although heavily bootlegged, were not officially released until *The Basement Tapes* in 1975.

[50] No such album was released in the States.

[51] The Fool's expensive and poorly-made designs were among the reasons for the boutique's closing.

[52] The Apple Boutique was an expensive failure, closing on July 31, 1968 in a giveaway of the remaining stock.

[53] The *Magical Mystery Tour* album – an EP in Britain, with only the songs from the film – was released in December 1967.

[54] "When I'm 64" appeared on *Sgt. Pepper*. "Baby You're a Rich Man" was the B-side of the single "All You Need Is Love". "In the First Place" appeared only on the *Wonderwall* soundtrack, as a George Harrison solo recording.

[55] Brian Jones did not appear on "Lady Madonna." The song features a horn section.

[56] The album peaked at Number Two on the *Billboard* album chart.

[57] Brian Jones was not present at Rishikesh.

[58] John Lennon fell out harshly with the Maharishi after – at the alleged instigation of "Magic Alex" Mardas – he accused the guru of making sexual advances on some of the female adherents.

[59] Bertha Lee Franklin shot Sam Cooke to death in the early morning hours of December 11, 1964 – she was armed with a gun rather than a club.

[60] James Earl Ray fatally shot Martin Luther King Jr. at the Lorraine Motel on April 4, 1968.

[61] Ray did not shoot a police officer. He fled the scene but was arrested later.

[62] Rioting occurred nationwide in the wake of King's assassination.

[63] John Lennon married Cynthia Powell on August 23, 1962, shortly after Cynthia discovered she was pregnant with her and John's son, Julian, who was born on April 8, 1963. They were divorced on November 8, 1968 due to Lennon's new relationship with Yoko Ono.

[64] Although John Lennon and Paul McCartney traveled to the United States after their return to India to promote Apple, there is no evidence that in the HC Universe John visited any independent movie theater.

[65] The Beatles freely invited submissions to Apple, which resulted in an avalanche of largely unusable material that no one ever managed to sort through. Apple was plagued from the beginning by hangers-on, some of whom literally lived in the offices, adding to the general chaos.

[66] "Child of Nature" was rewritten into "Jealous Guy" by Lennon several years later as an apology to Yoko Ono.

[67] There is no record in the HC Universe of Brian Jones playing with the Beatles at this time.

[68] There is no evidence in the HC Universe that Yoko Ono encouraged John Lennon to resume live appearances with the Beatles.

[69] The Beatles considered returning to live performances during the January 1969 *Get Back* sessions, but the idea never materialized, partly because of the increasing tensions within the group. The "rooftop concert" on January 30, 1969 proved to be their final live public appearance. Billy Preston sat in with the group as keyboardist, but no fifth member was formally added to the group.

[70] Brian Jones never received a formal songwriting credit at any time during his career with the Rolling Stones.

[71] Brian Jones did not officially leave the Rolling Stones until June 5, 1968, less than a month before his death.

[72] Shana Alexander did write a cover piece on "The New Rock" for *Life* magazine, but it is very different from the piece that appeared in our own universe.

[73] The Doors never completed "The Celebration of the Lizard," which was intended as the title track for their third album. A piece of the track, titled "Not to Touch the Earth," was released on their third album, which was titled *Waiting for the Sun.*

[74] Klein managed the Rolling Stones at this time. He took over management of the Beatles and Apple in early 1969, over Paul McCartney's objections – a division that was the final factor in the breakup of the group.

[75] The album cover controversy occurred in similar fashion in the HC Universe, but without Keith Richards' final message.

[76] John Lennon and Yoko Ono recorded an avant-garde album entitled *Two Virgins,* which featured a cover photo of both of them fully nude.

[77] The press and public were hostile to Yoko Ono almost from the start, as were the other Beatles – which tended to make John and Yoko more defensive and insular.

[78] The Beatles' "rooftop concert" in January 1969 – their final live performance – was the climax of the movie *Let It Be*.

[79] The Beatles appeared on the David Frost show, but made no appearance on the *Tonight Show*.

[80] John Lennon and George Harrison are the only Beatles whose voices can be heard on "Revolution #9."

[81] The lead guitar on "While My Guitar Gently Weeps" was played by Eric Clapton, sitting in with the Beatles. The saxophone on "Ob-La-Di, Ob-La-Da" was uncredited, while George Harrison played the slide guitar on "Yer Blues." None of the Beatles' various recordings of "Across the Universe" featured a sitar.

[82] The Apple Studios, built by "Magic Alex" Mardas, were not completed in a usable fashion.

[83] The Beatles' sessions for the *Get Back* album in January 1969 were extensively filmed and released as the movie *Let It Be* – which, because of the growing tensions in the group, turned out to be an inadvertent documentary of the Beatles' breakup.

[84] The only known reference to "Family" in the HC Universe was as the original title of a Rolling Stones song released in 1971 as "Sister Morphine." Brian Jones is not known to have participated in the writing of the song.

[85] George Harrison briefly quit the Beatles during the January 1969 sessions over his frustration at not having more of his songs included on the Beatles' albums, plus his difficulties with Paul McCartney. Although he was persuaded to return, no outlet was found for his songwriting, another factor in the breakup of the group.

[86] Paul McCartney and Linda Eastman were wed on March 12, 1969. The police that day raided the home of George Harrison and arrested him and wife Patti on drug charges. None of the other Beatles attended Paul's wedding.

[87] John Lennon and Yoko Ono were married in Gibraltar on March 20, 1969. None of the other Beatles were present, nor was Lennon's aunt, Mimi Smith.

[88] John Lennon and Yoko Ono famously used their "honeymoon" to stage a "bed-in for peace" at the Amsterdam Hilton. It was followed by a similar "bed-in" in Montreal.

[89] Richard Nixon was president of the United States at this time.

[90] Charles Manson based his crazed notions of "helter skelter" in part on the White Album and his insistence that the Beatles were the four angels mentioned in Revelation. His followers murdered several people at the home of actress Sharon Tate on August 9, 1969, including Tate herself, Jay Sebring, and Abigail Folger. The next day Leno and Rosemary LaBianca were murdered by the Manson "family" as well. Manson, along with a number of his followers, were initially sentenced to death, but their sentences were commuted to life in prison following California's withdrawal of the death penalty. "Squeaky" Fromme was not convicted of involvement with the murders but was imprisoned in 1975 after attempting to assassinate President Gerald Ford.

[91] The *Let It Be* album – not including a song called "Family" – was not released until May 1970.

[92] *Yellow Submarine* – which does not feature Brian Jones – debuted in London on July 17, 1968, and was released in the United States six months later. The villains in the film are called "Blue Meanies."

[93] Dick James' sale of Northern Songs to Sir Lew Grade effectively took the Beatles' songwriting copyrights out of the band's control. Allen Klein attempted to regain control of the company but was unsuccessful.

[94] The Woodstock event, held on Max Yasgur's farm at White Lake, New York, turned out to be the best-remembered rock festival event of the summer of 1969.

[95] Mick Jagger and Keith Richards were not notably at odds during this time period.

[96] "Midnight Rambler" appears on the *Let it Bleed* album.

[97] Ben Fong-Torres was an editor at *Rolling Stone* magazine, and Greil Marcus at the time also wrote for that publication.

[98] The Woodstock festival was overwhelmed by far more attendees than had been anticipated and was plagued by a shortage of food, sanitary facilities and medical supplies. Conditions were so severe that Governor Nelson Rockefeller of New York considered calling in the state National Guard.

[99] On Saturday, August 16, 1969, the festival was drenched by heavy rain.

[100] The Doors' membership was not in flux, but the Doors did not appear at Woodstock.

[101] Of the artists listed, the following did not appear at Woodstock: Tommy James and the Shondells, Paul Revere and the Raiders, Sam and Dave, the Moody Blues, James Brown, the Kinks, the Beach Boys, and Bob Dylan.

[102] Jimi Hendrix's comment at Monterey was interpreted by most people as a slap against the Beach Boys.

[103] Jimi Hendrix, succumbing to pressure, reformed the Jimi Hendrix Experience in 1970, performing with them until his death on September 18 of that year.

[104] Due to Cold War tensions, concerts by Western performers in Warsaw and Prague were very rare at the time.

[105] Peiping was renamed Beijing after the Communist victory in the Chinese civil war in 1949. As with Warsaw and Prague, performances by Westerners in Chinese cities were extremely rare at the time.

[106] There is no record of this performance in the HC Universe.

[107] Ringo Starr is the only Beatle ever to have appeared on *Laugh-In*.

[108] Goldie Hawn at the time was married to Gus Trikonis. They separated in 1973 and were divorced in 1975. She was then married to musician Bill Hudson, and since the 1980s has been in a relationship with actor Kurt Russell.

[109] The "Country Honk" version appears on the *Let it Bleed* album, but the rock version of "Honky Tonk Women" was released as a single and was a major hit for the Rolling Stones. Dick Taylor does not play on any version of the song.

[110] "Wild Horses" appears on the Rolling Stones' 1971 album *Sticky Fingers*.

[111] Keith Richards made no overtures to other managers at this time and enjoyed harmonious relations with Mick Jagger.

[112] Mick Taylor remained a member of the Rolling Stones until December 1974.

[113] Robert Fripp never played with the Rolling Stones.

[114] Portions of the cheery exchange with the media were included in the film *Gimme Shelter*.

[115] The concert was held at the Altamont Speedway on December 6, 1969, with disastrous results – Hell's Angels, allegedly hired as security by the Rolling Stones, ran rampant through the crowd, with numerous people injured and one individual, Meredith Hunter, stabbed to death. During the Jefferson Airplane's set, singer Marty Balin was temporarily knocked unconscious when he tried to intervene in a fight at the foot of the stage. The Grateful Dead refused to play due to the violent situation; the Rolling Stones' set was interrupted several times by violence near the stage, including Hunter's stabbing.

[116] The Rolling Stones' film *Gimme Shelter* chronicles their 1969 tour, including the climactic – and disastrous – final free concert at Altamont. The live album *Get Yer Ya-Ya's Out*, released in 1970, is made up of performances from the 1969 tour.

[117] The Rolling Stones, including both Mick Jagger and Keith Richards, are still a functional act as of 2018.

[118] Ronnie Lane remained in the Faces until June 1973.

[119] Ian McLagan, Rod Stewart, Ron Wood, and Kenney Jones all remained members of the Faces until the band's breakup in 1975.

[120] No record of the band "Best of Faces" exists in the HC Universe.

[121] *Abbey Road*, the final album recorded by all four Beatles, was released in September 1969.

[122] The rumor and most of the clues were similar in our universe, although since Brian Jones was not a member of the band and was in fact dead by that time, he was obviously not part of the rumor.

[123] John Lennon stated that similar advice was given by an Asian doctor to him regarding his and Yoko's desire to have a child in the mid-1970s.

[124] Sean Lennon is the name of John Lennon and Yoko Ono's son, born on October 9, 1975.

[125] The *Woodstock* film and soundtrack album were released in 1970.

[126] George Harrison left the melody of "My Sweet Lord" as it was – and he was subsequently sued by Bright Tunes, the publisher of "He's So Fine." The court settlement required that a portion of George's royalties be turned over to the plaintiff.

[127] "My Sweet Lord" and "Hear Me Lord" appeared on George Harrison's first post-Beatles solo album, *All Things Must Pass*, released in November 1970.

[128] No article matching this description was found in the HC Universe.
[129] No such article was found in *Crawdaddy* in the HC Universe, although a number of rock writers commented on the "death of rock" around this time.
[130] *John Wesley Harding* was released on December 27, 1967.
[131] Bob Dylan released a country album titled *Nashville Skyline* on April 9, 1969, but it was not a duet album with Johnny Cash. No track called "On the Third Day" is on this album in the HC Universe.
[132] Jimi Hendrix had not completed *The First Rays of the New Rising Sun* at the time of his death on September 18, 1970.
[133] Doug Lubahn was a studio musician who played on the first Doors albums, but he was not a member of the group. The Miami "exposure" incident took place in March 1969 and had a significant negative impact on the group's career.
[134] Marc Benno played bass guitar on *Morrison Hotel* but was not a member of the Doors. Jim Morrison never overcame his alcohol and drug problems. He was found dead in his Paris apartment on July 3, 1971.
[135] Sam Cooke and Richie Valens were both dead by 1970.
[136] The Who toured almost constantly during 1967 and 1968.
[137] No Who album entitled *Substitute* was released in the HC Universe. *Happy Jack* was the U.S. title for their second album, *A Quick One*.
[138] By 1970, in the wake of the Beatles' breakup, Apple had jettisoned all divisions outside of the record division. Janis Joplin died on October 4, 1970, before the release of *Pearl* (not on Apple). James Taylor was briefly an Apple artist but moved to Columbia; Deep Purple were never signed to Apple.
[139] No such organization as the Life Spiritual Center was found in connection with Apple in the HC Universe.
[140] "Cold Turkey" was released as a single by John Lennon's "conceptual" act, the Plastic Ono Band, in late 1969.
[141] "Isn't it a Pity" appeared in two versions on *All Things Must Pass*.
[142] "Oh My Love" appeared on John Lennon's *Imagine* album, released in October 1971. "Instant Karma" was released as a Plastic Ono Band single in February 1970.
[143] "Jealous Guy" appears on *Imagine*.
[144] "Another Day" was released as Paul McCartney's first solo single in February 1971. The other three songs listed appeared on his first solo album, *McCartney*, released in April 1970.
[145] *Every Picture Tells a Story*, featuring "Maggie May," was a solo album for Rod Stewart released in May 1971.
[146] David Bowie never signed with Apple.
[147] The Who never completed *Lifehouse*. Some of the songs intended for the opera were released in August 1971 as the album *Who's Next*, but with no storyline.
[148] *Sentimental Journey* was released in March 1970.
[149] John Lennon did not have a daughter in the HC Universe.
[150] "Dead Flowers" appears on the Rolling Stones' 1971 album *Sticky Fingers*. Mick Jagger never recorded the other two songs.
[151] Bowie gave "All the Young Dudes" to Mott the Hoople to record.
[152] *Exile on Main Street* is the title of the Rolling Stones' June 1972 double album.
[153] *Ram* is the title of Paul and Linda McCartney's May 1971 album.
[154] "Heart of the Country" appears on *Ram*.
[155] All three songs appear on *Ram*.
[156] "All Things Must Pass" is the title track of George's November 1970 album.
[157] Both songs appear on *All Things Must Pass*.
[158] "It Don't Come Easy" was released as a Ringo Starr solo single in April 1971.

[159] John Lennon never finished "Brother Sam."
[160] "Crippled Inside" and "It's So Hard" appear on *Imagine*.
[161] Elvis Presley was touted for the lead role in *Dirty Harry*, but that role was played by Clint Eastwood. *Butch Cassidy and the Sundance Kid* starred Paul Newman. Roy Scheider played the role in *The French Connection* that in our universe was played by Presley.
[162] Paul McCartney lived out his fantasy with his new group, Wings, in 1972 by performing an impromptu British tour along the same lines.
[163] Bianca Jagger filed for divorce from Mick Jagger in May 1978.
[164] During John Lennon's separation from Yoko Ono in 1973-74, he socialized with Keith Moon and Harry Nilsson, leading a life of dissipation similar to that described here. The Troubadour Club incident is the same in both universes.
[165] Paul McCartney and Wings recorded their May 1975 album *Venus and Mars* in New Orleans.
[166] "Nobody Loves You (When You're Down and Out)" appears on John's September 1974 album *Walls and Bridges*.
[167] The title track for John's October 1971 solo album.
[168] "I Found Out" appeared on the solo album *John Lennon/Plastic Ono Band*, released in December 1970.
[169] "Band on the Run" was the title track of Wings' November 1973 album.
[170] The three songs listed appear on Wings' *Band on the Run*.
[171] "Give Me Love" appears on George's June 1973 album *Living in the Material World*.
[172] "Has Anybody Seen My Baby" is the title of a song allegedly recorded by Brian Jones just before his death in July 1969.
[173] Released as a single by Wings in June 1973.
[174] "Photograph" appears on Ringo's November 1973 *Ringo* album.
[175] *One Flew Over the Cuckoo's Nest* was directed by Milos Forman.
[176] *Ooh La La* was an album by the Faces released in March 1973.
[177] John Lennon read *The Primal Scream* and undertook the primal therapy program in early 1970. Primal therapy was the central inspiration for his solo album *John Lennon/Plastic Ono Band*.
[178] Kit Lambert undertook no major projects after parting ways with the Who; he died on April 7, 1981.
[179] Don Kirshner was not involved in the creation of MTV, which debuted on August 1, 1981.
[180] "Scared" appears on *Walls and Bridges*, "How?" on *Imagine*, both with "icing."
[181] John never completed "Now and Then." The other three songs appear on *John Lennon/Plastic Ono Band*.
[182] The Gladys Presley Center does not exist in the HC Universe. Presley died on August 16, 1977.
[183] MTV adopted a "heavy rotation" format for videos. None of the programs listed were featured on MTV.
[184] *Night Flight* aired on the USA Network.
[185] Neither program appeared on MTV.
[186] Gerald Ford was the president of the United States during the time period indicated. Ronald Reagan was elected to the presidency in 1980. On March 30, 1981, John Hinckley attempted to assassinate Reagan; he survived the attempt. (Arthur Bremer made an attempt on the life of presidential candidate George Wallace on May 15, 1972.) Reagan joked that he hoped that the doctors who would be performing surgery on him were Republicans (his party).
[187] *Goodnight Vienna* is the title of Ringo Starr's November 1974 album.
[188] "Venus and Mars" and "Rock Show" appear on Wings' album *Venus and Mars*.

[189] "My Love" appears on Wings' April 1973 album *Red Rose Speedway*. "Picasso's Last Words" and "Bluebird" appear on Wings' *Band on the Run*. "Letting Go" appears on *Venus and Mars*. "Junior's Farm" was released as a Wings single in October 1974.

[190] "You" appears on George's September 1975 album *Extra Texture – Read All About It*. "Dark Horse" is the title track of George's December 1974 album. "Be Here Now" appears on *Living in the Material World*.

[191] "Mind Games" is the title track of John's October 1973 album.

[192] "One Day at a Time" and "Intuition" appear on *Mind Games*; the other tracks listed appear on *Walls and Bridges*.

[193] "Mull of Kintyre" was released as a single by Wings in November 1977.

[194] The "Crossroads Theme" closes Wings' *Venus and Mars*.

[195] Bob Geldof began the Live Aid effort in response to a famine in Ethiopia rather than China.

[196] The effort was dubbed "USA for Africa" in the HC Universe.

[197] Huey Lewis, rather than Sam Cooke, sang on "We Are the World."

[198] Several European countries, the Soviet Union, Japan, Australia and a number of others participated in Live Aid.

[199] There were a few other relief efforts outside of Live Aid, but nothing organized as part of Geldof's effort, and none involving musicians from other genres.

[200] Comic Relief is a telethon begun in the 1980s as a charity for the homeless.

[201] Live Aid was a single-day event – July 13, 1985.

[202] No benediction opened Live Aid in the HC Universe.

[203] Of the acts listed, only the Boomtown Rats appeared at Live Aid.

[204] Of the acts listed, only Black Sabbath appeared at Live Aid.

[205] *L.A. Woman* was the final Doors album with Jim Morrison. *An American Prayer* was a spoken-word recording of Morrison's poems released after his death.

[206] None of these artists appeared at Live Aid.

[207] Chuck Berry and Little Richard did not appear at Live Aid.

[208] The Beach Boys appeared at Live Aid – but without Dennis Wilson, who died on December 28, 1983.

[209] Of the performers listed in this paragraph, only Kenny Loggins and Teddy Pendergrass appeared at Live Aid.

[210] During his set at Live Aid, Bob Dylan remarked that perhaps "one or two million" of the money raised could be used to help American farmers who were in danger of losing their farms. His remarks led to the "Farm Aid" series of benefit concerts, which began that September.

[211] Neither the Hollies nor Donovan appeared at Live Aid. The exchange between Donovan and an audience member as described took place during the Concerts for Kampuchea in 1979.

[212] The Kinks did not appear at Live Aid.

[213] Keith Moon's descent into drug and alcohol problems was never arrested, and he died on September 6, 1978, of an overdose of a prescription medication that he was taking, ironically, in an effort to overcome his alcohol problems. The Who performed at Live Aid, and were plagued by technical issues, but Pete Townshend did not smash his guitar.

[214] Mick Jagger performed at Live Aid as a solo artist, because the Rolling Stones were temporarily split up at the time. Keith Richards and Stones guitarist Ron Wood accompanied Bob Dylan during his set.

[215] Tina Turner joined Mick Jagger onstage at Live Aid.

[216] Wings released *Wings Over America*, a live triple album from their 1976 tour, in December 1976. *The Beatles at the Hollywood Bowl* and *Live at the Star*

Club were both issued in 1977, the latter over the ex-Beatles' objections. *Live at the BBC* was not released until 1994.

[217] *Skywriting by Word of Mouth* was the title of a book of John Lennon's writings, published posthumously in 1986. The title "*119th and Menlove*" refers to the childhood street addresses of Brian Wilson and John Lennon: 119th Street in Hawthorne, California, and Menlove Avenue in Liverpool, England. John Lennon's *Rock 'n' Roll* album was released in March 1975.

[218] Paul McCartney was the final performer at the London Live Aid show, and he was joined onstage by Bob Geldof, Pete Townshend, David Bowie, and Alison Moyet.

[219] Although the Germans came very close to Moscow, besieged Leningrad for two years, and penetrated into the suburbs of both cities, they both remained in Soviet hands throughout World War II.

[220] The Germans, after losing the battle of Stalingrad, were driven from the Volga region. They attempted a new offensive in 1943 that resulted in the battle of Kursk.

[221] By the time of the Normandy landings, the Red Army had penetrated into prewar eastern Poland.

[222] The Free French movement was limited in scope, in part because the Communists represented a rival center of resistance to the Nazis.

[223] The Soviet Union (under Stalin) at the end of World War II retained most of the territory taken from Poland in 1939, compensating Poland by allowing that country to annex German territory east of the Oder-Neisse river line, the present-day border between Germany and Poland. The Soviets annexed part of German East Prussia along with the Baltic States, which did not regain independence until 1991.

[224] Pope Pius XII remained in the Vatican throughout the war, although Hitler on a number of occasions did express a desire to arrest him. The Pope, it was later revealed, was working with the German army intelligence unit, Abwehr (the center of an anti-Hitler plot) and other contacts within Germany in an attempt to have Hitler assassinated.

[225] General George Patton died on December 21, 1945, after a jeep accident in Germany.

[226] Hitler's final offensive was directed at the Western Allies, not the Soviets, and resulted in the "Battle of the Bulge" in December 1944 – January 1945.

[227] The attempt by the British and Americans to cross the Rhine per Montgomery's plan, dubbed "Operation Market-Garden," ended in failure.

[228] Patton advanced into Czechoslovakia, but the United States was unable to prevent the establishment of a Communist government there in 1948. A Communist government was imposed on Poland by the advancing Soviets in 1945.

[229] In the fall of 1944, as the Soviets approached Warsaw, the Polish Home Army led a revolt against the Nazis. The Red Army, controversially, stopped outside Warsaw for several months while the Home Army revolt was crushed by the Nazis. The Soviets did not resume their advance on the Polish capital until January 1945.

[230] McAuliffe's famous reply was to the German general who had surrounded the 101st Airborne at Bastogne, Belgium, during the Battle of the Bulge.

[231] The Soviets engaged in the final battle for Berlin, rather than the Western Allies, after General Eisenhower agreed to stop Allied forces at the Elbe River in keeping with the agreements on postwar occupation zones. Hitler killed himself on April 30, 1945, and the city surrendered the following day. Germany surrendered unconditionally on May 8.

[232] The Potsdam Conference was held from July 17 to August 2, 1945.

[233] Initially, there were only three occupation zones: the Soviet in eastern Germany, the British in northwestern Germany, and the American in southwestern Germany. A French occupation zone was later carved out of portions of the British and American zones.

[234] West Berlin – made up of the Western Allies' occupation zones within the city – was encircled by the Soviet occupation zone, which later became East Germany. The Berlin Wall, built in 1961, was not intended to keep people within the city, but to keep would-be defectors from using West Berlin as a means of fleeing to the West.

[235] At Potsdam, the Soviet government committed to entering the war against Japan within 90 days of the end of the war in Europe.

[236] The Soviets obtained an occupation zone north of the 38th parallel in Korea. This led to the establishment of the North Korean state and to the Korean War of 1950-53.

[237] Despite some success against the Communists in 1946-47, the Kuomintang was unable to defeat the Communist armies in Manchuria, and the United States refused to provide significant aid, instead attempting to arrange peace parleys between the two sides. The Communists finally succeeded in occupying the whole of mainland China in the fall of 1949 and in driving the KMT armies to the island of Taiwan (Formosa).

[238] Pakistan, during most of the Cold War era, aligned itself with the United States.

[239] Despite pressure from the Soviets, Iran resisted Soviet attempts to install pro-Soviet governments or to establish breakaway pro-Soviet states. Mossadegh became prime minister of Iran in 1951; after nationalizing the British-owned oil industry and taking other actions that led the United States to fear he was drawing closer to the Soviet Union, he was overthrown in a CIA-backed coup in August 1953.

[240] Iraq, Syria, Egypt, and Libya at one time or another during the Cold War era were formally or informally allied to the Soviet Union, though never as a cohesive bloc. Saudi Arabia remained allied to the United States during this period. Turkey, like Iran, came under Soviet pressure but resisted it with help from the United States, and Turkey joined NATO.

[241] The Warsaw Pact, created formally in 1955, consisted of the Soviet Union, Poland, East Germany, Czechoslovakia, Hungary, Romania, and Bulgaria. North Vietnam was a Communist ally of the Soviet Union but not part of the Pact. Sukarno was pro-Soviet but was overthrown in 1967.

[242] No such organization as PITO was found in the HC Universe.

[243] Alger Hiss was convicted of perjury in connection with his spy activities in 1950, although defenders continued to assert his innocence until the fall of the Soviet Union, when it was finally confirmed that he was a Soviet spy. The key members of the Cambridge spy ring managed to defect to the Soviet Union.

[244] The Soviets exploded their first atomic bomb in August 1949.

[245] The Attlee government remained in power in Britain until 1951.

[246] The Republicans nominated Dewey, who lost narrowly to Truman. Eisenhower was elected in 1952, defeating Adlai Stevenson.

[247] Joseph McCarthy became the lead figure in combating Communist infiltration, and his heavy-handed approach had the effect of discrediting the effort. The "Hollywood Ten," despite evidence of Communist connections, have defenders – particularly in Hollywood – to the present day.

[248] Oil shortages not being considered a major issue until the 1970s, none of these developments came to pass in the HC Universe.

[249] The cities mentioned have been in a perennially depressed state for many years due to the decline of their coal industry.

[250] The Three Mile Island facility was closed in 1979 following an accident there which nearly resulted in a meltdown. No new nuclear plants have been built in the United States since that time.

[251] These developments did not occur in the HC Universe.

[252] Eisenhower was instrumental in creating the act which authorized the construction of the Interstate Highway System, signed in 1956. Construction of the Interstates was substantially completed by the 1970s.

[253] The DOT was established in 1967; the agencies listed are under its aegis, though the FRA primarily handles railroad safety issues. The railroads were not deregulated until the Staggers Act passed in October 1980, and the ICC was not abolished until 1996 (it was replaced by the Surface Transportation Board). The CAB was abolished in 1984.

[254] Cabooses were phased out on American railroads during the 1980s.

[255] The railroads, which held approximately two-thirds of both the freight and passenger markets at the end of World War II, have declined significantly since then, although they have rebounded somewhat since the passage of the Staggers Act.

[256] In 1971, after years of decline, the remainder of American passenger trains was taken over by the federal government under the authority of Amtrak, which has operated them since then. Regional transit authorities operate most commuter trains. Amtrak is widely considered inferior to both predecessor services and to services in other nations.

[257] Fidel Castro came to power in Cuba in 1959.

[258] Ho Chi Minh died in 1969.

[259] The Viet Cong, or "Vietnamese Communists," formally the National Liberation Front, were a guerrilla army that operated in South Vietnam to overthrow the Saigon regime.

[260] Eisenhower won a second term in 1956, again defeating Stevenson.

[261] Kennedy won the presidency in 1960 by defeating Richard Nixon.

[262] Mob involvement in the assassination of both Kennedy brothers has long been rumored. Oswald made an attempt on the life of Walker in April 1963.

[263] Humphrey lost the 1968 election to Richard Nixon.

[264] In the 1972 election, Nixon defeated George McGovern in a landslide.

[265] The Kennedy-Nixon debates in 1960 were considered to have an influence on Kennedy's victory.

[266] The debate as described was between Reagan and Jimmy Carter during the 1980 election campaign.

[267] Jimmy Carter defeated Gerald Ford (successor to Nixon, who resigned in 1974 amid the Watergate scandal) in 1976.

[268] Reagan defeated Carter in 1980. Robert Kennedy was assassinated on June 5, 1968.

[269] Leonid Brezhnev died on November 10, 1982. He was succeeded initially by Yuri Andropov, then by Konstantin Chernenko, before Mikhail Gorbachev – the last Soviet leader – came to power in 1985.

[270] The Saigon regime fell in April 1975.

[271] Gorbachev instituted similar reforms in the Soviet Union in the late 1980s.

[272] The Warsaw Pact unraveled in similar fashion during the course of 1989. Konigsberg was in the portion of German East Prussia allocated to the Soviet Union; it is today the Russian city of Kaliningrad.

[273] A similar attempt to depose Gorbachev took place in 1991 in the HC Universe.

[274] Boris Yeltsin was the first president of the Republic of Russia.

[275] Ukraine became an independent state.

[276] Belarus and Moldova both became independent states.

Printed in Great Britain
by Amazon